The Art of Becoming

The Art of Becoming

CHARLOTTE KLUSKENS

THE ART OF BECOMING

Copyright © 2021 by Charlotte Productions

All rights reserved. No part of this publication may be reproduced, distributed, or
transmitted in any form or by any means, including photocopying, recording, or
other electronic or mechanical methods, without the prior written permission of the
publisher, except in the case of brief quotations embodied in critical reviews and
certain other noncommercial uses permitted by copyright law. For permission
requests, contact the author.

Book cover design by Fredericke Decoster

ISBN: 9789464204902

www.charlottekluskens.com

CHAPTER ONE

PLAYING the piano felt like coming home, in the sense that it represented everything that was familiar to Jack. His slender fingers touched the keys effortlessly. They moved from left to right, with precision and skill. He enjoyed the sound of the music he produced. Although the thing he enjoyed most was the not thinking, the not feeling.

"Jack!" his mother shouted. The music came to an abrupt stop. "Come and wash your hands, dear. Lunch is ready."

Seated on the piano bench in the dining room, Jack looked to his right into the kitchen. His mother finished up her traditional Sunday roast, which smelled delicious. With care she added a sprig of rosemary after which she wiped her hands on her blue apron. She caught Jack's eye and returned his gaze with a gentle smile, revealing the dimples in her cheeks. Jack resembled his mother in many ways and didn't only share the dimples in his cheeks but also her green eyes and light brown hair colour.

As Jack made an attempt to get up, his father shouted from the sofa behind him, "Let him finish, Margaret. He still has two passages to complete." With a sigh, he motioned for Jack to go on. Dressed comfortably in an old concert t-shirt, Jack's father settled back in his armchair from where he could observe Jack. For being in his early fifties, Mr Lewis was muscular and looked younger than he was. The only thing that gave away his age was his hair that had turned grey at a young age.

Music filled the house once again. Next to Jack a fan was blowing, making this hot summer day more bearable. The clock was ticking, almost like a metronome, guiding the rhythm. The last note lingered on. They waited a few seconds until the sound had vanished completely.

Jack's mother finished setting up the table in the dining room where the piano stood against the wall. She used the nice china, something she only did on Sundays or on the rare occasion they had Dad's friend Sean over for dinner.

"The sermon was lovely, wasn't it?" Mrs Lewis asked both of them.

Mr Lewis nodded as he chewed away his roast beef. "Father O'Connell gave us a lot of food for thought. It was good of him to address you at the end, wasn't it, Jack? Very considerate."

"It was," Jack replied. He hadn't paid much attention to Father O'Connell or the sermon. "Very considerate indeed."

His mother agreed, "Pass me the—"

Jack's father narrowed his dark eyes, the wrinkles on his face prominent and deep. "I've told you a million times to pay more attention in church, Jack."

"I'm sorry, Dad. My mind is all over the place. I can't concentrate on anything anymore today." Jack's mind drifted to the packed boxes that waited for him in his room. All of his belongings tucked away in no more than six cardboard boxes. The clock ticked on mercilessly, seconds feeling more like minutes, as Jack waited for his family to finish their lunch. He glanced towards the opened letter on top of the piano. His heart threatened to break out of his ribcage at the thought of what was to come. Moving to London had been anticipated and dreamed about at length, yet Jack could not control the nerves that rushed through his body now that it was actually time to leave. He forced himself to stop tapping his foot to the ground.

Jack's mother cleared the table. "Are you ready? We should be leaving soon."

With a nod, Jack jumped up. "I'll get my stuff." He snatched the letter from the piano on his way to his bedroom, where his father was already taking the boxes down. He walked through his room one final time to make sure he hadn't forgotten anything. He opened the letter for what must have been the hundredth time this summer. *After internal deliberation we are pleased to inform you of your acceptance into the undergraduate BA Piano performance program at the London Institute of Arts. On behalf of the faculty, staff—*

A car horn honked twice. Jack took his time in walking outside, leaving the familiarity of his parental home behind. When he closed the front door behind him, Jack didn't look back.

THE STREETS and landscapes Jack had called home for the last eight years passed by. Moving from America it had taken him some time to adjust to England. Jack had only just turned ten by the time they left Boston, but he had grown fond of Alston. It took leaving to make him realise how familiar everything had become. Jack stared outside in a desperate attempt to etch every last impression to his memory. Father O'Connell waved them off from the steps of the church. Miss Smith carried a large basket of bread into the bakery. The sheep grazed lazily in the sun on Mr Dickinson's farm. The oak tree, high and mighty, in which Jack used to climb to the top. He hadn't admitted it at first, he was too busy leaving, but he'd miss this place.

Alston disappeared and changed into the monotonous view of motorways. With a few hours to kill before they'd reach London, Jack closed his eyes and made himself comfortable for the long drive. The perfect opportunity had arrived for him to leave his everyday life behind in search of something that mattered. Living in the countryside most of his life had made him hungry to discover what else was out there. More than anything he wanted to become someone. He didn't know who yet, but London seemed like the right place to figure that out.

Jack opened his heavy eyelids when the car came to a sudden halt in front of a traffic light. The outstretched landscapes had traded place with tall buildings, people, and a whole lot of traffic. Jack yawned, stretching his body that had been stuck in the same position for too long. He opened his window, allowing fresh air to flow through the car. He observed the city he would soon call home with a sense of excitement that was new to him.

From the rear mirror his mother offered Jack a smile, contradicted by her glossy eyes. With a knot in his stomach Jack returned the smile and hoped it looked reassuring. He ran his hand through his, already messy, light brown hair to put it somewhat into place. No matter what he tried to do with it, his wavy hair had a life of its own and stuck out to all sides.

Mr Lewis parked the car in one of the few reserved parking spots of the residence hall at Soho Square, situated right in the heart of London. If all went well, this was to be Jack's home for the next four years. The final efforts of the summer sun warmed Jack's face as soon as he got out of the car. He closed his eyes and welcomed the pleasant feeling of the sun hitting his face. It was unusually hot for English weather.

Jack's father grunted as he got out of the car. "Absolutely horrendous traffic. Where did these people learn how to drive?" He stretched his arms and pushed a strand of grey hair to the back. "Sean already warned me about this. We were in the shop the other day. Remember that day when we sold the new Steinway?"

Jack and his mother nodded. They had heard the story before. Sean was Jack's father's best friend and business partner. They co-owned a music shop in Carlisle, Lewis & Burton's Instruments, where they sold all kinds of instruments and musical equipment. People came a long way for their expertise. Having a well-known last name did wonders for business. Explaining every day how *'yes, I really am his son'* somehow never seemed to bore Mr Lewis.

"Well, he already warned me London traffic would be crazy during rush hour. Even on a Sunday. We should have left earlier."

Jack muttered something in agreement whilst examining the building. Clutching his suspenders, Jack entered the residence hall through the glass door, followed by his parents who were still discussing traffic. The building's caretaker showed them around and pointed out Jack's room on the top floor of the building. Jack held his head up high when he used his key that first time to open the door to his room. As he stepped inside, a huge grin stretched out across his face. The room itself was quite small and nothing spectacular, but it was his and his alone. In the far-right corner stood a single bed with a desk to its left underneath the window. On the other side of the room by the door stood a wardrobe and dresser. That was about it. The walls were painted in a light shade of blue and the floorboards consisted of dark wood that gave a slight squeak when walked on. As long as you didn't look too close at the paint which had worn of in certain places, or at the curtains which had a burn mark on them, the room looked fine.

Mr Lewis motioned for his wife to come over to the window. "The view could have been better, don't you think? From up so high."

Jack joined them by the window. The view was pretty much non-existent as it got blocked by the brick wall of the building next door. "The room itself is quite nice, though."

"Hmm," Jack's father answered. "Let's get you unpacked."

In silence, Jack and his parents returned to the car. "Gently, Jack, that box is fragile!" his father cried out when he handed Jack a box from the boot of the car.

Jack readjusted his grip. Drops of sweat trickled down his body. Unpacking all of his belongings with his parents wasn't how Jack had hoped to settle in. He preferred to take his time to decide where to place his things. Now he'd have to redo the whole room. Besides, there was something about being in a small space in the middle of a busy city, his parents watching his every move, that made the whole experience feel rushed.

5

Jack cleared his throat. He didn't want to say goodbye yet longed for the solitude to explore his surroundings at his own pace.

As Jack's mother returned to the car to retrieve the final box, Jack and his father were left alone for a couple of minutes. The faint sound of a siren rushing by filled the silence that hung between them, sharp as a knife. Jack gulped down large sips of water to quench his thirst.

His father looked at him with that stern look of his and took a seat on the chair by Jack's desk. "I don't need to tell you to do your best. I know you'll make us proud. We already are."

Jack's father had a strange way of showing affection, but Jack smiled when he realised this was as close to an *I love you* as he was going to get.

Jack's mother had to catch her breath as she put the last box in the room. She started unpacking and hung Jack's clothes in the wardrobe. "They all have creases in them from the journey." She bit the inside of her cheek and ruffled Jack's hair which made it even messier. "You need to get a haircut." She returned to the wardrobe and took one of his shirts in her hands for inspection. "You should re-iron your clothes before you wear them, or you'll look like a slob." Silence. "And go to church if you can spare the time. If not, say your prayers at night." She fiddled with the hangers, but there was no point delaying the inevitable. The time had come for Jack's parents to return home.

Before they left, Jack's father unpacked a framed photo which he placed on the corner of Jack's desk. On it was Raymond Lewis, Jack's grandfather, who smiled brightly towards a little version of Jack as they both sat behind the piano. Little Jack looked up to him in awe, his fingers positioned on the keys, eager to play.

Jack's father and grandfather looked a lot alike in the way they presented themselves. They had the same sturdy posture and the same grey hair combed to the back. Wherever Raymond went, he had radiated a sense of authority, as did Jack's father. If it wouldn't have been for his grandfather, Jack would have never

6

been able to play as well as he did. He had always been Jack's hero and remained so even in death.

Jack himself, being tall and slender, couldn't be more different in appearance. He had a, what his parents would call, peculiar sense of style. A distinctive array of predominantly classic clothes. Tailored trousers with a waistcoat one day. A loose linen shirt the next.

"Thanks for…" Jack didn't finish his sentence. His mother's eyes had teared up and even his father looked uncomfortable. Seeing his parents next to the car, ready to leave, made Jack more emotional than anticipated. At that point, the only thing he wanted to do was to hug his parents and drive right back home with them. He barely knew how to do anything for himself… he had never had to.

Jack's mother took her son's face between her hands and looked him straight in the eye. "I'm going to miss you, darling." She stood on the tips of her toes and gave him a quick kiss on his cheek.

Jack smelled the familiar perfume he associated with her and had a hard time watching her get in the car. Tears prickled behind his eyes, threatening to fall down. He forced them back with some difficulty. Jack waved them off, as they disappeared from sight. Back to Alston it was for them. Jack stayed behind, torn by mixed feelings of doubt and relief. Most of all he felt the overpowering loneliness of being alone in a place where he knew absolutely nobody.

CHAPTER TWO

JACK TOOK a minute in front of the steps leading up to the London Institute of Arts to catch his breath. He looked at his phone to check the time. Six minutes almost to the second from the residence hall on Soho Square. Anticipation had kept him up all night and had made him count the minutes until his alarm would go off.

The walls of the enormous industrial building were lined with copper panelling on one side and black brick on the other. Large windows took up most of its facade. Located on the far end of Shaftesbury Avenue, right in front of Shaftesbury Theatre, the school stood right in the creative hub of the West End. Jack mounted the steps to the entrance and had a hard time refraining himself from grinning like an idiot. There was something nice about not knowing what was about to happen, about doing something for the first time.

Once inside, Jack removed his circular sunglasses and allowed his eyes to adjust to the light. An enormous chandelier hung from the high white ceiling of the lobby. Spiral stairways on either side led towards the classrooms. The lobby was filled with sofas and armchairs on the left, and an information desk next to the lifts on the right. Behind the large glass door in front of him was a little courtyard with some trees and benches. Large windows surrounded the entire courtyard, giving the impression of it being in the same room as the lobby. A couple of students were scattered across the grass, enjoying the sunlight and talking amiably to one another.

Jack checked the welcome e-mail yet another time to make sure he had the room number correct for the introduction class. He buried his hands in the pockets of his shorts and headed for the stairway. His shorts were held up by his favourite navy blue suspenders. These suspenders had been an important part of his morning. Ever since his grandfather had given him his first pair for his fifteenth birthday, Jack was rarely seen without. Sadly, his grandfather died less than a year later. Jack's father had made it a tradition ever since to buy him a new pair for his birthday. Jack had received his latest pair only a couple of weeks ago when he had turned eighteen.

Well in advance, Jack took a seat in the lecture hall on the top floor of the building. He glanced out of the window which occupied the entire wall. The view over West End caught his attention. Lost in thought he stared at the world outside as the noise of laughter and footsteps grew louder by the minute.

A loud bang filled the room, leaving the classroom in a pin drop silence. Everyone turned to the front as a tiny, chubby man with a bald head and a grey suit that looked too tight for his figure entered. He walked over to the desk in front, his shoes clacking on the floor, and put his briefcase next to it. He scanned the room left to right. Still in silence, he took a piece of chalk and wrote his name on the board. The chalk squeaked. *Robert Norbury.* "Right. Welcome, first-years."

Jack had the urge to laugh but contained himself. Mr Norbury had a high-pitched voice which changed his entire appearance. He was no longer the grumpy looking old man he had appeared to be earlier. A small smile now played on Mr Norbury's lips. He took a seat on top of the wooden desk, which squeaked dangerously under his weight.

"Great batch this year!" Mr Norbury joked as he looked around at the eager students. This earned him some chuckles. "Let's get introductions out of the way, shall we? I'm Mr Norbury, head of the Music department and teacher for all the conducting students. Can I see some hands please?" He nodded in approval as a group of people raised their hands. "Joining me are Mrs Hendrix, head of the Drama department, and Mrs Rostov, head of the Dance department." Both teachers waved as their names were called out.

Mr Norbury continued. "Being accepted to the London Institute of Arts is a privilege not given to many. Let me tell you a little truth. By this time next year, half of you won't be here anymore. Some will crack under the pressure and some will simply not meet the expectations. Our aim is to shape you into true artists. It's your job to prove that we did right in singling you out."

Mr Norbury took a piece of chalk and wrote on the blackboard. *Annual creative recital.* "Throughout the year each department will have several performances, recitals, and ensembles to perform. In June we perform our creative recital, a show put together entirely by students. It's the opportunity to create something of your own, either by yourself or in group. For this endeavour we recommend and appreciate the partnership between departments, so don't be afraid to reach out to other students." Mrs Hendrix and Mrs Rostov, who sat at his side, both nodded.

"One little catch," Mr Norbury concluded. "Not every submitted piece can make it in the recital. Right after our Christmas break the most promising pieces will be selected by a panel of teachers. Now on to the best bit. Among the audience you'll find acclaimed people from all over the art industry looking for new talent. If you want to make it in this world, it's your job to impress them. And if I can give one piece of solid advice: this is an opportunity you want to seize with both hands."

Jack listened, but soon found his thoughts wandering

elsewhere. He had noticed upon entering that the lecture hall was positioned right next to the cafeteria. And for someone who hadn't taken the time to have breakfast, the smell of freshly cooked food invading the classroom made Jack's hungry stomach growl. Loudly.

"Are you starving as well?" a voice whispered next to Jack in a cockney accent.

A flush crept to his cheeks as Jack turned his head to look at the guy who had addressed him. He nodded sheepishly. "I am."

"Can't wait to get a proper bite to eat. I overslept big time."

They returned their attention to the front, but Jack couldn't help himself. "We need to prove them they did right in singling us out," he whispered to the guy next to him, imitating Mr Norbury.

A gasp escaped the guy's lips. "We are the chosen ones." They both chuckled.

"I'm Jack. Piano." He extended his hand to his neighbour.

"Cool, I'm Omar, I play the violin." Omar had afro pitch-black hair and wore black jeans and a hoody which read: *Blink if you like me*. He was rather skinny but had a nice face with long lashes and eyes almost as dark as his hair. His mischievous crooked smile became him well.

Jack smiled. He could have guessed Omar played the violin without him having to say a word. Jack wondered if strangers could tell that he was a pianist from the way he looked and moved. He was his music, and his music was him. As if the two were entwined in a way that could not be broken.

———

JACK TURNED over the cold doorknob and entered the classroom where he'd spend most of his time the coming years. A Steinway wing piano on a little stage caught his eye. The room was dark, without any windows, and illuminated by spots that hung from the black ceiling. A girl flipping through some sheet music occupied one of the chairs which stood in a circle next to the piano. Jack stepped up to her and introduced himself.

She had a firm handshake and a sly smile. "Christina." She returned her attention to her sheet music and sighed a little too loudly. Now how to describe Christina. In one word you could call her beautiful. An intimidating kind of beautiful. Perhaps beautiful wasn't even the right word to describe her. There was something alluring about her dark skin and her black sleek hair falling down against her stern-looking face.

Jack took the seat next to her, unsure of how to behave. Although she seemed to have already forgotten he was there.

One by one, the rest of the class poured in. They were a total of twelve students, coming from hundreds of applications for the Piano department alone. A world of perfectionists and overachievers. They were the ones who had made it. Yet they were only about to begin.

Their piano teacher entered last and walked towards them with a confident stride. She was a petite woman and looked rather fragile, with pale skin and blonde hair. She introduced herself as Filippa Lundqvist. From the moment she opened her mouth she radiated a sense of authority, grabbing everyone's immediate attention. Jack allowed himself a sideways glance at Christina, who sat at the edge of her seat.

A hand rose up in the air, interrupting the introduction. "Yes?" Mrs Lundqvist exclaimed. "You can all call me Mrs Lund if that's easier to pronounce." A few sighs of relief went around the classroom. Mrs Lund turned towards the girl who had now dropped her hand. "Does that answer your question?" The girl nodded.

Christina sighed. "How is that difficult to pronounce? You pronounce it Lund-k-vist but then faster."

Mrs Lund ignored Christina and reclaimed the attention. "I'm sure you're all itching to play by now. Did everyone receive my e-mail? Does everybody have their sheet music with them?" Mrs

Lund nodded in approval as everyone reached for their backpack's.

"For today you all prepared a piece of your own choosing. I want to use this first day to get to know each other and determine the level everyone's at." Mrs Lund walked over to the wing piano and played first. She might have looked fragile, but this all vanished the moment her fingers touched the keys. "Don't forget to have fun!" she exclaimed upon seeing the frightened looks on everyone's faces.

When a volunteer was asked to start, Jack's hand was the first and only to rise. He walked over to the piano and cleared his throat, staring at the unfamiliar faces in front of him. "I'm presenting Chopin's Nocturne number 20 in C-sharp minor."

Jack's fingers touched the keys as he began the opening of one of his grandfather's favourite pieces. It took him a few seconds to adjust to the piano as the keys were heavier than his own. Particular pieces brought him back to a specific memory and this was a good one. He could vividly see himself as a child on the sofa as he listened to his grandfather's rendition of the song. He had been enchanted and tried to convey that same feeling in his own rendition. Having played this piece so many times he barely had to think about which chords to play next. The music flowed out of him. After the introduction came the more haunting part of the song. He played it as precise and clean as he could. The result pleased him. When he let the final note linger, he looked up to see a smile on Mrs Lund's face.

Mrs Lund scribbled something on her notepad and nodded in approval. "We just heard a beautiful nocturne by Chopin. He composed it for his older sister Ludwika and is sometimes referred to as the *Reminiscence* Nocturne." She turned to Jack. "I can see you've inherited your grandfather's talent. Maybe later on you can play one of Raymond's own compositions. Do you know how to play them?"

"I do." Jack shifted uncomfortably in his seat. His earlier confidence evaporated as soon as the subject had come up. "You knew him then?" Up until now Jack had been successful in keeping this particular detail to himself. He knew the others would find out eventually but hoped it would have lasted longer than a day. At least that would have given him the chance to make friends at his own merit first.

"I had the pleasure of meeting him when I was still performing in Sweden. And a second time here at the school." Mrs Lund smiled as if the memory gave her great pleasure. "Let's continue around the room clockwise." She looked towards the girl on Jack's left. "Katie, you're next."

As Katie took her place behind the piano, Jack heard Christina whisper to the person next to her, "I didn't need a famous grandfather to get me in."

Jack pretended not to hear but couldn't suppress a sting of disappointment. He almost spoke up. *Why don't you try living under the pressure?*

When it was Christina's turn to play, Jack could put a finger on why he had found her alluring. She brought *Voices of Spring* by Johann Strauss, which scored her great points. With the music she played she invited you to explore her deepest secrets in the most beautiful way. She invited you to see a part of herself that she would otherwise never reveal. The amount of passion she played with astounded Jack and rendered him speechless. Christina's body moved in sync with her music. Her face wasn't stern anymore, but surprisingly soft, with her brow creased in concentration. Slowly, the song came to an end. They were brought back to the dark, silent classroom. Christina stood up and smiled in such a conceited way it broke the spell. She knew perfectly well how good she was. *What a pity.*

JACK HALTED at the middle of Soho Square before entering the residence hall, enjoying the warmth of the setting sun on his face. Something about London intimidated yet exhilarated him at the same time. Being a city full of promise, the streets of London thrummed with a never-ending energy.

"Jack, wait up!" Christina's voice woke Jack from his reveries. He opened his eyes to look at her stern face. "Do you want to have dinner together? I was about to go up and cook something if you wanted to join." She sounded friendlier than earlier.

Jack narrowed his eyes. "Why?" Remembering the way she had talked about him in class didn't make him want to be in her company any more than necessary.

She shrugged. "Because school is over and I'm hungry." She started walking towards their building and Jack found himself following her.

Stepping out of the lift you came in a long hallway filled with bedrooms. On the far end of the corridor was the common room, filled with comfortable sofas and a huge rug. Lined against the wall were white tables for the students to work at. Jack and Christina were headed next-door to the large kitchen with a big communal table in the middle. Each student had a designated cupboard for their cooking supplies and a place in one of the fridges to store their food. Lunch was served daily in the cafeteria, but Jack would have to fend for himself at night. And for Jack, who had never cooked a meal in his life, it was a struggle to follow Christina's most basic instructions.

Christina shot him sideway glances from time to time. "Not much of a chef, are you?"

"That obvious, huh?" Jack didn't meet Christina's gaze, but continued slicing the courgette for her vegetable lasagne.

"Try and cut the pieces evenly," she intervened.

"I'm trying!"

By the time he had gotten through one courgette, Christina had done pretty much everything else.

"I swear to God, this is delicious!" Jack said as he took another bite. He was in no way jealous of the people on the other side of the table eating instant noodles, which was exactly what he'd be eating if it wouldn't have been for Christina.

Christina smirked. "I know, right!" She edged her seat closer to the table. "I liked your piece today, earlier in class. I had no idea you were related to Raymond Lewis." She tilted her head to the side as she observed him. "I looked through the list of names to see who'd be in our class, but it's such a common surname that I hadn't thought...." She paused. "It must have been like living a dream, having him as your grandfather."

"Not always a dream."

Christina didn't pay much attention to what he said. "I knew from the moment you played we had to hang out." She lowered her voice. "Between you and me, the rest of the class was a little mediocre, don't you think?" She didn't wait for his response. "Anyway. I don't mind that we're a little ahead of the group, but I have to say I'm disappointed in the level. We can help each other out though. I love a good challenge."

Jack stared at her with wide eyes. "It was only the first day. I rather liked hearing what everyone chose to play. It says a lot about a person, doesn't it?"

"It does indeed," Christina had to admit.

"I must say I enjoyed hearing you play as well. The way you brought your piece, all that emotion, it blew me away." He didn't know why, but Jack found himself being truthful to Christina even if he didn't like her all that much.

She smiled at him. "I do believe it turned out OK. I'm so excited that we finally got started. My mind was all over the place. Which piece do I want to interpret? How am I going to play it? And then when I play I just... get carried away. I get in my own head and spill everything I'm feeling through the keys of a piano. How extraordinary is that?"

Jack's lips tightened. "That's beautiful," was all he could muster. It really was extraordinary.

"Anyway, I'm going to prepare for Singing class tomorrow. See you later!"

Jack bid her goodnight and wondered what she could be preparing after one day of class.

CHAPTER THREE

THE STREET LANTERNS switched on as the setting sun disappeared behind the buildings. Jack waited for Christina outside of school on a Thursday night. In the two weeks they had been there, Christina had somehow managed to drag him into rehearsing together most nights after school. They didn't talk much about anything other than music. Jack had to practice anyway and didn't mind the company. Despite the huge differences in their personalities, they worked well together as a team.

Jack shivered, bouncing from one foot to the other in order to keep warm. Goosebumps formed all over his arms and a chill ran down his spine. He hadn't brought a jacket, underestimating how chilly it would get at night. In about two weeks he found his thoughts about London and life in the city almost completely altered. The loudness of the city now felt consoling. Consoling in the way that you were never alone. That there were others going through similar experiences.

People dressed up for the theatre filled the busy street, laughing amiably and having fun. Jack spotted Christina amongst them, making her way through a mass of people who were queuing in front of Palace Theatre. She always looked impeccable and today was no exception. She had not forgotten to dress warm enough and wore a long grey coat which almost reached the ground.

Christina rummaged through her handbag in search of her student ID. They walked around the corner, to the side entrance of the school. She held her card against the electronic lock of the door, giving them access to the basement level of the school. This part was always open after hours for the students to practice. They stepped into the long, dark, and narrow corridor. Doors on either side led to small individual studios or working spaces.

Christina opened the door to a piano studio, a small room consisting of a piano, a table, and some chairs. She removed a delicate blue scarf from her neck and handed it to Jack, who hung it over the coat rack next to him. She positioned her sheet music on the music desk in front of her and let her fingers hover above the keys before touching them. She had this way about her where she touched the keys in such a gentle way they could have been made of porcelain. Jack might have had the better technique, but Christina had something equally valuable.

Jack sighed when she had finished. "I can't play like that." He had been playing the piano every day of his life from before he could remember. He played his songs to the point of perfection, but something was always missing. Christina had a certain je-ne-sais-quoi about her that didn't come from talent alone. "It's mesmerising when you play."

Christina stood up and stretched her arms with that sly smile of hers. She ignored the compliment and made way for Jack to sit. Christina was conceited in the way that she knew how good she was. She made sure everybody else knew it too. "Of course you can. Your turn!"

They took turns playing and only stopped when they were satisfied with their work. Christina grabbed her coat and addressed Jack with a creased brow. "I think you're unable to hear how good you are." She sounded sincerer than Jack had ever heard her. She turned to look at him with a smile. "When you play, you leave the whole room in amazement. You make it seem so effortless." She opened the door. "Let's get out of here."

The fresh air made it easier for Jack to clear his head as they returned to the residence hall. Nobody could hear themselves play. Nobody could see themselves as others could. That thought lifted his spirits.

───────────

THE INCREASING sound of laughter emerged from the common room next to the kitchen. Jack, who had successfully prepared instant mac and cheese ate faster, burning his tongue in the process. He should have gone to bed, but the laughter was infectious and the curiosity too great.

"Hey, guys, how's everything going?" The words were out before he knew it. There he stood, in the doorway of the common room, addressing a group of strangers.

One guy pointed at him. "I know you, don't I? You're Jack, piano."

Jack grinned upon recognition. "Omar, violin. Right?"

"Do you want to join us?" Omar asked. He wore one of his colourful hoodies again, paired with joggers and fluffy slippers.

"If I'm not intruding?" Jack walked over and plopped down on the sofa next to Omar before anyone could protest. Across from them, seated in armchairs, were two guys whom he got introduced to. There was Christian, a first-year acting student with long ginger hair pulled back into a bun. His pale face was covered in freckles, making his blue eyes pop. Then there was Alexander, a playwright student. He was a fit guy with bright amber eyes and a light stubble around his jaw. He had a tapered haircut where his hair was longer on top and shorter on the sides. It was brushed to the side, but a single lock had fallen out of place.

"A piano student? That's cool," Christian said. "Have you had a whirlwind start of the year like the rest of us?"

Jack settled on the sofa. "Oh, yes. There doesn't seem to be much room for figuring stuff out, I've noticed that much."

Omar laughed. "I'd go even further than that and say this place is bonkers. But it's even better than I expected, you know? It's nice to be surrounded by likeminded people."

Alexander jumped in. He brushed the loose strand of hair behind his ear with his fingers. "However nice it is to be surrounded by likeminded souls, these people are also your competition and they can't wait to see you fail."

"Please," Omar dragged out. "Not everyone is waiting for us to fail."

Alexander shrugged. "Just you wait and see. You're too optimistic."

"And proud to be!" Omar retorted with a smile on his face.

"I have to agree with Omar," said Christian. "So far it's a nice kind of crazy. It beats secondary school any day. God was that an uninspiring place." He scrunched up his nose as if the memory pained him.

"Secondary school was alright for me. Being home-schooled however, that's the real pain." Jack elaborated at the sight of three pairs of curious eyes. "I was home-schooled until I was ten. My parents used to say they were able to give me a higher quality of education in that way. Something I'd never get in a public school."

Omar shuddered. "That wouldn't have been my type of thing. I lived for playground talk."

"Oh, it wasn't my thing either. Luckily, they caved in after a few years. When we moved to England my grandfather was able to convince my parents to let me go to school." Jack smiled at the memory. At times where his parents were ruffling his hair but not listening to what he was saying, it had been great to have his grandfather as his advocate.

"You moved here? Don't tell me where you're from, I'm going to guess," Omar said.

"He's clearly American. You have a slight accent," Christian explained upon seeing the look on Jack's face.

Jack nodded. "Dual citizenship. My father's English and my mother's American. I moved around quite a bit as a child."

"Where did you live in America?" Alexander asked. It was the first time he addressed Jack.

Omar grinned and turned to Jack before he could answer. "He's been to New York once and thinks he knows all about America."

Alexander threw his hands in the air. "Never mind."

"Come on, I'm kidding," Omar tried to plead with him, still laughing.

Jack laughed along but answered Alexander's question anyway. "I was born in Sunnyvale, Texas, a small village in the outskirts of Dallas. I grew up there near the ranch of my grandparents on my mother's side." Jack's Mammaw and Pappaw, as he had called them, had been closely involved in Jack's early upbringing. "They both died when I was six. That's when we moved to Boston to be closer to my other grandfather. We lived there for around four years before moving to England."

"That is a lot of moving around for a kid," Alexander remarked.

"I was so young I didn't really mind. It was all a big adventure at the time. My father and grandfather were born and raised in York, so that's why we moved to that area. I live in Alston now."

Nobody seemed to know Alston. Omar and Alexander had both lived in greater London their entire lives and Christian came from the south.

Christian got up. "Well, that's me off for tonight. Mrs Hendrix is expecting us to be in top shape tomorrow morning. We're working on Shakespearean plays this term."

They watched Christian leave in silence. Alexander shot Omar a knowing look and heaved a sigh when Christian was out of sight.

Omar shook his head in reply. "Come on, it wasn't that bad this time round."

Alexander looked like he wanted to say something but glanced towards Jack and thought the better of it.

Jack shot Alexander an annoyed look and took this as his cue to leave, but Omar addressed him before he could.

"Alexander can't stand Christian. That's why he's being obnoxious. They had to work together last week on a scene and let's just say that Christian wasn't very nice about Alexander's script."

Alexander's eyes widened. "Oh, please, don't say it like that. You don't like him either, admit it."

Omar shook his head. "I won't. I see him all the time in The Golden Lion. I'm determined to keep the peace."

"In the what?" Jack asked, unable the follow the conversation

"The Golden Lion is a pub where I work. Great atmosphere, great beers. You should check it out. It's always jam-packed with people from the Institute."

"By the way, it's not that he wasn't nice about the script. He was being a complete jerk all around. It's not my fault the guy only wants to do comedy. He has to be more versatile."

"So do you," Omar joked.

AFTER ANOTHER BUSY day of classes Jack ventured outside and didn't feel like going straight to the residence hall. He enjoyed exploring the city that slowly unravelled itself, revealing bits here and there the more he got to know it. He walked around the neighbourhood and came across Russel Square, which looked a lot like Soho Square, but bigger and greener. He sat on one of the benches and observed the people passing by, a lot of whom were in a rush to get home after their working days. Everybody minded their own business, ignoring the rustling of the leaves or the cry of the wind between the trees. Amidst the trees something caught Jack's attention. *The Imagination Factory.* The illuminated letters and the chill of the day invited Jack to take a closer look.

The tinkle of the bell above the door announced Jack's entrance in the small café. The smell of freshly baked pastries and the warmth welcomed him inside. He rubbed his hands together as a hint of cinnamon filled his nostrils. He took a seat at one of the round tables by the window and hung his scarf over the edge of his chair. The café had an intimate atmosphere and felt homey with its abundance of plants scattered around the place. Not two tables or chairs were identical. A mismatch of colourful furniture that somehow worked perfectly together.

"Can I get you anything, dear?" A steady voice broke him out of his reveries. The waitress had a strong American accent and looked to be in her forties. She had thin high arched eyebrows and coloured blonde hair in a bob haircut. With a pair of ripped mom jeans and trainers her overall appearance came across as young and hip for her age.

A couple of minutes later she returned with the pot of tea Jack had ordered. She placed it gently on the tiny table in front of him. "There you go. I haven't seen you here before, have I?" She continued when Jack shook his head. "I'm the owner of The Imagination Factory. It's always nice to meet new customers."

"Likewise. What a great place you have here. I think I'll be coming here more often."

The waitress smiled. "That's nice of you to say. What brings you to London? I can hear you're not from around, if you don't mind me prying?"

"Not at all!" Jack was happy for the conversation. "I'm a student at the London Institute of Arts, not far from here. I just enrolled."

"Oh!" she exclaimed. "We regularly get art students here. How's life in the city treating you?"

"Pretty well. Kind of hectic to be honest. Haven't found much time for myself since school is quite demanding. Long hours and such."

The bell rang as a young couple entered. The waitress greeted them amiably and returned her attention to Jack. "I can imagine so. What is it that you're studying? Are you an actor, a dancer, or a musician?"

Jack smiled, impressed by her knowledge of the school. "I'm a pianist." He took a sip of his tea, which was still too hot, and forced himself to swallow it down.

Again she looked up to the new customers. "I should get to work. It was a pleasure to meet you. Do come back if you find the time." She stood up and held out her hand. "I'm Grace Davis by the way."

He shook her hand. "Jack."

Grace left to tend to her other customers with as much enthusiasm as she had greeted Jack.

Jack's pocket buzzed with a text message from Christina, asking if he wanted to join her for a quick rehearsal in the morning before classes. Jack sighed but agreed anyway. They had each been working on a different piece during their weekly private piano lessons with Mrs Lund. At the end of every week they came together and listened to each other's pieces in a group session. Since tomorrow was that day, getting some extra practice in wasn't a bad idea.

Jack returned home in a daze and had trouble falling asleep. With classes, homework, and daily piano practices going on, he had scarcely found any time for himself. Jack had always known how life at the Institute would be demanding. To actually be in that position made him struggle more than he had anticipated. Not in the way that he had a hard time keeping up with his classes. The problem was that with each new day he could feel a distance between himself and his classmates, and it was a pretty significant one. Everybody put their heart and soul into their pieces. And while technically Jack was by far top of his class, he didn't seem able to give his music that extra spark it needed.

The pressure of living up to the expectations of his teachers and most importantly his parents was getting to him. He turned his head to look at his grandfather's photo on his desk, the last thing he saw before closing his eyes.

CHAPTER FOUR

MORNING ARRIVED SOONER than Jack would have liked. Still half asleep he stifled a yawn as he met up with Christina at the side entrance of the school. Christina sipped her takeaway coffee and tapped her foot to the ground. She sighed when he reached her as if saying, *Finally... You made it...*, even though Jack was right on time.

They walked towards their favourite piano studio, the only one with a similar Steinway to the one they had in their classroom. Their classmates Jessica and Imani had had the same thought and beat them to it. At the sight of Christina and Jack, Jessica had hurried, almost dragging Imani behind her. When Jessica closed the door behind them, Imani shot Christina and Jack an apologetic look.

Christina remained frozen where she stood. Her mouth fell open and she stuttered to find her words. "She did that on purpose to vex me!"

Jack tugged Christina towards another studio, too tired to care. "It doesn't matter. Let's get started. We don't have much time."

"Of course there is competition among the class and she knows I'm better than her." Christina had to hurry to keep in pace with Jack. Jack didn't pay much attention to her ramblings, but she went on regardless. "I don't know why she hates me like that... It bothers me."

Jack rolled his eyes and opened the door to the nearest piano studio. "I'm sure she doesn't hate you. Just don't show her that it gets to you," he suggested, to shut her up on the subject.

Christina laughed. "Oh, she doesn't get to me, trust me. I reckon she despises the both of us for being top of our class."

Jack, having never heard a bad word from Jessica doubted this, but didn't feel like discussing it any further. He was tired, it was early, and he wasn't in the mood to play. Still, he gave it his best shot. Once he got in the rhythm, his fingers flowed smoothly over the keys. He went over the fingering and hand positions one last time and decided he was ready.

Christina seemed to be more appreciative of his performance than himself. "You're such a quick study." A jealous undertone shone through in her voice. "I'm sure you must have had an amazing tutor. That plus your grandfather being the genius he is."

"My grandfather was my tutor."

Christina's jaw dropped. "How on earth did he have time for that?"

Some of the happiest moments from Jack's childhood were of the time when they lived with his grandfather in Boston. "He taught me how to play in between concerts and tours when we lived in Boston. The last years of his life he got sick and stopped performing and travelling. That's why we moved to England. Back to his roots. He had plenty of time to teach me one on one." Jack had been too young to realise that his grandfather had eventually stopped performing because of his illness. Moving to England had been nothing more than another big adventure in Jack's eyes. With no other relatives on Jack's mother's side nothing tied them to America anymore.

"Lucky you," Christina said. "That must have been amazing. I'm sure he taught you all kind of intricate techniques."

Jack's face reddened. He took a calming breath and tried to relax his tensed up muscles. "He was my grandfather first of all, before being my tutor." The words came out more harshly than intended.

"Don't tell your father, alright?" Raymond looked down at the little boy with the mischievous smile on his face. Coming straight from the airport he still wore his grey suit with a chequered vest and matching chequered socks underneath.

Jack giggled and held his hand in front of his mouth to keep quiet. He was wearing his favourite Christmas themed pyjamas even if it was full-on summer.

Raymond put a finger against his lips as he motioned for Jack to follow him. Nothing but the bags underneath his eyes and the pale tone of his skin gave away how tired and ill he was. As long as the boy didn't notice he wouldn't tell him a thing. It kept him energised and the thought of inflicting pain and worry to his grandchild was too much to handle.

"Grandpa, wait!" Panic crept through Jack's voice, which came out higher than expected. "It's past curfew. Mom and Dad will get angry if they see us out of bed."

"Then we'll have to be very quiet, won't we? Come on, I've got something to show you."

Jack decided to show his grandfather how brave he was and got out of bed. He slipped into his robe and slippers and followed his grandfather downstairs where his enormous suitcase stood by the door. Jack got comfortable on the sofa while his grandfather switched on the television.

Jack snuggled close to him. "I'm glad you're back, Grandpa. How long will you stay for?"

Raymond ruffled the boy's hair. "I'm here to stay, buddy. And I told you I'd make it to your birthday, didn't I?"

Jack turned serious and crossed his arms. "I thought you had forgotten."

"Oh, I could never. There was a hold up at the airport, but I'm here now. I have a surprise for you, little man."

Jack frowned. "I turned eleven today," he said with dignity. He softened his gaze. "Surprise?"

Raymond nodded. "I wrote a new piece. It's my Sonata number 17 in A minor. And I wrote it especially for you. Do you want to hear it?"

Jack's mouth fell open. "Just for me?"

"Just for you," Raymond assured him. "I played it last night in Brussels for your birthday. Shall we watch it together?"

Jack nodded vigorously.

Raymond pressed play and there he was, in a dark concert hall illuminated by a single spot. Jack listened with great fascination. It had a cheerful tune to it. It started of slow and picked up in pace by the middle and end. Jack loved the smile on his grandfather's face whenever he played. As the crowd broke into applause, Raymond paused the TV.

"That was beautiful!" Jack said, completely in awe. "Don't you ever get scared to go up there and play for so many people all by yourself?"

Raymond shook his head. "Not anymore. I was at first, until I realised everything I was scared of was only in my head."

Jack thought it over but didn't quite understand what his grandfather meant.

"If you want, I can teach you how to play the song. We can start tomorrow. Is that something you'd like?"

"Can't we start now?"

Raymond smiled. "We can't wake your parents, remember? We'll get started in the morning." He got up and took his grandson back to his room. He sat at the edge of his bed and tucked him in. "Would you like that? To be on stage and play your songs for everyone?"

Jack had to think about this for a moment. "Maybe," he contemplated, "But only if you're there with me."

Christina noticed the change in behaviour. "You must miss him."

Jack nodded. "Terribly."

Right when Christina was about to play again, Jack's pocket vibrated. He apologised to Christina as he mouthed *phone* to her.

Christina narrowed her eyes and waited for him to leave the studio before getting started.

Jack rushed into the hallway and was just in time to answer.

Hearing his mother's voice could always soothe him. His chest tightened at the thought of home.

"I'm not calling too early, am I? I thought I'd try and catch you before you start class."

Jack shook his head but realised his mother couldn't see him. "No, it's fine. Christina and I are rehearsing. I'm already at the school."

"Getting practice in before classes. You know we're proud of you, don't you? And I'm sure your grandfather would have been proud as well. Bless his soul." She sighed happily. "Your father is always talking about you since you left. Always talking about his son and how he is making it down in London. To everyone who'll hear him. But don't tell him I told you this."

Jack smiled involuntarily. "I won't!" He had always worked hard to gain his father's approval but didn't feel worthy of it now that he had it. Jack suddenly missed his parents terribly. "How come you're up so early anyway? Special day?"

"Oh no, nothing of that sort. Your father has to get to work early because some oversea shipments are going to be delivered early morning. Some new Italian violins that are just out on the market. I'm going to the shop to help him out today. Sean has been down with the flu all week."

Mrs Lewis didn't have a job of her own and had always been a stay-at-home mom. Jack worried for her now that he lived in London and hoped she wouldn't get too lonely. "You've been going there more often lately, haven't you?"

"I have. It wasn't part of the plan, but business is booming so your father and Sean can use an extra set of hands from time to time. I help them with all the administration work. Ah, here he comes. He'd love to talk to you."

Jack could perfectly imagine how his mother passed the phone to his father. She would stay close by in hope to hear the rest of the conversation. A few seconds later Jack heard his father's heavy voice. "Great to catch you this morning."

"Hi, Dad! Mom just told me about your busy day."

29

"The shop has been doing great. We've had a lot of international interest these past few months."

"Congratulations, I'm happy for you!"

"That's also the reason why I have to go down to London for business for a couple of days. What do you say we catch up over lunch on Monday?"

"Sounds great!" Jack longed to see his father again.

Meanwhile Christina had exited the rehearsal studio. She pointed towards her watch and mouthed for Jack to hurry up.

With a wave of his hand he shut her up. "I have to go. Class is about to start. See you Monday."

———

DURING HIS MUSIC Theory class Jack found his mind wandering elsewhere. A full day of Piano and Ear Training classes had exhausted him too much to pay any more attention. He wondered if his grandfather would be as proud as his mother tried to make him believe. Coming from a poor family, Raymond Lewis had had to work hard to become the pianist he had become. He had always chased his dreams and had never given up. His career started out by making recompositions of pieces by the great pianists from back in the day. Think Vivaldi, Chopin, Strauss, Tchaikovsky. Only when he started making his own compositions did word of his talent spread across the country and later the world. Touring took up most of his time at the peak of his career. As most of them were based through America, he had eventually moved there with Jack's father. A story of a man, coming from nothing, who had made something of himself. Jack couldn't not be in awe of his achievements.

The chuckles from his classmates brought Jack's attention back to the room. He couldn't bring himself to engage in the class and stared at his empty notepad.

"Split up in pairs of two," his teacher instructed. "Divide

yourselves around the classroom and pick one of the subjects we discussed."

Tumult broke out when everybody shoved their chairs around and looked for a partner to work with. Jessica, who sat next to Jack, etched closer to him. "Do you want to work together on this one?" She flashed him a smile, revealing her braces. She had layered blonde hair with bangs, a big nose, and always wore t-shirts tucked away in a pair of jeans.

Christina stood by his side in no time. "Move along, Jack and I will work together." She gestured with her hand, signalling that Jessica should leave.

Jessica pursed her lips and stormed off without saying anything. Her glare reached Christina from across the room.

"You didn't have to do that," Jack hissed. "That was so rude."

Christina shrugged. "Whatever. She deserves it." She flipped open her textbook. "Is there any subject that sparked your interest?"

Jack shook his head. "The choice is all yours."

"Let's go for Mozart versus Beethoven, a comparison of their style and technique." She typed the words on her laptop as if someone chased her. She stared at Jack's empty notepad. "Unless you'd rather write a paper on the development of musical instruments? That's fine too."

"Beethoven and Mozart are fine," Jack assured her. His phone lit up with a text from Omar. *What are you up to tonight?*

Jack grinned and texted back. *Taking a break?*

———

JACK WASTED no time in hurrying to the residence hall after class. He changed and tried his best to look decent in a loose buttoned-up shirt with black suspenders. With his hands he tried to put his wavy hair into place. Satisfied, Jack took one final look in the mirror. On his way out he ran into Christina, who had only just returned from school.

31

"Looking fancy tonight," she said, eyeing him up and down in approval.

Jack smiled. "I'm headed out. There's supposed to be this great pub nearby called The Golden Lion. I'm meeting up with a friend."

Christina clasped her hands together and continued in a friendlier tone than usual, "We have been working hard, haven't we? Every now and then we need to make sure to take a break, or we'll go crazy."

Ready to leave, Jack only nodded as he buried his hands in the pockets of his coat.

"I've heard great things about The Golden Lion, you know?" Christina added. "Loads of people from school hang out there in the weekends."

An uneasiness overcame Jack. He hadn't wanted to invite Christina but didn't seem to have much choice. "Do you want to join us?"

Christina pretended to be surprised. "Well... since you're asking. Why not? Can you wait ten minutes while I go freshen up?" A little spark ignited in her eyes.

True to her word, Christina reappeared downstairs almost exactly ten minutes later. She had dressed up for the occasion and wore an elegant black dress that came mid-thigh. "Next one to the right." Christina looked on her phone as she followed the directions.

Jack nudged her in the side and pointed further down the street. "There's Omar!"

"I recognise him! Doesn't he live on our floor?"

Jack nodded and quickened his pace to catch up with Omar. Christina took hold of Jack's arm to avoid stumbling in her high heels.

The warmth of the pub greeted them inside. It smelled of beer and chips and oozed that typical brown pub charm. In atmosphere it was like a big communal living room, open for whoever needed an escape from their day. People were laughing and had to shout to understand each other. The floor was covered in beer-drenched red carpet. The latest Manchester United - Liverpool football match played on the television while the Pixies blasted through the stereo.

Jack, Omar, and Christina stood in the doorway for a minute or so, scanning the pub for an empty table. Christina shifted from one foot to the other, clearly not in her comfort zone no matter how she tried to hide it.

Omar pointed towards the only available table, next to the window in the corner. "What do you guys want? First round is on me! Beers?"

Jack nodded. "Sure, why not!"

They both looked at Christina. "Sounds good." She unbuttoned her long coat and walked over to the table, squeezing past the other customers.

"Be right back!" Omar headed to the bar, which had barstools in front of it and a huge cupboard of liquor behind it.

Christina bopped her head to the music. "I love this song," she half-shouted.

Jack's eyes widened. "You do? I didn't know that." Who would have thought he would be able to bond with Christina over a mutual love of alternative rock music?

Christina smiled. It even looked genuine. "We don't know each other that well. Apart from what goes on in our classes, of course."

"Fair enough. Let's change that tonight."

Omar returned and clinked his glass against Jack's and Christina's. "Cheers, mate!" He spilled some beer in the process.

"How about the creative recital?" Christina asked them after a comfortable silence, much more at ease since they sat down. "Are your families coming?"

Omar sipped his beer and nodded. "The whole bunch is going to be there. My parents, brother, aunt and uncle, and my grandparents. They wouldn't miss it. They threatened to make t-shirts." His face turned grim for a moment.

Jack laughed aloud at the idea. "That would be brilliant, I want one of those. With a big photo of your head on it." The creative recital had escaped Jack's mind. They had until the new year to present an idea, which was plenty of time. It had only just turned October after all. "My parents are coming as well. We haven't really discussed it yet."

"No family support team with t-shirts for you?" Omar addressed Christina.

Christina shrugged. "I'm not even sure if anyone is coming to see me play. I have the busiest parents imaginable. They're always travelling for work."

Jack put his glass to his lips and drank the remainder of his pint. The now warm beer tasted disgusting. He locked eyes with the bartender and motioned for him to bring them another round.

"It's such a shame your grandparents aren't here anymore, Jack," Christina continued dreamily. "Just imagine your grandfather coming to watch us all."

Omar gasped as realisation hit him. "Wait a minute. Jack Lewis." He pronounced Jack's name slowly. "You are not telling me you are the grandson of Raymond Lewis, the piano legend?"

Jack only nodded.

Omar was all amazement. He received an annoyed look from Christina. "What?" he asked her. "Lewis is not an uncommon last name. How was I supposed to know Jack is related to a bloody genius?"

Christina merely rolled her eyes at him and changed the subject, for which Jack was grateful.

As the beers kept coming their conversation turned lighter and sillier. They were shouting at least as hard if not harder than the other customers, who got drunker the more the night progressed. Even Christina wasn't too bad once she got loose. Soon enough Jack's head spun and he couldn't contain his laughter anymore. He wished more nights could be like that one. Nights where you could forget about all the serious stuff and just laugh and talk away. No consequences. No time limit. No pressure.

"Do you guys want to head back to the residence with me?" Christina asked when the bar was emptying out.

Jack shook his head although he had a hard time to keep his eyes open and focused. "I don't want to go." He slurred his words, which made him laugh.

She directed her attention towards Omar.

"Sure, let's go." He downed his beer. His cockney accent became heavier after a few drinks.

Jack still had half a pint in front of him. He scrunched up his face. "What are you guys talking about? We just got here." Why did Christina have to be such a spoilsport all the time?

"We've been here for hours; everyone is going home." Christina turned to Omar for support.

Jack sighed. "Fine." He dragged the word out.

"He's just drunk," Omar responded. "Let's get him to bed."

Jack got up but had to hold on to the table to keep his balance. On their way out, the bartender was shaking his head. "Keep that one under control, will you?" he shouted towards Omar.

"Will do!" Omar shouted in return. "See you, Arthur!"

Jack linked arms with Christina on one side and Omar on the other. He had a hard time keeping his eyes focused and his feet going straight. A sudden emptiness consumed him. That was the last thing he remembered before waking up in his bed in yesterday's clothes, his head hurting like hell.

CHAPTER FIVE

BY MONDAY MORNING Jack hadn't seen or heard anything from Christina and Omar. Shame filled him up when he thought of his behaviour in the pub. What a way to make new friends. The last thing he remembered was Christina and Omar carrying him inside. He hadn't known his boundaries and hadn't known when to stop. Jack had never been drunk before that night. The experience had been more painful than he had hoped it to be.

Jack arrived right on time in class and took a seat next to Christina. He had a hard time meeting her gaze and looked away from her prying eyes.

Mrs Lund called the class to attention and explained their assignment of the week. They were free to pick any piece they liked, but it had to have a personal meaning to it. They had all week to prepare and would have to bring their songs in front of the class on Friday.

Christina straightened her back as Mrs Lund went over the details. She winked at Jack and nodded as if to say, 'we've got this'.

Jack returned the wink.

"We should get rehearsing straight away!" Christina exclaimed after Mrs Lund dismissed them.

Whatever Jack had expected, it wasn't this. "Christina, relax. We didn't even choose what to play yet."

"Jack, can you hang on for a second?" Mrs Lund called out to Jack from the doorway of their classroom. "I'd like to talk to you in private."

Jack stopped walking and turned around to face his teacher. "Of course!"

"Good afternoon, Mrs Lundqvist. See you tomorrow!" Christina exclaimed in a cheerful voice.

Jack followed Mrs Lund back inside but not before rolling his eyes at Christina upon passing her. His heart beat rapidly. The now empty classroom looked a lot more daunting than it had minutes ago.

"Any progress on your idea for the creative recital yet?" Mrs Lund asked him.

Jack wracked his brain to think if he had missed any deadlines. He shook his head slowly, horror written all over his face. "I'm afraid I haven't found the time yet."

Mrs Lund's expression remained neutral. "You're one of the most promising students I've ever had, so I'm going to be completely honest. I'm worried about you, Jack. I've been following your progress closely and feel you could do with some guidance."

So they had noticed how he was struggling. Great. Jack tried to keep a smile on his face but wanted nothing more than this conversation to be over with as soon as possible.

"Did you know your grandfather played a concerto here in the school? Back when the school celebrated its 50th anniversary? I was still a student of my own back then."

Jack nodded. How could he not, when his father reminded him every chance he got?

"You remind me of him in some ways. He must have been a good teacher."

An involuntary smile appeared on Jack's face. "He taught me

from the moment I could walk until the day he died." Jack rarely talked about his grandfather's death to others.

Mrs Lund gave Jack all the time he needed. She motioned for him to sit down before replying. "There is one major thing you've got to work on. I'm sure you already know it and if not, I'll give you some friendly advice. Your grandfather has been successful in teaching you the technical part. But when he played, he left the whole room in amazement. There was something almost magical about it."

"I do know what you mean," Jack admitted with a straight face. Mrs Lund discussing Jack's lack of passion in his work filled him with embarrassment. "And I know this is something I've got to work on. Please believe me when I say that I am working on it, hard."

"I'm not here to reprimand you," Mrs Lund assured him. "Merely to give you some advice now that we're still early in the year. It's only October, you have plenty of time. But now, with our next assignment, would be the best time to step it up a notch. Make sure that the piece you choose overflows with personality and emotion. Step up your game and prove yourself. In this case, talent alone isn't going to cut it."

Jack's head spun. *I know all this. I'm trying. Just let me be.*

"My advice is to broaden your horizon."

Jack's brow creased. "Excuse me?"

"I presume playing the piano has been your main focus, your only hobby?" When Jack nodded, she went on. "This school has so much creativity to offer it's hard not to get inspired. Why don't you take a look around the school? See what's going on. Art comes in many different forms. Allow them to inspire you."

Jack scratched the back of his neck. He left with a sinking feeling in his stomach. No matter where he went, he couldn't escape the fact that he never seemed to be good enough. His grandfather had fought for what he wanted and had gotten famous for it in the end. His last name was enough for young aspiring pianists to wish they had been born in Jack's shoes. Because how lucky was he, to be born as the grandson of such a legend. Luckier even, to have inherited his talent. Everyone expected such great things from him, while he didn't even know if he wanted that for himself.

It had been easy to get swept up in things and ignore the reality of it all. But right now, when he actually took the time to think things over, it was so easy to see. He had been blinded by his family, his teachers, and even by himself. He needed to play the piano because his grandfather did. He needed to make his father proud, who wanted Jack to become as good as his own father had been. But Jack couldn't pretend any longer. In a place like this, surrounded by the most passionate young musicians of the world, he couldn't deny one simple fact. That he didn't enjoy playing the piano as much as he needed to.

CHRISTINA INTERCEPTED Jack right before he had to leave for lunch with his father. "Let's talk." She pulled him into an empty classroom and closed the door behind them. "Are you quite alright? I mean, I get having fun and letting go every once in a while, but you can tell me if anything is wrong. Omar as well. He's a good guy."

"I know, I know." Jack grew tired of his own excuses. It had been naive of him to think he had heard the last about his behaviour of last weekend. "I'm having a rough time to be honest. I didn't mean to work it out on you guys. I'm sorry." He found that he wanted to confide in Christina. "Lately I've been wondering if I'm in the right place here…"

Christina's eyebrows shot upwards. "Of course you belong here! You don't need to have any doubts about that. You and me, we're top of our year. You can't… Oh, sorry, go on."

Hesitantly, Jack continued. "I'm not sure if I actually like playing the piano anymore." He avoided making eye contact. He had so wished to avoid telling her this, telling anyone this, but he didn't know what else to do. "I do love playing. Or I loved playing, with my grandfather. After he passed away it became even more important to my dad that I succeeded. Even if by that time I didn't want it as much as he did anymore... I feel like it's more my father's dream than mine to be honest."

Christina offered him an understanding nod and continued in a soothing tone of voice. "That must have been hard. If it's so important for your father, why didn't he pursue it himself?"

"He can play, but not very well. He never had any real talent for it, no matter how he tried to make up for it with hard work. That's why he's selling instruments right now."

Christina stayed silent for a minute, considering what to say.

The more Jack thought about it the more it made sense. He could no longer ignore the nagging feeling in his chest. It was tugging and tugging, trying to get some acknowledgment out of him. The time had come for the harsh reality to come out. He simply didn't enjoy playing the piano anymore. He wasn't even sure if he had ever wanted to become a pianist. "In coming here," Jack continued, "I started to realise it's not my dream I'm chasing. I think I already figured that out on the first day... after hearing you play."

"Me?" For once Christina didn't know what to say. She blinked slowly, her eyebrows furrowing as she tried to comprehend the meaning of it all.

"You play with such passion that I've been starting to realise how much I don't. I can play any piece but let's be honest, I lack motivation. I had to fight to get in here, just like you guys. The difference is you fought out of love, while I fought because I had to. Because it made sense." Jack rubbed his chin and let out a sigh.

For a full minute, complete silence hung between them. Jack heard the distant chatter of other students going for lunch. It was one of the longest silences he had ever had to endure. And no matter how much he hated silences, he didn't dare break it.

Much to Jack's surprise Christina smiled and clasped her hands together. "You know what? I wish you would have come to me sooner."

Baffled, Jack glanced at the message that popped up on his phone. His father was on his way. "I have to go get lunch with my dad soon."

"I also have lunch plans," Christina said. She looked at her watch. "I still have a few minutes though."

"Who do you have lunch plans with?"

"You know Carlos Matthews, right?" She looked at him expectedly.

"Carlos Matthews…" The name sounded familiar. "The third-year piano student? How do you know him?"

She nodded. "I met him during rehearsal yesterday. I thought I was alone until he popped his head around the door and nearly scared me to death. Anyway, he sat down with me and gave me some great pointers. Plus, he asked me to lunch today."

Jack wiggled his eyebrows. "Like in a date?"

Christina rolled her eyes, but Jack could clearly see a smile playing around her lips.

"Carlos Matthews," Jack said again. "He has one of those names you have to pronounce fully, don't you think? You can't just say Carlos."

"Did you know he is actually going to quit school?" She went on before Jack could interfere. "I know, I know. He got offered a job with the London Symphony, which he of course accepted. How crazy is that? He leaves in a month."

Jack shook his head. "That's amazing! The London Symphony…"

"Right? It's so prestigious. He has been scouted during a performance the third-years did last week." She sighed dreamily. "He told me I have a great technique. How nice is that?"

"Like you didn't already know that," Jack joked.

They fell into a comfortable silence.

"Look," Christina said after a while. "About what you told me earlier. It's not because you have always been pushed to play the piano so to speak that you can't enjoy it. It might seem like something you have to do. I can only imagine how things must be like in your family. But listen to this. You are good, great even, and you need to start putting your heritage to your advantage. Maybe you feel like pushing away from it because you lost your grandfather. From what I hear it hit you pretty bad."

The vivid image of his grandfather and himself behind the piano popped up in Jack's mind. "That could make sense." He admired Christina's ambition and hoped one day to be able to speak with the same level of confidence she did.

"Imagine this," she went on. "You quit this school, quit the program, then what? Would you regret it? What would you do?"

Jack's chest tightened at the thought of having to give it all up. He sometimes felt like he didn't belong here yet at the same time he did. He knew he did. These were his kind of people. People whom he could relate to. In such a short time this had become his second home. Part of him knew this was exactly the right place for him. "Of course I'd regret it! If you put it like that. In the short time we've been here, I've grown to care about this place so much. I wouldn't know what I'd do without it." He spoke with certainty. The only other option he had was to return home, which was the last thing Jack wanted. This was a good thing. Him, by himself, figuring out his life.

This encouraged Christina. "Exactly! What about the thought of you not being an artist? Sure, your family pushes you to be the best. But what about yourself? I thought you wanted to move people with your work?" She looked at him with high hopes. "You'd just be ordinary. No more than normal." She made it sound like an insult.

I don't want to be ordinary. "I don't... I do want to be an artist." He sounded certain once more. No doubts.

"Of course you do," Christina exclaimed. "We tell stories with our instruments. We press the right keys at the right time, and we tell a complex and beautiful story. What could be better than that?" When she spoke like that, she looked more radiant than ever. Jack even believed what she said. He wished Christina could see herself like this or see herself shine whenever she played. Too bad people never got to see themselves like that, with all their virtues and all their flaws. Not as someone else might anyway. You could never truly see yourself, not ever, and that was kind of sad. "What is it that you want to achieve?"

Jack hesitated. "I'd love to share and evoke emotion. Like you do. Like my grandfather did."

Christina seemed pleased. "If you ask me, I think you need to find your passion again. Stop doing things for other people and start living for yourself. Nothing is going to change if you keep sulking all the time. I'll help you. But you have got to do it for yourself."

Jack had never wanted to hug anyone that badly in his life. In that moment and for the first time, Jack saw Christina as a real friend.

———

JACK WALKED down the stairs of the school's main entrance. His appetite had completely disappeared. *It's just my dad.* Yet somehow the sight of his father rendered him speechless. What was he supposed to tell him? He knew one thing, and that was not to be honest about his feelings. Jack walked up to his father and joined him under his big umbrella to escape the drizzling rain.

"Great to see you, Son." Jack's father pulled Jack in a quick hug. Something he usually never did. "Let's go for lunch, shall we?"

They walked in silence. It wasn't uncomfortable. Jack just wasn't sure of what to say. After a short walk they stopped in front of The Imagination Factory. "This is the place I wanted to show you. They're supposed to serve some nice lunch."

Jack's father peeked inside and observed the café. He took a step back and looked at Jack in horror. "Wait a minute…" He looked inside again; disbelief evident in his voice. He clenched his jaw. "You know what? Let's go somewhere else. I know just the place."

"Go somewhere else? Alright… But, why?" Jack peered inside to see what the problem could be but couldn't find anything out of the ordinary. "What's wrong with it?"

Jack's father pulled him by the arm until they were past the café. "I'm in the mood to eat somewhere else." He walked on at a brisk pace. Jack had to hurry to keep up with him.

Mr Lewis settled on going to a nearby restaurant which Jack had to admit was excellent. A more formal choice of venue than The Imagination Factory, instrumental jazz music played through speakers and the soft chatter of customers filled the room. Their coats were hung up by a staff member who showed them to their table. Jack followed his father's example and placed the white cloth napkin on his lap.

It didn't often happen that Jack went out with his father alone, but they had a pleasant time. Jack's father was eager to know everything Jack had learned so far and inquired after the classes, the teachers, and the pieces he had had to play. And even though Jack had already told his parents most of this information over the phone, he obliged his father in telling him all about it again.

Mr Lewis chewed away a piece of his steak. "Who knows? One day when you need a steadier job between tours and concerts, you could come work in the shop with Sean and I."

"Dad, hold up." Jack wiped the corners of his mouth with his napkin before placing it on the table. "I think you're a bit hasty in assuming that I'll be touring the world, having piano concerts everywhere."

His father shook his head. He wouldn't have it. "You are going to make it one day. Just you wait and see."

Jack looked up at his father with wide eyes. He seemed so certain. "Do you really think so?"

"Without a doubt. You have to keep on going and you'll get there, I promise."

"Wow, thanks, Dad." Jack had rarely seen his father like this, all praise and compliments. He sat up a little straighter and couldn't wipe the grin off his face. He took a deep breath. Maybe he could do this after all.

CHAPTER SIX

THE CAFETERIA, situated on the top floor of the Institute, ran the entire length of the building. The most amazing views over the West End and beyond were visible through the huge windows that lined the wall. Modern round tables filled the room. The ones by the windows were always first to be taken.

Jack made his choice at the self-service buffet before joining Omar. "I do love me some rice pilaf." Jack dove in before he had taken a proper seat.

"Hello to you too," Omar greeted him. "How's it going?"

Jack, too busy chewing, put a thumb up in the air. He didn't mean that everything was fine. Things were far from fine. But they were better than yesterday. So overall everything was fine enough to give him a thumbs up.

Students poured in and the noise of people talking grew louder. Jessica took a seat behind the old piano in the corner of the room. She played a cheerful tune, which earned her some attention as people gathered around her.

Omar observed Jessica. "Christina should see this. Where is she anyway?"

Jack's signature grin appeared on his face at the thought of Christina seeing Jessica play a piece for so many people without paying attention to her technical execution. "She doesn't like to lose focus during lunch. She's in the library."

Omar nodded. "Fair enough." The boys continued to eat in silence. In the background, Jessica entertained whoever would listen.

"I almost forgot to tell you. I've discovered the most brilliant thing." Omar looked around suspiciously and continued in a low voice. "You know the fire exit in the residence hall? I checked it out and it's basically a stairwell that goes all the way down. But from our floor, there's a ladder which goes up onto the roof through a skylight which opens out. How wicked is that?"

"That sounds amazing." Jack looked around him to make sure nobody was listening in on them. "Kind of dangerous though, don't you think?"

Omar shook his head. "I tested it out and it seems quite safe to be honest. What do you reckon? Should we give it a try?"

"I'm in!" Jack finished his plate. "Speaking of things to try... I have something I'd like to try out. I'm preparing a piece for my Piano class and I could use your help."

"My help? What do you need a violinist for in Piano class?"

"Do you know any of my grandfather's sonatas by any chance? There's one in particular which holds a special place in my heart. I'm going to perform it in class this Friday and I'd like you to perform it with me."

"I'm not entirely following. What do you mean, perform it with you? Is that even allowed?"

Jack shrugged. "I'm not sure. Our task is to present a piece which means something to us and bring it with emotion. Adding the support of a violin to the piece will enhance its meaning and give it a different vibe than how it was originally written."

After a few seconds of internal debating, Omar gave him a thoughtful nod of the head. "If I can be of assistance, sure. I'd be happy to help."

They looked up as the cafeteria bust out in a round of

applause for Jessica. That's the moment Christina appeared in the doorway.

She came over and took a seat at their table. "She's embarrassing herself." Her eyes hadn't left Jessica since she had entered. "Why does everyone seem to love her so much? If I would go up there—" She stopped mid-sentence and shook her head. Christina pretended not to be bothered, but Jack and Omar knew better than that. Even Jack, who would never admit it, discovered a nasty feeling inside of him. Jealousy. He was jealous of Jessica. She didn't give a perfect performance, but what did that even mean? Jack himself could've played it better, but it still wouldn't have attracted so much ambience. Jessica smiled and had fun the entire time she played and her smile reached her eyes. Jack shook it off and filled Christina and Omar in on the conversation he had had with Mrs Lund the previous day.

"Broaden your horizon? Get inspired by the rest of the school?" Christina looked at Jack like he was an idiot. "Well that's easy, isn't it? I sometimes go and watch the dancers when I can spare the time. It can be quite inspiring to see them move on the music. That's some solid advice from Mrs Lundqvist."

Jack rolled his eyes. "I wish you would just call her Mrs Lund like everyone else."

Christina pretended not to hear him. "Come on, I'll take you if you want. I need to get out of here before I get sick of this." She stood up and glanced towards Jessica. "Actually sick." She turned around and left, without waiting to see if Jack followed her.

Omar and Jack shared a look.

THE DANCE DEPARTMENT was similar to the Music department in the way it looked, but the atmosphere was completely different. The sound of a piano filled Jack's ears. He heard something else, something he couldn't place. Loud thuds on the floor. A man shouting in French.

He followed Christina further down the hall. The closer they got, the louder the music got. They halted at a large bright dancing studio and tiptoed inside, staying close to the wall. They sat down on the floor, next to two other students who were also observing the class.

After a while Christina got up to leave. "Are you coming?" she whispered.

Jack shook his head and stayed for the remainder of the Ballet class. They took turns in dancing an exercise in the centre while the others waited their turn by the side, gulping down water but never losing sight on whoever was dancing.

Jack's eyes fell on a guy he recognised from the common room, who had come across as careless at first. Now he was in total focus, his face dead serious. He focused solely on his movements and was oblivious to the world around him. Moving around gracefully, he told a story with nothing but his body. In a smooth motion, his foot slid backwards across the linoleum dance floor. He jumped and spun from one side of the room to the other in total control. He made it look almost easy, but the sweat that trickled down his back gave him away. Jack couldn't keep his eyes off him and traced the lines of his muscles with his gaze, in awe of the sheer strength he possessed. His flexed muscles relaxed when the music came to an end, his chest rising and falling from the exertion. His gaze met Jacks for a brief moment.

Heart beating fast and with a flushed face, Jack left in a hurry after the Ballet class and got inside the lift once more. He pressed the button for the ground floor but changed his mind. *I'm not done broadening my horizon just yet.*

The hallways of the Drama department were deserted, making him wonder if he should come back another time. He passed an acting studio, which looked similar to the music rooms, only without all the instruments in it. To his disappointment he found it empty. He would have loved to see some actors at work. Finally, he walked past an occupied classroom. He peered through the window in the door at the dozen or so students seated across the room. Notes on script structure filled the blackboard and Jack realised it was a playwright class. He almost cried out in surprise when he saw Alexander amongst the students.

Alexander fiddled with his pen in his hand as he stared towards the board, a blank expression on his face. Jack easily distinguished his black hair and posture from the others. Alexander had something about him which set him apart, but Jack couldn't quite put his finger on what it was. As if he could sense that he was being watched, Alexander turned around to look right into Jack's eyes. Jack winked at him, making Alexander turn away quickly.

Jack walked on and reached a final studio at the end of the hallway, smaller and darker than the other ones had been. He didn't see a class in action as he had hoped, but there was a girl rehearsing by herself. Jack peeked inside, careful not to be discovered, and took her in. From the back you'd guess she was much younger than she probably was. She was small and had blonde hair that fell in curls unto her shoulders. A beige top tucked in a long pink skirt hugged her curvy body. She held on to a few papers that were folded in half and peered at them through a pair of cat-eye reading glasses.

She faced the mirror and tried the same line from her script a couple of times over again in different tones. Each time she finished, she sighed in frustration.

"My lord, why do you keep alone..." she repeated the line. This time very softly, in a way that sounded as fragile as she looked. On first sight, she looked too timid to be an actress, but she spoke her lines with confidence.

Jack smiled; he had liked this last try. It sounded right.

"No, no, no," she muttered again.

Something inside of him pushed Jack forward, revealing him from his hiding place. It would have been nice to call it fate or destiny. It was however probably just his inability to stay out of things that weren't his business. "I liked the last try."

The girl gave a little shriek and jumped up at the sight of him.

50

"Good heavens, I thought I was alone." She clutched the script to her chest.

Jack stepped up to her. She barely reached his shoulder and had to look up to meet his eye. "I didn't mean to startle you."

"I'm having such trouble to get these lines right. I'm not really feeling it, if you know what I mean." Despite her soft tone of voice, frustration was evident.

"I do, actually. I know exactly what you mean." A sudden seriousness overcame Jack. He had imposed long enough. "I should let you to it."

He turned around to leave, but the girl called out to him, her blue innocent eyes pleading. "If you've got any time to spare. You're here at a most convenient time. Help a struggling girl out."

Jack hesitated. He was only discovering what else the school had to offer, not participating in it. He couldn't afford to lose any more time and was supposed to get to the rehearsal studio as soon as possible. On the other hand, helping this girl out did mean broadening his horizon.

A chuckle broke the silence between them. "You seem to need an awful long time to make up your mind."

Jack laughed aloud. "Sure, I'd love to help you. What are you working on?"

"It's this scene we have to present in class. We're doing a lot of Shakespeare this semester." She handed him the script. "I'm Lady Macbeth, you're Macbeth. You just killed King Duncan."

Jack nodded along, although he had no idea what the play was about. "I might need a minute to get into character." He put on an angry face and straightened his back, making her laugh.

It didn't take Jack as long as he had expected to get into the character. They practised and paused whenever something didn't feel right. Horrified, Jack noticed one hour later just how much time had flown by. They decided to go through it one final time.

"Let's play as we'd do in front of an audience," the girl suggested, and so they did. They pretended the empty chairs against the wall were filled with people.

51

Jack threw the script to the front of the room. "I think I know it by heart now." He tried to give everything he could, even if he had no clue what he was doing. He couldn't grasp what went on inside of him, but he enjoyed putting on a different face for a little while. Something about it made him feel satisfied in a way that he hadn't felt in a long time.

Approaching footsteps made them look up. Jack tensed up as if caught somewhere he wasn't supposed to be. A woman in her mid-thirties entered the studio. Her chestnut brown hair was pulled up in a loose bun and she wore an all-white outfit with an orange kimono styled vest on top. "You seem to be getting on well, Ava. You're doing a good job implementing the advice I gave you in class."

"Thank you, Mrs Hendrix. I rehearsed all afternoon and feel like it's going a lot smoother than before." Ava's Irish accent, which had disappeared while acting, rushed back.

Mrs Hendrix, Ava's teacher, frowned as she looked towards Jack.

Ava jumped in. "Oh, this is my friend..."

"Jack," Jack filled in, a smile on his face.

"He's helping me practice. Christian couldn't make it."

Mrs Hendrix nodded. "No worries. May I ask which class you're in?" The question was aimed at Jack.

There was something prying in her eyes that Jack couldn't place. The only thing he did know was that he felt exposed. "I'm a first-year piano student, ma'am."

"Did you ever take any acting classes?"

"No, never," Jack replied. "But I think it's a wonderful form of art and expression."

A smile broke the stern expression on Mrs Hendrix's face. "That scene you just did there was pretty good. Especially for someone without experience. It's nice of you to help out your friend like that."

A flush of adrenaline tingled through Jack's body. He couldn't wipe the grin off his face. "Thank you."

JACK'S favourite sound of leaves crunching underneath his feet followed Ava and himself all the way to The Imagination Factory. The street lanterns turned on and the chilly wind made them walk faster. The fresh autumn air offered a welcome change from being inside all day.

Jack paid close attention to his surroundings. A nagging feeling had been bothering him ever since he had brought his father here for lunch. Something had scared his father off and Jack wanted to find out what it could have been. Upon entering he looked around for anything out of the ordinary. The smell of cinnamon and coffee filled his nostrils. A perfect place of refuge where he could escape the hassle of the school.

Grace had yet to notice him and when she turned around, she seemed taken aback.

"I'll take the spicy pumpkin latte." Jack pointed towards a stand that promoted the special autumn offers with a grin on his face.

"And I'll have some chamomile tea," Ava added.

Grace recomposed herself and smiled. "Coming right up."

Jack followed her with his gaze and was brought back to attention by Ava. "Thank you again for helping me out this afternoon. I feel much better prepared."

"You're very welcome! I had lots of fun. More fun than I've had in a while, to be honest." He looked into her blue eyes and could see she didn't quite catch him. "How did you get into acting?"

Talking about acting made Ava's eyes lit up. "I grew up in a little village called Kilkenny on the farm of my parents. Pigs and such. When I was a kid, I wanted to be a princess. When that didn't turn out to be a solid plan, I started taking acting lessons. My acting teacher encouraged me to audition, and I got through! I could have never dreamt of it."

Meanwhile the tea and coffee had arrived. "I guess you can be a princess through acting so that worked out after all." Jack sipped his coffee and nearly burned his tongue. "Maybe I should have a closer look at Macbeth and see the whole play. I love the scene we rehearsed."

"It's a brilliant play, and a brilliant scene indeed. At the time of Macbeth, a few hundreds of years ago, kings were second only to God because it was believed that kings were chosen by God himself. And it reflects in the play when Macbeth says that the angels will weep when King Duncan dies."

Jack listened attentively. "That's interesting to hear. How does it go from there?"

Ava shook her head. "No spoilers. You should find out for yourself. But basically, a whole bunch of people die."

"That's cheerful," Jack joked.

Ava laughed. "Did you know that saying the word Macbeth inside a theatre is considered taboo? It's an old superstition, but it still goes around. A few unlucky accidents and deaths occurred ever since they first performed the play. Some believe Shakespeare cursed the play himself because of the dialogue of the three witches."

"You're joking," Jack exclaimed. "What do people think would happen to them if they say it?"

Ava shrugged. "Not sure, the superstition says that disaster will occur." She sipped her tea and relaxed back in the armchair. "There is a funny protocol, though. If someone accidentally says the word, they have to spin around three times, spit, and curse."

Jack couldn't contain his laughter any longer. "I'll refrain myself from saying Macbeth when I go to the theatre. I don't think they'd be happy to clean up my spit."

Ava laughed and excused herself to go to the restroom.

Jack called over the waitress for another round of coffee. Now was the perfect time to find out if his suspicions were true. He had to follow his gut feeling, right? Even if he'd make a fool of himself.

She halted by Jack's side. "Are you enjoying your latte?"

"I love it!" A small pause. Jack doubted himself for a second but decided to go for it. "There was something I wanted to ask."

Her smile faltered. "Oh?"

"I'm not sure if his name rings any bells for you but I wondered if you knew my father by any chance?" When Jack didn't receive an answer, he realised how ridiculous he must have sounded. "I was here with him yesterday. His name is Jim Lewis. I was just wondering…"

Grace furrowed her brow. "I don't remember you being in here yesterday."

"We didn't actually come inside," Jack said in a low voice. Dread filled him up as he heard the nonsense he proclaimed.

Grace shook her head. "I don't think so, no. But I do remember you. You've been here before, haven't you?"

Jack didn't buy it. Something was off.

The bell above the door rang. "I'm sorry I can't be of more help, dear." At that point, Ava returned from the restroom. Grace averted her eyes to the man that had entered. "Excuse me." She hurried away.

Jack's thoughts were racing. Somehow, he felt even more confused. Whatever it was, something didn't add up. He was sure of it.

FOR ONCE, Jack was early as he waited for Christina outside of the school for another one of their rehearsal sessions. The fresh air made it possible for him to think, to breathe. He was a skilled pianist, so used to playing from a young age that it almost came natural to him. When Mrs Hendrix had complimented his acting earlier it had done something to Jack. In a way it meant more than any praise from Mrs Lund. He had given his all for something he had tried out and ultimately sincerely enjoyed.

Christina installed herself behind the piano. She had made an effort these last few days to be helpful to Jack in whichever way she could, even if she had nothing to gain out of it. They took turns in playing and guided one another until their pieces sounded the way they wanted them to. Jack hadn't told Christina about his plan to involve Omar in his presentation. She'd nag on and on and force him to ask Mrs Lund's approval. He'd much rather see her face in class when he surprised everyone.

"I'm famished! Let's go eat." Christina stretched her arms and yawned.

Jack did not attempt to stand up. "You go. I'm going to play some more."

Christina opened her mouth to say something but closed it again. She snuck out of the room in silence.

Jack looked at the sheet music in front of him. The pages stared right back at him. The notes challenged him. Play. He closed his eyes. His fingers hovered above the keys, but he didn't touch them just yet. He cleared his mind. Pushed all thoughts into a corner. He didn't think, he just played. For hours on end he played without stopping to eat or take a restroom break. Sweat dripped from his hair and face, and his white t-shirt was soaked. His breath came out harsh and uneven. His fingers hurt as he had played the life out of them. Those would result in blisters for sure.

Enough.

Jack remained seated at the piano. His hands and fingers had no more strength in them. Jack had no more strength in him. For once he was good enough.

At eleven sharp the school's caretaker made his round to lock up the school. Jack got up and went for takeaway. Back at the residence hall he collapsed on one of the sofas in the common room. He ate his food on autopilot and dragged himself to bed straight after. In a way, the night had been rewarding. He had given so much that he was simply too empty to feel anything anymore. He stared up to his ceiling and smiled. He felt at peace. He felt nothing.

They would have been proud if they could have seen.

CHAPTER SEVEN

ON FRIDAY MORNING, Jack had a rough awakening. Christina pounded on his door before his alarm had even gone off. She barged into his room, coffee in hand, and shouted at him for not being ready yet. She was pacing up and down the hall when Jack came out of his room ten minutes later in a sour mood.

They arrived at class early. Jack used the time to wake up properly and played some games on his phone while they waited.

Mrs Lund didn't need to ask for a volunteer as Christina offered to go first. As expected, she played flawlessly. She got up, received her feedback, and returned to her chair with a smug look on her face.

Jack's pocket vibrated and that could mean only one thing. He took his phone and saw a text message from Omar saying, *I'm here*. He fumbled with his suspenders and felt his mouth go dry. For the very first time that year, nerves raced through Jack as he had to perform in front of the class.

"Am I boring you, Mr Lewis?" Mrs Lund's sharp voice pierced through the classroom. She glared at his phone. "Perhaps you'd like to go next."

Jack smiled. "I'd love to."

Whispers arose when Jack didn't walk to the piano but

towards the door. If he would go down for this, at least it would be for something he actually tried for. He ignored the whispers as Omar entered. It fazed Jack how Omar never seemed nervous, not even in the slightest. Calm as ever, Omar followed Jack up the stage, violin at the ready.

Before Mrs Lund, or anyone else, could protest, Jack addressed the class. He hoped they weren't able to see the tremble in his legs. "I hope you will forgive me, Mrs Lund, for thinking out of the box today. The piece I'll perform is Piano Sonata No. 17 in A minor, composed by my grandfather, Raymond Lewis. This piece is of great importance to me because it was the last piece my grandfather ever wrote." Jack looked around the class and noticed Christina's crossed arms. Everyone's attention was still directed towards Omar. "I was advised to broaden my horizon and see what else this school has to offer. I found that the sound of a violin strengthens that eerie feeling of hope which the song possesses. So here we both are to perform it for you."

Jack and Omar had only rehearsed the piece together a couple of times, which meant that performing it was a huge risk. Right from the start however, Jack knew that bringing in the violin had been the right decision. The song chilled him to the bone in a happy way. It brought him back to the first time he had heard it as a little boy. His grandfather had woken him up after his last ever performance in Brussels, saying he had a surprise for him.

"I wrote a new song. And I wrote it especially for you. Do you want to hear it?"

Jack's mouth fell open. "Just for me?"

"Just for you," Raymond assured him.

Unstoppable, Jack's fingers ran swiftly and precise over the keys. As the song was building up, Jack gave everything he had to offer. He hadn't played like that in a long time. He hadn't even played this piece in years. It had always been too painful to open the wound of losing his grandfather. To allow all the feelings back in. While the last note lingered, Jack opened his eyes and knew he had nailed it. Omar's chest rose and fell from the exertion and he too held a smile on his face.

Slowly but surely, his classmates clapped their hands. Mrs Lund smiled a smile that reached her eyes. "Beautifully played, Jack. You have made the performance personal and have given it a creative twist. Not everyone might appreciate that little rebel in you, but let's say that today it has worked out in your favour. Congratulations to you as well, Omar. And thank you for joining us today."

Jack showed Omar out and returned to his seat. Christina glared towards Jack and didn't even try to hide it. When her eyes met Jack's, she looked away stubbornly. That was how he knew he had truly succeeded.

JACK MADE a detour before lunch in search of Ava. He walked past a studio where an acting class was taking place. Retracing his steps, Jack peeked inside through the open door to observe them as discretely as he could. The actors were seated in a circle on the floor, dressed all in black, reading aloud from the scripts in their hands. Intrigued by the process, Jack tried to make sense of what they were reading. To his dismay, he couldn't understand them. He tried to get a little closer, but stumbled forward by accident, almost barging inside. He hid against the wall, eyes closed and heart beating fast. After about a minute he deemed it safe enough to look inside again, only to look straight into Mrs Hendrix's eyes. Jack turned around and hurried away. He looked over his shoulder to see if anyone was following him only to bump into someone.

"Jack, watch where you're going!" Ava rubbed her arm. "Why are you in such a hurry?"

Jack, relieved upon seeing her, tugged her along. He pushed the button of the lift repeatedly until the doors opened.

"What's going on?" Ava asked, as Jack motioned her to get inside. "Who's chasing you?"

Jack grinned and shook his head. People must have thought him a lunatic by now. "Nobody. I was looking for you."

"Well, you found me. Do you want to join me for lunch? I have Speech class in half an hour so I'm in a bit of a hurry."

The smell of spaghetti welcomed them in the cafeteria. Jack brought Ava over to the table where Omar and Christina were already seated. Once everyone had introduced themselves Omar started chatting with Ava. Christina didn't say anything aside from the necessary hello. Jack couldn't blame the intimidated look on Ava's face upon meeting Christina.

Jack turned to Christina, who hadn't looked at him since he had joined them. "Why are you angry?" he whispered.

This time she did look in his eyes. She raised one eyebrow. "I'm not angry." Silence.

"Fine." Jack dropped it and started eating.

"I thought I'd nail that piece," Christina said in a low voice, staring at her plate.

Jack swallowed his food and frowned. "You did nail that piece. What are you on about?"

She shrugged. Her eyes softened. "You were better," she admitted, which must have been a hard thing for her to do.

"I'm sure you did well," Ava interrupted. She meant it in a friendly way and offered Christina a shy smile. "If you did your best then that's all you can do."

Not having noticed that Omar and Ava had been listening to their conversation, Jack looked towards Christina who had directed her glare towards Ava. Christina straightened her back before she spoke. "I was talking to Jack." She sounded dangerously calm.

"I'm just saying," Ava continued in a steady voice, "Don't beat yourself up about it. We're all here to learn." The genuine smile she offered Christina didn't improve the situation.

Omar jumped in to help. "You're right," he told Ava. "You haven't heard her yet, but Christina plays like an angel."

Christina turned to Omar. "Don't talk about me like I'm not—" She paused. "You think so? When did you hear me play?"

Omar smiled. "I was waiting outside your class before coming in. I heard you play. You were bloody brilliant."

Christina's eyes beamed. "Thanks."

Ava nudged Jack's side. "I've got to get to my Speech class." She smiled towards Omar and Christina. The corners of Christina's mouth went upwards reluctantly. Ava noticed. "It was nice to meet you both."

"Wait up. I'll walk you to class." Jack gathered his stuff and followed Ava. He still hadn't had the chance to speak with her in private. "I can't stop thinking about that day when we practised that Macbeth scene together."

Ava smiled. "It was good fun, wasn't it? Thank you for that again by the way. I played it with Christian in class and it went great. If you ever have the time, I'd love to go through some more scenes with you. If you're interested of course."

"I'm happy to hear it and I'd love to practice more scenes with you, if you can use the help," Jack said, "I enjoyed rehearsing that scene. And I enjoyed those little acting exercises we did the last couple of days as well."

Ava laughed at Jack's enthusiasm. "I take from earlier that your piece today went well?"

Jack didn't know Ava that well, but he found himself opening up to her without having to think twice about it. "It went well indeed. It's the best work they've heard of me this year. But something doesn't sit right."

"That actually sounds pretty amazing, Jack." They had reached her classroom by now. People passed them to get inside.

"It isn't really," Jack confessed. "For this particular assignment, I had to find emotion and passion. The piece I played means everything to me. I guess that's why I was able to play it so well." At a loss for words, Jack couldn't describe the conflicted tug of war inside of him. "I had to think of the scene we did and how I enjoyed being someone else. I acted my performance, pretending to play a role."

He had lost her completely.

Jack scratched the back of his head. "What I mean is that I acted being a pianist in front of an audience. I'm sure that's not what I was supposed to do."

Ava struggled to find the right words. "I wouldn't say that's a bad thing. You're a creative guy. You can use anything you want to draw inspiration from. That's the beauty of art, isn't it? There aren't any textbooks that tell you how to become an artist. It's such a personal journey. Who knows, if becoming a pianist doesn't work out, you can always try your luck in acting."

Jack nodded. "Maybe." He needed time to think.

"My class is starting any minute. See you soon?"

"Definitely."

EXHAUSTED after a long day of classes Jack walked back to the residence hall. The day had gone well, and his classes had been a success. Then why did he feel so lost? He threw his backpack on his bed and walked straight towards the kitchen, hoping he'd find something edible in the fridge.

Jack halted in the doorway, surprised at the sight in front of him. Omar stood at the stove, cooking away. Christina, seated at the dining table, went through their Music History course. Jack had never seen Christina and Omar interact without him before. A sudden feeling of loneliness entered the pit of his stomach as he observed his friends together like an intruder. They hadn't even bothered to invite him.

"Don't burn the vegetables," Christina shouted. She couldn't help herself.

Omar turned around. "Yes, chef!" He saluted her and spotted Jack in the doorway. His smile widened. "Hi, Jack!"

Jack greeted his friends. The whole kitchen smelled of spices. "I didn't know you could cook."

Omar shrugged. "I usually have dinner with Alexander, but he is out tonight. Besides, Christina was tired of cooking every night, so I gave it a try." He stirred the pot in front of him. "I'm preparing a traditional Moroccan couscous with vegetables. Grandmother's recipe."

"That sounds delicious. Would you mind if I join you?" Jack remained in the doorway.

Omar frowned. "Of course! I already counted you in. Besides, by the looks of it I'm cooking for a whole army anyway. Measurements aren't my strong suit."

Jack laughed and took a seat at the table, offering Christina an apologetic smile. "I'd offer to cook for a change, but..."

"We all know how that turns out." Christina almost smiled. She changed the subject. "Your new friend seems interesting."

Jack rolled his eyes. "You didn't even try to like her. You'd see she's pretty nice if you'd give her a chance."

"I liked her," Omar said. "She's a sweet girl."

"Sweet isn't going to cut it here," Christina snapped. "And who said I didn't like her?"

The frustration was getting harder for Jack to hide. "The look on your face did."

"Whatever." She got up and set the table.

Omar installed his portable speakers and played an instrumental Moroccan playlist to suit the vibe. They were joined by a few others for dinner as Omar offered a plate to everyone who walked into the kitchen. Christina ate in speed tempo and left as soon as she had finished.

Omar followed Christina with his gaze. "What was that all about?"

Jack couldn't answer if he wanted to.

Everyone pitched in to do the dishes and thanked Omar for the delicious meal. The kitchen grew quiet as only Jack and Omar remained.

An idea popped up in Jack's head. "Would tonight be a good night to explore that rooftop you told me about?"

The two of them dressed warmly and sneaked over to the emergency exit next to the lift. When they were certain nobody was near, they hurried inside. The ladder was there just as Omar had described it. Omar went first and unlatched the safety pins keeping the skylight in place. It opened out to one side, giving Jack and Omar enough space to climb through. Once on the roof, Omar closed the skylight again quietly.

Jack's heart raced with excitement. Gobsmacked, he looked around, enjoying the cold, though not uncomfortable, wind against his face. The chill air and the night sky rendered him speechless. He walked around to take it all in. In a city like London, a good view was priceless. And this one was breath-taking.

Omar tossed Jack one of the beers he had brought up with him and broke the silence. "There was something I was wondering about. Something Alexander told me."

Jack thought of how he had seen Alexander in class the other day. "What did he have to say?"

Omar shrugged casually. "That he's seen you at the Drama department recently… quite a few times." Omar didn't sound judging, he never did. "He claims you were acting. Is there some special project you're working on?"

That little snitch. Jack shifted uncomfortably on the floor and felt the need to defend himself. "I was only helping out Ava with her acting exercises."

Omar held his hands up in the air. "I was just curious."

Jack stared at his legs as he opened up about his doubts to the second person that day. "What I say up here stays up here, agreed? Lately I feel drawn to acting in a way that I have never felt about playing the piano." The words came easily, revealing for the first time the whole truth about the doubts Jack had been struggling with. "I obviously like playing the piano, but I'm not sure if it's what I want to do with the rest of my life. It's hard to explain but I feel like I'm discovering a whole new side of myself. It excites me and I find myself going back there for more. It's stupid, I know."

Omar considered this for a moment. A small crease had set between his brows. Whatever he had expected, it wasn't this. "You talk about it like how I feel about the violin." And that said enough.

JACK SAT up in his bed and yawned. He stretched his arms and tried to get rid of the cramp in his neck. Sleep couldn't find him no matter how tired he was. He got out of bed and put on some joggers and a t-shirt. He dragged himself to the kitchen, where the light was still turned on, for a midnight snack. Alexander sat at the table, eating pizza and scrolling on his phone. He didn't say anything when Jack entered.

Jack poured himself a bowl of cereal with too much milk and took a seat. "Hey, Alexander."

Alexander grunted in return, as he had just taken a large bite of pizza. He stared at Jack's bowl of cereal.

Jack couldn't stand the silence and tried to make conversation. "Your room is next to mine, isn't it? I can usually hear your music playing."

Alexander placed his phone on the table. He moved slowly, the bags underneath his eyes clearly visible. "And I can usually hear your voice over my music."

Jack grinned. Someone was in a sour mood.

"I didn't mean that as a compliment," Alexander retorted.

Jack's grin disappeared. "No worries, you have great taste in music. I'm not usually in the jazz scene, but I have to admit that I like it. Who are your favourite artists?"

Alexander shrugged.

"Come on," Jack urged him. "You don't want to tell me because you don't feel like talking to me, am I right?" This made the corners of Alexander's mouth turn upwards ever so slightly. Alexander looked into Jack's eyes for the first time that night. Jack was taken aback by the brightness of his amber eyes that pierced into his own. He couldn't read him at all and found it impossible to avert his gaze. How Alexander and Omar were such close friends remained a mystery to him. They seemed so different. "How did you and Omar become friends?"

Alexander raised his eyebrows. "That's a bit personal, isn't it?"

"Omar is my friend." This guy was impossible, but Jack couldn't blame him for not wanting to make small talk in the middle of the night.

Alexander gave in. "I met him a couple of years ago right here in London. I guess we've been friends ever since. We auditioned together as well."

"How nice that must have been. It's hard to come to a place where you know absolutely nobody."

Alexander's expression softened. "You seem to be doing pretty well."

Jack didn't want to push his luck, but he simply had to ask. "Why did you tell Omar I've been hanging around on the drama floor?"

An incredulous look appeared on Alexander's face. "Why not? You told us you were a pianist the other night, yet I saw you on our floor almost every day this past week. Once I even saw you act when I had to walk past to get to class. I asked Omar what was up with that."

"Yeah, he told me..." A short silence fell between them. "Aren't you going to ask me what I've been doing there?"

Alexander shook his head. "That's not any of my business, and frankly I don't really care."

Alexander wasn't in a talkative mood, but Jack found his honesty refreshing. "The Playwright department seems pretty cool. It must be exciting to see your words come to life."

A spark ignited Alexander's eyes. "It really is. There are so many stories to tell... Everyone has their own version of the truth, you know? If you let, for example, five people tell a story, you'll end up with five different stories. That doesn't mean that one of them is wrong however."

At this Jack smiled. "I like how you talk about stories. That's what we're all doing here, aren't we?" Alexander didn't respond. "Somehow I had an entirely different vision of what this school would be like. And what the people would be like. You've seen the films, right? The ones with all those crazy over the top people and all the drama going on?"

"You thought the place would be full of stereotypes? All glittery gay people and anorexic ballerina's? I hate to disappoint, but it's a little more complicated than that."

Jack shrugged. "I'm figuring that out."

"Welcome to the world of overachievers and mentally conflicted people. You can't be an artist if you've got no shit going on. Here you get to see who's most fucked up."

Jack's voice lowered until it was nothing more than a whisper. "That's pretty dark."

Alexander merely shrugged and didn't say anything else. He averted his eyes and continued to eat.

Jack's phone buzzed with a text from Ava. *I know it's late, but if you're free I'd love to practice another scene with you this weekend. Stressing out over this new play. X*

Jack wrote a quick reply. He barely had to think it through. *Sure. What time do you want to meet?*

The message went straight to 'read'. A reply immediately followed. *Tomorrow 8 AM too early for you? X*

Jack's eyes widened as he saw the time. Still, he didn't feel like refusing, even if it meant waking up in a few short hours.

He glanced towards Alexander. He had imposed long enough. "I'm off. I guess I'll see you later, Alex."

Alexander's eyes narrowed. "It's Alexander."

CHAPTER EIGHT

AVA AND JACK sat under one of the few trees that occupied the school's courtyard with a script in hand. Jack wore a dotted wool jumper and a thick scarf in which he could hide away from the cold. He helped Ava with a final run-through of the scene they had practised over the weekend.

"I need you to know how much I appreciate—"

"I know," Jack intervened, before she could continue. "I enjoy doing this. So please, don't worry about it." Jack had spent most of his time during the weekend with Ava, acting out scenes and enjoying themselves by portraying all sort of characters.

"Anyway, after today I'll get partnered up with someone else than Christian. I won't have to bother you with these things anymore."

Jack frowned. The thought of Ava not needing him anymore to rehearse her scenes didn't sit right with him. It had become one of his favourite pastimes. "How come Christian isn't here rehearsing with you now? Or where was he this weekend?" Jack recalled the good-humoured ginger guy he had met in the common room. "He seems to be a nice guy."

"Oh, the best." She went on in a lower voice. "The thing is that he needs so little time to get the hang of this while for me it takes a lot longer to master a scene."

"There's no shame in that." Jack remembered how Alexander didn't like Christian because he was difficult to work with. "If it can make you feel any better, I think you're ready to play this part."

Ava gave him a grateful smile.

"I've got to take this." Jack pulled out his phone which had been buzzing for the last few seconds. "Hi, Mom." Even though he loved his new life, from time to time he missed the comfort of home where everything was familiar. At home, there was no need for doubts. The piano was the only certainty he had there, and it had been enough.

Ava told him a quick goodbye and went inside. "I'll see you this afternoon," she whispered.

He gave her a thumbs up and a big smile. "Break a leg," he whispered back before returning to the conversation with his mother. "I really do miss you, Mom… No, nothing is wrong. I just wanted you to know."

"I miss you too, darling. I'll pass your father along now. We have something fun to tell you."

"Hey there, champ. How are you doing?" Jack's father sounded too cheerful. He hadn't called him that in years.

A nostalgic wave rushed over Jack. "I'm fine, thanks, Dad."

"I wanted to let you know that we were browsing the website of the London Institute of Arts and found out about the recital at the end of the year. The big one, for all the first-years."

Jack closed his eyes in horror. He could hear his mother in the background. "That sneaky little boy didn't tell us a thing!"

"I didn't tell you yet because it's not even certain if I'll be in it." Jack cleared his throat as his voice came out uneven. He had deliberately tried to keep this from his parents. Not only had he not started working on an idea to submit yet. If he was completely honest with himself, he wasn't even sure if he wanted to play at all anymore. Thoughts of quitting the school and giving up the

69

piano all together had invaded his mind. And once the thoughts had entered his head, it was impossible to make them go away. Perhaps he could study a more regular course, like economics, and take up acting as a hobby. Maybe he could even make something of acting one day.

Mr Lewis snorted. "Please. I'm certain you'll be in it. How could they not let you? You're the best one there, I'm sure of it."

"Thanks for the vote of confidence, Dad." Jack paced around the courtyard. The tenseness in his stomach increased. Seeing how he had earned his father's confidence at last, made him happy and guilty all at once. This was what he wanted, right?

"We went ahead and bought tickets to come see it. I know it's a bit early, but we like to be prepared. It's been such a long time since we heard you play. When you come home for the holidays you can let us hear everything you've been working on."

Jack felt as if someone had punched him in the stomach. "I should go."

Then his father had to go and make the whole thing worse. "We're proud of you, Son. We love you."

A short pause. "I love you too." Jack hung up before anything else could be said. He took a deep breath. He rarely heard his parents saying they loved him out loud. Especially his father. Jack had dreaded hearing these words. It only meant the disappointment would be so much bigger.

JACK TAPPED his foot to the ground and bolted as soon as Mrs Lund dismissed them from class. He made it in time for the start of Ava's acting class. From the door he watched the students perform the scenes they had prepared in teams of two. It provided a welcome break to his day. He had to refrain from bursting out in applause along with the rest of the class. Ava and Christian had done an amazing job. *I helped! I helped make that happen!* Jack loved the custom of applauding for yourself and your classmates after each class. It never failed to bring a smile on his face. He got ready to leave and checked his timetable for the rest of his day.

"I was hoping I'd find you here today."

Jack turned around to stand face to face with Mrs Hendrix, Ava's teacher. His courage faltered upon the sight of her. "Me?" Meanwhile, her students walked out of the classroom. Ava passed him with a questionable look on her face.

Mrs Hendrix smiled, which revealed little wrinkles around her eyes. "Don't act so surprised. You've been here more than my own students lately."

Jack wasn't sure how to reply. He wished he was one of those people who always knew exactly what to say. Nothing ever came out as good as he prepared it in his head. "So you've noticed that?" He shifted from one foot to the other.

A few students passing by greeted Mrs Hendrix. "Let's go to my office, shall we?"

Jack had no idea what was going on. "Sure." He followed her with his gaze fixed to the floor. He knew he'd get into trouble. If anything, he was surprised it had taken this long.

Mrs Hendrix motioned for Jack to sit. "You can relax now." Her office was small and dark as there were no windows. The colourful decorations, consisting of fake plants and posters from theatre plays, livened the place up. "I've got an interesting proposition to present to you. One I'm sure you'll be interested in."

This spiked Jack's curiosity. "Oh?" Maybe he wasn't in trouble after all.

"One of my students had to quit the program, which means I've got an empty spot to fill."

She hadn't said much. She hadn't asked him anything. Then why did Jack's heart start racing as it did now?

"This… never happens. Ever. I must tell you that. It's only because we're so early on in the program that I've decided to let a new student enter our class. It would put him or her in a compromised position, having missed a month's worth of classes

71

already. But it's not impossible. I'd like to give someone the chance to try." She looked him straight in the eye the entire time she talked, gauging his every expression. "You may not have noticed that I was observing you, but I've seen what you can do. I saw a spark in you that I liked. Of course you would…. Wait, you told me you didn't have any theatre or acting experience, right?"

Jack, baffled, shook his head. He clutched the edges of his chair, barely able to form a response. "No, but I'm not—"

"Of course you would have to work as you've never worked before." She paused to look at him. "There is something about you that makes me want to give you a chance. So, if you want it, the spot is yours."

Jack couldn't believe his ears. "Really?" was his first and unprofessional answer.

Mrs Hendrix nodded, giving him time to process the news.

Jack's mind spun. His heart leapt in joy at the possibility that lay before him, but he didn't show it. "Why did this student have to leave the program?"

Mrs Hendrix's smile vanished. "She didn't quite cut it and decided to quit early on in the program so she could still enrol elsewhere. She didn't have what it takes." She looked genuinely sorry. "It's a hard world, Jack. You have to be prepared to give it everything you've got or it's never going to work."

Jack let out a deep breath he didn't know he was holding. "I don't get it," he had to say. "I'm a piano student. I'm already in a program. I didn't know anything like this was even possible. To switch programs once the year had already started."

"It's certainly unusual," Mrs Hendrix admitted. "I've never seen it happen. But, it's also unusual for people to like a different program better than their own. If I may be so bold, I'd like to say that I think you have made the wrong choice in applying for the Music department."

Jack was about to contradict this, but he couldn't. "Are you sure this is possible?"

She took her time to explain. "I see the unexplored potential in you. You're new in this, which we can take to our advantage. You can still be taught everything the right way and from what I've seen you're a quick study. Why would we go through the trouble of auditioning for somebody else when I already see a capable person in front of me?" She went on, as she saw the contradictory feelings it stirred in Jack. "I can give you one day to consider, but no more. There are hundreds of people eager to get in. People who wouldn't blink twice before accepting. You're in a privileged position here."

Jack's heart sank, realising how privileged he was indeed. He struggled to keep his voice even. "I don't need time to think it over, Mrs Hendrix. I'm honoured to have been considered, but I'm afraid I have to refuse." He had to force the words to come out of his mouth. It pained him to say it, but this was how it had to be. "I'm a pianist."

"Are you sure? You won't get this chance again." She looked disappointed but not nearly as disappointed as Jack felt.

No. "Yes."

Mrs Hendrix bid him goodbye. Frozen to the spot, Jack forced himself to get out of there. Tears welled up in his eyes. *One foot in front of the other. Just breathe.* There was no way on earth he could do this to his parents. He would be disowned. His parents had paid so much money to be able to give him this education. They wouldn't have done that if it wasn't for the piano. And after all they'd done for him, this would be a poor way to repay them.

Lips pursed together and head directed towards the floor, Jack walked away. He couldn't even try to hide the contempt he felt anymore. His hands clenched into fists by his sides. *We're proud of you, Son. We love you.* The words echoed in his head like poison.

CHAPTER NINE

JACK PRETENDED to be sick to skip class. After his conversation with Mrs Hendrix the previous day, he had sat through a whole afternoon of classes, coming home completely drained. He got out of bed when most people had left for school and got dressed in cropped trousers and a black turtleneck jumper paired with green suspenders. Having woken up with a lot of tension in his muscles he stretched one arm, then the other.

Out for breakfast in The Imagination Factory, Jack enjoyed his latte and bagel in silence, observing the people passing by and imagining what their lives could be like.

When he ordered another coffee, Grace stopped by his table. "I knew you'd be back."

Jack, caught up in his own world, looked up at her. "You did?" The last time Jack was here Grace had definitely acted strange. It was a hunch that wouldn't go away.

"Are you alright, dear? You look a little pale." She looked at him with warm, worried eyes. "Can I sit down?"

Jack gestured towards the chair next to him. He stirred his coffee and held it between his hands to warm them up. He was sure he must have looked horrendous. He hadn't gotten any sleep and his hair stuck out to all sides.

"Go on then, spit it out," she encouraged him, "I'm sure you'll feel better once you do."

"That obvious, huh?" Sometimes it could be easier to talk to a stranger, and Jack used that to his advantage. "You know I'm a pianist, right? My grandfather was Raymond Lewis, a classical pianist. It's important for my parents that I follow in his footsteps. Especially for my father. We never even looked at other possibilities. But yesterday I received the opportunity to switch to an acting program, which I would love to accept. But then again, I have no acting experience so how would I know it's not an impulsive decision? I've never known what I wanted to do with the piano after graduation. But acting... To play in those theatres on the West End... It's a silly dream."

"It's not a silly dream," Grace assured him. "That's quite an ordeal you're in. Family is important and of course it matters what they think. But in the end, it's you who needs to live your life and not them. You need to make sure you're happy with the decisions you make. Isn't that the most important thing? If you really want to give it a try, maybe you should go for it?"

Jack shook his head, his smile faltering. "My parents would never forgive me. They wouldn't allow it. And after everything they've done for me, I can't disappoint them like that."

Grace didn't reply.

"I'm sorry for dumping all this information on you." Jack already regretted letting everything out.

Grace sighed, shaking her head. She looked up in Jack's eyes, a serious expression on her face. "You look a lot like your mother."

Jack tensed up. Whatever he was expecting, this wasn't it. "Excuse me?" His voice came out high and sharp.

"From what I hear I can tell your parents haven't changed a bit." The frustration in her voice was evident.

Jack gasped. His eyes widened as a deep frown set on his face. "So, you do know my parents? I knew something wasn't right."

"Oh, I do," she confessed, a grim look on her face. "I recognised you from the first time you set foot in here. You told

75

me your first name and that you played the piano. That made me wonder. But I couldn't bear telling you the truth unless I knew for sure that I was right."

"Right about what?" Jack almost whispered. His heartbeat sped up. He didn't dare move.

"My name is Grace Davis. Does that ring any bells to you?"

Jack thought hard. He shook his head when realisation hit him. "Davis? Davis was my mother's maiden name." He looked straight into Grace's eyes to find the remarkable resemblance and understood why she had looked familiar to him.

"I had to promise them never to search any contact with you. Margaret is my sister. You look so much like her... It's only when I saw you with your father outside that I knew for sure. I've only seen your dad in photos but he looks—"

"Hold up! I never knew I had any family on my mother's side." Why would his parents lie about something like that? Why would they hide his own family from him?

"That makes me your aunt," Grace said. She remained calm while Jack's whole world turned upside down.

Jack shook his head. This couldn't be true. "How is it even possible I've never met you before? They never even mentioned you." He had trouble keeping his voice down.

"I haven't had contact with your mother in about twenty-three years. From before you were even born. We fell out of touch when we were younger. It's a long story. Your parents should be the ones to tell you."

Grace gave Jack all the time he needed to let the information sink in. He finally understood why she had acted strange before. She had the same green eye colour as his mother. The same as him. While Grace's more modern appearance stood in stark contrast to his mother's more traditional choice of style, there were many similarities to be found. He could see that now. That didn't explain the whole story though. If she was his aunt, why had he never seen her? Even if she and his mother had fallen out of touch, why hadn't he heard any stories about her?

"My parents won't tell me the truth." The cold tone in his voice surprised Jack. "They have been lying to me my whole life. They told me there wasn't any other family."

Grace wouldn't budge. "I would love to tell you everything, but I don't want to drive a wedge between you and your parents. Why don't you try and talk to them now that you know?"

Jack nodded. "So you're from Dallas like us? Your accent.... I could have known." He shook his head. "I should have known."

Grace sighed. "Born and raised. I moved here about twenty-five years ago. I figured travelling half the world would be sufficient to put some space between me and my family."

"Until we ended up moving to the same country," Jack remarked.

Grace laughed. "It's a small world, isn't it? I moved to Brighton first, but your mother always knew I dreamt of opening a café in London."

"She knew where you were going when you left? Why didn't you reach out to her again? Or she to you?"

She shook her head at him. "Please talk to your parents, Jack. Give them a chance to explain."

ON AN IMPULSE, Jack found himself in front of the school. An uncontrollable anger rose inside of him. He didn't get angry often, but when he did, he meant it. More than anything, it motivated him. Everything had been fine, until one day it wasn't enough anymore. Jack had tasted this other world, this other life, and wouldn't go back to how things were. The only way was forward and that was where he was headed. Even if it meant jumping in the unknown. It thrilled him. The only thing left to do was to cut the cord to the past. Make sure he couldn't go back anymore. And that was what he did.

Jack knocked on Mrs Hendrix's door and did something he hadn't done in a while. He said a little prayer. Barging into her office, Jack greeted her decidedly. He thought she'd be surprised to see him, but this was clearly not the case.

"I want in, Mrs Hendrix. I'm willing to do everything it takes." No doubt whatsoever came through in his voice. He was certain. He had been certain since the moment she had offered him to switch programs. Why would he live a lie for his parents' sake when they had been lying to him his whole life? Without their knowledge, they had provided him with the last push he needed.

Mrs Hendrix looked him in the eye. "I told you it was a one-time offer. You didn't take it."

Jack's heart sank. He straightened his back and held his head up high. "I had one day to consider. The day isn't over yet."

"You didn't need the time to consider. Five minutes. That's how long it takes me to find someone who wants a place in our program more than anything. This is the best drama program in Britain, and one of the best worldwide."

"Please." Desperation was now evident in Jack's voice. Mrs Hendrix opened her mouth to speak but he interrupted her. "You don't understand. I've never been happy playing the piano. I need this spot. I do want it more than anything, I'll prove it to you."

Mrs Hendrix raised her eyebrows but remained calm. "You cannot change your mind because you don't like playing the piano anymore. We're not a second choice. This isn't a game."

Jack shook his head. Still standing up, he placed his hands on top of the chair in front of him, leaning forward. "Acting makes me feel things I've never experienced in my life. It's new and exciting and I absolutely love it. It's not a second choice for me. It's my first and only choice. I only declined your offer because I didn't want to disappoint my parents." Jack took a deep breath and let go of the chair, his cheeks flushed. He couldn't bear the silence. It scared away the last confidence he had left.

Mrs Hendrix broke the silence in a calm voice. "Did you clear things with your parents now? Are you OK to transfer?"

"They're OK with it. I spoke to them earlier." The words came out a little too fast. His heart skipped a beat with the lie he produced.

Mrs Hendrix must have seen the change in his demeanour but didn't comment on it. She narrowed her eyes ever so slightly. "I'll set up the paperwork so we can get everything done. We'll also have to talk to Mrs Lundqvist and Mr Norbury tomorrow. Once that's done, I expect you in my class on Monday morning. It will be a big transition but I expect you to catch up as soon as you can. How it works in my class is that I don't consider you to be students, but professional actors. So make sure to act professionally. If you're late, you're out. That's my rule. You're going to have to work like you never have before."

Jack couldn't believe his ears. He thanked her about a dozen times before leaving her office in a daze. For once he did something because he wanted to and not because he had to. He had never been more excited about what the future would bring. When the door closed behind him, Jack clasped his hands to his chest as he closed his eyes and let out a squeal. His legs trembled while an incredulous grin broke out on his face. He could scarcely believe what he had just done.

JACK ENCOUNTERED Christina in the kitchen, cooking up some eggs.

"Do you want some?" She pointed towards Jack with her spatula while stifling a yawn. "I spent all of last night looking for inspiration. I'm stuck between two ideas to present for the creative recital."

Jack poured himself a glass of water. "No, thanks."

"Come again?" Christina asked.

"No, thanks," Jack repeated, louder. "I'm not that hungry." He sat down at the table. His stomach clenched together. Christina was the last person he wanted to encounter that day. *What did I do?*

"Are you feeling alright? You're spacing out again." Christina devoured her breakfast and glanced at her watch. "We need to leave in five."

Jack gathered his courage. "I'm not coming." The words were hard to say.

Christina raised her eyebrows. "Are you still sick?"

Jack nodded; his eyes glued to the table. "I feel like throwing up. I'm going to rest today."

Concern was written all over Christina's face. "I do hope you feel better soon." She squeezed his shoulder before cleaning up

Jack didn't trust his voice anymore and avoided looking her in the eye. He watched her leave and had the urge to go with her. Walk with her to class and listen to her stress over whatever it was they needed to do that day. Jack waited for two hours until he was sure everyone was gone before going to the Institute. He went to the administration desk to sort out his paperwork and received a new student ID and timetable. With a heavy heart he continued his day with the conversation he had least looked forward to.

The door to Mr Norbury's office was open, but Jack knocked anyway. Mr Norbury and Mrs Lund were deep in conversation but stopped talking at the sight of him. They were seated behind a massive mahogany desk that stood in the middle of the room. The desk seemed out of place in the otherwise small and bare office. Jack took a seat in front of them and felt ready for an interrogation. A tense atmosphere hung in the air as the extent of his actions only became clear to Jack in that moment.

Seeing the disbelief on Mrs Lund's face was the worst. Lost for words, her usual energetic self was nowhere to be found. Her lips were pressed together in a tight line. "I didn't know you wanted to become an actor?"

Jack sat on top of his hands to keep them from fidgeting. "Please forgive me, Mrs Lund. I never meant to be disrespectful towards you, or the time you have put into teaching me."

Surprisingly, she softened up. "I know you wouldn't do that. But I have to say I didn't expect you'd drop out. You're so well on your way to become a great pianist. It's a shame to throw such talent away. I'll ask you this one time and one time only. Are you sure?"

Jack forced the words to come out of his mouth. "I am." Even though the doubts were still there, he didn't regret it. Not even at that moment. If anything, for the first time in a while, he could finally breathe. He was the one making the decisions and he could be held accountable for them. He looked from Mr Norbury to Mrs Lund. "It's true that my interest in acting is a newfound passion, but that doesn't mean it isn't genuine. I've discovered a side of myself I didn't know existed and I cannot wait to explore it. I've always wanted to tell stories. Unfortunately, it took me this long to discover that it isn't through the piano that I want to do that. I sincerely apologise for the terrible timing."

Mrs Lund shook her head. "There's no way to time these things. Somehow you always know when something isn't right. It takes courage to face that reality, so for that you do not need to make any apologies."

The rest of the conversation went by in a blur. Outside the office, Jack heaved a deep sigh. At least Mrs Lund took the news better than expected. Jack planned on going back to the residence hall where he could lock himself in his room to let everything sink in.

"Wait up you! I heard the news!" Ava zig-zagged through some students to get to Jack. "Is it true? Please tell me it is!"

Jack smiled. Her happiness was infectious. He looked sideways to meet her curious eyes. "It is."

Ava shrieked and pulled Jack in a hug. "I'm over the moon! When do you start?"

Jack tried his best not to panic at the reality of it all. "Right after the weekend."

Ava clasped her hands together. "You know what? I'm taking you out for drinks tonight. We have to celebrate!"

Jack smiled and felt more determined than he had all day. He walked down the steps of the Institute when his pocket vibrated.

His whole body tensed up as his mother's picture appeared on the screen. The one person he was supposed to be able to trust unconditionally. He ignored the call and put his phone back inside his pocket. By the time he had reached his room, he had two more missed calls. When his phone rang again, Jack finally answered. It was a struggle to keep the irritation out of his voice.

"Jack!" The relief in Mrs Lewis' voice was obvious. "Are you alright? You hung up on me."

"To be honest, Mom, I'm not alright at all," Jack managed to say. He hated how fragile he sounded.

"What happened? You're worrying me. You can talk to me, you know."

"Can I? How about the truth? That's something I'd like to talk about." Jack went on before she could pretend nothing was going on. "I'd love to hear more about our relatives on your side of the family." Jack tried his best to remain calm while his heart was beating uncontrollably fast. There was no code of conduct for something like this, was there? How did you confront your parents after finding out they had kept your family a secret from you your whole life?

Taken by surprise, his mother sounded nervous. "Where is this coming from? You know we have a small family, Jack. You know it's just us."

Jack couldn't take it anymore. He knew he could talk the truth out of her. His father was too hard to crack, but his mother was a terrible liar. "What about your sister? What about Grace?"

It was silent on the other side of the line for a long time. "How did you find out?"

Jack's heart dropped. Part of him had still been hoping this would be a horrible mistake. That Grace had had it all wrong. That his mother hadn't been lying to him his whole life. "Your only concern is to know how I found out? That's totally beside the point." Light-headed, Jack took a seat on the edge of his bed. "Why would you lie about having a sister? That's just messed up."

"Please calm down, darling. I can explain. Give me a moment to process. How did you meet her? Did she try to contact you?"

Jack rolled his eyes but gave in. At least they were talking about it. "I met her by accident somehow. She owns a little café near the school. We got talking and I told her a bit about my life. She recognised Dad when I took him there. She's nice, Mom, I don't see the issue here…"

Jack could picture his mother nodding on the other end of the line. "We grew up on the ranch in Dallas. Me, my parents, and Gracey… My older sister."

Jack gasped. Finally.

"Grace had always been too rebellious for my parents. It started when she was a teenager and refused to join us to church. Your grandfather wouldn't have it and made her come along every week. One time she publicly humiliated him during the service. I don't think he ever forgave her after that incident. They rarely ever talked anymore.

"We were best friends when we were younger. She left right after she turned eighteen. I was only fourteen at the time. She begged me to go with her. She wanted to take care of me, but where would we have gone? I was only a child and I needed my parents. I loved my parents. That's the last time I ever saw her. And that's why we have never mentioned her." Mrs Lewis' voice had turned into a whisper by the end.

"So you chose to pretend she didn't exist?" Jack needed time to think. It was clearly difficult for his mother to talk about it. He tried to lower his voice. "Thank you for telling me. I understand a lot better now." He took a deep breath and went through his hair. "Are there any other family members I should know about? Now that we're on topic."

Mrs Lewis remained silent for a while. "No, it was just me and her. Grace never married or had any children."

Jack nodded to himself. His head was spinning. It didn't seem like a good enough reason to hide Grace's entire existence. How could he ever trust his parents again? Were there other things they were hiding? Also, how could his parents ever trust him again after what he did? *One step at a time.* It was alright to take baby steps. The execution of it… a little harder to accomplish. For now at least they had been able to have a conversation, no matter how difficult it had been for Jack's mother to open up. Jack respected that but hoped in time she'd tell him stories about Grace and their childhood. He'd have to find the right moment to tell his parents the truth about what he had done as well. Dreadful as it was, he owed it to them. Yet he couldn't find the strength to tell her right now.

Jack had dwelled on the subject long enough and vowed to himself to try and live in the moment. Tomorrow there would be plenty of time to worry. After a final look in the mirror, Jack plastered a smile on his face.

Rain drizzled down on Ava and Jack, and their breath was visible in the cold autumn night. They were in a merry mood when they entered the pub. To Jack's absolute surprise, Ava reached in her handbag and pulled out a wrapped gift. Jack tore the paper apart and got a lump in his throat as he looked at a copy of *Macbeth*. No words were needed, his face said it all.

Jack had found the off switch and he used it. They laughed and drank all night and just had fun. In a little over a month Jack had become a completely different person. That's how it seemed anyway. The truth was that he was becoming who he was supposed to be all along. He was becoming Jack. And while there was a long way to go, it was an open and unexpected road that he was eager to explore.

CHAPTER TEN

WALKING down Shaftesbury Avenue felt new and exciting all over again, as it had done the very first day of school. For some things you were never ready, not even as they were happening. Jack checked his reflection in the door of the lift. He went through his hair to make it look more alive.

The lift came to a halt. *Floor five. Music Department.*

Jack cursed as the doors started opening and attacked the button to make them close again. He sighed in relief as the lift descended. Seeing the panicked look on his face in the reflection made him chuckle. He shook his head. *Get a grip.*

It could be the coffee overload, the fact that it was early, or simply the nerves, but Jack felt giddy as he entered Mrs Hendrix's office. "Good morning."

She motioned for him to sit down. "Good morning, Jack. All set?" After a quick but nervous nod on Jack's end, Mrs Hendrix placed a folder in front of him. "I'm sure you did your research but I'll go over the course with you as a reminder before we start." She flipped through the pages and stopped at the timetable. "As you know we start our mornings at eight with Acting and Scene study classes taught by myself. We alternate between scenes from existing plays and scenes written by our playwrights. The afternoons are different each day and filled with Improvisation, Speech, Singing, and Movement classes. All drama students take Music Theory classes as well, but you are exempt from this class since it's more basic than the studies you've already had. You can use the extra time to study for your other classes." Mrs Hendrix flipped the page again. "Masterclasses. This month we have Mask classes, in November Stage Combat classes, and so on."

"Uhm…" Jack tried to stop her. "Stage Combat classes?"

Mrs Hendrix nodded. "You will catch up with all the terminology in no time, don't you worry. In the Stage Combat masterclass we learn how to act out fight scenes. Attacks, defences, choking, all of that good stuff."

Jack was excited at the look of his new curriculum but stayed silent and only nodded.

"You have all the necessary documentation. You're good to go," Mrs Hendrix concluded. "I know it will be hard and we're here to assist you in any way we can. Don't be afraid to reach out for help. But in the end, you're the one who has to do the work."

"I'm ready! Thank you for your time."

Mrs Hendrix got up. "Great, let's get started. I'll meet you in class in a few minutes."

About a dozen students were already in the studio, seated across the floor. They chatted amiably amongst one another. The studio was bright and airy, with a high ceiling and a front wall covered in mirrors. Among his new classmates, Jack spotted Ava. He smiled and went over to her after dropping his backpack by the wall. Despite the knot in his stomach and his weak legs, Jack hoped he succeeded in appearing calm and confident. The truth was that he felt none of those things. Everything, from the way you behaved in class to the clothing you wore, was different from his experience in Piano class. Dressed in comfortable stretchy trousers and a plain black t-shirt, Jack blended in with his new classmates.

Christian, with his ginger hair pulled back into a tight bun, plopped down on the floor next to Jack and Ava. "Who would've thought?"

"Not me, that's for sure," Jack had to say.

Christian laughed and patted Jack on the back. "How good of you to join us. Let's see what you can do."

Jack let out a nervous chuckle but didn't have time to respond as Mrs Hendrix entered the studio.

"Good morning, class. Hope you had a good rest this weekend because I've brought you all one chunk of a scene to work on this week." Mrs Hendrix took out some booklets that she waved up in the air. "Let's also welcome Jack to our group. He transferred to us from the Music department. Let's make him feel welcome."

Jack's eyes searched for Christina, longing to see her familiar face. He found Ava's instead. She gave him an encouraging smile as everyone scrambled to their feet.

They started class by doing some warm up acting exercises standing in a circle. Jack felt silly at first, trying to keep up with the others. His cheeks flushed whenever it was up to him to do something. The discovery that nobody cared if he made a fool of himself settled him down and made him enjoy the process a lot more. It was a big difference from the times he had rehearsed with Ava alone.

"Very well, class. If you weren't awake before, I'm sure you are now. Let's go through the monologues we prepared. Remember what's important here. You have been given a piece of text. Now how do you interpret that text? That's the exercise for today. I want each of you to bring your monologue in front of the class in two different ways. First very quietly, then very loudly in a strong voice. You can spin it however you like but pay close attention to your…?"

"Articulation," the whole class, except for Jack, said in unison.

"That's right. Christian, would you like to start?"

Christian took his place in the centre of the studio. Jack followed the others to the front where they took a seat by the mirrors.

"Did you receive the monologue I sent you?" Mrs Hendrix asked Jack. When Jack nodded, she went on, "I'll turn a blind eye if you want to use the text in front of you. Just this once. Pay close attention to the others first." She returned her attention to Christian. "Whenever you're ready."

Jack sighed in relief. One thing less that could go wrong, being so nervous he forgot his lines. He observed his classmates, getting a first impression of their personalities as they acted. They had all received Shakespearian monologues to present. Looking at the short text he had had to prepare, Mrs Hendrix had gone easy on him. How fitting that he was allowed to play Macbeth in his first-ever acting class.

One by one the class brought their monologues. Jack already felt a lot more at ease than when he had first entered the studio. People actively helped in providing each other feedback and were there for each other. Jack had had no clue what to expect, but this made him feel welcomed in the group. Even if he got more and more nervous by the time it was his turn to give it a go.

A new sense of self-awareness followed Jack to the middle of the studio. Whilst watching the others he had been determined not to use his script. He wanted to show Mrs Hendrix he could do it. Then came the nerves. Out of fear of forgetting his lines he snatched his script and took it with him after all. He cleared his throat and opened his monologue in a soft voice.

"Is this a dagger which I see before me, the handle towards my hand?"

FAMISHED, Jack sat down with his tray at lunch and was about to dig in when a handbag dropped loudly on the table. Jack flinched in surprise. He froze upon seeing Christina's glare. Being too absorbed in his own issues to pay attention to anything happening around him, he had been a terrible friend to her.

"Christina." Jack's face paled. *Does she even know I switched to*

"Jack, I don't know what's worse," she sneered, "The fact you lie and say you're sick when you're toying around in Acting class, or the fact you're throwing away all of your talent for nothing."

Jack got up from his seat to face her. "I'm so sorry. I didn't—"

"You didn't what?" Her voice sounded cold and distant. "Care to explain?"

Jack was lost for words. He could see the hurt in her eyes. "I'm not sure where to start." At least he was honest about that.

"Maybe you can start by telling me why you have been lying to me. I know you haven't been sick. I've known for days." She inhaled sharply. "I waited all weekend, and still you don't come up and talk to me? Not even a message? Mrs Lund said you quit?"

This had to be the worst Jack had felt in a long time. "You know I wasn't happy playing the piano anymore, right?" It sounded like a weak excuse, even to himself.

"Do you have any idea how much time I have spent, no wasted, trying to help you?" She was raging and other people started to notice. "I thought you were serious about playing the piano. I had better things to do than to throw away my time for someone who'd just use me."

"Use you?" Jack burst out. "You've got it all wrong. That's not—"

"You change programs and now I'm not even good enough for you to talk to anymore? Have you found someone to help you act, the way I helped you with the piano?"

Ava flashed across Jack's eyes for a second. He shook his head. It wasn't like that. Christina twisted everything around.

She went on mercilessly. "You don't want to be my friend anymore because you don't need me any longer?"

She was being unfair and it angered Jack. "If anybody used someone, it was you. I'm pretty sure you only chose to hang out with me because my grandfather is famous." It was out before he could take it back.

Christina gasped. She collected herself and swung her handbag over her shoulder. "You know what, Jack? I could always tell you didn't have it in you." She said it with the mere purpose to hurt Jack because she had been hurt herself. Jack could see that. But it worked. More than that, it fuelled his anger.

Jack looked her straight in the eye. "I never thought you were that great anyway."

She left.

JACK ENTERED Mrs Hendrix's office for the second time that day. To his surprise he wasn't alone. Alexander sat in front of her desk and another teacher was present as well, making the space feel cramped.

"I can come back later." The three of them turned around to look at Jack.

Mrs Hendrix shook her head. "Come in. You're right on time."

Alexander eyed Jack suspiciously when Jack stepped inside the dark office. It was clear that he hadn't expected Jack to show up any more than Jack hadn't expected Alexander to be present.

"Are we in trouble?" Jack whispered once he had taken a seat.

Alexander didn't reply and turned his gaze to the teachers in front of them.

Mrs Hendrix smiled. "It's only day one for you. I hope you didn't already get yourself in too much trouble."

Jack let out a dry chuckle and tried not to think about Christina.

"Mr Lang and I called you here to discuss the annual creative recital everyone is working on. Everyone but you two it seems. You're the final two students in our classes that have not yet started." She held up a finger when Jack wanted to intervene. "I know you haven't had time to think about it. That's why we're here together."

Mr Lang, Alexander's teacher, spoke up for the first time. He was a short and sturdy man and had his arms folded together. A low ponytail held together his long grey hair. "I know you've had your troubles last year, Alexander. This is why we want to assist you in helping you start a project."

Alexander shifted in his seat. "I didn't know participation was mandatory."

Jack's eyes widened. He'd never dare talk to Mrs Hendrix like that.

Unfazed, Mr Lang continued. "Not officially mandatory, no. But unofficially, yes. We do expect everybody to at least try to present a project to the panel of judges after Christmas."

"The same goes for you, Jack. I'd like to see how you get on working on an original project. Since you're new however we thought it best to pair you up with someone from the Playwright department. Alexander is one of our top playwrights. And since he doesn't have any actors yet, you two will have to work together."

"I prefer to work solo," Alexander said.

Jack smiled. "I'd love to work together." It was true. He could never do it by himself and everyone else was already involved in a play.

Mr Lang addressed Alexander. "You'll have to. Jack has missed a lot of classes. He has no experience as an actor yet and is going to struggle enough as it is."

Jack frowned. Was he being insulted? Mr Lang wasn't doing a particularly good job advertising Jack as a project partner.

Mr Lang went on. "After the year you've had, Jack can help give you a fresh look at things."

Mrs Hendrix agreed. "Working together with your actor from the beginning will give you a fresh set of eyes. As for you, Jack, it'll be nice to go through the process from beginning to end. Get your creative juices going."

"This is supposed to be fun guys," Mr Lang encouraged.

Alexander didn't look as if he was having much fun. He stared straight ahead and looked ready to flee from the moment they'd dismiss him.

Once outside Jack addressed Alexander before he could run off. "Were you already a student here last year?"

Alexander hesitated. "I was."

Jack frowned. "I didn't even know you were allowed to repeat your year? Usually people are sent away, aren't they, if they aren't good enough?"

"I was definitely good enough." Alexander started walking, but Jack followed him.

"What happened?"

Alexander sighed. "I missed a lot of classes."

Sensing Alexander's reluctance to talk about the subject, Jack decided to drop it. "Fair enough. When do we start working on our project?"

"You're very curious, aren't you?" Alexander asked.

Jack grinned. "Being curious lies in the nature of human beings. I simply can't help myself. It's a blessing and a curse."

Alexander shook his head, but the tips of his mouth curled upwards. "What do you say we meet Friday after class? We can take these few days to prepare and brainstorm on Friday?"

"That works perfectly for me, I finish classes early that day," Jack said. "Just one thing. It's Omar's birthday party that night so we should meet as early as possible."

Alexander nodded. "Why don't we meet around five? We can set up our project and go to the pub for his birthday after."

"Sounds like a plan. See, we're a great team already."

Alexander rolled his eyes, though not in an irritated manner. "We should get going. I'm pretty sure we're running late for our next classes."

A glance at his phone told Jack that Alexander was right. "I'm stuck with you too, you know?" he told Alexander before parting ways.

THE FAMILIAR WARMTH and cosiness of The Imagination Factory sheltered Jack from the rain. He had gladly accepted Grace's invitation to come over after school, even if it was past their opening time. After this whirlwind of a day, with second firsts and that horrible fight with Christina, Jack longed for a sense of familiarity. He couldn't stop replaying that fight over and over again in his head. At the end of the day, Christina was the one person Jack wanted to confide in. He wanted to cook dinner with her and listen to her obnoxious chatter about the piano all night long. He realised how much he had leaned on Christina these past few weeks and how much he cared for her.

Grace took a seat on the chair opposite Jack. "There's a reason why I've asked you here tonight, so I won't keep you waiting. There's someone I'd like you to meet."

Jack's curiosity spiked. "Who?"

"Well, it's my daughter. I haven't told you about her yet, but I'm sure you'll like her. She's quite amazing."

"Your daughter? I have a cousin?" He tried to mask the surprise in his voice as he recalled the last conversation with his mother. *It was just me and her. Grace never married or had any children.* Those were her exact words. Maybe his mother wasn't aware that her sister had a daughter. Or she was holding back even more information than she let on.

"There she is!" Grace jumped up and hugged the young woman by the front door. They greeted each other happily, then both turned towards Jack. Jack gave her an awkward little wave. His cousin looked straight at him with a huge smile plastered on her face. She had bright green eyes which popped beautifully against her dark brown hair, pulled back into a playful ponytail. She removed her coat as she came over, revealing the floral tattoos that covered her arms. She wore big golden earrings and dungarees with wide legs.

"Jack, meet Isabel."

Jack stood up and stretched out his hand. "It's such a pleasure to meet you, you have no idea."

Isabel took Jack's hand and pulled him into a tight hug. "You can call me Izzy. I hate it when people call me Isabel."

"Isabel, please," her mother scolded her. "I'll get us all some drinks."

"Only my mother gets away with it," Izzy whispered when Grace was out of sight. "It's so nice to finally meet you, Jack."

Jack needed time to process the shock of finding out about his new relatives. He couldn't stop looking at Izzy. There were clear indications they were related. They shared a similar green eye colour, although Izzy's was a lighter shade of green whereas Jack's eyes were darker closer to the iris. Izzy's hair had the same waves to it as Jack's although Jack's hair was a few shades lighter brown. Jack smiled. "So, Izzy, what do you do in life?"

"I study Psychology at Brighton university. I'm there most of the time, but I come over to London as often as I can. I'm here most weekends and sometimes during the week as well. I'm close with my mother, so I try not to let her get lonely too much." She studied his face. "I guess she has your company now. It's nice to have family nearby. We never had that."

"Me neither. I… I'm sorry, I don't know anything about you. How old are you?"

"Twenty-three," she said. Five years older than Jack.

Grace re-joined them and ruffled Izzy's hair as she had done with Jack's. "I'm happy to have some quiet time when you're in Brighton," she joked. She turned to Jack "She's quite a handful."

Izzy laughed and got up. "I'm going to settle in, I'll be back in a few."

"Please, take a seat," Grace urged Jack when Izzy had left the room. "Did you get a chance to talk to your parents?"

"I did." Jack paused. Where to start? He tried to ignore the nagging feeling in his chest. "I don't know what's going on to be honest. I don't know how to talk to them anymore. They've lied to me my whole life."

Grace nodded. "They told you the truth in the end, didn't they? Isn't that what matters?"

Jack shrugged. "Is it? I'm not sure. If I hadn't found out the truth for myself, they would've never told me. Mom practically confirmed that." A pang of jealousy went through Jack as he thought of the loving way Grace and Izzy had greeted each other. "I've always thought I had a good relationship with them. But all of that's twisted. I see that now. All my life I've listened to them, never acted out, always tried to please them. I thought we were good. But now I'm not sure anymore."

Grace put her hand on Jack's arm and gave it a slight squeeze. "I hope you can all find a way to work it out. I honestly do."

Jack wanted to believe her. "I hope so too. But I doubt it. I messed things up as well. I haven't told you this yet, but I didn't tell them that I stopped playing the piano." Jack shook his head. "I guess I learned from the best."

Grace's eyes widened and her voice filled with shock. "They don't know you've switched programs?" She recomposed herself. "I mean... That's a pretty big decision to make without telling them."

"I know it's bad," Jack confessed, "but in the end, it's my decision to make. I don't trust them right now. I don't even know how to talk to them. It would break their hearts if they knew." He looked his aunt in the eye. "You're not going to tell them, are you? It'll only make things worse." A slight edge of panic entered Jack's voice.

Grace smiled and shook her head. "Of course not. You can trust me. Besides... I haven't spoken a word to your mother since I was twenty years old. I don't think that's going to change today."

"Thank you." A sigh of relief escaped him.

Jack stayed in The Imagination Factory for a little while longer. Grace made the three of them bagels for dinner. Jack enjoyed getting to know Izzy, who was funny, fierce, and didn't hold back on saying anything that crossed her mind. Jack felt lucky to be getting to know his lost relatives.

CHAPTER ELEVEN

BEFORE CLASS, Jack went up to the cafeteria for a quick coffee break with Alexander. He observed the busy road from the window. It's usually only after making a life-changing decision that you find out if you did the right thing or not. Things can either turn out wonderful or everything can blow up in your face. In the heat of the moment, you can never predict how things will eventually turn out. Jack's confidence grew every day and by the end of his first week in Acting class he was working like never before. The long hours didn't bother him. He had momentum and was determined to keep it going. Even if his classes were mentally and emotionally tiring.

Alexander walked over to Jack, carrying a few folders clutched to his chest. He took a seat and placed the folders on the table in between them.

"What are those?"

Alexander held one hand protectively on top of the folders. "My entire life." He removed his hand as Jack reached for them to read the titles on the front. *The Hammersmith Opera House.* He flipped to the next. *The Edge of the Orb. Window in the Mist. Death of an Angel.*

"You can go through them when you have the time. They're a couple of scenes and short plays I've written for the Institute. It's important to get familiar with each other's style of work." He rubbed the back of his neck and hesitated before going on. "It's important to get on the same page in terms of thematics and style in what we want to do for our project. This will give you an idea of what kind of scenarios I usually come up with."

Jack nodded. "Definitely. Thank you for this." He took the one on top and opened it. *The Hammersmith Opera House.* He flipped the title page.

"Not now!" Alexander cried out. He snatched the folder out of Jack's hands and clutched it to his chest. "Whenever you have some time."

Jack looked up, right in Alexander's horror-struck eyes, and grinned. "Are you embarrassed?"

Alexander let out a deep breath and relaxed his tensed shoulders, his expression softening. "The agony is real when someone reads your work in front of you." He slid the folder back to Jack's side of the table. "That's my blood, sweat, and tears you have there in your hands."

"I get it," Jack said. "You're embarrassed." Alexander opened his mouth to reply but Jack beat him to it. "I'll take good care of these."

Alexander nodded but didn't seem entirely confident. His eyes followed Jack's every movement as he put away the scripts in his backpack. "You better!"

———

DRAINED OF ENERGY, Jack changed his outfit in the dressing room. He was slow in changing, tired from the demanding class, and was last to get out. There wasn't much time to rest as he was about to meet Izzy. She had returned from Brighton and had invited Jack for lunch in a small Italian bistro. Stepping outside renewed Jack's energy. The sun shone brightly, making Jack squint against the light. The colours on the street were red, yellow, and golden. It was a crisp day where you could wear one of your most cosy jumpers while wearing sunglasses.

Christina walked towards the school when Jack had just come out. Their eyes locked for a split second. Christina averted her gaze and hurried past him. Jack ran after her, ready to try and make amends. "Christina!"

She pretended not to hear him and kept walking.

"Christina, wait, please!" Jack caught up with her.

She turned around to face him with her chin held high and folded her arms on top of each other. Her scarf matched her lipstick; both in a vibrant red which complimented her dark skin. She looked as beautiful as ever. "What do you want?" she sneered.

"I want to apologise," Jack pleaded. He couldn't blame her for being angry.

In reply, Christina turned around and walked away again.

"Christina, come on!" Jack shouted. To his surprise she listened. He stepped up to her once more. "I know I've been awful. I've been thinking of a way to make it up to you. So much has happened in the past week, and you're the one I want to talk to about it." Jack lowered his voice. "You're my friend, Christina. I miss you."

"You don't have to do this. We've drifted apart. That happens." It was impossible to guess what she was thinking. "By the way, someone's shouting out for you."

Jack turned around to see Izzy waving at him like a maniac from across the street. She stood on the tips of her toes, waving her arm in the air as she waited between a group of pedestrians for the light to turn green.

Jack waved back and returned his attention to Christina. "That's my cousin. I was about to meet up with her."

For a moment Christina was taken by genuine surprise. The anger vanished from her voice. "Your cousin?"

"Yes, I'll tell you all about it." Despite the fact that Christina looked frightful when angry, Jack put his hands on the side of her arms. "Do you want to join us? We have so much catching up to do."

Christina flinched away from Jack's touch. "I don't care. I've got things to do." She turned around and walked away.

This time Jack let her go. But not without a heavy heart.

"Who's that?" Izzy had jogged over to Jack and panted slightly. She looked colourful, wearing green trousers and an oversized orange jumper. Her hair was pulled back in her usual ponytail with strands of hair sticking out on all sides.

"That's Christina," Jack said. "I've been a bad friend to her, I'm afraid."

"If that's the case you should make it up to her."

"I'm trying." They watched Christina disappear in the school. She hadn't looked back. "I am!" Jack added when he saw the look on Izzy's face.

In the restaurant they took their time to order, talking about nothing much else than their taste in Italian food. Posters of Italian celebrities and film stars decorated the restaurant. The waiters were loud and Italian music played in the background. Jack took a glance at Izzy from over his menu with a sense of peculiarity. Here he sat, with someone who was until shortly nothing more than a stranger to him. She looked right back at him, her eyes smiling. Jack chuckled at their behaviour and Izzy laughed right along with him. That seemed to break the ice.

"I've thought about you a lot these last few days," Izzy said. "There are so many questions I have for you. My mother always told me that the rest of the family broke all communication with her. But I genuinely don't understand why. Why haven't we ever seen you before? Or your parents for that matter?" She looked at him expectedly. They were both looking for answers neither of them had.

"I wish I knew… My mom actually told me a different version of the story. She told me that your mother just left and that that's why they're out of touch. She told me she hasn't seen your mother since she left at eighteen…" Jack paused as the recollection of the conversation with his aunt rushed to mind. *I haven't spoken a word to your mother since I was twenty years old.* She did say that, right? It all became such a blur in his head that he could hardly think straight anymore.

"She left because she couldn't take it anymore, the way they treated her like a pariah," Izzy explained. "Our grandparents and your mother shunned her after that. At least that's how I heard it."

A frown was set on Jack's face. "I'd love to hear the full story from both of them. I can't wrap my head around the fact that they never spoke again since then. You don't know my mother, but she is a sweet and gentle woman. It doesn't seem like her to hold a grudge."

"It's such a shame." Izzy sipped her water as they waited for their food to arrive.

"Have you ever been to America?" Jack asked. "Wait… are you even American? I have dual citizenship since my father is English. But what about you?"

Izzy shook her head. "One hundred per cent English. I was born here, although I think my dad is American. I've never been myself though."

"You *think* your dad is American?" Jack looked at her. Now that he thought of it, Aunt Grace had never mentioned a husband before.

Izzy shrugged. "I don't know who my father is, and my mother doesn't either. It was a one-night stand with a man called Wyatt. That's all the info we have, so that doesn't narrow it down much. She left the States soon after."

Jack was speechless at first. "Do you think our grandparents might have sent her away because of it?"

"Who knows. It's certainly possible. From what I heard our grandparents were very conservative. It couldn't have been easy for my mother being pregnant in that kind of environment."

"They were conservative, sure. But to banish your own daughter like that... There must be another reason why things happened the way they did." The delicious scent of spaghetti with fresh pesto filled Jack's nostrils. "Things just don't add up," he continued after a while. "Did you know my mom only admitted to having a sister after I confronted her about it? And even then I didn't know about you until meeting you in person."

"That's horrid! At least my mother never kept me in the dark about it." Izzy took a bite of her pizza, deep in thought. "When did you move to England exactly?"

"When I was ten," Jack answered. "Mammaw and Pappaw... our grandparents... they died when I was six. We lived near their ranch, so we saw them all the time. We then moved to Boston to be closer to my grandfather on my father's side—"

"The pianist?"

Jack nodded; his chest heavy with guilt towards his grandfather. "After a few years living in Boston, we moved to Alston."

"How were they?" Izzy asked, barely audible. "Our grandparents?"

Jack shrugged. "I don't remember much of them. Mammaw stayed at home. The only real memories I have are baking brownies with her in the kitchen and eating them as dessert when Pappaw came back from working on the ranch all day."

"I'm sorry to burst your image of them. I don't want to ruin your memories." There was a sharp edge to her voice. "My mother tried and tried to get in touch with them, but they wouldn't talk to her. They treated her like a pariah. They're awful people as far as I know."

For Jack it didn't seem like they were talking about the same people. What he heard from Izzy and the stories he had heard from his parents didn't match up. "I can't believe my parents lied about it my whole life. There has to be a better reason as to why, right?"

"There must be," Izzy agreed.

They fell into a comfortable silence while they finished their lunch. Jack found Izzy easy to talk to. Easier than he would have expected. They parted ways as if they had known each other for years. And even if meeting her had been a strange turn of events, he was grateful for it.

JACK TOOK Alexander's stories out of his backpack, making sure to make no creases in the paper. He thought it brave of Alexander to share his work with him like that. With no classes in the afternoon, Jack took the free time to be amazed by Alexander's writing. Settled comfortably in one of the sofas in the common room, he read through the scripts in one sitting and barely noticed the passing of time. Jack hadn't read any work of the other playwrights, so he didn't have anything to compare it to, but he was impressed by Alexander's ability to move him with his words. When he finished reading, Jack counted the minutes until they were supposed to meet. Up until now, Jack had had zero ideas for a play, and he didn't want to disappoint Alexander. He hoped more than anything he would be valuable to their project and not a nuisance. Alexander was already great at what he was doing while Jack was all new to this. He couldn't see the outcome and that scared him. In those few minutes he waited for Alexander to arrive, he realised how he didn't know Alexander at all.

Alexander, dressed all in black with skinny jeans and a plain black t-shirt, opened the door to his room and plopped down on his bed. He started typing on his laptop but stopped to look at Jack, who still stood in the doorway. "Aren't you coming in?"

Jack smiled nervously and stepped inside, closing the door behind him. "Of course!" He took a seat on the chair behind Alexander's desk and couldn't keep his fumbling hands to stay still. "It was quite clear the other day that you don't want to work with me."

Alexander opened his mouth to interrupt him. He looked at Jack from over his laptop.

"Please let me finish," Jack added. Alexander frowned but Jack went on, nevertheless. "I know I'm new to all of this, but they asked me for a reason so there must be something good in my acting. You'll see."

"It's nothing personal and it's not because you're new. I just prefer to work alone. Which is impossible because I need an actor anyway. We're going to make it work. So how about we start talking about ideas and stop talking about things that don't matter?"

Jack held his hands up in surrender, already feeling much more at ease. "Fine by me."

Alexander jumped right into it. "I already have some ideas in mind, so I'd like to hear your thoughts on it. I'll write the script over the next few weeks and get your feedback on it."

Jack nodded. "And once that's finished, we start rehearsing."

"Exactly." Alexander continued typing but immediately paused again. "We don't have too much work today. The important thing is to get started. Besides, it's Omar's birthday party tonight so we have to leave on time."

Jack grinned. "I thought you might chicken out."

Alexander shrugged. "I at least have to make an appearance, right?" He almost smiled.

"Being his friend, it would be pretty rude not to." Jack took a moment to observe Alexander's room. Everything looked neat and organised. It looked the same as Jack's. Same size and same furniture. Some black and white posters of musicians livened up the room.

"Miles Davis," Alexander said, pointing towards the poster Jack had been looking at. "I like to write to his music." Alexander shrugged and returned his focus to the screen. "Whatever."

Jack grinned but Alexander ignored him. He opened his backpack and pulled out the folders Alexander had given him earlier that day. "All that listening to Miles Davis pays off. You're a great writer."

Puzzled, Alexander at Jack. "You finished reading? All of them?"

Jack nodded. "I have to say I'm impressed. *Window in the Mist* was my personal favourite. The relationship between the sisters was well played out."

"I'm happy you liked it," Alexander said in a soft, incredulous voice.

"The subjects though, they're quite heavy, aren't they?"

Alexander nodded. "They are. It's what I do best. If you want to do something light-hearted, I don't think we'll be a good match. It's just not my style." He reconsidered this for a moment. "Although I wouldn't mind giving dark comedy a try."

Jack shook his head. "I said it was heavy, but I like that. I think it gives more food for thought than a happy ending kind of script. I'm open to whatever you'd like to suggest."

Alexander heaved a relieved sigh. "I have to say, this is going smoother than I expected."

Jack grinned. "If I didn't know any better, I'd think you thought I'd be a complete idiot?"

Alexander ignored Jack and resumed typing.

Jack laughed aloud. "How do we start? Now that we know in which direction we're going. I want the audience to leave the theatre thinking about our play for long after it's over. I'd like to leave an impact on them. And I'd love to try and play a darker theme. It'll surprise people."

Alexander's eyes widened and he tipped his head to the side, observing Jack as if he saw him for the first time. "I usually get inspired by poems and letters. I recently wrote a poem I'd love to work with. Come here, I'll let you read it. It's called *Faceless Midnight*."

Jack took a seat next to Alexander on the bed with their backs against the wall. Jack couldn't not observe the way their sides touched. Couldn't not observe the way Alexander's warmth radiated against his body. Alexander placed his laptop in the middle.

With his breath stuck in his throat, Jack started reading. He had a hard time concentrating at first, but the haunting words of the poem sucked him in. Overcome by a sadness that came from within, Jack finished the poem.

"It's beautiful," he managed to say. "Sad, but strong. I can't believe you wrote this."

Alexander closed his laptop but remained close to Jack. "I'd like to work around this context. Explore these feelings and see what we can do with them."

Jack nodded. "If I understand correctly, it's about the loss of a loved one. How it impacts the ones he left behind."

"Exactly," Alexander encouraged him. His whole face lit up when he talked about his work. "About the immensity of grief. About one person's world collapsing while the world in fact carries on as if nothing happened."

"It's a powerful subject. I say we go for it."

A slow smile appeared on Alexander's face, barely visible. "I wanted to talk to you about something completely different as well. Omar's birthday party tonight." Alexander scratched the back of his head.

"What about it?"

"Arthur, the owner, is letting us decorate the pub. And since I'm low on time and extra hands I wondered if you could help me out?" He gestured towards two cardboard boxes near the door. Jack got up and looked inside of them to see they were full of decorations. "Don't say a word," Alexander warned him.

Jack, of course, couldn't resist. "I didn't know you cared so much for birthdays and parties to go decorating. That's sweet of you."

Alexander rolled his eyes. "This was not my idea whatsoever... But as Omar's friend I'll do him the favour. Luckily for me, it's only his birthday once a year." He looked annoyed. "Is that a yes for the help? Because if not, we're done here for today and I'll see you tonight."

"Of course I'll help! Did you make him a crown?"

Alexander sighed, rummaged in the box, and pulled out a party head.

Jack laughed. "Wicked."

"Just to get one thing straight," Alexander said. "This… was all Omar's brother's idea." He gestured towards the boxes. "It turns out he can't make it in time to decorate so he put me in charge."

"Whatever helps you sleep at night."

"DID YOU PUT WEIGHTS IN HERE?" The walk to the pub took less than ten minutes but Jack grunted when he dropped the box on one of the tables in the pub. Only a few other customers were present. Arthur showed them upstairs where they were allowed to decorate the first floor. It was a cramped little place, but it was perfect for what they needed. Two microphones and a screen for karaoke were already set up in the corner.

Alexander unpacked the boxes. "We have about an hour before everyone arrives."

Jack pulled out a pack of balloons "Omar's brother really went out of his way for this."

"Give me a hand will you." With the assistance of Jack, Alexander hung up a banner with Omar's name and the number twenty on it.

"It looks a bit crooked, doesn't it?" Jack took a step back and looked at the banner questionably.

"It's fine," Alexander grunted without looking.

They worked in silence. Jack couldn't wait until Omar arrived. He was going to love this.

"It looks horrible." Alexander concluded. He looked at his

watch and took a seat on a wooden stool in the corner, from where he could observe the whole room.

Jack got them a pint and joined Alexander while they waited. It didn't take long for the pub to fill up with twenty-something people from the Institute including Ava, who had joined last minute.

Omar appeared on the staircase. Everyone cheered and burst out singing *For he's a jolly good fellow*. Omar laughed aloud as he made his way through his friends, receiving birthday wishes left and right.

"Did you do all this?" Omar asked Alexander when he had reached the other side of the room.

Alexander nodded. "My birthday present to you. Happy birthday." He let Omar pull him into a hug.

Omar greeted Jack and Ava and joined their little table. "Oh, Alexander, you must have hated that."

"It wasn't too bad. But as soon as people start singing, I'm out of here," Alexander said gloomily.

Ava looked at Jack and mouthed *karaoke*?

Jack nodded and lifted his beer. "To you, Omar!" Ava and Alexander joined in.

After a few sips of his beer Omar turned to Jack. "I've invited Christina to come. Will you be nice to her?"

"Me? Nice?" Jack exclaimed. "Of course I'll be nice. She's the one who is being mean at this point."

Omar shook his head. "Sure, but you know her, don't you? I've got the impression she's a bit lost, to be honest."

Jack felt a pang of guilt inside his chest. He had no idea how she was doing lately.

"My brother is here! I'll be back." Omar exclaimed out of nowhere. He jumped up and hurried over to his brother, who looked a few years older and had short, shaved hair instead of an afro haircut. Nevertheless, the resemblance was astounding.

When Ava left to greet some friends, Alexander turned to Jack.

"An idea just came to me. Wouldn't it be nice to have original music to accompany our play?"

"Sure," Jack agreed. "But who would play it? Everyone is drowning in work as it is."

Alexander gestured towards the stairs. "I heard your friend Christina is pretty good."

When Jack turned to look over his shoulder, Christina had entered the pub. She stood at the top of the stairs, holding a little wrapped gift in her hands. She scanned the room. When her eyes met Jack's, she looked away quickly and walked over to Omar.

Jack returned his attention to Alexander. "I'm not sure if you've followed the previous conversation, but Christina and I aren't exactly on speaking terms."

Alexander shrugged. "Didn't you just say you were going to be nice to her? Push aside your pride and make up with her. This is about art, about a project. Differences should be set aside for that, don't you think?"

Jack sighed. "It's not my pride that's the problem."

"It's worth a try, right?"

"I guess so." Jack didn't sound convinced.

Alexander gulped down the remainder of his beer. "Right. That's me off for tonight."

"Already?" Jack gasped. "The party barely started."

"And I did my duty. See you next week! Do ask Christina about the music."

"But... Don't go yet!" Jack shouted in vain. Alexander made his way through the tables to say goodbye to Omar and left the pub. Jack followed him with his eyes until he was out of sight.

With nobody else to talk to, Jack mustered up all the courage he had and walked up to Christina and Omar, who now stood by the bar.

Omar took a step back so Jack could join them. "Here's your beer." Omar passed Jack a pint which he gladly accepted if only to have something in his hands. He had to raise his voice as Arthur had turned up the music a notch.

Christina gave Jack a sharp look and nodded towards his pint. "Go easy on the beer," she sneered.

Jack refrained from giving a remark and ignored her. He looked at Omar who didn't meet his gaze. He did say he'd try. "How are you?" he decided to ask Christina. Perhaps not the cleverest thing to ask, but at this point Jack was hopeless.

Christina glared at him and returned her attention to Omar. "I don't have time to stay, but I wanted to pass by and wish you a happy birthday."

"Are you sure you don't have time for one drink?" Omar pleaded.

She shook her head. "I wish I did. See you later." She turned around and made her way through the others to reach the staircase.

Jack spoke up before Omar could say anything. "I'm trying. You know I'm trying."

"I'll see if I can talk some sense into her," Omar said. "This has lasted long enough."

It was hard for Jack to get back into the party mood. It didn't look like Christina was planning to forgive him any time soon. He didn't want to disappoint Alexander, but Jack couldn't see himself asking Christina to play the music in their play.

A few pints and a few great songs later Jack managed to forget all that was on his mind. He sang *500 miles* twice. Once with Omar, and once with the whole group. At some point, he was rocking it out on top of one of the tables. It was fair to say that his first karaoke experience was a success. Or that's what he thought at least, but everyone was drunk at that point, so it didn't really matter.

About six of them were still present when Arthur kicked them out. "Alright, lads. Enough of this. Off to bed with you all!"

Nobody took the initiative to move until Omar suggested they went for a midnight snack. When they finally walked back to the residence hall a few hours later, Jack squinted as the morning sun greeted him. Together with the others, he slouched all the way back. Half asleep, Ava and Jack leaned on each other for support. Jack had rarely felt this shitty before, but there was something nice about walking drunk and half asleep through the streets of London in the first rays of sunshine. Eyes directed to the floor, while putting one foot in front of the other, they somehow got home safely.

CHAPTER TWELVE

"COME IN." Jack barely recognised his voice. Another knock. Jack managed to crack one eye open and took a look at his phone. It was well past midday. "Yes!" he tried to shout. His voice came out hoarse and uneven. He forced himself out of bed and slouched to the door.

"Christina?" It really was her. The absolute last person he had expected to see.

"I'd say good afternoon, but it looks like I woke you up. I can come back later." She took a step back. Finding Jack half naked and half asleep was probably not what she had expected.

"No!" Jack exclaimed. "Please come in." He opened the door so she could enter. He grabbed a shirt and joggers from his wardrobe and threw them on. He opened the curtains and window for some fresh air. The light that entered the room made Jack groan. His head pounded horribly.

"I assume you guys stayed for a while after I left?"

Jack could be hallucinating but she sounded calm. "You could say that," he said while making his bed. He had an inkling he had Omar to thank for Christina's visit.

"Jack, stop fussing around," Christina snapped.

"Sorry," Jack said sleepily. He closed the curtain halfway,

dimming the light in the room. "I wasn't ready for that," he admitted.

Christina laughed, and it pleased Jack so much to hear it. Silence hung between them for a moment. "Look—"

"No, let me go first," she interrupted him. "I want to apologise. I've been horrible towards you. I'm embarrassed to admit it but it's true. You were going through a difficult time and I completely abandoned you because... because I was hurt. The truth is that I don't have that many friends." She stared at the floor.

"Christina..." Jack whispered.

"It's true," she said. "I didn't want you to stop playing the piano because I needed you to challenge me. There are only a handful of people who make it through the program, and I intend to be one of them. With you in class there was someone to challenge me to be better. To make sure I didn't get overconfident."

Jack appreciated her honesty. "You don't need me for that," he assured her. "I know you, Christina. And I know that you challenge yourself to be the best every day. It's not because I do something different now that we can't be friends anymore. I miss you; you know?"

Christina's expression softened. "I miss you too. Even if you can be a total dickhead at times."

"I'm sure I'm your favourite dickhead." Jack engulfed her in a hug.

Christina pulled out of the hug. "I say this as a friend, but you need a shower."

Jack laughed. "We're good, right?"

Christina nodded; a smile plastered on her face. "I'll see you soon then." She turned around to leave.

"Wait, what are you up to today? Maybe we can catch up?"

Christina turned around to face him. "I'm headed to the rehearsal studios to practice the piece I'm writing for the creative recital. What about tomorrow?"

"Can I come?" Jack found himself asking to both his and Christina's surprise.

"Sure. I'll wait. But hurry."

Jack took an aspirin and got ready in no time. The shower had done him wonders. He was surprised to see Christina had indeed waited for him. Together they set off to the rehearsal studios.

Jack's hand rested on the doorknob for a few seconds before he found the strength to open the door. Old memories rushed back as he looked around the small room, feeling out of place and comfortable at the same time.

He had almost forgotten how radiant Christina looked behind the piano. It was sad that people never got to see themselves like that. In pure concentration, doing something they loved. She played for Jack as she had done hundreds of times. This time however, it felt like Jack heard her play for the first time all over again. He tried not to show her how much it did to him.

When Christina went out on a coffee run, Jack couldn't resist. He walked over to the piano and let his fingers run over the keys. They were aching to play. He pressed a note. Simple and pure. Jack closed his eyes as the note lingered on. Something stirred inside of him. He thought of his grandfather and what he would think of Jack. Would he resent him? Or would he be proud that Jack was standing up for what he wanted, as he had once done? Aware of his every movement, Jack positioned his fingers on the keys and allowed the familiarity to rush back to him. He was unsure of what to play but when his fingers touched the keys the answer was right in front of him. He allowed himself to get carried away by the sound of his music.

Jack jumped up, startled by the door that opened. He ended on a false note as Christina came in. He blushed. It almost felt as if she had walked in on an intimate moment. Was this how it was supposed to feel?

Christina handed Jack his coffee. "You haven't lost your touch. Do you want to have another listen to my piece? I'm better warmed up now."

Jack nodded but didn't say a word. He couldn't concentrate on Christina's piece. It was a peculiar thing, wasn't it? Take away the pressure, lift a burden of someone's shoulders and an almost magical thing happens. For once Jack was one with the music he produced. No one had ever told him that when he played, he had to play for himself. He could finally enjoy it now that it was no longer an obligation. Jack had played because he wanted to play. He had played for himself, and it turned out that that was the key.

"Do you miss it?" Christina had stopped playing.

"I do," Jack confessed. "I miss it terribly. But I'm sure I've made the right decision. I can play and enjoy it now that the pressure is gone. It reminds me of how it used to be when I listened to my grandfather play. It used to be relaxing. Something I looked forward to. He always had such fun playing and so did I." Jack smiled at the memory.

Christina nodded. "I think I get it now. And I do hope you made the right decision."

"I have no doubt I did, to be honest. I feel lighter now... in some ways."

"It was selfish of me not to listen to you," Christina admitted.

Jack raised his eyebrows. "Are you admitting you were selfish? I never thought I'd live to—"

Christina punched his arm, hard. "Only I get to say that!"

Jack rubbed the painful spot on his arm. "You should get into boxing." He held his hands up when he saw Christina's narrowed eyes. "Seriously though. I was a horrible person and a shitty friend for keeping you in the dark like that."

"At least you know it," Christina scoffed. Then she smiled

Jack had always been terrible in predicting the right time to do things but figured now was as good a time as any. "There's something I'd like to ask you. But you have to understand it's only a question and you are entitled to decline."

Christina rolled her eyes. "Just tell me what it is already."

"Alexander and I are working together on a play for the recital. Alexander thought, well we thought, how it would be nice to have somebody accompany us on the piano." It seemed like a big favour to ask when things were only just right between them again. But he didn't want to tell Alexander he hadn't even tried. "You can forget I even asked if you want. I know how busy you are."

"Do you ever shut up?" Christina waited a second before going on. "I've been working on my own piece non-stop. It's pretty much ready to go for the judges. Since there's so much time left, I'd love to work on something else as well. Because what if my piece doesn't get chosen? I want to double up my chances."

"There's no way your piece isn't going to be selected." Christina smiled at the compliment. "Wait," Jack continued. "Is that a yes? Was that a yes?"

Christina held her hands up. "It's a maybe. I should at least know what I'm signing up for, right?"

Jack grinned. "There's not much to tell you yet I'm afraid. We only just started. We're taking inspiration from a poem that Alexander wrote called *Faceless Midnight*. We want to create a play that deals with the consequence of death, the afterlife even. With the idea that a spirit or soul lives on after it ceases to exist in this world."

"That sounds good," Christina said, taken aback. "That sounds really good."

"It was Alexander's idea, but it's genius. I read some of his previous work and he has an extraordinary way with words."

"I'd love to accompany the play on the piano. If you believe in it, so do I."

Jack couldn't wait to tell Alexander the good news. He was in a strange sort of daze for the rest of that day and it wasn't because of the hangover. He mustered up the courage to call his parents. Playing the piano again had made him miss them. Never before had he gone so long without seeing or hearing them. He wished everything wouldn't have to be such a big mess. Jack missed how things used to be. Before all the secrets.

"YOU LOOK a lot better than the last time I saw you, lad," was Arthur's way of greeting Jack into the pub the next week. The floorboards creaked underneath Jack and Christina's feet as they took a seat behind the bar.

"Feel a lot better too," Jack replied. He waited for Omar to spot them. Once he did, he came over to take their order. Dressed in a white shirt and black bowtie he looked a world apart from his usual funny t-shirts and hoodies.

Christina ordered a pot of herbal tea. "It's the first time we see you in action."

Omar grinned. "Welcome to another episode of my life. Available every Thursday and Saturday."

"You are doing great, Omar, we believe in you!" Jack nudged Christina's side and pointed towards the tap. "Look at the way he holds that glass. The work of a professional, let me tell you."

Christina tilted her head to the side. "I see. The angle in which he pours that beer. Pure perfection." She couldn't hold it in any longer and let out a giddy laugh.

Omar shook his head. "I won't allow the art of pouring beer to be mocked." He gave Jack and Christina their drinks but couldn't keep the grin off his face as he took the order of another customer. "Here we have another prime example," Omar said as he took another glass. He held it under the tap. "It's more of a feeling. I treat every pint with the same amount of respect."

Jack couldn't contain his laughter and nearly fell off the barstool. "Is every beer the same?"

Omar shook his head in a serious manner. "They have different personalities." He tended to his customer and returned to Jack and Christina. "It's nice that we can all hang out together again. You two—" Omar looked at the door. "Idris!"

Jack turned around to see Omar's brother standing in the doorway. The similarity in their faces still caught him off guard. Idris walked over to the bar with the same crooked smile Omar had. He unbuttoned his long black coat and took a seat. "Another round on me, please." While their voice sounded similar in tone, Idris' cockney accent wasn't as strong as Omar's.

Omar's smile disappeared. "Are you alright? What are you doing here?"

Idris smiled and shrugged. "What do you think I'm doing? Visiting my little brother, of course. I was nearby and thought I'd pop in. Aren't you pleased to see me?"

Omar's smile returned. "Always." His accent became less understandable when talking to his family.

Jack listened to Christina talking about her piano lessons to Idris when panic overtook him. He cursed loudly. "What time is it?"

Startled, Christina replied. "Almost ten, why?"

Jack got to his feet and cursed under his breath. He passed his beer to a confused looking Christina. "I am so late."

"I think that's the first time I heard him curse," Omar said to Christina, loud enough for Jack to hear. "Do you reckon we're a bad influence on him?"

Jack threw on his coat in a hurry and groaned. "I was supposed to meet Alexander over an hour ago. How stupid of me to forget."

"I'm sure he'll understand if you explain," Christina offered.

Omar held a questionable look on his face.

Jack sprinted to the residence hall as fast as he could. He needed a minute in the lift to catch his breath. The common room was empty with no sign of Alexander anywhere. Jack ran over to Alexander's bedroom and knocked on the door. It opened a few seconds later.

"What do you want?" Alexander stood before him in a black jumper and grey joggers. He had clearly changed into something more comfortable. The only light in his room came from a night lamp. A book lay open on his bed.

Panting, Jack untangled his scarf. "Hi... I'm so sorry... for

117

being late. I lost track of time. Shall we start?" His face was flushed from the run.

Alexander raised his eyebrows at the sight of him. "You're not late exactly... You didn't show up at all."

"I know," Jack explained. "It was such a busy day at school and I went to the pub after with Christina and Omar, totally forgetting what day or time it was. I—"

Alexander heaved an annoyed sigh. "It's nice for you that you prefer to go out drinking over working on an important project. But I'm not a teacher. You don't need to come up here with all your excuses."

An anger arose in Jack. "I'm here now, aren't I?"

"Our meeting would have been over by now anyway, so let's call it a night," Alexander snapped.

Jack tried again. "I'm sorry. Honestly. We were having a pint and..." Jack struggled with the zipper of his coat. Why was it so hot inside? "Never mind. I came as soon as I realised how late it was. So can we just, please, start working?"

"I'm going to bed." Alexander closed the door slightly. "Always good to know you have your priorities sorted out, Jack. This is exactly why I prefer to work alone. At least I can count on myself to show up and not sit around waiting for someone who doesn't take this seriously."

Jack's heart sank. "Alex, come on. That's unfair."

"It's Alexander. And I don't have time for this shit." He slammed the door shut in Jack's face.

Someone must have punched Jack in the stomach since he couldn't breathe anymore.

THE FOLLOWING day Jack asked Omar for Alexander's timetable and tried to catch him at lunch. Jack was unsure if Alexander had spotted him, but he had suddenly disappeared from the crowd and Jack couldn't find him anymore. He went on to plan B and was prompt in waiting for him outside of the school building. When Alexander descended the stairs and saw Jack waiting for him, he quickened his pace.

Jack ran up to him. "Alexander!"

At first, he walked on without looking Jack in the eye, but he stopped walking abruptly after turning the corner. "Are you following me?"

Jack shrugged. "Kind of... Yes." Jack didn't expect an apology from Alexander for what he said last night. He knew he had been in the wrong by forgetting the time. It still hurt though, to be seen as a person who doesn't take things seriously when he did so very much.

Alexander opened his mouth to say something but closed it again. He had a frown set on his face.

"There's something I have to get off my chest," Jack said. "You can trust me when I say I've given up a lot to be able to act. I have not done so lightly and it's my main priority. I give it all my time and attention and take it very seriously."

"Jack—" Alexander started but got cut short by Jack who kept on talking.

"Everyone can forget something or make a mistake. And I'm sorry I did. It won't happen again. But you shouldn't be so upset about it. It's still—"

"You can stop," Alexander said. A silence fell between them as they had reached Soho Square. He scratched the back of his head. "I'm not good at this."

"Good at what?" Jack asked.

Alexander pointed between himself and Jack. "This. Depending on someone. I'm sorry for what I've said. Not that it makes anything better, but I had a shitty day yesterday."

Jack couldn't help himself but smile at the awkward manner Alexander had apologised.

"What do you say we go up and I let you read what I've come up with so far?"

Jack nodded. "Sounds great. Let's get to work."

CHAPTER THIRTEEN

AUTUMN WAS COMING to an end as Jack got used to his new schedule the following weeks. He spent most of his time acting and completing his coursework. The other time he spent with Alexander, working on their play for the creative recital. Alexander wasn't always the most talkative guy, but in the end, they worked well together as a team. For the first time Jack had a purpose. And that motivated him to be the best version of himself every single day. He was one of the fortunate ones, to be able to pursue his dreams. For the first time a long while he felt completely and utterly happy. Yet Christmas break was right around the corner and Jack dreaded going home for two full weeks to his parents and all the frustration that hung unresolved between them. That would make for an interesting holiday for sure. Time was moving fast. Much faster than he would have liked.

"Jack?" Christina woke him from his musings.

"Hmm?" Jack was seated in the common room, going through some notes of his Stage Combat masterclass.

"I asked if you wanted to join us? Omar and I are going to hang out on the roof for a bit."

Jack stretched his back. "Sure, I'll be there in a sec." He

dropped his notes in his room and dressed warmly in a thick scarf and hat, both knitted by his mother.

Jack greeted his friends as he climbed onto the roof. "You guys know it's freezing, right?"

"It's only cold if you believe it is," Omar joked. He patted the blanket which he and Christina used to sit on. "It's not too bad once you sit down."

They huddled together, their breath visible in the night sky. "I love how quiet it is up here." Jack snuggled up in one of the blankets and gladly accepted the cup of tea Omar handed him. The cold air against his face and the warm tea helped Jack relax.

Omar nudged his side. "We were discussing Christina's upcoming date with Carlos Matthews."

Jack grinned as Christina was about to protest. "What do we have here?" he teased her. "If it isn't the talented and famous Carlos Matthews. How's he doing? Is he working for the London Symphony yet?"

"I don't know how he's doing. Not in detail anyway. He's indeed working for the London Symphony. We ran into each other in the music shop and got talking again."

"How romantic." Jack wiggled his eyebrows to vex her.

It seemed to work. Christina rolled her eyes. "He's taking me to dinner on Thursday, right before we leave for Christmas break."

"To then leave him hanging for two weeks wanting more? Smart move." Jack grinned and winked at Christina.

"Of course not!" she exclaimed. "But it's a nice bonus, no?"

Omar laughed. "That guy had better prepare himself for an interrogation on life in the orchestra. A day in the life of Carlos Matthews: paid to play."

"Paid to play: an improbable love story," Jack added.

Christina changed the subject, but not without a playful smile on her face. "I can't wait until I get to tease you guys. You'll never hear the end of it. Come on, enlighten me. Nothing interesting happening on the love front? No secret crushes?"

Omar clasped his hands together. "Yes, Jack, why don't you spill the tea?"

Christina laughed heartily. "Nice try, Omar."

Omar shrugged. "I'm no Carlos Matthews, am I? There aren't any girls swooning over me." No response came. "I go out!" Omar defended himself. "Just not as often as I would like."

Christina laughed. "You went on a grand total of one date this year."

Omar held his hands up in defence. "Hence the not as often as I would like." He refilled his cup of tea from the thermos beside him before going on in a more serious tone. "I'm a hopeless romantic I'm afraid. I need to feel a connection with someone first."

"You don't need to be a Carlos Matthews," Jack assured Omar. "You're better than him." He looked towards Christina for support.

"You are," she agreed. She went on when Omar shot her a look. "You're... funnier. You're the funniest person I've ever met."

A smile tugged at Omar's lips. He turned to Jack. "We'll have to turn our luck around, won't we? Put ourselves out there a bit more. The school is full of brilliant girls. Heck, the whole of London is full of brilliant girls."

"Or guys," Christina added.

"Or guys," Omar corrected himself. "London's full of brilliant people." Both of them looked at Jack expectedly.

"You can leave my love life, or lack thereof, to me. To be honest, I've never even been in a relationship," Jack admitted. "There, happy?"

Christina laughed at Jack's defensiveness. "Me neither. Nothing serious anyway. But you must have been dating, for sure?

"I guess. A while ago." Jack pulled the blanket closer around him and stared at the open sky in front of him. "It never felt right though, and I didn't pursue anything seriously."

"Why didn't it feel right?" Christina asked, a frown on her face.

Jack shrugged. "I don't know." But he had the inkling that he did know. Months, maybe years, of suppressed thoughts and feelings stirred inside of him. "If there's anyone of interest I'll update you guys with all the juicy details, don't you worry." But Jack did worry a bit.

JACK SPENT the last night before Christmas break with Alexander, going over their script. As per usual, they installed themselves in Alexander's room. Alexander on his bed with his laptop in his lap, surrounded by different versions of the script. Jack behind Alexander's desk, notepad and pen at the ready.

Jack pulled out a form from his backpack and waved it in the air. "Look what I brought. We're one step away from officially taking part in the preselection show in January."

Alexander didn't look quite as excited as Jack. "Let's fill it in."

Jack inspected the form. "There's one requirement we didn't discuss yet."

"The title," Alexander said.

Jack nodded. "That's right. Why don't we go for *Faceless Midnight*? We used the poem as our inspiration after all."

"Only if you like that title," Alexander said quickly.

Jack smiled. "I love it! It completes the eerie feeling of the play, doesn't it? Adds a bit of mystery. I don't say this often enough, but sometimes you're a genius."

Alexander looked up in Jack's eyes. "Only sometimes?" He almost smiled.

Jack turned his attention to the form and filled in their title in the best handwriting he could muster. "This makes it look so official. I'll have to drop it off tomorrow morning. My parents are already in town and will be here early to meet me."

"Why don't you give it to me? I have nowhere to be tomorrow."

"That would be great, thanks." Jack handed Alexander the form.

"I'm going to edit the script one last time over the weekend and send you the final version as soon as that's done."

"Make sure not to overdo yourself. You should take a break and enjoy your holidays." It was kindly meant.

"We're art students, Jack, of course we overdo ourselves. We don't take breaks." Alexander sighed. "By the way, I'll be pretty much on my own here, so I'll have plenty of time to write."

"You're staying here?" Jack's eyes widened. "Why don't you go home to your family? Didn't they live somewhere in London?"

Alexander's expression hardened as he pursed his lips.

"Fine, I'm sorry." Jack's voice came out a little harder than intended. No matter how he tried to get closer to Alexander, Alexander wouldn't let him.

Alexander changed the subject. "Do you want to go through the script one more time together?"

Jack nodded and took out his printed version of the script. He read it out loud to Alexander, who listened and typed notes on his laptop. Jack tried his best to convey the right emotion, but when they were finished, Jack was left in doubt. "Please don't kill me, but there's a thought that keeps popping up in my head and I have to spit it out." Alexander raised his eyebrows. "I know the script is nearly finished and it's written as a monologue. But I feel like we might need to bring in an actress as well. Correct me if I'm wrong."

"I was thinking the same," Alexander said to Jack's surprise. "We haven't discussed it for the sole reason that we were signed up together. But that doesn't mean we can't bring more people in. Looking back at the essence of our play, I agree that we might need to bring in a second actor."

"I have to say I thought you would argue me on this one. It's fine as a monologue but we could do more with it if it was played by two characters."

"It'll change the whole feel of the play." Alexander stretched his back and arms, lifting his shirt up in the process.

Jack tried and failed not to stare at the visible skin underneath Alexander's t-shirt, his cheeks flushing red. He took a deep breath.

"I hope you don't have anywhere to be tonight," Alexander said in a low voice.

Jack shook his head, staring right into Alexander's eyes. "I'm good right here," he said softly.

That night they rewrote the entire play. Well... Alexander wrote, and Jack gave input. They had seldom had such a productive night.

"Can you sit still for like two minutes?" Alexander snapped.

They were seated next to each other on Alexander's bed with their backs against the wall, both gazing at the screen of Alexander's laptop. "I'll try, but no promises." Jack took hold of the laptop and turned it his way. "Hold still, will you."

Alexander pushed Jack's hand to the side. "No dirty fingers on my screen!"

"I need to be able to read, right?"

Alexander sighed. "I'll mail you a copy. I'm getting tired."

"I'm thinking of Ava," Jack blurted out.

Alexander tilted his head to the side. "What for?"

"For the play of course. She's working on a project with Kim, but I think she'd be willing to take on the extra work. They're pretty much finished anyway. We could ask her as our female lead." Jack had wanted to suggest Ava from the second they had decided to change the script.

Alexander opened his mouth and closed it again. "We don't have to decide right now, do we?"

Jack frowned. "If not now, when? We're running out of time. The preselection is already one week after Christmas break."

Alexander stopped typing. "You're right. It's just that... I didn't quite see her as the character."

"Don't you like Ava?"

Alexander raised his eyebrows. "It has nothing to do with liking on a personal level. The thing is... she's not the best in your class." He looked Jack straight in the eye.

"I'm not the best of my class either," Jack said. "Are you saying we're not good enough for you?"

Alexander shook his head. "Never mind. And by the way, you are better than you think. Let's ask Ava. You're right. We need someone as soon as possible."

Although still confused, a grin broke out on Jack's face. "Can you repeat that?"

Alexander rolled his eyes in a playful way. "You're better than you think?"

Jack laughed. "What about the other part?"

"You're never hearing that again."

"Hearing what again? That I'm right? That you think I'm right?" Jack was joking. It was hard to get Alexander to smile but Jack loved trying.

Alexander remained serious. "Will you ask her, or should I?"

Jack got up from the bed and stretched his body. He had been sitting in the same position for too long. "I will. You don't like her anyway."

"I don't... It's not." Alexander sighed. "She's fine. Drop it."

"It's fun to see you struggle." Jack laughed aloud. "Let's end the night with some music, shall we?" When no protest came, Jack turned on the speakers on the desk and pressed play. *Motorcycle Emptiness* started playing. It took Jack a few seconds to recognise the song. Surprised, he turned to Alexander. "You've been listening to my suggestions?"

Alexander avoided looking into Jack's eyes. "I like the sound of this one. And the meaning behind it."

"Me too." Jack swayed lightly to the rhythm of the music, left to right. "I've been listening to Miles Davis as well. A bit of a change from what I usually listen to, but I'm into it."

Alexander smiled. It was only a small smile, but Jack had finally done it.

Humming along to the song, Jack swayed more enthusiastically. He returned Alexander's smile. "Look at us, enriching each other's taste in music."

Alexander watched Jack in silence with a look of amusement in his amber eyes.

Jack felt scrutinised by Alexander's gaze. It somehow urged him to keep dancing, even if he made a fool of himself. Jack extended his hands and moved closer to Alexander. "Come on! You know you want to."

Alexander shook his head. "You should know me better than that by now. I don't dance." A small pause. "Or at least not when people are watching." He didn't budge.

Jack wasn't discouraged. "It's only me." He got closer and extended his hands far enough for Alexander to take them. "I do know you. And I'm sure you're tempted."

Right when he was about to give up Alexander surprised him. He allowed himself to be pulled up to his feet, closing his hands around Jack's.

Jack swayed in circles around Alexander who held a sly grin on his face. Alexander turned around with Jack, his eyes never leaving him until he finally gave in and started dancing. Alexander sang along to the lyrics, pretending to have an imaginary microphone. Jack whistled in encouragement.

When the song came to an end, Jack gathered his belongings. They both panted from the exertion. There was something in the air which had Jack feeling elated. He couldn't keep the grin off his face. Couldn't keep his eyes off Alexander. "I have to go pack," he said in a low voice. "I won't have time tomorrow morning."

"It'll be a short night for you in that case. Don't look at the time."

Jack looked at the screen of his phone and groaned. Two in the morning.

"Do you ever listen?"

Jack had to grin. "You can't tell me not to do something. It'll only make me want to do it more." He walked over to the door, followed closely by Alexander. "I'll see you after Christmas, yeah?"

Alexander opened the door for Jack to leave. "See you after Christmas. But we'll hear each other sooner. We'll talk every day."

Jack walked outside. "About the project?"

"No, about our feelings…" Alexander grinned upon seeing the bewildered look on Jack's face. "Of course about the project. You'll need to rehearse by yourself over the holidays. But we can check in with each other for progress. Don't forget to ask Ava! Oh, and I'll make a rehearsal timetable for the week after the holidays."

"Aye, aye, captain." Jack saluted Alexander and walked away before he got tempted to get back inside.

CHAPTER FOURTEEN

"THANK you again for the ride home, Mr and Mrs Lewis." Seated on the backseat of Jack's parent's car, on their way home for the holidays, Christina was uncharacteristically friendly.

Jack's mother, who hadn't stopped smiling since picking them up, brushed her off. "It's our pleasure, dear. Leeds is on our route anyway. And it's a pleasure to meet one of Jack's friends."

Off to Alston it was for Jack. He longed to be home again. To take a long walk over the hills and country lanes that surrounded their house. To put his presents underneath the Christmas tree. To see the people of the village again. Yet at the same time he dreaded it. How was he supposed to rehearse the play while his parents didn't even know he was acting? How was he supposed to hide the fact that he wasn't playing the piano anymore? Jack could think of only one feasible solution. He had to tell them the truth. He had put it off for such a long time that he had nestled himself in a nasty position and it was hard to find a way out.

"Will your parents be home?" Jack asked Christina when they had left the hustle and bustle of the city well behind them.

Christina spoke in a low voice. "Probably. My mother is working in Australia this month, so I won't see her. She promised to Skype on Christmas though, so there's that." A trace of bitterness was audible in her voice. "My father is also working, but from Leeds. So at least I'll get to see him."

Jack had never much inquired after Christina's family and didn't dare elaborate on the subject with his parents in the car.

Mrs Lewis turned to face Jack and Christina. She had picked up bits and pieces from their conversation. "Is your father by any chance Mr Clarke from Clarkes Industries?"

"He is indeed," Christina confirmed.

This spiked even Mr Lewis' interest. He looked at Christina from the rear mirror before returning his attention to the road. "Clarkes Industries? Your father owns companies all over the country. All over Britain even." He clearly approved. "I take it you are adopted then?"

Christina shifted in her seat but smiled. "I am, yes. My parents couldn't have children of their own, so they opted for adoption."

Jack shot Christina an apologetic look for his parents acting snobbish. Luckily, Christina didn't seem to mind.

"Don't talk about stuff like that, Jim." Jack's mother sounded curt and final. It was one of the rare times Jack heard his mother raise her voice with his father.

Jack decided it was time to come in between. "I appreciate you two scheduling a trip to London to pick us up."

"Not just to pick you up," said Mr Lewis. "There was another reason for going to London this week."

Mrs Lewis gasped. "I thought you were going to wait until we got home."

"It'll be of Christina's interest as well," Mr Lewis said.

"Very well. Go on," Mrs Lewis urged him. She clasped her hands together and brought them up to her face, hiding her smile.

Mr Lewis wasted no time in obliging. "You know how business has been going great, right, Jack? We sell a wider variety of instruments now than we did last year. I'm happy to say the hard work is paying off." Mr Lewis could hardly contain the grin that spread across his face. "Sean and I have had a lot of meetings lately and the decision came through yesterday that.... We're opening a second shop in London."

Jack's mouth dropped open. He looked from his father to his mother, both of them beaming with pride. "That's fantastic news."

"Congratulations," Christina said with a bright smile.

"When is this happening?" Jack asked.

Mr Lewis happily received the compliments. "As soon as possible. We're looking for a property as we speak and will arrange everything as soon as we do. But not to worry, Sean and I will stay in Alston and travel back and forth to London to check up on things."

"I'm happy for you, Dad." Jack meant it. "I never knew you had plans to expand the business though."

Mr Lewis shrugged. "Neither did I at first. Yet when the opportunity presented itself, we didn't need to think twice." He glanced at Jack in the rear mirror. "I meant what I said when I was last in town. It could be nice for you to manage your own branch of the business in a couple of years. You could handle the London one. Your expertise in pianos is invaluable."

Jack's brain went in total lockdown. He opened his mouth to speak but no words came out. He shot Christina a panicked look and shook his head lightly, warning her not to say anything.

"Jim," Jack's mother urged her husband. "Let them rest for a bit." She turned to her son. "You must be tired, aren't you, darling?"

Grateful for his mother's interference, Jack rested his head against the window. The cold glass felt comfortable against his skin. His heartbeat returned to beating at a normal pace, but his stomach still clenched together at the thought of telling his parents the truth. He would break his father's heart if he knew. More than anything, Jack wished he could talk to his grandfather one last time. He would have known the right thing to say.

Too soon, it was time to say goodbye to Christina. Jack heaved her suitcase out of the boot. They engulfed each other in a long hug in front of her house, both of them realising they faced two difficult weeks.

"Stay sane," were Christina's parting words.

Jack watched her get inside the house as he and his parents drove off to Alston.

GLANCING AROUND HIS BEDROOM, Jack noticed how it was exactly as he had left it a few months earlier. Only a few hints gave away that he hadn't been there for some time. The bed was made a little too neatly, the row of books on the shelf above his desk was organised alphabetically, and the photos on his dresser were straightened. He unpacked in silence. There was no noise at all. No music from his neighbours, no shouting, no street noises.

He plastered a smile on his face and walked to the kitchen where his mother was preparing dinner. Wearing her blue apron, working three hobs and the oven at the same time, Mrs Lewis looked to be right in her element. She hummed along to a song on the radio and cooked in a way that looked almost rehearsed. Jack kissed her cheek in passing her and took three plates from the overhead cabinet above the sink.

Jack's mother stopped stirring the soup and turned to face Jack. "What are you doing? Since when do you help out in the kitchen?"

Jack halted on his way to the dining room. "Since I live alone?"

His mother stared at the plates in Jack's hands. "Thanks for the help, darling. But don't break anything."

Adamant to keep the peace, Jack tried his best not to let out a sigh. It amazed him how quickly he had gotten used to living alone. And how much everything had remained the same back home. Almost like he had never left.

Jack leaned against the half wall that separated the kitchen from the open plan living and dining room. From where he stood, Jack could see his father in his armchair, watching television. The sound of the hood and the oven, mixed with the sound from the television, would make sure his father wouldn't hear what Jack had to say. "I was hoping we could talk a bit about Aunt Grace, Mom."

Facing the stove, Jack's mother had her back turned to Jack. At first it appeared she hadn't heard him, but the muscles in her shoulders visibly tensed up.

"We don't have to go into detail now," Jack added in a hurry. "I know for some reason you don't like to talk about her. But I'd love to hear stories about both of you. About what it was like growing up together. About why you two really fell out of touch." Jack held his breath in anticipation. She still hadn't told him about Izzy. Did she even know of her existence?

Hands clenched together; Jack's mother turned around with a sigh. "I'll try to talk about her, no matter how hard it is. But please, not now. Let's have a nice dinner to celebrate the start of our holidays. We'll have plenty of time to talk later."

Even if Jack hadn't gotten any wiser, he viewed his talk with his mother as a success. He hoped he would finally be able to make sense of it all. That she would finally tell him the whole truth. He couldn't believe that they would hide his family from him just because his aunt ran away. Jack knew there had to be more to the story.

THE FIRST FEW days were pretty eventless, much to Jack's enjoyment. Mr Lewis worked long hours in the shop. A detailed report of that day's events were relayed to Jack and his mother every night. Mrs Lewis on the other hand helped out Father O'Connell with a Christmas charity event in the church. So far Jack had gotten out of accompanying her with the excuse that he needed every spare minute to practice his pieces. This meant Jack was home alone quite often, which worked out well for him.

He couldn't wait until his parents were out of the house in the morning. He'd rush upstairs to get out his script and practice his lines in front of the full-length mirror in the corner of his room. Ava had readily accepted the part and was excited to join Jack and Alexander in their endeavours. Every other day Jack and Ava rehearsed their lines in one of their video chats until Alexander was satisfied. Those video calls pulled Jack through the days. After their rehearsal, Alexander and Jack often remained just the two of them. Both of them didn't have a lot going on so they talked on and on about their project, eventually deviating to all kinds of subjects. Jack enjoyed these talks and tried to make them last for as long as possible, often until his parents came home.

Jack had only been gone for a few months. And although everything seemed fine on the surface, many things weren't. Despite what his mother had said, his parents didn't bring up Aunt Grace, or the fact he had a cousin at all. Not even once. While this frustrated Jack, he was trying far too hard to keep the peace in the house. Every day Jack planned to tell his parents that he stopped playing the piano and every day he couldn't bring himself to do it. Somehow living in a state of denial and pretending things to be fine had become a habit for them all. And once it became a habit, it was too easy to go on to start a row.

The closer it got to Christmas the more Jack's parents remained at home, enjoying their holiday by the cosy warmth of their fireplace. They spent their nights reminiscing, drinking hot chocolate, and playing board games. They had fallen back into old routines and Jack started playing the piano again. It did him well to play. He couldn't however avoid his parents' questions about his classes. Those were the times where he was simply lying to their faces. He answered questions about his supposed piano classes until he couldn't take it anymore. He couldn't keep living a lie. It was becoming too much. He owed it to his parents, who were so happy to have him home again, to be honest. If only he could find the right moment.

The awkward stuff didn't happen until Christmas Eve. That's where it all went wrong. Something was bound to happen eventually. They had been tiptoeing around each other, hoping in vain the bomb wouldn't drop. But of course, it did.

As per usual they spent Christmas Eve with the three of them and Mr Lewis' friend Sean, his wife, Helen, and their annoying eleven-year-old, Tommy. Jack didn't dislike a lot of people, but this kid managed to get on his nerves every single time.

The night started off fine. They were all in a jolly spirit, enjoying the delicious meal Jack's mother had prepared. The house was beautifully decorated with lots of candles and fairy lights spread around the room. A decorated evergreen wreath hung above the upright piano. On the piano itself stood a nativity scene surrounded by Christmas branches and red ribbons. Glass ornaments decorated the huge Christmas tree that looked too big for the room it was in. It stood proud in the corner of the dining room, next to the piano.

Things only started going in the wrong direction when the main course had been served. A delicious roast chicken with mash and carrots. Jack loved Christina's cooking, but nothing could beat his mother's food. Jack helped everyone fill their plate. They laughed and talked about all sorts of unimportant things. Tommy's grades, Tommy's perfect behaviour, Tommy's friends.

Jack's mother was fishing for an opportunity to change the conversation from Tommy to Jack. Was this something all mothers had to do? Make sure that their child was the best at something? "We met Jack's friend Christina the other day. Such a lovely and polite girl. Wasn't she lovely, Jim?"

Jack tried to suppress a grin.

"Hmm." Jack's father grunted with a mouth full of food. "It's true that she's a lovely girl. According to Jack she is top of their class. Her parents own Clarkes Industries."

Jack frowned and looked up from his plate. He found that, for the first time since arriving home, he couldn't keep his mouth shut. "It's not a competition. Even if she wasn't all those things, she would still be my friend."

His father shot him a warning look.

Mrs Lewis turned her attention back to Helen and smiled weakly. "Jack's been working really hard. He's top of his class as well. Although we can hardly be surprised at that."

"It's one of the finest schools in the world for aspiring musicians," Mr Lewis added. "They have to watch out if they want to keep their good reputation though. I'll tell you, the ideals they have there…"

Sean nodded. "Quite right." Sean never seemed to understand what Mr Lewis was talking about.

The answer satisfied Mr Lewis. "Margaret, the carrots." This meant the subject was closed.

Meanwhile, Jack's desire to speak his mind to his parents had never been greater. Sean and Helen had turned quiet. Tommy who sat across from Jack, grinned at him like the little devil he was. Jack ignored the kid and took a deep breath. He returned his attention to his plate of food and relaxed his grasp around his cutlery.

It wasn't until dessert that things got out of control.

"Your grandfather would be so proud if he could hear you play just one more time." Jack's mother offered him a smile.

"And I would be honoured to play for him," Jack said. He took a spoonful of his Christmas pudding. "This is delicious."

"Thank you, Jack. And while it's not for your grandfather, you can play for us when you're finished."

Jack's father nodded. "I'm thinking Bach." He turned to Sean. "Jack plays it very well. Not as well as his grandfather, but he's getting there."

Sometimes you had to make a judgement call for yourself. And while this might not have been the perfect moment Jack was waiting for, he couldn't take it anymore. All these lies made it impossible to breathe at times. The time had come to finally tell his parents that he had stopped playing the piano. That he had changed to the Drama department. They would have to understand, right? It was one of the best decisions Jack had ever made. They should be happy to see him following his dreams. That's what he should have said.

"He's our own little Mozart," his mother added.

I quit playing the piano. "I'm gay." Jack paled as soon as the words left his mouth. He didn't dare breathe. Didn't dare make another sound. Did he really just say that out loud? Everyone had stopped eating and was now staring at him in utter shock.

The only thing worse than any response his parents could have given him was not responding at all. The most awkward of awkward silences hung in the air. The radio filled the room with Christmas carols that were too cheerful for the situation, making the silence even more painful to endure.

Jack's father started eating again and everyone followed suit, except for Jack. A tight knot formed in his stomach. He wouldn't be able to eat another bite and put his spoon down on the table. He hadn't known these words were the ones he was going to say aloud. He had shocked everyone including himself, but it made perfect sense. In a way he had always known, and he wasn't ashamed of it. Yet when he looked around the table, everyone was so focused on their pudding you'd think they hadn't eaten in days.

Everyone but Tommy. He had finished eating and was smirking at Jack with his arms crossed over his chest. Remainders of his pudding were smeared around his mouth. "Ew. Do you want to kiss boys on the lips?"

Helen shot Tommy a sharp look.

Jack didn't know at that point whether he wanted to laugh or cry. Possibly both. Was the thought of him being into other guys that disgusting? Living under the strict rules of his parents all his life it had never been possible to show much individuality outside what was expected of him. Everything had changed now that he was living on his own, surrounded by people of all colours, nationalities, and sexualities. At a place like the London Institute of Arts nobody cared if you were different. It was something to be celebrated, not hidden away.

Nobody looked him in the eye anymore until coffee was served. Finally. The end of the most awful Christmas dinner had almost arrived. Although the cherry on top of the cake was still to come.

Mrs Lewis tried to restart the conversation with her small talk about the weather and the food. Jack allowed himself to relax ever so slightly. At least that horrible silence had come to an end. Soon everyone would be going home.

"How's that horrific brother of yours?" Mr Lewis asked Sean. "Is he still in the middle of his divorce?"

Mrs Lewis shook her head. "A union between a man and a woman made by God is a sacred thing. Not something to be broken."

Helen answered. "They are still fighting over who gets what. Latest argument: the cat. Who gets the cat? Of course we're the ones they complain to. It's driving us both crazy, isn't it, Sean?"

"It sure is, Helen."

Helen continued. "Praise yourself lucky on that front. Siblings sound like fun until you have them. My sisters aren't any better."

After everything that had already happened, Jack should have kept his mouth shut. On the other hand, he was already in so deep that things couldn't get any worse. Or so he thought. "Having a small family is nice indeed." It was the first time in almost half an hour they looked at him. As if they'd forgotten he was there. Jack looked his mother, who was clearing the table, in the eye. Her eyes begged him not to go on. "It's only us, Aunt Grace, and her daughter Izzy. A nice little family indeed."

Jack's mother froze dead in her tracks. The plates she was holding slipped right through her fingers, breaking in a million pieces on the floor. She gave a little shriek and bent over to clean up the shards, whispering incoherently. Even Jack's father had turned pale.

"Are you quite alright?" Sean asked.

"I didn't know you had a sister? Or a niece?" Helen asked at the same time.

Mr Lewis took over as his wife was in no state to talk. "We don't talk about her. We don't even talk to her. It's been twenty-five years." When Helen opened her mouth to ask more questions he quickly went on. "She's even worse than Sean's brother. That's why we never told you about her."

Jack had had it with his parents. First, they flat out lie about her existence, and now they were spreading ugly talk about her. "She's actually pretty great, Dad. She is one of the nicest people I've ever met. Both of them are."

His father looked Jack in the eye, his own eyes blazing with anger. He tried to compose himself. "How would you know that?"

Jack shrugged, not breaking the eye contact. "I see her all the time. I'm often in her café, to work on school assignments, or to hang out with Izzy in the weekend."

"Now I see why you've changed. That woman is doing it again."

A SOFT KNOCK on the door. Jack laid on his bed, clutching a pillow. The only source of light was his little night lamp. He didn't have to look up to know it was his mother. He had recognised the sound of her footsteps coming up the stairs. For those few seconds the door was open Jack could understand every word his father said downstairs. He was in the hallway, letting out Sean, Helen, and Tommy. "…rebellious until now. I thought we raised that boy well." The noise was reduced to muffled voices as soon as his mother closed the door. Jack sighed and kept his gaze fixed to the ceiling even when his mother took a seat on the edge of his bed.

"Darling," his mother said, "I hate to see you like this."

"Like what?" Jack finally looked her in the eye only to see that she was struggling as well. He heaved another sigh and went on.

"He talks about me like I'm a terrible person. Like he has to apologise for my behaviour."

"It's hard on him too. He wants to end the night smoothly."

"You don't have to be perfect in everything, you know?"

"It's OK to strive for perfection. That's what we always do."

Jack looked up at the ceiling again. "It would be nice if you could let me do my own thing. To be supportive. But it's clear that you're embarrassed." He continued in a shaky voice, "I feel like I'm living in this constant struggle between being too much or not enough. I can't handle it anymore. I know who you want me to be, who you need me to be—"

"You need to be nothing but yourself," Jack's mother interrupted him.

Jack snorted. "Are you sure? What if one day I didn't like playing the piano anymore?" He observed his mother's expression closely.

"You're tired. Don't fret. You've been working so hard that…" Jack's mother was taken aback and couldn't complete her string of thoughts. "Let's not say stuff like that to your father, alright?"

"So much for being myself," Jack added bitterly.

"What did you think, Jack? You didn't handle tonight as an adult, as much as you like to be one." She put her hand on Jack's ankle and squeezed it. She continued in a softer tone of voice. "You're gone for less than four months and already you stopped going to church—" She held her hand up as Jack tried to interrupt her. "You don't think I haven't noticed how you worm your way out of going to church with me every single time? You used to love helping me out with these charity events. Especially at Christmas."

Jack didn't have anything to say. She was right.

"You don't call us as often as you did anymore and now you tell us that you're… gay? Of course we'd be—"

"Disappointed?" The silence was sharp as a knife.

Mrs Lewis shook her head but didn't correct him. "For the record, I don't hate your aunt. You have to know that. It's confronting to talk about her. You cornered us a bit with it. After she had been gone from our lives for so long."

Jack sat up straight in his bed, still clutching the pillow. "But why? I don't see the problem. She is such a nice person."

His mother smiled. "I'm happy to hear that."

Something happened Jack never saw coming, especially after how the night had gone. His mother opened up about her past.

"We lived a secluded life, Grace and I. The community we grew up in was not a forgiving one. Anyone who made one misstep became a pariah. So you followed the rules and made sure not to step out of line."

"I understand why Aunt Grace wanted to leave."

Mrs Lewis nodded. "Exactly. It was nothing for Gracey. I didn't want her out of my life, but she just left. Even though she knew I couldn't join her. I loved our parents too much and would have never done anything to disappoint them. I was too young, and I didn't mind the community we lived in. I was, and still am, a devoted Christian. The values I was taught still apply to me now. While I understand that Gracey wanted to leave that environment behind, she still left me... her little sister. I never got over that. We got in a horrible fight when she left. We only got in touch once, when you were born."

His mother's story moved Jack. He had a million questions but didn't want to scare her off. "Why didn't you make amends with her? Surely there is nothing to be mad about anymore?"

"It's not about being mad anymore," she said sadly. "Sometimes when things happen time goes by and you... grow apart."

"What about Izzy?"

"Izzy." His mother smiled while saying her name. A single tear fell down her cheek.

"You told me Aunt Grace never had any children."

"I didn't know," she whispered. The front door slammed shut. "Shall we keep your father company now they left?"

Jack nodded and followed his mother downstairs.

"What a wretched night." Jack's father sounded beaten.

"Shall I play you something?" Jack was surprised by his own words.

His father nodded but had a hard time looking Jack in the eye. "Please."

With a sense of calmness, Jack took a seat behind the piano and started playing. He thought about all the times he had been seated at that exact spot wishing he wouldn't have to play anymore. Today was the opposite. He enjoyed the music he produced and made sure to put as much emotion into it as possible.

Mr Lewis walked over to his wife and stretched out his hand. Surprised, she took her husband's hand and let herself be guided to the side of the room, next to a few remaining broken shards.

Jack glanced sideways at his parents, careful not to miss a note, as they started slow dancing. He smiled and refocused his attention to the piano. A peaceful ending to a unique night.

CHAPTER FIFTEEN

"I'VE NEVER BEEN HAPPIER to see someone in my life." Jack engulfed Christina in a big hug. They stood in the middle of Leeds station amidst people hurrying to catch their trains. Jack let go of Christina and double-checked the departures to make sure they were headed to the right track. "How was your holiday?"

"Let's say I'm happy to get back to London. Or in other words… shitty. Yours?"

Jack couldn't stop grinning at her. "Same."

Waiting for Christina to order her takeaway coffee before boarding the train, they ended up running not to miss it. Safe and sound in their seats, Jack told her all about his holiday and the grand Christmas fiasco as he now decided to call it.

Christina stayed silent for a full minute before responding to Jack's story. "That sounds… insane? I'm lost for words here."

Jack stared out of the window to see the rolling hills of the South Yorkshire countryside pass by. "Your turn to tell me about your holiday, it's only fair."

Christina's spirit dropped. "Fine, I'll tell you all there is to know and then I'm closing the subject forever."

Jack's eyes widened at her serious tone. "Very well, my lady," he joked to lighten the mood.

Christina gave Jack a playful kick under the table. "You're an idiot, do you know that?"

Jack grinned. "An idiot you've missed!"

She didn't deny it. "You already know my mother had to work in Australia during Christmas…. I shouldn't be so upset over it, but she promised to call and she forgot. On Christmas nonetheless." There was a bitterness to the edge of her voice. "Don't get me wrong. They're loving parents but they're so focused on work all the time. I get scared, you know? When I look at myself. I see what I'm turning into. Do you think it's true when they say the apple doesn't fall far from the tree? Do you think we'll end up like our parents?"

Jack took hold of her hand which lay on the little table. "I guess a lot of people do. And there's nothing wrong with that I suppose, as long as you're happy with yourself. But you and me…. We're going to be different. Trust me."

"You don't know this, but I've only lived with my parents for nine years. I grew up in foster homes before they came along. Nobody wanted a ten-year-old. They all wanted the cute toddlers. Except for my parents. We clicked instantly. I loved them from the start."

"I never knew all that," was all Jack could muster as he stared at Christina with wide eyes.

Christina shrugged and downed the remainder of her coffee. "Nobody does. It's the piano that helped me through it all. When they took me home the first thing I noticed was this amazing Steinway standing in the living room. The funny part is that neither one of them could play. When they saw my admiration for that piano, they sent me to Piano class straight away. I was sold from the start."

Jack felt honoured that Christina trusted him enough to open up to him. He was touched but didn't have the right words to express it. Christina went on before he could, eager to put an end to the subject.

"I'm going to help you, you know?" she told him out of the blue.

"Help me with what?"

"Your family. After all the stories you told me I want to help you discover the things they're hiding."

Jack frowned. "Maybe they're not hiding anything anymore. I finally got them to talk."

Christina shook her head. "It doesn't explain everything, does it?"

Jack thought long and hard. "You know what's weird? My mother told me she hadn't seen my aunt in twenty-five years. My aunt told me she hadn't seen my mother in twenty-three years. I figured they must have forgotten how long it had been. But my parents said it again at Christmas… Twenty-five years. In such a significant situation it's peculiar to be off by two years, isn't it?"

Christina's eyes widened. "That can't be a coincidence. I'm willing to bet you they're holding something back. All of them. Something that happened in those years."

Jack nodded thoughtfully. "I was so happy that my mother opened up to me. She sounded so genuine. But there has to be more. Aunt Grace might be more willing to tell me her side of the story. I'm going to try and talk to her again."

Meanwhile they arrived in St-Pancras station. London welcomed Jack with open arms. Stepping out of the train, he felt right at home.

SAVE FOR ALEXANDER, the common room was empty as many people had yet to return from their holidays. Alexander was early and already waiting for Jack as he entered. He flipped through the script and barely acknowledged Jack as he plopped down beside him. He wore a wool jumper, black skinny jeans, and big combat boots. He checked the time on his phone. "You're late, again."

It seemed there was no room for small talk for Alexander

today. "By two minutes, that doesn't count," Jack cried out. He uncrossed his legs and leaned forward, trying to catch Alexander's expression which looked more tense than usual. "There's no need to be nervous."

"I'm not nervous," Alexander said, a little too quickly. He looked at Jack for the first time that night. "Can we go through the script?"

Jack sighed. "You're all business and no pleasure. Why don't we catch up for a bit? We can—" Jack stopped talking when he saw the look on Alexander's face. "Fine, let's start... Alex."

Alexander got up to his feet. "I'm happy you want to jump right in."

Jack rolled his eyes but held a grin on his face. He allowed Alexander to pull him to his feet.

"Why did you get a haircut?" Alexander asked, staring at Jack's hair. He stepped up to Jack and ran his fingers through Jack's short waves. "I liked your crazy hair."

Jack's breath hitched in his throat. He swallowed while studying Alexander's face, which was inches away from his own. Alexander had shaved the stubble that usually ran along his jawline. Standing close to Alexander was enough to send Jack's mind in overdrive. "I don't have crazy hair. It just doesn't like to do as it's told." His voice didn't come out as confident as he wanted it too.

Alexander took a step back, seemingly oblivious to the feelings he stirred in Jack. "Much like yourself," he joked. He turned around to take the script from the sofa.

Jack continued to stare at Alexander with wide eyes, his lips slightly parted. He'd never allow himself to think... He'd never allow himself to hope...

"Ready?" Alexander asked, hands in his sides.

In a daze, Jack nodded. There was no avoiding getting started. A tight knot had formed in his stomach. With only one week left, what if Jack couldn't live up to Alexander's expectations? What if this had all been a terrible mistake? An impulsive misstep.

Everything had happened so quickly. If Ava would have been there to act alongside him, he wouldn't feel so exposed. Too bad she still had to fly in from Ireland that night.

Jack took a deep breath and started acting. Much to his frustration, he had to start over several times for the simple fact that he couldn't get into his role. Looking into Alexander's expectant eyes made Jack self-conscious about the way he acted. He shook his head after stumbling over his words on the fifth try. "I can do it," he muttered to himself and shook his arms to loosen up.

"Jack, stop." Alexander came up to him. "Relax."

"I'm not used to failing," Jack said in a sharp voice. "I'm just nervous."

Alexander on the other hand remained as calm as ever. "Weren't you the one that suggested *I* was nervous?"

Jack had no idea what to make of Alexander tonight.

"Look," Alexander continued, before Jack could reply. "It's only our first in-person rehearsal. We still have the whole week to perfect it and it'll go easier when Ava joins us tomorrow. We are going to practice this play until we are sick of it. There's no need to despair."

Jack heaved a relieved sigh. "You're right. I'll try again."

"Hang on. Let's not go again straight away. You need to find the right energy before you do. It'll help you settle in the story."

Jack frowned as he looked at Alexander. "When did you get so wise?"

This was one of the rare occasions Jack saw Alexander smile. "I've always been wise." Alexander started pacing up and down the room. "You need to get into the skin of the longing and aching of the character who reflects on the person he has lost. We need to feel his despair through your words. The character needs to undergo an evolution throughout the ten minutes playtime we have. We want to end on a hopeful note. The people who leave us never really leave us. They leave their mark on the world." Alexander paused and stopped pacing. "I need you to focus on not only looking, but actually seeing. Seeing things and people for what they are. Open your eyes. Get conscious of what's happening around you. It will help you get into character."

Jack nodded, in awe of the way Alexander handled things. He couldn't stop looking at Alexander and tried to really see him. There was more to his cold exterior than met the eye. Alexander's face was a handsome one. He had strong cheekbones and nicely shaped lips which were set in a tight line. His eyes seemed to hold many secrets, like he carried the weight of the world on his shoulders. And whenever those eyes met Jack's, Jack's breath hitched in his throat.

They gave it another go, which went a lot better with Jack at ease. Right in the middle of a third run of the play they got interrupted by Alexander's phone. His brow creased. "It's Omar." He took the call, talking in a low and hushed voice. "I have to go. I'm going to pick Omar up from the train station."

Jack jumped up in no time. "Is he alright?"

Alexander didn't seem keen to answer. "Something's wrong with his brother Idris and—" He paused for a moment. "Never you mind. I'll see you tomorrow, yes?"

Jack gathered his belongings. "I'm coming with you. If something is wrong with Omar, I want to be there for him."

Alexander shook his head. He had already put on his coat. "I don't think that's a good idea. I'd rather go by myself."

Jack didn't have any time to answer as Alexander bolted out of the common room without so much as a goodbye.

NERVES RUSHED through Jack like a high fever. He couldn't sit still and after a morning of fidgeting and worrying it was finally time to leave for the theatre. The week had flown by much faster than Jack would have liked. He double-checked his appearance in the mirror before leaving. Despite being well on time, he hurried over there and arrived at the theatre hot and sweaty. He waited outside for Alexander and Ava to arrive. He took off his scarf and unbuttoned his coat. It was freezing but the chill of the winter wind did him good.

After about ten minutes Jack walked inside to see Ava and Alexander sitting right there on the steps. "Guys!" Jack ran over to them, a slight edge of panic in his voice. "We were supposed to meet in front of the theatre."

Ava got to her feet. "You didn't wait out in the cold, did you?"

Jack threw his hands in the air. "I was waiting for you two!"

"Relax. Everything will be fine." Ava came over and greeted him with a hug. They made their way backstage where they had plenty of time to prepare themselves.

They took a seat in their dressing room, which sounded fancier than it was. The tiny square room housed a couple of chairs and a table with a small mirror on it. In silence they each did their thing. Jack rubbed his cold hands together and paced around. Alexander went on a coffee run. Ava waved her arms in circles to warm up. She sped up her pace, doing a little dance which made no sense whatsoever. She jumped around, waving her arms like a maniac. "Come on, Jack, loosen up." She smiled and continued spinning around. She roared.

Jack laughed and got to his feet. He jumped towards Ava, roaring back at her. He pounded his fists to his chest. They jumped around each other until they ran out of breath and collapsed on the floor with fits of laughter.

Alexander came in with the drinks and shook his head. "You guys are lunatics."

After some last-minute pointers from Alexander, Ava had to go. She was part of a different project as well. The boys wished her luck and used their spare time to watch her from the audience. They snuck inside the theatre and found two empty seats on the last row. By the looks of it, most of the school had turned up, despite it being a show for the first-years only. This didn't help settle Jack's nerves.

Jack burst out in applause as his classmates entered the stage.

"That's Christian with Rachel!" In less than an hour he would be up there himself. "I'm nervous." Maybe if he said it out loud, it would go away.

Alexander leaned closer to Jack, his eyes never leaving the stage. "There's no need to, you'll be brilliant. You need to have a little faith in yourself."

Goosebumps formed all over Jack's neck and arms when Alexander whispered in his ear. They watched a couple of the plays together, including the one with Ava and Kim. Jack gasped as she messed up one of her lines. She recovered as gracefully as she could, but Jack hoped it wouldn't cost her a place in the recital.

"You have to go and get ready," Alexander told Jack over the sound of the applause. "I'm staying here to watch. I'll meet you guys after."

Jack stopped clapping and looked Alexander in his eyes. "OK," he said with as much confidence as he could manage.

"Break a leg." Alexander encouraged him.

Jack dressed in his costume which consisted of a simple tweed pair of trousers and a linen shirt. Jack had suggested a pair of suspenders would complete the costume. He blocked out all the noise around him and walked backstage, clutching his suspenders tightly. Ava would enter from the opposite side of the stage. Jack waved over to her. Ava's costume was a simple blue dress that reached the middle of her calves.

Something strange happened to Jack as he watched the performance before theirs. He shivered to the bone and folded his arms together to get warm. Actual goosebumps formed all over his arms. Time seemed to go twice as fast. He tore away his gaze and closed his eyes. The sound of applause pierced his ears. His heart hammered inside his chest. The lights went dark and the curtain closed.

The stage manager passed Jack, talking rapidly in her earpiece. She motioned her assistant to hurry up. The props of the previous play were cleared off and replaced by theirs. The picnic basket was organised in the middle of the stage on top of the plaid blanket. A big tree which Alexander had selected was projected on the screen in the back. They cleared the stage.

Everything around Jack had gone quiet. He stepped out onto the stage and took his position right behind the blanket. He would open the piece with a monologue and Ava would join in for the second half. Jack squinted, just a little bit, to be able to see the audience. It was impossible to recognise any faces through the blinding lights, so he looked straight ahead with his chin held up high. He tried to relax his clammy hands that hung by his sides. He took a deep calming breath and let it escape his lungs. The stage lights gave off an agreeable heat all over his body. *I'm doing this.* And he did.

Jack tuned out his surroundings and focused on his character and his lines. Nothing could disturb him as he performed in pure concentration. The flow of the play took over his body and mind. He wasn't himself anymore, but the character, portraying a believable message. The energy of the audience moved him forward. He took a seat on the blanket and opened the basket out of which he took a picture of a little boy. He placed it on the stage for the audience to see. Ava stepped onto the stage and took a seat beside Jack on the blanket. It surprised Jack how well in sync they were and how comfortable he felt playing. Much too soon they had come to the end.

The applause of the audience when they took their bow was the biggest gift Jack could ever ask for. All the hard work and all the long hours. It was all worth it. Jack took another bow; a grin already tugging at the corners of his mouth. This was definitely the best day he had had in his life so far.

Ava and Jack hurried back to their dressing room, talking in hushed and excited voices. Adrenaline raced through Jack like a drug.

Alexander waited for them when they entered, his hands clasped to his mouth and his eyes beaming. "You guys were great! Everyone loved it."

"Did *you* love it?" Ava asked.

A smile broke out on Alexander's face. "I did. You two made it come alive."

Ava engulfed Alexander in a hug. To everyone's surprise he let it happen. Then she hugged Jack. "I was so afraid after messing up my first play. But this was amazing." She sighed happily and gathered her clothes to change. A few minutes later she got back. In the meantime, Jack had changed as well. He handed his costume to Ava, who stored their costumes into the garment bags. "The Music department is about to go next. Do you guys want to come and watch?"

Jack nodded. "Wouldn't miss it. I need a few more minutes to get ready."

Ava was already by the door. "I'm going to catch up with the rest of our class, see you in a bit." She ran off.

"Are you joining as well?" Jack asked Alexander. He couldn't keep the grin off his face. An electric sort of energy filled him up.

Alexander seemed deep in thought. His eyes shone brightly as he looked at Jack. "No, I don't think so. I'm quite hungry to be honest. It's been ages since we had lunch."

Jack's stomach growled right on cue. "Talking about food... I could have a bite myself."

"What do you say we bolt and get out of here?" Alexander suggested mischievously.

Jack gasped. "Christina will kill me."

Alexander shrugged, a hint of disappointment in his eyes. "Fine. See you later." He left the room.

Jack contemplated for a moment. "Wait!" he shouted. He grabbed his coat and backpack and ran after Alexander into the hallway.

"YOU WERE BORN to be on stage, Jack. It was exactly how I envisioned it." Alexander smiled in a way which made his eyes lit up. He held out his pint. "Cheers."

"Cheers," Jack said. "To the absolute best day ever. Is it possible that I have peaked already? Maybe I should die now that I'm at my best. Young and great."

"Oh, please," Alexander said. "You have not peaked. You have just begun."

Jack had never seen Alexander as relaxed and easy-going as that night. They had found this great little pub a bit further from the theatre where the streets were quieter. Despite the dimmed lights in the pub, Jack could see Alexander's eyes shine with happiness. Absolutely stuffed from the delicious burgers they had devoured, Jack heaved a contented sigh.

"Do you have somewhere to be?" Alexander asked. He picked up the drink menu again. "If not, I wouldn't mind having a glass of wine."

"No," Jack exclaimed. "I'm good right here." Alexander passed him the menu, but Jack put it down without looking. "I'll have some wine as well. Red." He had only had wine a few times with Christina over dinner but found that he quite enjoyed it.

Alexander called the waiter. "You can make that a bottle."

Jack raised his eyebrows. "I didn't know that's how you like to order your glasses of wine," he joked once the waiter was out of sight.

Alexander shrugged. "We'll save money ordering a bottle."

Jack laughed aloud. "Whatever excuse works for you." Their wine was brought to the table. "I..." Jack started. He hadn't been able to wipe the grin of his face all day. "I feel alive... I am alive. And it's the most wonderful feeling."

Alexander smiled and nodded. He stared at his glass. "It's a good day."

And so it was. A comfortable silence hung between them. By the time their bottle was half empty Jack's cheeks glowed with a bright red blush. They talked about all sort of nonsense and all sort of important stuff at the same time. Jack found himself opening up to Alexander more than he had expected. Despite their differences in personality they understood one another.

The bell for the final round rung. Alexander topped up their glasses with the remainder of the wine. They stayed behind until the bartender had to ask them to leave. With reluctance Jack got up, not wanting this surreal night to come to an end.

They stumbled outside and Alexander managed to open the lock of his bicycle. "Shall we try?"

Jack could hardly contain his laughter as he managed to swing his leg over the bike. Alexander tried to cycle but couldn't get any movement in the bike. Jack tried to help by pushing off with his legs. Finally, after some weird hops and near falls, they were off.

Jack closed his eyes and enjoyed the chill of the wind against his face. The cold didn't bother him, he hardly even felt it. Both of them were quiet as they cycled through the streets of London. At one with the world with every fibre of his being, Jack felt more alive than he had ever done. Acting on stage had given him a high. That and hanging out with Alexander which was just the way how he had wanted to celebrate. The beer and wine could have had something to do with it as well.

At that moment, Jack felt happy. Truly happy. He knew what people meant when they said they were on top of the world. And now that he did, he wished the moment would never end. He wished he could pause time and stay right then and there, feeling as he did in that exact moment. But before Jack realised it, they had reached the residence hall.

Jack couldn't stop laughing anymore and held on to Alexander's arm to steady himself while they waited for the lift to take them up. The doors opened and Jack pulled Alexander inside. His breath hitched in his throat when Alexander's hand touched his face, removing a tear that had escaped while laughing. Jack held on to the handrail just behind his back and looked at the rising and falling of Alexander's chest. Everything got quiet. The only sound came from the closing of the doors.

"There," Alexander whispered. He didn't step back.

Alexander stood close enough that Jack could feel his breath against his face. Without fully processing what he did he looked towards Alexander's lips. They were slightly parted, the ghost of his smile still lingering. Jack looked up again, to see Alexander's amber eyes staring into Jack's own with an intensity that sent his legs trembling. Alexander's lips found his only seconds later as he kissed Jack softly. Jack closed his eyes and leaned in. Feeling Jack's eagerness, Alexander deepened the kiss and pushed Jack against the wall. Jack gasped for air as their bodies pressed against each other. His brain barely had time to process what was happening. Trapped in Alexander's embrace, he had never before felt so liberated.

Alexander pulled away, looking straight into Jack's eyes as if he was searching for something. Jack looked right back at him and was surprised to find his own desire mirrored in Alexander's eyes.

They both panted, their chests rising and falling. Jack closed his eyes and found Alexander's lips. He kissed him softly, tenderly, and was surprised by the feelings it stirred inside of him. Jack tugged at Alexander's t-shirt, pulling him as close as possible and almost grunted of sheer pleasure. How could he ever get enough of him?

People shouting broke them apart as the doors opened. Alexander drew back, the expression on his face changing into one of utter shock. They stepped out in a different world. The hallway was filled with people. Some were talking in corners; others were simply dancing wherever they could. Music blasted through portable speakers.

"Where have you been? So good that you're finally here!" Omar's voice broke the spell between them.

"Hey, Omar," Jack's voice came out hoarser than expected. His hammering heart wouldn't settle down. "How are you?"

Omar swayed from left to right. "Amazing! Come join the party."

"I'm off to bed," Alexander said as he turned to leave. Jack watched him go with mixed emotions.

"Goodnight," Jack shouted after him. He couldn't help himself.

Alexander stopped and turned around. His eyes met Jack's. "Goodnight."

Jack sobered up at once. "You know Omar, I'm off as well. I'm pretty tired."

"Fine," he slurred. "Jack missing a party, that's a first. What happened to you?"

Jack didn't answer and escorted Omar to the kitchen where he filled him a large glass of water. He then hurried into his room before anyone else could talk to him. The hushed sound of music and chatter filled Jack's room but at least he was alone. He was very aware that only one wall separated him from Alexander. He leaned on his desk for support as he tried to recollect how the night could have ended in such a way. He undressed himself, tripping over his trousers multiple times, and got into bed. He vividly remembered the touch of a pair of soft lips as he fell asleep.

CHAPTER SIXTEEN

JACK WAS EARLY in taking place in the lecture hall on Monday morning. Soon enough he spotted Christina, who rushed over to take the seat beside him.

"Why are you sitting so far to the back?" was her way of greeting him.

Jack rolled his eyes, then smiled. For the first time since changing departments he and Christina were in the same classroom again. "We'll hear fine, don't worry."

The room filled up with first-years, all waiting anxiously for the Heads of Department to arrive. In mere minutes they'd reveal whose pieces made it through the preselection and would perform at the creative recital in June.

Jack fixated his eyes on the door, counting the minutes for their teachers to arrive. Alexander entered first. Their eyes met briefly but Alexander averted his gaze before Jack could even smile at him. Jack tried not to worry about the fact that he hadn't seen Alexander around all weekend.

Christina nudged Jack's side. "Here we go."

Mr Norbury shut the door. The lecture hall was crammed with students. Not all of them had a place to sit. Some were sitting on the stairs and some were still standing.

The dancers were up first. Their Head of Department, Mrs Rostov, read out a list of the eight performances that had been chosen. The atmosphere tensed up. While some people broke out in ecstatic cheers, some had trouble to hide their disappointment and tears. One girl with long ginger hair ran out of the lecture hall, sobbing in her handkerchief.

Until this point Jack had focused solely on getting to the day of the judging. Everything he had worked for had been building up to that. He hadn't thought much further down the line. Until now. They had done everything they could but what if that wasn't enough? They should have done more. They should have worked harder. Jack's heart sank as Mrs Hendrix stood up. She grabbed a list from the table and held it out in front of her.

Mrs Hendrix congratulated the whole year on the show they had put up. She went on about the importance of stage experience. Out of the eighteen submitted plays only eight would get chosen. That was less than a fifty per cent chance. Jack stared at Alexander's back with a knot in his stomach. If their play wouldn't get chosen, there would be no more reason to work together anymore.

"The first play to get chosen is *Twenty Steps Forward* by Milo Harper, played by Christian Foster and Rachel Phillips." Mrs Hendrix paused for the applause. Rachel and Christian gave each other a high-five. "Next up we have *Faceless Midnight* by Alexander Henderson, played by Jack Lewis and Ava Gallagher. Supported on the piano by Christina Clarke."

Jack let out a breath he didn't know he had been holding. Christina shook his arm excitedly. At this point Alexander did turn around. His eyes found Jack's immediately. A small smile played around his lips and Jack saw in his eyes how proud he must have felt at that point. Ava climbed over the chairs from the row behind him and took the vacant seat on Jack's left. "We did it, we did it." She hugged him and kissed his cheek. "I have to go call mum at once." She sneaked off.

Jack remained seated next to Christina, who could barely keep it together. He took hold of her hand and didn't let go until Mr Norbury read out the list for the musicians. Jack didn't have a single doubt she would make it and, of course, she did. She radiated happiness; a genuine smile spread out over her face. Jack cheered when Omar's name was called out as part of a string quartet.

Jack rushed out of the lecture hall as soon as it was over. He wanted, no needed, to talk to Alexander. Jack wasn't willing to tiptoe around him for the coming months. He had no idea what to expect from Alexander. At the very least he aimed to clear the air between them so they could be professional around each other. Maybe even for something more. Either way, they needed to talk. He found Alexander in the hallway. Jack made his way through the other students to get to him. "Congratulations."

Alexander turned around to greet Jack. "Same for you."

A silence hung between them for a couple of seconds. "I want to talk to you," Jack blurted out. His heart was ready to burst out of his chest. He forced himself to keep looking straight into Alexander's eyes and straightened his back. At least he'd look more confident than he felt.

Alexander glanced at his phone. "I actually have to get to my next class now."

"It won't take long."

Alexander seemed lost for words. His tense demeanour didn't go by unnoticed. "Fine. Let's go in here." He motioned towards an empty classroom around the corner.

Jack got the odd feeling Alexander had been avoiding him on purpose. He had wanted so badly to talk to him. Yet here he stood, unable to utter a word. While Alexander was looking at everything but Jack, Jack couldn't stop looking right at him. He tried to get his brain to work again and gathered his courage. "Can't you even look at me?" This wasn't the way he had wanted to start the conversation, but the words were out before he could help himself. Jack remembered the chills he had gotten from the way Alexander had looked at him only a couple of days ago.

159

Seeing the distant and cold look on Alexander's face, that seemed like a lifetime ago.

Finally, Alexander gave in. "What?"

Jack's confidence faltered as he struggled to find the right words. "I wanted... Have you been avoiding me?" He dreaded the answer.

"I have," Alexander confessed. He scratched the back of his head. At least he was honest.

Jack hopped on one of the desks. His hands clutched the edge of the table, his knuckles turning white. "But you kissed me." He spoke in a soft, fragile voice.

"Yes." Alexander didn't move. "And I'm sorry."

"You're sorry," Jack stated slowly. He tried to keep a straight face.

"Listen, Jack..." Alexander averted his eyes again, looking at the bare wall behind Jack. "What happened on Friday was a mistake."

Jack's heart sank. He hadn't expected much, but hearing the actual words come out of Alexander's mouth felt like a kick in the stomach.

Alexander went on. "I might have had a bit too much to drink since I hardly drink otherwise. We were there, and the wine was there, and you were there... It was such a fun night. But I never should have given in. It never should have happened."

Jack nodded along until he realised Alexander was waiting for a reply. "Fine." He tried to make it sound light. "I don't think you should blame the wine though. It's too easy of an excuse. It was still just you and me."

"You're right. I shouldn't have said that." But he didn't say anything else. He had shut down completely.

Jack's body felt heavy. He had expected more than this. He didn't know what exactly, but more. He swallowed and heaved a sigh. He didn't want to give the impression that he would be left hurting. He didn't want Alexander to look at him with pity. "I'm

160

glad we sorted that out. It's a... relief." He even forced out a smile.

At this Alexander did look surprised. He glanced towards his phone again. "I really have to get to class."

Jack nodded. "Of course. I didn't mean to keep you for long. See you later."

Alexander opened his mouth to say something else but closed it again.

Jack watched him go and stayed in the classroom for several more minutes. With closed eyes, Jack let his head hung low and focused on breathing in, breathing out. He let out a sob but refused to let the tears, that prickled behind his eyes, flow.

It had been Alexander who had kissed Jack, not the other way around. Jack would have never dared. He would have never even suspected Alexander to be into Jack. But when Alexander had kissed him, he couldn't help but get his hopes up. Only to have them crushed down like this. One way or another, they still had to work together for the rest of the year. Jack was determined not to let this situation ruin their friendship, if he could even call it that.

JACK WAS first to arrive in the studio and started his warm up exercises. He watched himself in the mirror as if he observed himself from a distance. He walked over to the mirror, glancing around to make sure he was alone. He tried to push aside the empty disappointment Alexander had left him with. He took one step closer to the mirror, observing the face that mimicked his expressions. He ducked and got up again. How silly. Who was this person looking back at him? The truth: he was free to choose. Last month he had portrayed Macbeth. Yesterday he was an elderly man, proclaiming his dying wish. In a few minutes he'd be someone else. That's what happened in Drama class. He took another step closer. Who was underneath all these characters? Could he still take of the many masks he had created for himself? His green eyes stared back at him, empty and full of stories at the same time. Jack's vision went blurry after a while. His breath had created a foggy condensation on the mirror. Slowly, he took a step back. A deep breath filled his lungs. Jack brought his hand up and went through his wavy brown hair, trying to catch his own movement in the mirror. Tears glistened in his eyes. He forced himself to look away from his reflection.

Jack stretched his body and let it all go. With his back turned towards the mirror he waited for his classmates to arrive. He now knew what it was like to be on a stage and that was invaluable. It gave him newfound energy and motivation to be better and try harder than ever before. He was officially not the newbie anymore.

For their Improvisation class a cardboard box stood on a chair in the middle of the studio. Inside were folded pieces of paper with character names on them from scenes they had previously played in class. They took turns in drawing a character card. The assignment was to act out that character while the others had to guess who you were. Jack found the strength to let go of himself completely, to leave his worries behind. That was one of the things he loved most about acting.

"Great work today," Mrs Hendrix said. "Let me please also take this moment to tell you how much I enjoyed the preselection for the creative recital last Friday. It gave me great joy to see the hard work you have all put in. Congratulations to everyone. And while I know some of you are disappointed, which is understandable, please don't let it get you down. Learn from the experience to get better."

A round of applause filled the room before everyone packed up to leave class. Ava and Jack remained in the studio as they had a rehearsal scheduled right after. They planned to rehearse the play one more time and see what could do with improvement. If they were early in making a to-do list, they'd have plenty of time to get everything ready by June.

Jack overheard Mrs Hendrix talking to Ava. "I need to have a word with you once everyone has left."

Jack took this as his cue to wait outside and offered Ava a reassuring smile upon passing her.

Mrs Hendrix hurried over to Jack. "A quick word with you too, Jack. I want to take this moment to say how proud you have made me. You have an amazing energy on stage. I hardly recognised you from the boy who walked in here a few months ago with no experience whatsoever." Her smile revealed the crow's feet around her eyes.

Jack couldn't believe his ears and nodded in a grateful manner. Mrs Hendrix seldom praised people, which is why it meant so much when she did.

"You are working hard to catch up and your performance was top notch. We gave you high marks." Mrs Hendrix frowned when she did not receive the exuberant response she expected. "Are you alright?"

"Everything is fine," Jack lied. He felt suddenly calm and at ease. "Thank you, again. It's such a relief to hear that all the work I put in is showing."

Mrs Hendrix opened her mouth to say something else but only winked at Jack as Ava re-joined them.

"I'll wait for you in the hall," Jack told Ava.

Alexander was already waiting by the door when Jack stepped out in the hallway. "Why aren't we going in?" he asked Jack. "You guys didn't forget about our rehearsal, did you?"

Jack ignored him and waited until everyone was out of sight to lean closer to the door. He tried to understand what Mrs Hendrix had to say.

"Haven't you learned it's not nice to eavesdrop?"

Jack held a finger to his lips, motioning Alexander to tone it down. "I'm curious," he whispered. Jack pointed towards the door and mouthed *Ava* to him. Alexander followed suit, although a frown set on his face, and got closer to the door.

"—beneath average." They picked up Mrs Hendrix's voice.

They listened on opposite sides of the door. "You're falling behind on the rest of the class. You think too much when you act. It doesn't come naturally."

"I'll work harder." It was Ava, barely audible, who sounded close to tears.

It almost broke Jack's heart, hearing the vulnerability in her voice. He met Alexander's eyes and saw a sympathetic look in them. That was more than what he had offered Jack that morning. Jack narrowed his eyes and lowered his gaze to the floor.

"You have been working hard. I'm not sure that's going to cut it," Mrs Hendrix said in a gentle voice. "Maybe you don't have what it takes to pursue acting on this level. Perhaps a different school, or—"

"I'll prove you that I have!"

Footsteps approached the door. Jack and Alexander jumped up and pretended to be waiting. Ava stormed out of the classroom, tears streaming down her cheeks. Jack called out to her as she rushed past them. She didn't stop, didn't even look at them. Jack wanted to run after her but felt Alexander's hand around his arm pulling him back.

"Let her be alone for a while," Alexander said in a low voice.

Jack yanked his arm out of Alexander's grip with as much force as possible. "I should be there for her. That was awful."

Alexander really did look sorry. "That's how it is. It's a hard life, the life of an artist. You are lucky to be so talented, in more than one field even. Unfortunately, some people don't have what it takes, despite all the hard work they put in."

"Don't have what it takes?" The sharpness of his voice surprised Jack. "She doesn't deserve to be talked to like this. She works like nobody else in the entire class. You're taking Mrs Hendrix's side in this?"

Alexander shook his head. "Of course she doesn't deserve it." His voice came out steady. "I've noticed it too. She's falling behind on you guys. I'm not saying this to be mean and it has nothing to do with taking sides. But it's true."

164

"Let's agree to disagree." Jack was fuming at Alexander. How could he talk like that?

Alexander tried to reason with Jack, who wouldn't hear it. "It's painful to see, but only the lucky few make it through." Alexander sighed, seeing it was pointless. "Let's reschedule our rehearsal."

Jack couldn't listen to him anymore. "Yes. Let's," he said, and marched off.

CHAPTER SEVENTEEN

"TAKE THAT!" Omar put the controller on the floor and smirked. He took a large bite of his burger, hanging above the cardboard box as not to spill any dripping sauce to the floor. "This is fun."

Jack scoffed. "Easy to say when you're the one always winning." The ice cubes of his coke had melted by now, making it taste bland. He dipped a chip in ketchup. "Want to go again?"

"Do you even have to ask?" Omar grinned and pressed play. "I'm Mario this time. I'm pretty sure we've established you don't need to be him to win."

"Fine, Browser will lead me to victory." They were seated on the floor with their backs against Omar's bed. Spring had just arrived, and Jack and Omar were in another one of their late-night gaming sessions. With some of the money he had earned working in The Golden Lion, Omar had bought a TV and PlayStation for his room, making the space feel even more cramped. Omar had shoved everything he could in there, leaving little floor space available. With the huge oriental patterned rug, the dark wooden floorboards were only visible here and there. "You're too good at this. Now I know what you do with your free time."

Omar laughed. "You caught me. As little kids Idris and I played Mario Kart day in, day out. We never got sick of it."

Jack smiled. "It sounds like so much fun, having a brother who is also one of your best friends."

Omar's smile faltered. "He's the best." He pressed play and turned his focus to the game.

It was the first time Jack won anything playing against Omar. He didn't feel the victory though. Omar had lost interest in the game and was deep in thought.

"Are you alright? Something I said?" Jack hadn't really seen Omar as anything other than a happy, goofy guy who owned a broad collection of funny hoodies and t-shirts. Today was no exception. He wore a hoodie which had a big square with the letters *Ah!* written in them in the same format as the periodic table. The words *The element of surprise* were written underneath. That was Omar, always comfortable and always in a good mood. Yet Jack got the impression Omar had let him win on purpose; which was not like him. "I didn't mean to offend you or anything…"

"You haven't said anything wrong. I'm just going through a shitty time." Omar hesitated before he went on. "Mentioning my brother makes me miss him. Makes me miss my family. It's nothing, though."

Jack was at a loss for words, which seemed to overcome him often lately. He had been so caught up in his own reality, he had become oblivious to the fact his friends were struggling too. A wave of guilt overcame him. "You go home almost every weekend, right? That's something."

Omar smiled. "Yes, that's something."

No matter how curious Jack was, he was adamant not to push Omar. Omar was hiding something, whatever it was. "I'm always here to listen if you want to talk about something. You do know that, right?" Jack wasn't sure if he did. Talking about serious stuff wasn't 'their thing'.

"Thanks, Jack. I appreciate that." He didn't elaborate on the subject. A knock on the door meant the definite end of the subject altogether. "Come in!"

"Mind if I join you?" It was Christina, in satin floral pyjamas and a white robe, who didn't wait for an answer to come in and plop down on Omar's bed. "How is it that everyone keeps complaining about our workload?" Jack and Omar shared a knowing look before turning to Christina. "It's that Jessica again. I don't know what's wrong with her. If she doesn't want to put in the work, she shouldn't be here." She sighed. "Anyway. What are you guys doing?"

Jack waved the controller in the air. "Playing Mario Kart."

"Beating his arse," Omar said at the same time.

Jack chuckled and gave him a slight shove in the side. All seemed to be well again. Omar gave Christina his controller and climbed on his bed to sit next to her. He explained briefly how to play, patient as ever. Christina was competitive but so was Jack. "I won!" Jack exclaimed after their first round. "I won! Fair and square."

"I'm going again. This was only a warm-up," Christina said in a sharp tone. She went up against Omar but lost again. "I want to switch controllers. You have a better one."

They played for a little while longer but decided to stop as Christina was a sore loser. Or in her words, because she was tired.

Jack turned to Omar. "Quick question. Just out of curiosity." He tried to sound indifferent and saw this as the perfect opportunity to pry. "You know what I was wondering lately? How you and Alexander met? Since you guys know each other from before."

Omar frowned, surprised by the change of subject. "We both live in London. We've been friends for years." A smile appeared on his face. "Did you know I tried applying two years ago? He and I both did. He got through immediately, but I didn't make it. So I tried again last year and that was that."

"I didn't know that," Christina said, suddenly not so tired anymore. "Did they give you any feedback on why?"

Omar nodded. "Oh, yes. They liked what they saw but thought I was too inexperienced. They advised me to take an extra

168

year to grow. I reapplied the year after and they accepted me. Alexander was already here by then, but he had to repeat his first year."

"That's right," Jack said thoughtfully. Alexander had indeed told him that but hadn't confided in Jack to relay the details. Now that he thought of it, Alexander had talked about a great deal of stuff, but nothing deeply personal, nothing about his past. "I still don't understand how he managed to do it though. Normally people get sent away when they fail their classes, they don't get to repeat here."

"Jack is right," Christina stated. "It must have been a special circumstance in his case."

They both looked towards Omar for answers.

Omar shook his head and held up his hands in surrender. "He wouldn't like me discussing his personal life."

"We're all friends, aren't we?" Jack pushed on.

Omar laughed. "Then I'm sure he wouldn't mind telling you himself. It's not my place to tell." Omar got up and stretched his back. "I'm going to take a shower."

"Can we play a bit more while you're gone?" Christina asked. "I think I'm getting the hang of it."

"Sure! See you in a bit."

The door slammed shut. Christina got down from the bed and took a seat on the floor next to Jack. "Can you imagine if Omar got accepted last year instead of this one? We would have never been as close with him as we are now."

Jack nodded. "That would have been such a pity."

"It would have been," Christina agreed. "I can't even think about it, life at the Institute without him."

An incredulous look appeared on Jack's face upon hearing Christina talk this way. He turned his head to her, trying to catch her expression.

Christina went on. "Why the sudden interest in Omar's friendship with Alexander by the way? Do you know something I don't?"

Jack had managed to keep what had happened all those weeks ago to himself but found he didn't want to anymore. "I kissed Alexander," he blurted out. Jack watched Christina freeze, a look of utter disbelief forming on her face. Saying the words out loud for the first time made it more real. Not something that existed only in his imagination. "Well, he kissed me," Jack corrected himself when Christina didn't say anything. "I kissed him back though."

This made her snap back to reality. "You did what?" she shouted. She went on in a whisper. "I didn't know you liked him?"

"I didn't know myself until—" Jack started.

"Wait, what?" Christina shouted once more. "He was the one who initiated the kiss? I can't believe it."

Jack rolled his eyes. "Thanks," he said, fake offended. He continued before Christina could shout again. "But seriously, that makes two of us… I couldn't believe it either. Anyway, he said it was a mistake."

Christina shook her head. "I can't believe it," she said again. "Alexander doesn't seem like the kind of guy who would kiss someone on an impulse."

Jack shrugged. "We had quite a lot to drink that night."

"Even so… Wait. That night? When did this happen?"

"The night of the preselection."

"The night of the preselection? And you're only telling me now? That was over two months ago!" Christina slapped him playfully on the shoulder. "That's the real reason you didn't stay to hear me play that night." She shook her head once more, as if she still couldn't believe the story to be true. "Seriously though. Do you like him? I didn't even know you were gay. Or bisexual? I suspected, but then you never told me."

Jack laughed. Despite the hammering of his heart, he was relieved to talk to someone about what had happened. He didn't have to carry the weight of it alone anymore. "I do like him. That's the worst part. I didn't tell you because I wanted it to go away. But it doesn't work like that I'm afraid. When I get into a room, my eyes always search for him. I find myself drawn to him in a way that I've never been drawn to anyone else. I'm keeping my distance though." Jack sighed. "You're the first person I tell. Technically my parents know I'm gay, but—"

"What?" Christina shouted. Jack shot her a look that shut her up. She held her hands up in the air. "I can't help that you're dropping one bomb after the other. Your parents. I bet that didn't go down well, did it?"

"It obviously didn't, no. Did you know what their reaction was though? Nothing. Absolutely nothing. No reaction whatsoever. Nothing good, nothing bad."

"How cruel." The frown on Christina's face disappeared. "Don't feel like you ever need to hold back though, OK? Or at least not to me. You're a great guy, Jack. And you'll find someone right for you, I know you will!"

Jack threw his arm around Christina. "You're a good friend, do you know that?"

She rested her head on his shoulder. "Obviously."

THAT WEEKEND IZZY got back to town. Jack couldn't think of a better time to introduce her to Christina. It pleased, and surprised, him to see how they got along from the start. He could never be sure with Christina, her being very particular in who she chose to like. Christina wore black culottes and a white fitted turtle neck jumper. She held out her hand for Izzy to shake, making Izzy laugh and pull her into a friendly hug. Izzy wore another one of her colourful outfits which looked mismatched at first. Izzy had this way about her where she lit up the whole room as soon as she entered.

Aunt Grace came up to them. "Isabel, dear, I have to go to the bank. I'll be back in half an hour. Please don't burn the place down."

Izzy grinned as she received a kiss on the head from her mother. "We'll try not to."

Jack watched the simple interaction with a longing he hadn't known was inside of him. He thought of his mother, of her smile and her way of moving, and felt a sting in his chest. Aunt Grace supported Izzy through thick and thin, that much was obvious. He was sure that, should she tell her mother she was gay, Aunt Grace would be as supportive as ever.

They settled comfortably around one of the tables. Jack didn't waste any time to jump right in. "We finally deserve some answers about our family situation, wouldn't you agree? What's the real reason we didn't meet before? There has to be more to the story. There just has to be." He slapped his hand to the table, causing the people from the table next to them to look up. Jack turned towards Christina who gave him a reassuring smile. He went on in a calmer voice. "I want to take action and find out exactly what happened. No more speculation, but the truth."

Izzy sighed. "I would love nothing more than to put this to rest once and for all. To finally get someone to tell us the full story."

"I was hoping you could talk to your mother again. See if she'll open up? I doubt we'll get two more words out of my parents, so Aunt Grace is our last resort."

"Oh, Jack. Believe me when I say that I've tried. I don't know what to do anymore."

"It's a bit sneaky, but I might have a plan," Christina said in a low voice. She put her cup of coffee on the table and leaned in closer. "It's a bit dodgy, I'll admit that. But you can always go through your mother's stuff."

Jack raised his eyebrows. "A *bit* dodgy?"

Christina ignored Jack. "Just through the drawers where she keeps the important documentation and such. See if you can find any letters she kept from that time. There's a chance they didn't use e-mails yet."

"Christina," Jack called out. "I don't think that's an

appropriate thing to ask." He didn't know Izzy well enough and was afraid to upset her.

Izzy ignored Jack and looked Christina straight in the eye. "It's perfect."

Jack sighed loudly and leaned back in his chair. "Fine. If they don't want to tell us, measures have to be taken."

"I'll do it now, while she's gone," Izzy whispered. She turned to Jack with doubt in her eyes. "I'm doing this because it's about time we found out the truth, but I need you to know I'm not comfortable snooping around."

Jack nodded. "I have no better ideas myself."

Jack and Izzy shared a look before Izzy got up to check if any of the customers needed any refills. She beckoned Jack and Christina. "If anyone asks something, you serve them OK? Get behind the counter! Give me a sign if my mother comes back early. I'll be quick."

Jack obediently stepped behind the bar. "Izzy, wait! I don't know how to prepare any of these drinks." But Izzy had already left. Jack looked around with fear in his eyes and leaned in to whisper to Christina, "What if they want to order something?" He moved to the edge of the bar and tried to hide behind the coffee machine.

Christina rolled her eyes. "You'll be fine." She studied the menu. "I'll order a chai latte."

Jack opened his mouth to protest but saw she was mocking him. He laughed dryly. "Very funny."

Izzy stayed up for a long time. Too long. After about twenty minutes Grace crossed the street. There was no time to give Izzy a sign. Grace frowned at the sight of Jack behind the bar. "Are you looking for a job? Where's Izzy?"

Jack moved aside for her. "Well, she…"

"She went to the restroom," Christina said politely.

Jack nodded. A few minutes later Izzy re-joined them, startled by the sight of her mother.

"You stayed away for such a long time," Jack remarked in a low voice when they were back at their table.

Izzy held her hands up apologetically. "I wanted to be thorough. I had no luck though. I searched everywhere I could think of, but I found nothing besides documents regarding the bar or insurance papers."

Jack sighed in frustration. "That's it then. We'll never find out. We should just accept it and be happy to have found each other."

"Don't say that. What if I told you I have a plan B?"

A grin appeared on Jack's face. "More like a plan Z you mean?"

Izzy grinned. "You could say that. Our family home is in Brighton, where I grew up. My mother only moved to London a few years ago when she started the business. She kept the house in case the café would fail, but the café has been a huge success. I still live in the house since I go to uni there. Mum goes there over the holidays and some weekends whenever she doesn't need to work. Most of our stuff is still there."

Jack could see where this was going. He could hardly keep the excitement out of his voice. "You should have a look around when you get back."

"Why don't we all go? The three of us? We can make a nice weekend by the beach out of it and see if we get any wiser."

Jack nodded, a grin stretching out over his face. Things were looking up. Jack had never been south of the country and longed to see where Izzy grew up.

TWO WEEKS LATER, a few days before their trip to Brighton, Jack walked up to Christina in the common room. She closed her book when Jack took the seat beside her. "I asked Ava to come along. She's feeling quite blue lately and I thought this trip would do her good." Ava had been out of spirits ever since her conversation with Mrs Hendrix a couple of weeks ago. She pretended things to be fine, but Jack could see how hurt she was.

Christina raised one eyebrow and let out a dramatic sigh but didn't make a fuss like Jack expected she would. "Fine, let her come." It was no secret that Christina didn't like Ava.

"I still have to double-check with Izzy but I'm sure she wouldn't mind if one more person came along."

"One more person." Christina chuckled nervously. "Actually, I've—"

"Omar, over here," Jack interrupted her. Omar had just entered the common room and stood by the door, scanning the room. Jack waved and gestured for him to come over.

Christina grabbed Jack's arm and scooted closer to him. She spoke in a rapid hushed voice. "Please don't be mad. I asked Omar to come as well."

"When were you planning on telling me this?" Jack whispered, while keeping a smile on his face.

"Right now."

"You guys excited for the weekend?" Omar greeted his friends. "I know I am!"

Jack shot Christina a look although he didn't mind bringing Omar along at all.

Instead of taking a seat on the sofa next to his friends, Omar got down on his knees and turned to Jack. "I need to ask you a big favour," he pleaded. He brought his hands together. "Can we bring Alexander along?"

Christina shot Jack a worried look. He ignored it. "Are you sure he even wants to join? It doesn't sound like him."

Omar nodded, not convinced. "He's been so down lately. I want to cheer him up a bit. A little road trip would do him wonders, I'm sure of it!" Omar smiled his bright crooked smile and looked at Jack with big puppy eyes.

Jack almost snorted. "So he's coming because you told him to..." He sighed. "It's fine, I guess. But let me check with Izzy if she's fine with bringing so many people along."

175

Omar nodded. "Thank you, Jack." He jumped to his feet to leave but couldn't hide the smile from his face.

That was the story of how their little party became bigger than anticipated. Not that it mattered much. Jack was happy to bring his friends along, even Alexander. He was determined to act normal towards Alexander to show that all was forgotten. Or if not forgotten, at least buried to never be talked of again.

CHAPTER EIGHTEEN

FRIDAY, late in the afternoon, the five of them met up in front of the Institute. Classes had just finished for the day and everyone had brought their overnight bags. Jack glanced around their little group with a smile as they set off towards London Victoria to catch the coach to Brighton. Christina and Alexander huddled together and checked the timetable for what must have been the third time in a row. Less than three hours later they got out of the bus in the pouring rain. Alexander and Ava had been smart enough to bring their raincoats and Christina had an umbrella. Jack and Omar huddled together and walked as fast as they could, shivering to the bone. Soaking wet and out of breath, they finally reached their destination.

Izzy greeted them by the front door with a steaming cup of tea in her hands. "My oh my," she said upon the sight of them, trying her best not to burst out laughing. She was dressed in a cosy oversized jumper and black leggings. "Can you guys go around the back? There's a mudroom."

The house itself was small but cosy. A squeaky fence brought them round to the garden which overlooked the sea. Jack couldn't quite make it out in the dark, but the sound of the waves guided his gaze to the pitch-black vastness of the sea. Already soaked to the bone, the rain didn't bother him anymore. He opened his eyes and hurried inside where he took off his wet boots and jacket.

Still in good spirits, the group gathered around the fireplace and warmed up with hot tea. An arrange of board games waited for them on the dining table. They played and laughed the night away and crawled in bed early. Christina and Ava shared a room, much to Christina's dismay, and Izzy and Jack shared one. Omar and Alexander had to sleep on the sofas in the living room due to a lack of space. They didn't seem to mind and got comfortable in sleeping bags and blankets.

Jack awoke to the sound of Christina and Ava, who slept in the room next to his. He opened his eyes, adjusting to the morning light that peeped in from behind the curtains. He heard it again. They were laughing, giggling like two little girls. Jack sneaked out of bed and tiptoed to the door, which squeaked when he opened it. He froze. Izzy made a noise that sounded like a snore and turned around. Jack relaxed and slipped into the bathroom.

Christina and Ava were cooking up some eggs in the kitchen. The scent made Jack's stomach growl as he entered. "That smells divine."

"You spend a long time getting ready in the morning, do you know that?" Christina observed.

Ava, still in her pyjamas, seconded her. She left to go to the bathroom that had been occupied every time she wanted to use it but came back a minute later. She shrugged when she saw Christina and Jack's questionable looks. "Omar beat me to it."

"Girls, have you seen what a beautiful day it is?" Jack gestured outside. The sun was out, shining high and bright. The day was crisp and chilly but warm enough to go out in a jumper. The first real sunny day of the year. "It's been ages since I've been at the seaside."

Ava joined in on the excitement. "It's gorgeous here, isn't it? What do you reckon we do today?"

Christina didn't need any time to think it over. "We obviously need to take a walk on the beach." She returned to the pan where their breakfast sizzled away.

"And a visit to the pier," Jack added.

Alexander entered the kitchen. He too was still in his pyjamas with a black t-shirt and red and black chequered trousers. He went with his hand through his hair, but it didn't help him hide the just out of bed look. "Omar is in the bathroom," he grunted. He washed his hands and started setting the table.

"Thanks, Alexander," Christina said loudly. She turned to Jack, pointing at him with the spatula. "At least someone is being helpful."

"I'm always helpful," Jack retorted. He snatched the last plate out of Alexander's hand and placed it on the table. "There. I helped."

It took ages for everyone to get ready. By the time they left for the beach it was almost noon. By that time Izzy looked human again. Jack pulled her aside. "When should we start looking through the house?"

"It's a bit hectic right now, isn't it?" she whispered as Alexander walked past them into the hallway.

Jack nodded. "Let's do it when we get back."

It took them a mere fifteen-minute walk to reach the beach. Other than the occasional dog walker or jogger there weren't many people around. They strolled along the pebbled beach and played badminton. After three rounds Jack was exhausted. He plopped down in between Christina and Alexander, both of whom were absorbed in their books.

"What are you reading?" Jack asked both of them.

Christina, too deep into her book, ignored him. Alexander sighed and mumbled, "*Les Misérables*." He laid on his stomach, propped up to his elbows. He was about halfway through the enormous book. A crease of concentration was set on his forehead as he was immersed in the story.

"I didn't know you liked to read," Jack couldn't help but add.

This made Alexander look up from his book. "Let me tell you

what the most annoying thing is for readers. It's when people interrupt their reading."

Christina chuckled.

"Point taken." Jack shut up but found it hard to stop sneaking glances towards Alexander. The expression in his eyes was surprisingly soft. His dark hair moved in all directions with gushes of wind. It had grown since Jack had met him. The stubble around his jaw was longer as well. Jack forced himself to look away. He observed Omar and Ava who were finishing up another game of badminton. Izzy played the most enthusiastic referee he had ever seen.

Jack's eyes drifted towards Alexander once more, taking in the sharp features of his face. He looked right at home at the beach with his book, with his scarf around his neck, with his beautiful amber eyes.

Jack leaned back and supported himself on his elbow, getting eye to eye with Alexander. He opened his mouth to speak but had no idea what he was supposed to say. "Are you enjoying the story?" He nodded towards *Les Misérables*.

Alexander rolled his eyes, though not in an irritated manner, and closed his book. He held one finger between the pages to remember the page he was on. "It's a pain to get through because of its length but I do enjoy it. Victor Hugo is a brilliant writer. Amazing descriptions, compelling characters, what more could I ask for?" His eyes lit up.

Jack smiled. "I only know the story from the musical on West End, I'd love to go see it."

"You should!" Alexander sounded more excited. "In fact... I'd love to go see it as well. See how it compares to the novel. The theatre is only a short walk from the Institute. We'd be fools not to get tickets."

Jack nodded, unsure of what to reply next. Alexander hadn't implied for the two of them to go together, had he? He couldn't have. The sea glistened underneath the sun, its soft waves crawling to shore. Getting his hopes up again was the last thing

Jack needed.

To his surprise, Alexander broke the silence. "It's the complicated stories I like best. Not the happy ending ones."

Jack smiled carefully; his gaze still fixed on the sea. "I think I know that about you by now."

"I want all the heartache and the longing. I want the characters' hopes to be crushed. Meaningful lessons learned. I want to feel their pain through the pages."

"Make it linger for long after it's over," Jack added.

"Exactly."

A comfortable silence passed between them, broken by the others who approached them. Jack turned around to take a glance at Christina, who he had completely shut out. The others got seated in front of them, creating a circle. Jack sat up straight and scooted away from Alexander.

"What are you two whispering about?" Omar asked curiously.

"*Les Misérables.*" Alexander nodded towards his book.

Jack wondered. Could he? He could definitely try. "We were thinking about going to see it, weren't we?" Jack turned to Alexander with a knot in his stomach.

Alexander nodded. "We were, yes."

Jack tried not to grin and turned his head so Alexander wouldn't see the satisfied look on his face.

"What a wonderful idea," Ava beamed. "We have to see both a musical and a play for school anyway. I hadn't thought of *Les Misérables* yet. I was personally leaning towards *The Phantom of the Opera* but maybe *Les Misérables* is an even better choice."

"*The Phantom of the Opera* is an outstanding musical," Alexander told her calmly.

"Anyone else getting hungry?" Izzy intervened.

Alexander turned to Jack again and whispered, "Do you know which play you want to see yet?"

Izzy continued. "I know this little stand which sells the most amazing fish and chips."

Jack shook his head towards Alexander. "Not yet, no."

At the mention of fish and chips everyone scrambled to their feet. "I won't say no to that," said Omar, who was always either eating or hungry. How he stayed slim remained a mystery.

"I can give you some recommendations," Alexander said, when they had gotten to their feet. "If you need them of course." He started walking.

Jack hurried behind him. "That would be great."

They strolled along the pier. Alexander and Jack stayed a few steps behind on the others, discussing various plays and musicals currently running in London. Squabbling seagulls flew over their heads, on the hunt for abandoned food. The fiery sun made its way down, disappearing in the sea and colouring the sky as if it was an ever-changing canvas. They enjoyed the view that went on for miles and only returned to the house when darkness surrounded them.

THE PERFECT OPPORTUNITY TO sneak away from the others finally presented itself. While everyone was setting up a campfire in the garden, Izzy opened the door to her mother's office. "It feels weird to sneak in here. This was the one room growing up that was off limits."

Jack's eyes widened. "Because your mother keeps secrets in here?"

Izzy laughed and shook her head. "This was the only quiet place in the house. I was a noisy kid growing up if you can believe it."

Jack grinned. "Oh, I can."

Laughter and music coming from the garden broke the heavy silence in the office.

"Now what?" Jack asked. "We just go through her stuff?" It felt weird and invasive. "Maybe we already know everything. Maybe there is nothing more to it."

Izzy gave him a sharp look. "You don't believe that for a

second." She bit her lip. "I don't want to do this either. It's inexcusable. But we've come this far..." She opened the first cabinet she saw and took out a stack of books. One by one Izzy opened them without saying a word. There was no going back anymore.

Jack started with the desk, situated on a red woven carpet in the middle of the room, and pulled open one of the drawers. He smiled as he realised what was inside of them. He nudged Izzy. "Look. Photo albums."

Izzy looked at him like he had won the jackpot. She hurried over to him. "There might be photos of our mothers together."

"I hadn't even thought that far ahead. He handed her one of the albums and took one of his own. He was invited to Izzy's childhood as he flipped through the pages, almost forgetting he was supposed to be looking for something. While cute, the album didn't reveal anything new to them.

"This is strange," Izzy mumbled, more to herself than Jack.

Jack took a look at the album she was holding. There were some pictures of Izzy as a new-born baby. Jack smiled.

Izzy turned the page. "Look, one of them is missing."

One of the photos was indeed missing. The edges where it was torn off were still visible, leaving a big gap on the page. After a while of thorough searching Jack heaved a heavy sigh. There were no photos of their mothers together. Jack's mother wasn't even in them at all. And while they looked for the missing photo, they couldn't find it anywhere.

"She might have taken it out to frame it," Jack suggested. "It wouldn't surprise me if it was another adorable photo of you as a baby."

They returned all the albums to the exact same place as where they had found them.

"This is pointless," Jack said. "We should join the others."

Izzy made no attempt to get up and leave. "You go ahead," she muttered, absent-minded. "I want to double check some things."

Jack had had enough of it. How could he ever face his aunt

again, who had been nothing but good to him? He squeezed Izzy's shoulder. "Don't fret over it."

Jack joined his friends in the circle of chairs around the fire. About ten minutes later Izzy came outside. She shook her head towards Jack. "Nothing," she whispered when she had taken the seat next to him.

They were a funny little group, thrown together by chance and coincidence. Although Jack didn't believe in coincidences anymore. Each of them was different from the other both in character and spirit. On first sight it was hard to believe they were friends, but somehow they clicked together.

Jack looked around, left to right, and took in his friends. The campfire illuminated their faces and made them look serene under the starry sky.

Next to him Ava, whose eyes he couldn't see but who laughed at a joke being made. Her curly blonde hair fell in front of her face as she laughed. She pulled it up into a messy bun and hugged her legs which were popped up in the chair. Next to her Christina, fierce like a storm. Getting close to her had been a long process but Jack found her friendship invaluable. Across from Jack sat Alexander. Jack could make him out through the flames that illuminated his face. He wished he could unravel the layers one by one that made up Alexander's hard exterior. Jack longed to know what his thoughts were late at night. Longed to know if he was ever on his mind. Next to him Omar, trustworthy and funny. Always the life of the group. Yet Jack got a hunch that Omar wasn't as happy as he made everyone believe. Omar caught Jack looking and winked at him. Finally, Izzy, to his right, who Jack was fortunate to call his family. Her green eyes looked straight into Jack's own. He offered her a smile which she didn't return. Her eyes looked distant and Jack knew she had hoped their outing to be more successful. As had he.

In the background they heard faint noises of the sea, overshadowed by the campfire logs that crackled away. It was a good night to spend with friends. Jack poured himself a cup of red wine and passed the bottle along to Izzy. He vividly remembered the last time he drank red wine with Alexander. What a perfect night that had been. He glanced at Alexander to find him already looking at Jack. Alexander looked away quickly.

"I only met Izzy a couple of months ago." Jack found himself sharing his family story before he had properly thought about it. Up until now he had only told Christina. He hadn't planned on telling the others but at that particular moment the atmosphere was just right for it. Everyone was sharing stories and that made it easy to join in. The more they drank, the more they talked. The wine made sure they were slowly but surely letting their walls down.

"How come?" Ava asked.

A little voice in his head told Jack not to give away too much, to be cautious. "My parents never told me about my family. I always thought it was just us. I'm trying to find out why."

To Jack's surprise, talking about his family made Christina share her adoption story which she had only been able to tell Jack. He offered her a warm smile when she looked over, assuring her he was there when she needed him.

"No matter how good I am, or which prizes I win, my parents are barely ever there for me." The tone was bitter and left a contemplative silence in the circle.

The crackling logs of the campfire rustled and turned to ash. Six pairs of eyes followed the enchanting spectacle, hypnotised by the flickering flames. Alexander, who had been quiet for most of the night, spoke up. "Family has the power to destroy you." He kept looking at the dancing flames. "Often without realising the pain they're conflicting."

Jack wished for Alexander to go on, to talk a bit about himself. To let them in.

It was Ava who spoke next. "I never knew how many of you have troublesome situations at home. I'm sad to hear it. I love my family to bits. They're the best support someone can wish for."

"Lucky you," Alexander said, looking up into Ava's eyes.

She returned his gaze coldly. Now it was her turn to sound bitter. "Lucky me, lucky me," she said a little crazily. "It doesn't have to be the people around you that destroy you. Sometimes you destroy yourself. By wanting too much... but not ever being good enough." Tears glistened in her eyes, threatening to fall.

Jack reached for her hand and squeezed it. "You are good enough." It wasn't much, but he didn't know what else to say.

During the day they goofed and joked around, whatever worked to keep them going. They were always so busy, working on their assignments, that they barely had any time to stand still and think everything through. Only in moments like these, in the glistening light of the fire underneath the night sky, were their deepest thoughts and insecurities revealed. Everyone had their own story, their own version of the truth. And everyone was hurting and trying to hide it some way or other. Sometimes it was OK not to be OK.

Jack refilled his cup with wine, letting the liquid cloud his judgement but making him feel giddy.

His thoughts had wandered off until Omar called him out of it. "It was a brave move of you, Jack, changing to the Drama department. We should do more of that, stand up for what we want. All of us."

"Thanks, Omar." Jack smiled. "We have to stop waiting for things to happen and learn to be our own hero first."

Christina raised her cup in the air, spilling a few drops as she did so. "Here's to standing up for what we want." She took a large sip but struggled to swallow it down. "It's only such a pity you have to keep it a secret from your family."

"Christina!" Jack yelled out. But it was too late.

Christina clasped her hand to her mouth. "I'm sorry."

Jack glared at her until he saw the sorrowful look in her eyes. This was the one thing he had wanted to keep private. The one thing nobody was supposed to find out. He had lied about it to the whole world, even his teachers. They could never find out.

"Your parents don't know you're acting?" Alexander frowned.

"Jack!" Izzy exclaimed. She shot him a look. "You still didn't tell them? We're not supposed to stoop to their level by hiding stuff."

"I know, I know," Jack exclaimed. "Can we not talk about this please?" He sighed as he saw everyone's expectant looks. "If you've heard of my grandfather, you'll get the situation I'm in. My parents would take me off the school if they knew. They'd see it as utter betrayal. And who knows? Maybe it is." He was being serious. Izzy looked as if she was going to say something else, but Jack held his hand up "Please, drop it. I don't want to talk about it."

To Jack's relief nobody uttered another word on the matter. The subject changed and Jack's heart returned to beating at a normal pace. It wasn't until well after midnight when Jack noticed Omar had been gone for over half an hour. He excused himself and went looking for him in the house.

Warmth engulfed Jack when he got inside. He rubbed his hands together and involuntarily shivered. Light came under the cracks of the living room door. The door was ajar. Jack pushed it open and saw Omar on the sofa with his head in his hands.

"Omar?" It was barely a whisper.

Omar lifted his head and looked at Jack. "Oh, come in!"

Jack took a seat next to Omar, who had dark circles underneath his eyes. "Are you alright?"

Omar nodded. "I was about to come join you guys again. I lost track of time." He offered Jack a smile, but it didn't look convincing.

Jack was taken aback. He wasn't used to seeing Omar out of his cheerful state and wasn't sure of what to say to him. Jack had already told him he could talk to him about anything. Surely he'd do that if he wanted to, right?

"Everything OK?" Alexander entered the room and closed the door to the kitchen behind him. He looked at Omar questionably.

"I was just about to get back outside." To Jack's surprise Omar sounded annoyed. He got up and hurried outside without saying another word.

"I'm headed for bed," Alexander said.

"Right." Jack was about to get up from the sofa so Alexander could get comfortable in his sleeping bag. To his surprise Alexander took a seat next to him and faced him.

"You never told me you kept changing departments a secret? That was a pretty big risk to take, wasn't it?"

Alexander's knee touched his own. "That's why it's called a secret," Jack said, a little too harshly. Hadn't he just told them he didn't want to talk about it? But this was Alexander. "I'm sorry. It's... I don't know what to do anymore. I know I have to tell them the truth, but I can't bring myself to do it."

Alexander spoke again, in a soft voice. "Do you really think your parents will take you off the school?"

Jack opened his mouth but closed it again. Alexander had placed his hand on the sofa, right next to Jack's. With a deep sense of longing, Jack looked down at their almost touching hands. "Part of me hopes that when they see me act, they'll see me as I truly am and forgive me. I hope they will understand and appreciate the fact I'm following my passion. But it's naive to think that way." Jack sighed.

"There must be something you can do," Alexander replied. He placed his hand on top of Jack's and let it sit there.

Jack tried his best to keep a straight face, but his heart was beating like crazy. He continued in a whisper. "I'm afraid they'll cut me off. And I can't afford it without their help. So I'm stuck, aren't I?" It was hard to look away from Alexander's eyes. He couldn't settle his thoughts that raced back to the moment when Alexander had kissed him. Jack forced himself not to look at his lips. He forced himself not to lean in. Not to give in. He wouldn't want to do something he'd regret so he forced himself to look away and took a deep breath. The warmth of Alexander's hand on his disappeared.

"Do you know what's going on with Omar?" Jack changed the subject.

Alexander frowned. "What do you mean?"

"I've noticed a change in him. He doesn't seem as cheerful all the time anymore."

"Nobody is cheerful all the time," Alexander retorted.

Jack rolled his eyes. What a typical thing for Alexander to say. "You know perfectly well what I'm talking about, Alex. Just tell me. I can help."

This made Alexander shut down completely. "As I told you, I don't know." He scooted away from Jack. "And stop calling me Alex. It annoys me."

Jack flinched. He didn't give in though. What could be so terrible that Alexander refused to tell him? "No, you didn't tell me. You didn't tell me a thing. But you do know what it is, don't you? I can see it in your eyes."

Alexander turned around. "Get out, I want to sleep."

Jack flinched at the harshness with which Alexander spoke and stormed off.

CHAPTER NINETEEN

ON THE COACH back to London Jack made sure to sit next to Izzy. While she wasn't the brightest person to be around in the morning, she had been uncharacteristically quiet all day. Jack tried to make eye contact, but Izzy continued to stare outside, her head resting against the bus window.

Jack got an uneasy feeling in the pit of his stomach. He leaned in a bit so she would be able to hear him. "Penny for your thoughts."

Izzy shrugged, her gaze intent on the passing traffic. "I'm going to take a little nap."

Jack settled back in his chair without another word. Either she was exhausted, or she didn't want to talk to him for some reason.

Christina and Ava giggled and whispered to each other all the way back. Behind them were Alexander and Omar. Omar's head bounced on Alexander's shoulder. He was sleeping like a rock, his mouth wide open. Alexander tried and failed to push Omar to the other side. He noticed Jack's gaze and rolled his eyes playfully.

Jack laughed and returned to the front. He popped in his earphones and closed his eyes.

The coach came to a rapid halt in front of a stoplight, waking Jack up. They were driving through the outskirts of London.

Everyone but Izzy was fast asleep. Jack turned towards her and caught her eye. "There's something on your mind, isn't there?"

"I don't want to talk about it."

Jack folded his arms across his chest and tried his best to remain patient. "Does it have something to do with what we planned to discover this weekend? Because in that case you should know that I'm as bummed as you are. I hoped we would have found something useful."

Izzy didn't reply.

"Come on, talk to me. Where do we go from here? It frustrates me that we still don't know the truth."

"Maybe you should talk to your parents again."

Jack raised his eyebrows. "Are you serious? You know that didn't work all the previous times I tried. Same for you."

Izzy shrugged and returned her gaze towards the window.

Jack didn't budge. "Is there something you're not telling me?" His voice trembled. "I knew it. I just knew it. Care to share it with me?" It was hard to keep the anger out of his voice. "Izzy!"

"Fine! Maybe I did find something. I don't have to tell you everything."

"That's so unfair! Why are you being so secretive all of a sudden?" Jack clutched the handrail of his seat. He had to do his best to keep his voice down.

"Not everything concerns you, Jack. Can you please mind your own business?" She had a hard time looking Jack in the eye.

"Fine," Jack spat out. He looked away from her.

When Izzy next spoke she was pleading with him. "I need some time. Will you please just give me some time?"

Jack didn't reply. They spent the remainder of the ride in silence. Every fibre in his body urged him to keep asking questions. He had waited and longed for the truth for such a long time it was hard to hold back when a missing piece of the puzzle could have been uncovered. Jack would have never held back from Izzy and that was exactly why it hurt.

Once arrived in the coach station in the late afternoon it was time to say goodbye to Izzy. She hugged everyone and paused for a few seconds in front of Jack before pulling him into a hug as well. "I'll see you next weekend, right?"

Jack nodded reluctantly and waved her off.

On their walk to the tube station Alexander walked up to Jack. He pulled the sleeve of Jack's arm to guide him away from the others. Jack hadn't expected Alexander to talk to him after their little discussion last night. When they had created a little distance from the others Alexander spoke up. "I hope you don't mind me intruding, but I noticed you were arguing with Isabel on the coach." He paused to take a look at Jack. When he didn't object, he went on. "I'm not sure what you were arguing about, but I got the impression this weekend you were on to something, am I right?"

Jack frowned, surprised Alexander had even noticed. "How would you know that?" As far as he was aware nobody but Christina knew about their plan.

"Come on. You can't honestly think it wasn't obvious? You disappeared. You talked in quiet voices all weekend. You know being subtle is not your strong suit."

Jacked laughed. He had no idea where this was going. Again, Jack found himself confiding to Alexander. "We were looking for something this weekend, but we weren't successful. At least that's what I think. I'm not sure." He remembered Izzy's words on the bus. Whatever she found, even if it didn't concern Jack, it was the not knowing that was the hardest.

They halted in front of a stoplight. Locals and tourists alike passed them left and right. Alexander spoke up so Jack would hear him amidst the noise of the city. "That's where I think you're wrong. I think she did find something; whatever it was you were looking for."

They crossed the street, trying not to bump into the mass of people coming from the other side. Ava, Christina, and Omar walked way ahead of them. Jack could just make out Omar's frizzy hair in the distance.

Alexander went on, oblivious of the distance they had created from their friends. "I could be wrong, of course. When I walked in the hallway earlier this morning Isabel was seated on the floor in an office. She was reading some kind of document, crying."

Jack's mind was racing. This meant that she had indeed found something. Why wouldn't she share it with Jack though, whatever it was? They were in this together. He could have helped her. "Why are you telling me this?"

Alexander shrugged. He put his hands in the pockets of his coat. "I thought you should know." He quickened his pace to try and catch up with the others.

"Wait," Jack called out. He hurried behind Alexander. "Did you see what it could be, whatever she was reading?"

Alexander shook his head. "Not sure." They got on the escalator to go underground. "It looked official. It had a stamp."

A CHANGE of scenery in Brighton had done Jack wonders. It had allowed him to realise he had gotten distracted by personal issues while he should have only been focused on his acting progress. Izzy hadn't called or even texted Jack since they got back. If she wanted to push him away, then that was her choice. He had other things to focus on. Succeeding wouldn't cut it anymore. He wanted to strive to be the best. He wanted to shine as an actor. Jack had never been more determined than he was at that point and would do everything in his power to achieve his goals.

Meanwhile, Jack tried to clear his head of Alexander. There was no use in holding on to something that wasn't going to happen. Something that only caused a distraction. It would be fine to settle for being friends. It had been nice how Jack and Alexander had been able to interact with each other over the weekend. An involuntary smile appeared on Jack's face when he thought of the talks they had had.

He dropped his backpack against the wall and hung his jacket over the coatrack. Most of his classmates were already in the studio, waiting for Mrs Hendrix who entered only moments later.

"Let's start with some improvisation. Crawl into the skin of the character from the scenes you're working on."

Jack got himself in the zone. He closed his eyes, stretched his body, and spaced out his surroundings. The terrible, unwanted sound of a ringtone interrupted the whole class. All eyes shot towards the wall where the backpacks were lined up. With a jolt Jack realised it was his.

"Whose phone is that?" Mrs Hendrix, who had zero tolerance for phones during class, shouted out.

At that point Jack was already running to the front. "I forgot to put it on silent mode, I'm so sorry."

Mrs Hendrix pursed her lips but continued the exercise. Jack crouched beside his backpack and frantically reached for his phone, seeing several missed calls from his mother. What if something happened?

"Is this class boring you, Mr Lewis?" Mrs Hendrix asked in a tense voice.

"Of course not," Jack replied, before glancing at his phone in doubt. He was very aware of a dozen eyes staring at him. "I have to take this call."

A few silent gasps went around the room. Mrs Hendrix's expression remained unchanged. "Go ahead and make that call," she said.

Jack sighed in relief. "Thank you, it's—"

"And don't bother coming back after."

Jack's heart sank. There was no use in protesting. He left the studio and closed the door behind him. He looked through the window in the door at his classmates who continued the improvisation exercise. An overwhelming feeling of loneliness took hold of Jack. He felt like an outsider, seeing them practise. Like he was observing his own life from a distance, unable to grasp the reality of it.

This call had better be important.

"Mom, thank God," was the first thing Jack said when she answered the phone. Relief flooded over him. "Is everything alright?"

"Jack." Something was definitely not right.

"What?" Jack got a horrid feeling in his stomach. The feeling that he had done something wrong and was being called out for it. He leaned against the wall for support.

"You've lied to us, haven't you?" Mrs Lewis rarely sounded this stern.

Jack's heart raced. It was finally happening. His lies were catching up on him. Part of him felt relieved. Being forced to get it out in the open was cowardly, but much easier than mustering up the courage to tell them on his own.

His mother went on before Jack could reply. "We bought tickets to the recital. I was looking online at the Music department but couldn't find your name anywhere. You told us your piece got selected, but it's not there."

Jack swallowed and reminded himself to breathe. The right thing would be to finally get it all over with. But like this? Over the phone? Everything was going too fast and the words poured out of his mouth before he actually thought them through. "I can explain, Mom. They forgot to include my name. It will be rectified, don't you worry. You'll see me play at the recital."

His mother let out a sigh of relief. "You cannot imagine how happy I am to hear that, darling. All sorts of scenarios were forming in our heads. I was afraid you were ashamed about your piece not getting chosen and that you felt the need to lie about it." She sighed again. "No grandson of Raymond Lewis would go by unnoticed."

Jack bit his lip. He shouldn't have left class for this. "Right," was all he could manage at that point.

"Please know that I'm sorry for calling you out like that. Know that we're proud of what you're achieving. It's a huge deal. These kinds of recitals can jumpstart your career. According to your dad head-hunters will come to the show. It's the best way to get discovered."

Hearing his mother's voice was exactly how Jack remembered it. Sweet, soft, and caring. Jack hesitated before answering. He had dragged this out for long enough. He could still tell her the truth. She was his mother after all. Surely she'd understand. "I…" he started. Why couldn't he tell her the truth? "Listen, Mom, we need to talk." For a moment Jack wondered if she had hung up on him.

"You're absolutely right."

"I am?" A sense of relief washed over him.

He could almost hear his mother nod on the other end. "We need to sit down as a family and be open about everything. I feel like we're growing apart. This has gone too far for my liking."

A smile broke out on Jack's face. There might still be a fighting chance that he and his parents could work things out on their own. They'd tell him the truth about his family, and he'd tell them the truth about acting. He let out a deep sigh as tears welled up in his eyes. "Thanks, Mom. I needed to hear this. I miss you."

"I miss you too, darling." Her voice trembled. "I wish I could hug you right now. We have to talk face to face, the three of us. I'm going to have a word with your father and see if we can get down to London soon. What do you say?"

Jack nodded but realised his mother couldn't see him. "As soon as possible!"

Jack loved his parents. He just had no idea how to communicate with them. The time had finally come to tell them about acting. Telling them in person would be scarier than telling his mother over the phone. Yet delaying the inevitable had been the only thing Jack had managed to do. He wasn't proud of it. Things already were irreversible but somehow he kept on digging a deeper hole for himself. There was no visible way out anymore. *I'm suffocating myself.*

Jack had trouble sleeping that night. Not only his mother's

words were haunting him but Mrs Hendrix's as well. *Don't bother coming back.* He dreaded the morning, where he had to see her again and apologise. He went over the words in his head but couldn't find a decent apology. Acting had easily become everything to him. He hated for people to think he wasn't serious about it. Jack wished he could record his thoughts. Nothing ever came out as good as he prepared it in his head.

The insomnia rushed back to him, worse than before. He had woven himself in a web of lies which tightened around him every day. It made him wonder. Did he have the right to be angry with his parents for lying to him when he was doing the exact same thing? Tossing and turning in bed, Jack tried to think of a way out of the mess he had created for himself. The blankness of his mind terrified him.

THE ANNOYING SOUND of a ringtone pierced Jack's ears. He needed a moment to process what was going on. The ringtone rung again, loud and unwanted. Jack grunted. He really needed to change that cheerful tune. It made him anything but cheerful. He reached for his phone on his nightstand, eyes still closed. He forced one eye open and faintly saw Izzy's name on the screen. He picked up and held the phone to his ear, still laying in his bed. He tried to speak but only a low, incoherent grunt came out

"Jack? Are you there?" She sounded a bit hysterical.

Jack held the phone a little further away from his ear. "Izzy? It's four in the morning." His voice cracked. In the dark, he reached for the switch of his little lamp and turned it on.

Izzy ignored him. "I've been up all night talking with my mom. I had to call you. This simply couldn't wait."

Jack needed some time to process what she was saying. Once he did, his heart rate sped up.

"I can't believe it, Jack. I know the whole story." Her voice was very loud, or Jack was very tired. "I can't tell you over the phone though."

Jack groaned. "Izzy, come on. Don't wake me up to leave me hanging."

"Can I come over?"

CHAPTER TWENTY

WIDE AWAKE, Jack paced around his room. The seconds ticked away like minutes. He forced himself to sit on the edge of his bed but found himself pacing again a few seconds later. He checked the time. It wouldn't take long for Izzy to get there. In the bathroom Jack splashed his face with cold water. He took a look in the mirror and hardly recognised himself. He had changed so much from where he had started that year. His whole life had been turned upside down. In an effort to calm down he jumped in the shower and got dressed. There was no way he'd get any more sleep that night.

Izzy texted him while he was drying his hair. Jack shivered in the chilly hallway and had to suppress a yawn, even if he didn't feel tired anymore.

Izzy didn't look at him until they were in his room, seated across from each other on Jack's bed. She looked like a mess with her uncombed hair, her mismatched socks, and her smeared mascara.

Jack looked at her expectedly. He wanted to be patient but the time for that was long gone. To his frustration she didn't say a word. "How are you? How's Aunt Grace?"

She crossed her legs. "I'm not on speaking terms with her at the moment."

He opened his mouth but couldn't think of anything to say. Izzy and Aunt Grace were the closest mother-daughter duo Jack had ever seen.

"When I tell you the story," Izzy said, "I need you to listen and stay quiet until the very end. No questions."

Jack stopped fidgeting at the edge of his blanket when he saw Izzy's glare. Did he even want to know the truth?

There was no time to doubt any longer as Izzy started talking. "Our mothers grew up together in Dallas on the ranch with our grandparents who were… let's say… quite strict and conventional in their upbringing. Grace had a hard time as a teenager and moved away when she turned eighteen. She couldn't take it anymore. This we already knew." She sounded formal, talking quickly without any pauses. "She begged your mother to join her, but she refused. They had a huge fight and that seemed to be the end. But that wasn't the end at all. She didn't hear from your mother until your mother was pregnant."

Jack nodded, letting the words sink in. "My mother told me she wrote Aunt Grace when I was born."

Izzy crossed her arms, making Jack shut up immediately. "Not when you were born," she contradicted him. "Margaret wrote a letter while she was still pregnant, but not with you. Your mother had a lover. Not one that our grandparents approved of. They weren't married. Weren't even dating. Above all, he was engaged to another woman."

Jack's thoughts were racing, a deep frown set on his face. His mouth was set in a thin line. He wanted to speak up, shout even, but all he could do was shake his head.

"More than that, your mother was only sixteen years old at the time."

Jack's eyes shot upwards and found Izzy's. He searched her face for any signs she was making some sort of sick joke.

Izzy went on regardless, her eyes red and puffy. "Of course

abortion was out of the question, with them being so religious. Your mother had to give the child up…." Silent tears rolled down her face, one after the other. "Had to give me up."

All sort of emotions caught up with Jack. He didn't know what to feel first. He sat there, frozen, his hands clenched into fists. A lump formed in his throat.

Izzy stared at the empty space between them. "At that point she wrote my… she wrote Grace and asked for her help. She begged her to take me far away and raise me as her own. Apparently, she can't have any children of her own. They knew that by then…"

Jack's mother had indeed told him how Aunt Grace was unable to have children. At least that part hadn't been a lie.

"After I was born, our mothers met again for the first and last time. Grace was disgusted with the whole situation. She made a vow to raise the child as her own. She had only one condition, that your mother didn't seek any contact with her or me ever again." Izzy's voice broke. "And she hasn't." Izzy's head hung low as her body trembled with her sobs.

Jack reached for a tissue and handed it over. What else could he do? He took a deep breath but couldn't keep his own emotions under control. He could hardly believe his own ears. A tear escaped his eye and then another. He dried them angrily with his sleeve.

"Thanks," Izzy mumbled. She dried her tears and blew her nose. Only then was she ready to look into Jack's eyes again. "Great. We're both crying like babies now."

Jack laughed, but it made him cry harder.

"We're siblings." She offered him a weak smile. "Oh, and you can talk again," she added when Jack remained silent.

She was trying to defuse the tension and Jack loved her for it. He would've smiled if the situation hadn't been so utterly messed up. "I'm…" he started. How could he say anything when he didn't even know what to think? When he felt both nothing and everything at once. "I'm angry. I'm disgusted. I'm disappointed with my parents," he uttered, a sharp edge to his voice. "I'm embarrassed being the son of someone giving up their child like that. Who does that?" He took another tissue. This time for himself. The image of his mother that he had built up throughout his life burst like a balloon.

"I feel the same with... Grace... my mother. I can hardly call her that anymore. She has lied to me my whole life."

"Don't be too angry with your mother. And yes, Aunt Grace is, and will always be, your mother."

"I feel disappointed more than anything else," Izzy admitted. "Hurt. Confused."

"The bond you and she have is a rare one. I'll admit I've been envious of it more than once. Please don't let it go to waste, even if she lied. She took you in. She raised and loved you. She's always there for you, no matter what. If you look at what my mother did... Aunt Grace is a blessing." Jack hesitated. "Or should I say *our* mother now?"

"Never call that woman my mother," Izzy snapped. Her gaze softened upon hearing the sharpness of her tone. "I'm sorry."

Jack shook his head. "Don't be." He clasped his hand in front of his mouth. "My poor dad. What about my dad?"

"I'm not sure," Izzy said, "but from what I understand, he knows what happened."

Jack heaved a deep sigh. "What now?" he mumbled, more to himself than to Izzy. Jack scooted over to her and threw his arm around her. "At least I have the most brilliant sister in the world."

Izzy rested her head on his shoulder. How long they sat there he had no idea. Jack replayed the conversation over and over again in his head. While some questions had been answered, new ones had already formed.

JACK CONSIDERED SKIPPING school that day. He wasn't in the mood to face everyone and act like everything was fine. He considered the alternatives. He could lock himself up in his room. He could shave his hair and take a different identity. He could call his parents and confront them. Jack shuddered at the thought. When the clock struck six in the morning, he went to the kitchen for breakfast, but halted in the doorway. Omar and Alexander were seated at the table, whispering rapidly to one another.

Alexander noticed him first. He stopped talking in the middle of his sentence. "Jack."

This made Omar turn around. "Morning!" His smile looked forced and out of place.

Jack didn't feel quite welcome but stepped inside anyway and poured himself a bowl of cereal. "I'll eat in my room," he mumbled.

"Nonsense," Omar said. "Join us."

Jack looked from Alexander to Omar and back and hesitantly took a seat next to Alexander.

"Why are you up this early?" Omar observed. "You look awful."

Jack looked up and observed the dark circles underneath Omar's eyes. "So do you," Jack said. A horrible feeling still tugged at his stomach. "It's a long story," he said apologetically. A silence fell between the three of them.

"Was that Izzy I saw leaving earlier?" Omar asked.

Jack nodded. "She came over." He ignored Alexander's questionable look. It's not that he didn't want to tell them what happened. He didn't know himself what to make of it yet. The shock hadn't worn off.

Omar's phone buzzed on the wooden table. Three pairs of eyes looked at it. Omar took it and read the message.

"And?" Alexander pressed.

Omar sighed in relief. "They got there safely. He's in surgery now." Part of the tension left the room.

Jack looked from Alexander to Omar with wide eyes. "Who is?"

Omar hesitated for a few seconds before he spoke. "Idris is."

Jack was taken aback. "Your brother? How terrible! Are you alright?"

Omar smiled. "I'll be fine. He'll be fine." He stared again at his phone, reading the message over and over. "I can't go to school today. I need to go to the hospital."

Alexander nodded. "You should. He won't be out for quite some time, but at least you can keep your mother company. She'll be freaking out."

"She will," Omar agreed. He still stared at his phone, his chest rising and falling at a steady pace. "I should pass by school to tell them I won't attend any classes today."

"School's not open yet," Alexander reminded him. "Call them from the hospital. Is there anything I can do for you?"

"Or me?" Jack chimed in, even if he felt out of place in the conversation.

Omar shook his head. He got up and walked out in a daze.

Jack was left speechless. He turned to Alexander who looked right at him. "I don't know what to…" Jack started. He tried to gather his thoughts. "What just happened?"

Alexander shook his head. "Look—"

"I know, I know. It's not your place to tell. Don't worry, I get it by now." Jack sighed. Could this day get any worse?

"I think you already know what's going on," Alexander said softly. He stayed right where he was and made no attempt to leave, giving Jack time to think.

"I've been a horrible friend, haven't I?" Jack whispered. "How can I be so absorbed in my own problems when someone else has got it much worse? I'm so caught up in my own world that I seem oblivious to what's happening around me." He hadn't meant to spill his guts like that. But it had been the strangest morning he had ever had, and he didn't know what to do anymore.

Alexander remained calm. "Everyone has what they have. There's nothing to change about that. You have your shit and I have mine. Even if one can seem worse in perspective, that doesn't mean that you don't have what you have."

"But how could I not have noticed something was up? He talks about his brother all the time. He isn't well, is he?"

Alexander sighed and finally gave in. "Don't beat yourself up over it. He doesn't want the pity. He wanted things to be normal, even if he had to pretend nothing was wrong. That's why he never told anyone."

Jack closed his eyes. He had never heard Alexander talk in such a caring voice. "I still should have been there for him more than I have been."

"Be there for him now."

Jack nodded. He resisted the urge to get closer to Alexander. He wanted nothing more in that moment than to let go of himself completely and find comfort in Alexander's arms. He had promised himself to stop thinking of him in that way but found that he couldn't. He was drawn to him. He leaned back in his chair instead. "What's wrong with Idris exactly?" he asked.

Alexander took a moment to consider. "I can't tell you. You should talk to Omar."

Jack sighed. "You two are so secretive." He looked into Alexander's eyes. A thought popped up in his head.

"What is it?" Alexander asked before Jack had said anything. Was he that easy to read?

"You and Omar. How did you meet? I know you have been friends for several years, but..."

Alexander seemed torn. His usual composed attitude crumbled down for a few seconds. "I can't tell you," he said once more. "I just can't."

Jack left it at that. He had learned that while he was curious, he didn't always want to know the answer to everything. He changed the subject. "You were right about Izzy yesterday." He looked up in Alexander's eyes. "About the document she found. It was something official. It was..." he struggled to go on and had trouble swallowing.

"You don't have to tell me," Alexander told him.

"But I want to," Jack found himself saying, "I trust you."

Alexander's eyes widened. "You do?" His voice was almost a whisper.

Jack nodded. The first rays of sunlight peeked through the window, setting an orange morning glow all over the kitchen. "It was her birth certificate. She's my sister. Our parents have kept it from us our entire lives." He hardly knew how to go on.

Alexander put his hand over Jack's arm, which lay on the table, and squeezed it lightly. "Didn't you only meet her recently?"

Jack nodded. "They told us we were cousins. It was a teenage pregnancy. My mother... she gave her up." He didn't dare look Alexander in the eye anymore. "My aunt took her in."

"I'm sorry," Alexander said softly. "Have you talked to your mother? It might help."

Jack shook his head. He opened his mouth to speak but found that he couldn't go on anymore. If he did, the tears would fall and he didn't want Alexander to see him cry. He looked towards Alexander's hand, caressing his arm in a repetitive motion.

"It's going to be alright," he said. "You'll be fine."

The door of the kitchen opened, revealing a humming Christina. As always she looked impeccable, with a grey knitted dress and wet hair from the shower.

Alexander pulled his arm back, but Christina had already seen them.

"Morning, early birds," Christina greeted them. She grinned as she walked over to the fridge.

Alexander turned to look at Christina, who was cutting up some fruit, and leaned in closer to Jack. "What do you say we turn this awful day around?" he suggested in a low voice.

Jack smiled. "I'm up for that. How?"

Alexander took his phone out of his jeans and started typing. "Why don't we book those tickets for *Les Misérables* we were talking about? See when they have some seats left?" Jack barely had time to respond when Alexander pushed his phone under his nose. "Here, what do you say? First Wednesday of May."

"Sure. The seats look good." Jack mentally slapped himself for being such an idiot.

Christina took a seat opposite from them and ate her bowl of yoghurt. She pretended to be interested in the table.

Alexander almost smiled. "I'll book the tickets." He glanced towards Christina, got up, and left the kitchen.

Christina grinned from the moment Alexander was gone and put her spoon down. "The seats look good?" she imitated Jack. "Is that what you say when someone asks you out?"

"Lower your voice," Jack warned her. "It's not a date by the way. It has been an awful morning and Alexander has been supportive. We were both planning on seeing it anyway."

Christina was still smiling. "I know for a fact that you were planning to see *The Phantom of the Opera* with Ava."

Jack tried to remain indifferent. "I changed my mind. That happens."

"Of course it does." It was clear she didn't believe him. "Don't think I haven't noticed the puppy eyes you're throwing at him."

"Christina, don't!" Jack cried out. "You know what happened in January."

She shrugged. "I'm telling you. I can see the way he looks at you." She went on when she saw Jack's look. "Oh please. He barely says anything to anyone, but he's always talking to you."

"About our work, mostly." Jack didn't want to get his hopes up.

"He's gay, in case you weren't sure," Christina went on upon seeing the look on Jack's face. "Omar told me. I asked him. It's not a secret or anything. He doesn't hide it."

Jack raised his eyebrows. "He doesn't?"

"Well… It's Alexander we're talking about. He hides everything." Christina went on when Jack didn't reply. "Do you want to know what I think? I think you should stop running away from everything in your life. Face up to it. Tell your parents the truth. And tell Alexander the truth."

She was right. Of course she was right.

CHAPTER TWENTY-ONE

THE CRISPNESS of the evening air filled Jack's lungs as he and Alexander walked side by side to the theatre. They were early and chatted in anticipation before they could go in and take their seats. Even Alexander couldn't stop talking. He had finished reading the book that same afternoon and hoped the musical would live up to his expectations. Jack enjoyed listening to Alexander, who wasn't often in such a talkative mood. Jack had made an effort and wore tailored trousers and a black long-sleeved shirt with his grandfather's suspenders on top. He could see Alexander had dressed up for the occasion as well. He wore grey trousers with a green knitted jumper. One of the rare occasions Jack saw him out of his usual black on black combinations. Through the intercom they were instructed to take their seats. Having been in that theatre before, Alexander led the way.

They observed the program booklet page by page as they waited for the show to start. They went through the cast members, seeing what kind of acting schools they came from and what experience they had. Jack sneaked a sideways glance at Alexander, who was reading intently. He looked up into Jack's eyes and nudged him with his arm. Jack looked down again.

Alexander had turned the page and pointed towards the lead actors who were playing the roles of Jean Valjean and Javert.

The lights dimmed. The chatter of the audience ebbed away. Jack looked towards the stage, a weird sense of excitement entering his stomach. The curtains opened. Goosebumps formed on Jack's arms and he got chills all over hearing the orchestra play. Unable to stop smiling, Jack clung to every word. He was amazed by every change of décor and by the impeccable singing of the actors. It was like dreaming with his eyes wide open. Jack loved the thrill of watching a story unfold in front of him in real life. Nothing could compare to the spectacle of experiencing the wonder of theatre from the audience. Films, television, and even books could be rewatched or reread. Live theatre could only be watched in that exact time and space. After it ended, it continued to exist forever in your mind. Even if you went back for a second viewing, it wouldn't be the same.

The musical came to an end before Jack knew it. Where did the time go?

Jack and Alexander left the theatre with the show still in their minds. They strolled towards The Golden Lion which was still open for another hour or so. Jack hummed the last melody of the show aloud, enjoying the aftermath of the musical.

"How did it compare to the book?" Jack broke Alexander out of his musings. He tried his best to keep the humming to a minimum.

"It was different, certainly. But the main aspects were there. They did a brilliant job portraying the original story. It's one of the most well-known and longest running musicals of all time so that stands for something." He looked towards Jack.

"I'm impressed, to say the least," Jack said. His cheeks hurt from smiling all night. "I love coming out of the theatre. It makes me see the world in a different light." He let out a contented sigh. "I'm excited to get back to class and learn everything there is to know about acting. I'd love to work in these big West End productions." He smiled at the thought. "One day."

"You might," Alexander said. And it sounded like he meant it. "Or you can act in my plays."

They turned the corner to a street that was much quieter and more dimly lit, away from the big crowds. "Oh, but I was talking about your plays," Jack joked in a serious way. "They'll be on West End in no time. You'll leave the audience crying every single time. They'll be shouting your name for more."

Alexander smirked. "That sounds like a nice future."

"It does, doesn't it?"

In a comfortable silence, they recognised the pub from afar by people drinking their beers on the pavement. They halted a few hundred meters before the pub, not ready to step inside and burst their bubble just yet.

Jack couldn't keep the grin off his face. "Seeing plays or musicals," he said, "they make me feel alive." He leaned against the wall of a building and breathed in the fresh air with closed eyes. "It makes me want something. I just... want something." Jack laughed aloud.

Even Alexander had a little smile playing around his lips. "You want something?"

"I need something. I can feel it inside of me. I feel nostalgic for a world I'll never even know."

Alexander took Jack's hand and spun him around. Before Jack could process it, Alexander pressed his lips to his. It was a sweet and gentle kiss. The kiss Jack had longed for months.

"You kissed me," Jack whispered, breathless. His chest rose and fell as his mind tried to process what had just happened. The proximity of Alexander's body to his made him want to get even closer.

"I did," Alexander whispered against Jack's lips. He rested his forehead against Jack's, his eyes closed, and brought his hand up to stroke Jack's cheek.

Jack leaned into Alexander's hand. When his brain caught up with what had happened, he pulled back. "Again..."

"Yes," Alexander stated. He searched Jack's eyes, his own vulnerable and pleading.

"Can I kiss you back?" Jack's voice was low and quiet, but Alexander had heard him just fine. He tried to keep the eagerness out of his voice.

Alexander nodded as he looked at Jack's lips. He took a step closer to Jack until their faces almost touched.

Jack's breath got stuck in his throat. His hands travelled around Alexander's back in a tight grip, closing the space between them as he pulled his body close to his own. He kissed Alexander softly on the lips once, twice, three times, before pulling back. He swallowed and took another deep breath before he opened his eyes to look at Alexander. "You always look so calm and collected."

Alexander took hold of Jack's hand and brought it up. He placed it over his heart. Jack could feel Alexander's heartbeat underneath his fingertips, racing like crazy. Much like Jack's own heart in that moment. Drops of rain fell on their faces, slowly at first but speeding up until it poured down on them.

"Let's get inside," Jack said.

Already ahead of him, Alexander ran towards the pub. "Come on!" he shouted back to Jack.

Jack braced himself and ran after him. Laughing, they opened the door and stepped inside the warm, noisy pub. Omar and Christina were seated at a table in the far corner, deep in conversation. Omar looked tired and worn out, despite having gotten the news Idris' surgery had gone well.

"Should we join them?" Jack asked Alexander.

At that point Omar waved at them. "I don't think we have a choice," Alexander replied. He turned to look at Jack. They still stood in the doorway. Alexander's hand closed in around Jack's. "We can pretend we didn't see them."

Jack wanted nothing more than to kiss Alexander again, right there and then. From the corner of his eye he saw Omar waving at them. Alexander let go of Jack's hand and walked over to Omar and Christina.

Jack followed him, taking of his wet coat, perplexed the night could even be real. As soon as they sat down they got questioned about the musical. They obliged in telling them all about it. Especially Jack. Giddy and elated as he felt, he couldn't stop talking anymore. They continued speculating about the future. About how they'd all work together in big productions one day. They talked about anything they could think of that would cheer up Omar.

"I would have loved to see it," Omar said about the musical. "I'm hurt you didn't even think to invite me."

Jack's eyes shot towards Alexander, who didn't meet his gaze. That meant he hadn't told Omar anything about what was going on between them.

"Next time we will," Alexander said.

Omar turned to Jack. "Well, Alexander is smiling in public. You must have done something right."

Alexander opened his mouth to say something, to come to his defence, but he relaxed and softened his gaze.

Jack laughed heartily and winked at Alexander. "It's not like we received an invitation for drinks tonight. Or at least I didn't." He looked at Alexander who shrugged.

"My invitation got lost in the post too."

Jack smiled at him. He wasn't used to seeing Alexander so carefree.

Jack tried to ignore Christina's *I told you so* look. She turned serious after that. "It wasn't planned or anything. I ran into Omar earlier and thought I'd cheer him up."

Omar nodded. "I told her..." he said, mostly to Alexander, "about Idris. More people will find out as well. I'm not sure if I'm ready for that to happen."

Alexander's smile vanished. "They don't have to know if you don't want tell them."

"I'm not as good at hiding my emotions as you are," Omar said.

Alexander crossed his arms and looked away.

"You are a bit like an open book," Jack told Omar. "It's not necessarily a bad thing if people know, is it? Especially if it's only Christina and me. We're here for you. We can support you."

Christina nodded and put her arm around Omar, holding on to the back of his chair. "Jack is right, Omar. We are here for you. You do know that, right? Always will be."

Alexander abruptly got up to his feet and excused himself. He walked over to the bar and ordered more drinks from Arthur.

Omar waited until Alexander was out of sight. "It's nice to see you and Alexander getting along," he told Jack. "At first I thought your bluntness might be a little too much for him, but I'm surprised to see him opening up to you. He hardly ever makes new friends. But he's the most amazing friend to have, I promise. You just need to have a little patience with him." He shut up as Alexander made his way back to the table with a new round of drinks.

"Me? Blunt," Jack scoffed. "I'm not too much, I'm the perfect amount of me."

"That's the truth," Omar admitted. "Cheers mate."

"Can I ask...?" Jack started, although Omar already knew what Jack was going to ask. "What is wrong with your brother exactly?"

Christina tensed up. Alexander held a dubious look on his face. To everyone's surprise Omar nodded. "Sure." It took him a moment to get the words over his lips. "He has cancer... Leukaemia." He sighed when none of the others responded. "They had it under control for a while, but he had a serious relapse. The doctors don't think he has much time anymore." The frustration was evident in his voice.

Christina's eyes glistened with tears that refused to fall down. "But he's in recovery now, isn't he? That's good news, right?"

"For a little bit." Omar's voice cracked. He coughed and

recomposed himself. He stared at the pint in front of him, not meeting anyone's eyes. "He was alright at first. As alright as he could be. Until Christmas break. He went to the hospital for a check-up... It all went downhill from there."

"I'm so incredibly sorry for you..." Jack felt like a terrible friend. He had absolutely no idea how to console Omar. What did one say in a situation like this? Problems could seem important one moment, but trivial the next. The things Jack had been worrying about vanished like ice in front of the sun in the face of Omar's misery. "I wish we could do something," Jack muttered. "It's so unfair."

Omar smiled at him. "It is unfair. Life always is. Idris he... he doesn't deserve it. He's a good person. Then there's me. I just had to apply to the Institute and play the violin. I couldn't wait and be there for them."

"Omar," Christina snapped. "You can't blame yourself. That won't help anyone. You have to live your life. I'm sure you do everything you can for your family."

Omar nodded. "You sound like Alexander."

Alexander had been quiet for a long time. He was sitting there with crossed arms and didn't reply to the comment. Jack wanted to reach out to him but thought better of it. Alexander had clearly crawled back into his shell.

Omar looked towards Alexander. "He's been there for me through it all." He raised his pint, but nobody joined him. "Alexander has been there for me from the start."

Alexander didn't reply but shot Omar a warning look.

Christina intervened. "If there's anything at all you ever need help with, let us know, alright?"

Jack stepped in. "That's right. If you ever need to talk to someone, if you ever need to vent; we're here. It's not healthy to keep it all inside."

Omar shook his head. "Sometimes it seems like all I ever do is talk about it. Sometimes it's nice to not talk about it for a change."

"We can do that too," Jack added quickly. Christina agreed.

"Thanks, guys. I'm in one of these groups…" Omar stopped talking mid-sentence and looked towards Alexander. "Bloody hell. I'm sorry. You don't like me talking about that."

Jack shot Christina a questionable look. He had no idea what was going on. "One of these groups?" he asked. "You mean like a support group?"

Omar nodded.

Alexander shoved back his chair and got up. "Alexander," Jack cried out. But Alexander was already storming outside. Time stood still for a moment. Jack looked from Christina to Omar.

Christina motioned to the door. "Go after him."

"I messed up," Omar said at the same time. He dropped his head in his hands.

Jack didn't want to leave Omar like that. Not in that state.

"Go!"

Jack followed Alexander out on the street. Alexander didn't stop when Jack ran after him. Jack tried to grab his arm, but Alexander yanked it back forcefully and kept walking.

"Alexander, wait!" Jack pleaded as he followed him in the rain. "I'm sorry. We're all sorry. We're all idiots." Jack sounded helpless, but at least Alexander stopped walking. The street was dark and quiet. They heard only the distant sound of laughter in the pub, the traffic nearby, and rain falling on the parked cars.

"Why would you run away when Omar…" Jack couldn't go on.

Alexander turned around to face Jack, tears and raindrops falling down his cheeks. Standing there in the middle of the street, he looked so helpless.

Jack took a hesitant step towards him. "Alex," he whispered, too quiet for Alexander to hear him. Alexander stared at Jack with pleading eyes. But for what? Jack took another step closer. "Are you alright?" It was a stupid question. The truth was that it unsettled him to see Alexander this way.

"It's nobody's bloody business but mine," Alexander spat out.

Jack didn't flinch. "You're right." His voice was soft, trying not to scare Alexander off. "Come here," he said. He found shelter from the rain under a small roof at the side of an office building.

Alexander averted his gaze and looked down at the street. "Don't look at me like that." His voice sounded broken.

Jack stepped closer to him and put his hands on his shoulders, pulling Alexander into a hug.

The door of the pub opened, filling the street with the noise of people shouting and laughing. Omar ran out on the street. "Are you guys crazy?" He popped open an umbrella as he ran towards them. "I'm so sorry for all that. Can I help?"

Alexander shook his head and remained silent. Jack stepped in, surprising both himself and Omar. "We're fine. We're heading back to the residence."

Omar looked towards Alexander with wide eyes. "Will you be OK? Do you want me to come?"

Alexander shook his head.

"Fine," Omar said with a worried look on his face. He pushed his umbrella in Jack's hands before running back to the pub, but not without looking over his shoulder.

Jack searched Alexander's eyes. "Do you want to go?"

Alexander nodded. "Are you going to share that umbrella?"

———

"THANKS, JACK." They paused by their bedroom doors, where Jack had to go one way and Alexander the other. The umbrella hadn't helped much. They had already been soaked and now left a trail of dripping water on the carpet in the hallway. Jack shivered from the cold and used his arms to keep him warm. His clothes were wet and he felt it to the bone. Alexander had barely spoken a word on the way back and Jack was afraid to push him away. "Do you want to talk?"

Alexander shook his head. "If there's anything you can do it's to forget all this."

A heavy feeling filled Jack's chest. "All this?" Jack was being stubborn and he knew it.

"I got emotional. Just forget it. It won't happen again."

Jack frowned. "That's not at all—"

"Goodnight, Jack."

Jack threw his hands up in the air. "Fine." He wanted so badly to get Alexander to open up to him. How could anyone get through to him? Stubbornly, Jack didn't move until Alexander was in his room.

Changed into something dry and warm, Jack got into bed. Wide awake, he tossed and turned. How was he supposed to sleep?

Less than a minute later he found himself knocking on Alexander's door. He couldn't go to bed. Not like that.

Alexander didn't seem surprised to see him. "That was quicker than expected." He didn't invite Jack inside, however.

"Come on. I'm not that predictable," Jack cried out. He had to calm himself down. "I can't go to sleep like this."

"You told me you trusted me," Alexander said out of nowhere.

Jack wasn't sure if it was a question or a statement. "I do." He made sure to look into Alexander's eyes with every word he said. "I do trust you. And you can trust me too."

"You're too curious for your own good," Alexander muttered.

Jack almost smiled. "You don't have to tell me anything you don't want to share," Jack assured him. "But you don't have to push me away either." He walked inside, closed the door behind him and took a seat on Alexander's bed. At first, he feared Alexander would throw him out.

At last Alexander gave in and took a seat next to Jack. "This is not at all how I expected the night would go."

Jack didn't reply. He wasn't prepared to be let down by Alexander. Not again.

"The last part at least. The first part was better."

Jack looked up in surprise. He couldn't refrain himself from smiling. "I have to ask though... Are you well? You aren't sick, are you? Like Idris?" Jack dreaded to know the answer and couldn't suppress the hint of fear in his voice.

"Oh." Alexander hadn't expected the question. He shook his head. "No, I'm not."

Jack let out a breath he didn't know he was holding. "Thank God. I thought... for a moment... Isn't that how you met Omar?"

"You don't give up, do you?" Alexander turned towards Jack. "I don't think I can tell you. I haven't told anyone. I don't know how."

Jack scooted closer to Alexander and grabbed his hand between his. "I'm prying, again. I seriously have to stop doing that." He stared at Alexander. "There was one other thing I was wondering though."

Alexander rolled his eyes. "Go on."

"Are you and Idris...?" he asked suggestively. "Or were you ever...?"

"What? No!" Alexander cried out. "No, definitely not."

"OK." Jack tried not to sound too relieved.

"No," Alexander said once more, shaking his head. He looked at Jack for a long time. Neither of them broke the eye contact. Alexander went on in a whisper, his eyes wide and insecure. "I met Omar in our support group. I was there because of my brother." His voice broke as he let his head hang low, as if it caused him too much effort to support it. "He died in a car crash."

Jack's eyes widened. His breath got stuck in his throat. He did the only thing he could think of. He pulled Alexander close and engulfed him in a hug that neither one of them let go of. Jack tightened his grip around Alexander, clinging on to him as if his life depended on it, and hoped Alexander felt consoled. He wanted to try and protect Alexander from his pain. Save him from the hurt he had been feeling for years. Jack kissed the top of Alexander's head and caressed his hair.

Alexander drew back, a wretched look etched on his face. "I was in the car too. How can it be that I got out with a broken leg and some bruised ribs? I still don't... It shouldn't have been that way."

Jack swallowed deeply and blinked away his tears. "What was his name?" he asked carefully.

"Viktor," Alexander whispered. "He was only fifteen." Once Alexander had started, he couldn't stop. He had opened his own box of pandora and it all had to get out. "They put him in an induced coma which lasted for months. I joined a support group at that time. That's where I met Omar. He was there through everything. After they... unplugged Victor, we got the idea to apply for the Institute together."

"Omar didn't get through the first time he applied," Jack said thoughtfully, his voice no more than a whisper. "I didn't mean to interrupt you." He brought Alexander's hand up to his lips to kiss it.

"It's alright," Alexander said. "You're right. But I did, I got through. I never should have applied that year though. I couldn't focus, didn't attend most of the classes. I was a total wreck. But I did write some plays and scenes they liked. Considering the circumstances, they allowed me to repeat the year."

Jack nodded. Everything was falling into place. "It's a good thing you had someone to go through it with you."

"I couldn't have done it without Omar."

Jack sighed and scratched the back of his head. "You are an incredibly strong person. I can't imagine how you got through it."

Alexander's vulnerable eyes looked up into Jack's. "I didn't." His voice trembled. Trying so hard to stay strong, Alexander couldn't hold up appearances any longer. A sob escaped his lips. "And I'm not strong. I never chose to be strong. I had no other choice but to put one foot in front of the other. He never should have died. I was in the exact same car. How am I still here? Why am I still here?"

Jack kissed Alexander's hand once more, leaving a wet tear behind. "Don't talk like that," he pleaded. "It isn't fair. Not one bit. But please, I'm happy you're here. I'm happy you survived.

That's a good thing. For your parents too. They could have lost both of their children."

"They can barely stand to look at me," Alexander admitted. He looked away, hiding his face from Jack.

Jack put his hands on either side of Alexander's face and brought it up so he was looking at Jack. "You're beautiful. And strong. Much stronger than you think. Even if it wasn't by choice."

"I—" Alexander started. He didn't continue.

Jack kissed him softly on the lips.

CHAPTER TWENTY-TWO

WITH EXAMS APPROACHING FAST they spent every free moment studying and working on assignments. Despite still having a full month to study, Christina was a walking ball of stress, making her even more obnoxious than usual. Omar commuted back and forth between school and home to spend as much time as possible with his brother. Ava was afraid of failing and had trouble believing in herself ever since Mrs Hendrix had called her out on her performance in January. Her confidence had visually crumbled down. They were a sad little group. Jack had no idea how to be a good friend or how to give solid advice. All he could do was try. Alexander had told him to be there for Omar. So that's what Jack did. He tried to lift everyone's spirits by organising a little study group. They met regularly in the common room and set study and break times.

During one of their study sessions, Jack and his friends got outside to grab a quick lunch. They chatted excitedly as they stepped outside in the fresh air, a welcome surprise from sitting inside all day.

"Anyone up for Mexican?" Omar suggested.

Positive replies followed.

"Jack," Christina said, horror struck. She linked her arm in his and whispered low enough so only he could hear. "Are those your parents?"

Jack followed her gaze. *Impossible.* But she was right. He took out his phone, which he had put on silent mode while studying. A few missed calls from his mother. "They were only supposed to arrive tomorrow," Jack said, a lump forming in his throat. "I was supposed to prepare what to say." He clung to Christina's arm as if his life depended on it. "Quick, hide me."

Christina laughed. "You can do it, Jack. Just talk to them."

His parents walked over Soho Square in direction of the residence hall. It was a weird image, seeing them both there. One that didn't fit in Jack's head. "Guys, I have to go," he told Ava and Omar. He tried to sound as casual as possible, not letting them notice the fear inside. He gave Christina a knowing look and walked towards his parents. Jack wanted to clear the air between them more than anything. He'd finally get this over with once and for all. No secrets would remain after this day.

Jack urged his feet to move forward until his parents caught sight of him. The look on their faces took away what little confidence Jack had left. He felt like a little kid all over again, after having done something they wouldn't approve of.

The silence that hung in the air was sharp as a knife. Jack sat on the edge of his bed while his parents stood in front of him.

"I quite frankly don't know where to begin," his mother said.

"Oh, but I do," Jack's father burst out, not caring who heard him. "When were you planning on telling us you quit playing the piano? You're a disgrace to this family. An absolute disgrace! And for what? For acting? Actors are the centre of ridicule and gossip. First you tell us that you're gay, and now this? Is that the life you want for yourself? I don't recognise you anymore. I had set out great things for you. Absolute greatness! And you threw everything away!"

"A disgrace for our family?" Jack involuntarily let out a dry chuckle. "Who is our family, Dad? Our family revolves around a dead grandfather on your side and a hidden family on Mom's side and yet I'm the disgrace?" Jack looked at his mother, who had been silent until now.

"Darling, why did you lie to us like that?" she pleaded with him.

Jack rolled his eyes. She was one to talk. "How did you find out?"

Mr Lewis took over again. "That's what you want to know? That's what's important to you? I don't know what sort of phase you're in, but you need to go back to normal."

Mrs Lewis shushed her husband. "The neighbours," she said in a low voice. She turned to Jack. "Why on earth did you do it?"

Again, Jack's father interrupted her. "I for one would like to know how long this circus has been going on for."

"I changed at the end of October." Jack ignored his father's glare. This might be the one chance he'd get to advocate for his decision. "I love acting, with all my heart. I don't have any dreams of pursuing a career as a pianist. I never have. When I act I can give my all. It's what I want to do with my life. I like playing the piano as a hobby, as—"

"Enough of this nonsense," Mr Lewis shouted. "We're taking you out of this school. This isn't who we raised you to be."

Jack clenched his hands into fists and looked up into his father's eyes with a glare of his own. "Who you raised me to be, or who you want me to be? There's a difference."

"Now listen to me—" his father started.

Jack went on. "It's not because you failed in the eyes of your father that I have to be the son you never were to him. I'm not you. I don't want to be a copy of Grandpa. That's your dream, not mine. I want to be my own person."

His father's jaw dropped open. His face turned red.

Mrs Lewis stepped in before her husband could start shouting again. "We should go. This isn't going anywhere. Let's all take some time to calm down and we can meet up later." She turned to Jack. "We'll let the school know you drop out."

Jack jumped up from his bed to face his parents. "I'm eighteen.

That's my decision to make." There was no chance whatsoever of Jack giving in. Not when everything he had worked for was on the verge of falling apart.

"Oh?" His father said, disturbingly calm. "With what money?"

They made their way to the door when Jack spoke up. "I know the truth about Izzy." Both his voice and body trembled at this point. "I'm not the only liar in this family."

Jack's parents froze. "We already told you that story Jack," Mr Lewis said, still faced to the door.

"The real version, Dad." Jack turned towards his mother. "We found Izzy's birth certificate."

Mrs Lewis shook her head. A single tear trailed down her cheek. "You have to believe me when I say I never wanted to give her up." She had to sit down and took a seat on the chair behind Jack's desk. Mr. Lewis put a supporting hand on her shoulder. "My father threatened to throw me out," she explained in a soft voice. "He wasn't a man you said no to. After already having a scandal of a daughter who ran away, I was his scandal of a daughter who got pregnant at sixteen. He pressured me into giving her up. It broke my heart. But what could I do? I was only a child on my own. I didn't know what to do with a baby. I couldn't take care of her."

At this point Mr Lewis took a seat as well.

Jack sighed. This was too messed up for words. "Why didn't you ever tell me?"

"I was happy when I met your father, ready to move on after years of grief. Not a day went by that I didn't think about Isabel, but I was finally happy again after a long time. You were born a few years later and everything was perfect. We moved to Boston after Mammaw and Pappaw passed away and our life was good there. You grew up an only child and... Telling you about Isabel became too painful. I had never even met her. You'd want to see her and I promised Grace that... Well, she made me promise not to contact them again."

"That wasn't nice of her," Jack said, torn. What his mother told him made sense, but still... "You should have told me the truth from the moment I met them. It was horrible, finding out on our own."

"I should have," Mrs Lewis agreed. "As you should have been honest with us from the start."

"I know," said Jack. "I wanted to, but I couldn't be honest with you. If I was, I would have had to tell you months ago that I didn't want to keep playing the piano. I loved playing with Grandpa and I still enjoy it, but not in the way the other students here do." Jack was grateful they let him speak his mind. He had had months to think about the right words, but they failed him when he needed them most. Jack turned to his father again, almost pleading. "When you talk about the pressure your father put on you." He then turned to his mother. "And the pressure your father put on you." He hoped they'd understand him. "Didn't you ever realise that you do the same to me? Your expectations are impossible to achieve. It drives me crazy." Tears welled up in his eyes. "Is it because your own fathers have been so awful to you in the past, that you're trying to push something impossible on me?"

His mother looked sympathetic. "You are so talented. It's such a shame to throw that all away."

"Have you ever asked me if I wanted to play the piano? No. You forced it on me." The words came out stronger than Jack intended them to.

"This has got to be enough," Jack's father exclaimed. "Has your life been that much of a disappointment? Were you always that unhappy, when we gave you everything? Snap out of it already. Go back to doing what you're supposed to do. Play the piano. And for heaven's sake, go back to church."

Jack's mother got up and put her hand on Jack's shoulder. "It's true that God forgives those who ask for his forgiveness."

"What would I need forgiveness for? Following my heart?" One of Jack's talents was to make things worse, even when that seemed impossible. He didn't even care anymore. His parents were impossible to get through. "I'm actually not even religious."

Mrs Lewis gasped. Her face turned pale.

Mr Lewis was fuming again. "That's it. We're out of here."

Jack watched them leave. Had they even heard anything he had said? Wasn't it important what he thought too? The frustration and anger grew until a they hit a boiling point. With no other way to release it, Jack clenched his fist and hit the wall as hard as he could. A sharp pain erupted as his fist collided with the brick of the wall. Jack pulled his hand back and cursed loudly. He dropped to his knees in pain, breathing heavily with his fist clenched against his chest. Part of him was waiting to wake up, realise it had all been a nightmare. He only moved again when he heard a knock on his door.

"Alexander?" The shock was evident in Jack's voice. Alexander must have heard what happened. Jack dropped his throbbing hand to his side but cringed as he tried to relax his fingers.

"Can I come in?"

Jack tried to keep his emotions under control. His head was all over the place. "It's not the best time. Could you come back later?" His voice sounded strained. He was still trembling. All he wanted was to be alone at that point.

Alexander came in anyway. "Are you alright? I must confess the walls aren't quite thick. There was a lot of shouting."

Breathe in. Breathe out. "Everything is falling apart, Alex."

"I understand."

Jack believed him. Alexander stepped up to Jack and put his arms around him. Jack took a deep breath and relaxed his head against Alexander's chest.

"Do you think they'll take you away from the school?" The words were muffled against Jack's shoulder.

Jack let go and took a step back. "How much did you hear?"

Alexander shook his head and shrugged. "Not much. I honestly wasn't eavesdropping. I tried not to listen, but…"

Jack looked at his feet. He wanted to curl up in his bed and stay there forever. "I think they're serious. They can't exactly take me off school, but they can cut me off and I think they will." Jack tried his best not to panic. "Even if I work a part-time job there is no way I can cover everything myself. Not even half."

"That sucks," said Alexander, his eyes full of worry "I hope you can turn them around."

Jack looked Alexander in the eye. "Who are you and what did you do with Alexander?"

A smile played around Alexander's lips. "I'm his evil twin, Alex."

Jack laughed aloud. That felt good. Since when did Alexander joke around? "I thought it annoyed you when I call you Alex?"

"It did." Alexander took a step closer to Jack. All playfulness had disappeared. Jack took a step backwards and felt the edge of his desk against his back. "There's something I need to tell you."

"You can tell me anything," Jack whispered.

"It doesn't annoy me anymore when you call me Alex." Alexander looked straight into Jack's eyes. "My brother used to call me that when we were children. I couldn't bear hearing it anymore after he…"

Jack was overcome by a sudden feeling of guilt. "If I'd known… I wouldn't have—"

Alexander held his finger against Jack's lips, silencing him. "With you it's different." Was Alexander saying what Jack thought he was saying? Could he really?

Jack's hands found support on the desk behind him. He swallowed as Alexander came even closer, letting his forehead rest against Jack's. Jack wanted nothing more than to give in to Alexander completely. Mind, body, soul. He closed his eyes as he remembered the soft touch of Alexander's lips on his, until that actually happened again.

It was nothing more than a brush of the lips, but it was enough to make Jack shiver and yearn for more. "I like you, Jack. A lot. I

227

can't stop thinking about you," Alexander whispered against his lips.

"I can't stop thinking about you either, but..." Jack pulled away and turned his head. He sighed. Why did this have to happen now?

"I thought..." Alexander stumbled.

Everything Jack had worked for was falling apart and Alexander clouded his mind. "I can't think," Jack said. "I'm a complete mess."

"But that's OK," Alexander said quickly. His voice sounded soft, almost pleading. "I'm sorry I pushed you away the other time, after the preselection. I was so afraid for how I felt, for how I feel. I don't let people in. I don't trust people. But you... I want to try to let you in. Please let me try to let you in." He grabbed Jack's hand.

Jack flinched in pain and pulled back his hand. He held it up painfully. Bruises were already forming around his knuckles.

"Are you alright? What happened?" Alexander reached for Jack's hand, but Jack held back.

"I can't," Jack whispered, barely audible. It was too much. This day was too much. He couldn't take anymore. This was the worst possible timing. "Can't you see I've had enough?"

Alexander's expression visibly hardened, his eyes turning cold. He stepped back and held his hands up. "Fine."

Jack flinched at the change in his voice. "I didn't mean it like that, I'm sorry!" Alexander needed someone who'd be there for him, who was strong. Jack felt far from strong and soon he'd be forced to leave London.

Alexander turned around and stormed out of the room, slamming the door shut behind him.

Jack threw himself onto his bed. If it was up to him, he'd never get up again.

CHAPTER TWENTY-THREE

YOU COULD CUT the tension with a knife. Barely any words were said since Jack had taken a seat. He forced himself to eat even if he was far from hungry. Jack's mother had suggested a restaurant, which was probably the safest option. Less chance of shouting, more chance of awkward silences.

They sat around a round table, waiting for their lunch to arrive, in the same restaurant Jack's father had taken him months ago. The restaurant was packed with customers, not a single table empty. Soft chatter coming together in an incoherent buzz filled the restaurant. A vast contrast to the quiet, tense atmosphere at their own table.

Jack and his father both eyed Mrs Lewis, whose mouth was set in a tight line. There was something different about her demeanour. Something unpredictable. She opened the conversation in a sharp voice. "Things were said yesterday in the heat of the moment that all of us regret. We're going to sit here together as adults and discuss what is going to happen."

Jack and his father remained silent, unaccustomed to Mrs Lewis' direct language.

"We came to London a day earlier than expected, Jack. Your

father had a business meeting. You know the business has been thriving this past year."

Jack nodded. "Congratulations." He forced himself to take another mouthful of his salad. He could barely chew it down, despite it being delicious.

"Thank you, Jack," Mrs Lewis replied. She looked towards her husband expectedly. "There's actually reason for celebration this weekend."

Jack's father straightened his back. "After talking about it for months it's finally happening. We're expanding the store. We'll open a branch in London by the end of this year. And that's not the end of it. We're going international." His eyes lit up, forgetting the situation they were in. "We're opening a branch in Boston as well. Our family name is well-known there because your grandfather lived there for so many years. It'll be a lot of work and a lot of travelling back and forth to get everything up and running, but it's a massive step forward for us."

Jack looked up to meet his father's eyes for the first time since they sat down for lunch. "That's great news. I'm happy for you."

Mr Lewis smiled towards his son. He loved to talk about his accomplishments. His smile soon faltered. The gleam in his eyes disappeared. His dream of expanding his business had always included his son by his side, working together. That dream crumbled down before his eyes as his son drew further and further away from him.

The three of them raised their glass. "To you," Mrs Lewis said. She turned to her son. "Now, Jack, why don't you tell us what you're working on at the moment?"

Jack observed his mother, who he had never seen take control like this.

"Well?" she urged him. "We'll ignore the fact that you've been fighting."

Jack followed her gaze towards his bruised hand. Even holding a grip on his fork hurt. He'd been biting through the pain all day. "I haven't been... Yes, Mom." He told them about the classes he took, about Mrs Hendrix believing in him, and about the play he would perform on the night of the creative recital. His throat felt dry as he talked. This was the only chance he'd have to make them listen.

Jack's father had clenched his hands around his cutlery and his mother nodded along while trying to keep a poker face.

"It's called *Faceless Midnight.* A story about... Viktor," Jack ended in a whisper. His eyes widened. How could he have been so stupid?

"Speak up," his father grunted.

"About deceased loved ones," Jack continued. "How their spirit still lingers on after they die. How they leave their mark on the world. It's based on this beautiful poem..."

"I can't listen to this nonsense," Mr Lewis gritted through his teeth. "You're dropping out."

"I am not," Jack said forcefully. He straightened his back, as his father had done, making himself as tall as possible.

"Enough," said his mother. "Shut up, both of you."

Both Jack and his father turned to look at Mrs Lewis with wide eyes.

"Jack, it sounds like a lovely play. But I'm afraid your father is right. You will have to drop out."

Jack wouldn't have it. "Why don't you give it an honest chance?" If he could convince any of them, it was her. "Come and see me play at the recital, then make up your mind. It would mean the absolute world to me. If you could just come and see me play, it'll all make sense. Can you please do that?"

Mrs Lewis looked at her husband for a few seconds. Jack couldn't read either of them. She turned to Jack; her expression much softer than before. "We can, darling. We will. But—"

"You won't regret this, Mom. I love you!" A huge grin appeared on Jack's face. "You'll understand when you see me play. I'm sure you'll understand why I did it."

"We'll come and watch you play," his mother assured him. "But you'll still have to drop out."

At a loss for words, Jack's smile faltered.

"We're moving back to Boston, darling."

A CLOUD of smoke filled the air when Christina opened the oven. She swore and waved her hand frantically in front of her.

Jack, who had just entered the kitchen, ran over to the window and opened it.

"You're late," Christina greeted him, "Ava and Omar are already in the common room. How was lunch with your parents?" She slipped in her oven gloves and took a cake out of the oven.

"About that—"

"Damn it," Christina swore again. She ran over to the table where she dropped the cake. "It's garbage. The worst thing I ever baked."

Jack took a look at the cake. "It's still edible. Only the edges are burned." He took a knife from the drawer and cut away the burned edges. "There, that's better, isn't it? Lunch was awful by the way. I just went for a walk to clear my head. That's why I'm a bit late."

Christina still glared at the cake, not listening to a word Jack said. She had been in a sour mood all week.

"Come on, it's not that bad." Jack continued to cut the cake in pieces and plated them.

Christina took a deep calming breath and lowered her voice. "I'm not on top of everything anymore and that scares me. It's a bit much to handle at the moment to be honest. With exams, Piano class, and the recital it all gets too much. It drains my energy."

Jack knew exactly what she was talking about. "Try not to worry, we'll get there. We have to tackle this one day at a time or we'll go mental."

"I feel like I'm already mental," she grunted. "I'm sorry for interrupting you, you were saying? Wait, what happened to your hand?" Christina reached for Jack's hand, but Jack pulled it back instinctively.

Jack held out his hand and looked down at his bruised knuckles, avoiding Christina's gaze. "I hit a wall."

"That looks ugly. Did you ice that?" The look on Jack's face was all the answer she needed. She hurried over to the freezer and handed him a cold-pack which she wrapped in a kitchen towel.

"Thanks," Jack mumbled. He winced in pain as he held the ice pack to his hand.

"Cake!" Omar exclaimed upon entering the kitchen. He grabbed a piece of cake from the plate and shoved it in his mouth. "Delicious!"

"You think so?" Christina asked, a smile appearing on her face.

Omar nodded "That's the most brilliant cake I've had in my life." He threw his arm around Christina and guided her to the common room.

Jack, now by himself in the kitchen, took a deep breath and closed his eyes. He sat down for a few minutes as his hand went numb. When the ice pack had turned lukewarm, Jack joined his friends in the common room. They didn't talk much, each of them working on their own assignments.

With the creative recital only weeks away, Jack worked on a to-do list. They had worked on their play consistently throughout the year. Yet there was somehow still a ton of work to be done. Jack nudged Ava in the side. He slid her the timetable. "Are you free for rehearsals on these dates?"

Ava marked the dates in her calendar. "There's only two of these I'll have to miss. But you and Alexander can use the time to prepare the decor, can't you? I see you still need to get that done. Did you decide on how to do it?"

"We did." Jack kept his voice to a whisper not to disturb the others. "We are using the picnic blanket and basket as we did during the preselection. For the background we're going to project a big tree divided on three screens that seem to be floating mid-air. We still need to get out to film the footage."

"It'll be brilliant if it works. What about the screens? Do you have a solution for those?"

Jack nodded. "Mr Lang is helping us with the screens. We'll make it work." Jack's thoughts wandered to Alexander. He was supposed to check the timetable with him but felt reluctant to do so. Jack was afraid he had really hurt Alexander, without intending to, and wasn't sure how he would react. "Why don't we go out tonight? Like properly go out for once?" Jack whispered so only Ava would hear him.

"Oh, I'm not sure about that," Ava said apologetically. "You mean to something like a club?"

"Yes! Great idea." Jack saw the hesitation in her eyes. "Why not?"

"Sorry, Jack. I'm exhausted from these crazy past few weeks. Exams are right around the corner and I want to get some rest now that I still can."

Jack nodded and even smiled although a strange sort of panic arose in him. "Omar, what are you up to tonight?"

Omar looked up from his notes. "I'm working tonight," he said with a shrug, "and going to my parents' house straight after."

"That's right, I forgot you were working." Jack tried to calm himself down. He had no idea why it was so important for him to go out that night, but the thought of being alone with his thoughts terrified him. He turned to Christina and plastered a grin on his face. "What do you think, Christina? You and me? Why don't we go out dancing tonight?"

"Seriously? You're thinking about going out right now?"

He was taken aback by the sharpness of her tone. "It is Saturday, isn't it? Plus we can both use the distraction. We've been working so hard."

She sighed loudly. "Now is not the time to get distracted. I have tons of work still to do this weekend. I need to be fresh. You too, in case you've forgotten. You should do something useful instead."

Jack didn't smile anymore. He gathered his things. Omar shot him an apologetic look, but nobody said anything. Jack marched out of the common room without looking back. In the hallway he nearly bumped into Alexander. A sense of relief washed over Jack at the sight of him until he remembered how he had messed everything up. Whatever he and Alexander had was already fragile to begin with. The fear of having ruined that terrified Jack.

Alexander had stopped and turned to face Jack. His eyes gave Jack a sharp, almost unapproachable look. That wouldn't stop Jack from trying to make up with him. He knew by now that Alexander felt much more than he let on.

"Hey Alex," Jack tried carefully. He took a step in Alexander's direction, searching for the right words.

"Hey? Are you serious? Piss off, Jack," was all the reply he received before Alexander stormed off.

Jack watched him leave with a heavy heart. He couldn't stay in the residence hall for another minute. Back in his room he observed himself in the mirror. The longer he looked, the less he seemed to recognise himself. He threw on a light jacket and left the room. He dialled Izzy's number.

———

LOCALS AND TOURISTS alike filled the streets of Camden that were always buzzing with a never-ending energy. The long walk through Regent Park had been a nice distraction that had allowed Jack to clear his mind. The contrast of Camden's busy streets was a welcome one. Whenever Jack came here, he seemed to arrive in London for the first time all over again. A youthful excitement filled every little corner of the area. Amidst the hustle and bustle of the city it was almost easier to find peace. Jack was happy to blend into the crowd, shuffling along on their slow rhythm.

Izzy's colourful outfit made her easy to spot. She hadn't noticed Jack as she leaned against the wall of a pub, chewing gum and scrolling down her phone with an almost bored expression on her face. She lit up at the sight of Jack. Seeing the look on her face made Jack feel more appreciated than he had all day. The big hug she gave him filled him with warmth. She squeezed him hard, making him chuckle.

"What's wrong my darling brother?" she asked. Her smile was infectious.

"People are horrible!"

They went for a bite to eat in Camden Market which was already closing down by the time they got there. Street food vendors desperately tried to get their attention by offering discounts. Jack and Izzy bought noodles which they enjoyed on a little bench. People around them were leaving the market in a hurry, hands full of shopping bags. Jack and Izzy on the other hand had time on their side and enjoyed the setting of the sun around them.

Arm in arm they strolled the streets. Queues were already forming outside of the venues. They were lucky to find a bar that had a table by the window available. They observed the streets as nightfall set. Umbrellas opened as it started drizzling. They ordered a cocktail and filled each other in on the latest news. At last Jack had found someone who would listen as he talked about the horrible confrontation he had had with his parents. *We're moving back to Boston, darling.* He didn't want to freak her out with that thought before he was sure there was no option for him to stay, and conveniently left it out of his story.

They moved to a club soon after. entering through a long narrow corridor. Izzy took Jack's hand and guided him through the crowd. People dancing harmoniously to the beat filled the dance floor, moving on the rhythm from left to right, up and down. Eyes open or eyes closed. Drinks in hand, swaying like they had no care in the world. Jack closed his eyes and let himself be guided by the rhythm of the music and the floor that bounced up and down. The room was circular, its walls lined with mirrors, making the place seem enormous while in reality it was more intimate than that. Around the dance floor were booths to sit in, illuminated with sconces hung against the wall.

The vibrant sound of a violin grabbed Jack's attention. He looked up towards the DJ booth, situated on a platform above the crowd. The DJ got accompanied by none other than Emma, Omar's classmate. She was a petite girl full of tattoos and a large pair of glasses. Her purple hair hung in front of her face as she played. Lost in time and space, she played her violin to the beat and created a perfect harmony between the electronic and classical music. The crowd went wild. Her every movement radiated a strength that hit Jack deep inside, making him nostalgic for something he couldn't quite place.

Jack laughed aloud when he saw Izzy's idea of dancing. Her arms flew everywhere, making people around her duck once or twice. She stuck out her tongue at Jack and motioned for him to follow her as she led him to the centre of the dance floor. Jack allowed himself to let go completely, a lopsided grin etched on his face. At that point the music and beer took over all sense of rational thinking. He felt included and invisible to the outer world all at once. With closed eyes he felt the bass travel through his whole body. Nothing mattered anymore but being there, being present.

Sweating and panting Jack pulled Izzy to the side, looking for an empty booth. Jack struggled through the crowd, bumping into people left and right. He stopped by a booth occupied by two others. Jack made eye contact with the girl and she motioned for them to sit down. He couldn't quite place her, but he had definitely seen her before. She had one of those faces to never forget. Dark freckles stood out against her pale skin. She had ginger hair that came mid-thigh and big blue eyes that seemed too bright to be real.

"You're from the Institute, aren't you?" Jack shouted at her.

She nodded and held out her hand with long fingers full of rings. "Nice to meet you, I'm Léna." She spoke with a heavy French accent. Her voice was much softer than Jack would have expected. "You're Jack, aren't you? I saw your performance in January. It was very good."

Jack had a little trouble understanding her accent through the noise of the club but nodded when the words had sunken in. "Thank you!" It hit him where he had seen her before. She was one of the ballerinas. "I'm surprised to see so many of us represented here tonight."

"But of course. We're all here for Emma. She's fantastic, isn't she?" Jack could only agree. "Do you and your friend want to join us?"

Izzy, who had been talking to Léna's friend, nodded. Léna led the way to the dance floor with ease and started dancing in front of Jack. She twirled around to face him, winking at him in the process. Jack went along with it and danced with Léna who got closer and closer to him. Jack resisted the urge to laugh when realisation hit him. *She is flirting with me.* Having no idea how to make it clear that he wasn't interested he moved closer to Izzy until he was close enough to take her hand and swirl her around.

"What are you doing?" Izzy yelled in Jack's ear when they were dancing. "She seems like a nice girl."

Jack grinned. "I'm sure she is."

Izzy rolled her eyes. "You're weird, did anyone ever tell you that?"

Jack shook his head. "Not weird. Gay." He eyed Izzy to catch her reaction. "OK, maybe weird too."

Izzy stopped dancing. Her eyes widened and her mouth fell open in shock. "Jack," she exclaimed on top of her lungs. She hit him on the arm. "You're supposed to tell me these things." She started dancing again with a huge smile on her face. "Well in that case, take a look at her friend. His name is Maxence. He's been staring at you."

Jack eyed Maxence, who smiled when he noticed Jack observing him. Jack returned the smile.

"He doesn't speak a word of English, but there's no need to talk much," Izzy said suggestively. "Do you want me to check if he'd be into you? This falls under sisterly duties, right? Making sure your brother gets to snog the hot guy at the party?" She was enjoying this way too much.

Jack pulled her aside, a look of horror covering his face. Izzy burst out laughing which made Jack relax. He sneaked a curious glance towards Maxence, who was very handsome, and wondered what it would be like to dance with him instead of Izzy or Léna. Jack blushed when Maxence noticed him staring and averted his gaze. In the end he could only compare how different he was from Alexander.

Jack couldn't remember how many drinks he had had in the club. What he did remember was how dizzy he felt when exiting it. One foot in front of the other, he managed to slouch all the way back to Soho Square. He paused on the square and looked up at the sky. The stars were moving in circles and danced before his vision. Were they getting closer? The whole world spun around him and Jack had to steady himself. Bad idea.

Jack managed to get to his room in one piece. He kicked off his shoes, losing his balance in the process, and fell down on his bed. A wave of dizziness kept him down when he tried to get up again. He wiggled out of his trousers and managed to pull his shirt over his head. He pulled the covers on top of him and tried to lay still. Closing his eyes made the room around him spin even harder. He was falling through the earth.

The thoughts rushed back to him all at once. Disappointing his parents. Disappointing his friends. Disappointing Alexander. Moving to America. They played in his head over and over again. Bits of conversations that Jack would rather forget. A single tear escaped his eye and fell on his pillow.

CHAPTER TWENTY-FOUR

MUSIC BLASTED through Jack's earphones as he went outside for a walk. His usual suspenders were replaced by a comfortable hoodie in which he buried his hands. It was a chilly sort of day, but after a while of walking with no direction the exercise warmed him up. The headache he had woken up with disappeared as he walked through London streets he had never seen before. It was easy to get sucked into the rhythm of the city, the tumult of being one in a million. Most people were exactly like Jack. Headphones in, head cast downwards, disappearing in the crowd. But if that was all you looked for then that was all you could see. That day Jack paused to take a closer look. An old man reading his newspaper on a bench. Children playing in the park, their infectious laughter even louder than traffic. A dog wagging its tail as his owner picked him up for a hug. Two friends skipping through the streets, arm in arm. London was buzzing with life, hope, and fresh beginnings.

After a slow afternoon of meandering, Jack found himself in front of The Imagination Factory. The chilly air filled his lungs as he took a deep breath before entering. He hadn't seen or talked to his aunt since finding out Izzy was his sister and became apprehensive about his choice in coming here. Grace had already spotted him by the doorway. She looked at him with a smile and motioned him to come inside with a nod of her head. The familiar cosiness of The Imagination Factory welcomed him inside. He was met by Grace who engulfed him in a hug. He let himself be held and swallowed deeply when she released him.

Worry was written all over Grace's face. "I'm happy to see you, Jack. Why don't you take a seat?" She put her hand on his back and guided him to a table. "We're closing soon, so we'll be able to talk without interruptions. I'll bring you some coffee while you wait."

Sipping his coffee, time passed by. Spending time by himself that day, thinking about his actions and their consequences, actually standing still for a moment, made him realise that he needed a wake-up call. If Jack wanted to become an actor, if he wanted to stay in the school, he'd have to do something about it. If only he had the energy to take action. If only he knew what to do. In the end everything came down to himself. Everything he wanted was within his grasp and yet so far away. He would fight for what he wanted. He'd find a way to break through the fear and fight.

A hand on his shoulder made Jack turn around, startled. "You seem lost in thought." Izzy took the seat opposite to him with a delicious smelling hot chocolate. She was in joggers and an oversized t-shirt and didn't wear any make-up. Very different from her usual vibrant appearance. "Are you having an equally unproductive day as I am?"

"You could say that." Jack wasn't in a particularly talkative mood.

"It was loads of fun though yesterday." Izzy shifted her armchair closer to Jack. "I've been thinking about what you told me. I had no idea you were gay."

"No need to whisper Izzy, it's not a secret."

She chuckled and leaned back in her chair. "I'm sorry. But I should have known. I should have noticed something. Perhaps you can still track down Maxence from last night." She wiggled her eyebrows.

Jack smiled. "That would be great."

"Then why don't you sound more excited? Unless you're hiding a secret lover from me?" She eyed him for another moment. "Spill."

Jack went through his hair. His poker face needed work. "It's a little more complicated than that." He was reluctant to go on but he trusted Izzy. "The term secret lover is a bit overdramatic. I don't think Alexander would like it much."

Izzy turned white. "You're joking." She stared at him. "You're not joking." Her mouth fell open. "Well that changes things, doesn't it? I had no idea when we were in Brighton. Good choice though. He's very handsome." She put her empty cup on the table and licked some chocolate from her upper lip. "Then why do you look so sad?"

"I messed things up with him, I'm afraid. He won't talk to me anymore." Jack vividly remembered Alexander's cold look and almost shuddered. "I pushed him away when he finally opened up to me."

"If you hurt him you have to fix it," Izzy said. "I only met him that one time in Brighton, but he seems like a sensitive person."

Jack raised his eyebrows. Behind them Grace closed the shutters and locked the door. They were the only ones left.

"Yes, sensitive," Izzy continued. "He is a little closed off, sure. But that means if he chose to open up to you it's a big deal for him. You'll have to make him listen."

"It's not only Alexander," Jack said with a lump in his throat. "Nobody is talking to me these days. Everyone is so busy and everyone has their own problems, I know that. But I've been going through a rough patch, especially with my parents… Nobody seems to be there anymore. I didn't mean to unload on you like that. I'd usually tell Christina, but she has been so caught up in schoolwork that…" Jack didn't continue. He missed talking to her. "I didn't even like her at first. Now she's my best friend."

"I'll be your best friend," Izzy suggested, her smile sweet and caring.

"You're already my sister, you're stuck with me anyway."

Grace placed a steaming cup of tea on the table. "I'm ready to join you now." She put a hand on Izzy's shoulder. Izzy flinched away from her which didn't go by unnoticed by Jack. He averted his eyes from the hurt look on his aunt's face. Grace took place in the armchair between them. "A lot has happened since you were last here."

"There has," Jack agreed. He glanced towards Izzy who inspected her lap. At least Aunt Grace seemed ready to talk.

"How are you?" she asked. "Did you talk to your parents? To your mother?"

"Define talk," Jack said bitterly. Tears glistened in his eyes. "They were in London these past few days. They must have just left for Alston." He hadn't heard a single word from his parents since they had left the restaurant. Was that only yesterday? So much had happened since then.

"I'm sorry for you, Jack," Aunt Grace told him. "I know I have played a big role in this unfortunate story. The only thing I can say in my defence is that I did what I thought was right. I did what I did out of love." Indirectly, she was talking more to Izzy than to Jack. And while Izzy was still inspecting her lap, she listened intently. "Once I had picked Izzy up from that awful place my life was finally complete. I have always been independent. But I always wanted to have children. I never told Izzy the truth because I was too afraid she'd go away and look for her birthmother. She's a stubborn one, that one."

Izzy looked up for the first time since Grace had joined them, her expression unreadable. "I wouldn't have gone looking for that awful woman," she said, collected.

"That's Jack's mother you're talking about," Grace interjected.

"It's fine," Jack said. He understood Izzy's anger. He understood it because he felt it too. Not in the same way Izzy did, but he felt his parents' betrayal just as much. He turned to his

243

aunt. "It's not your fault either. It's my mother's. She was never as strong as you are."

"Your mother is strong in other ways," Aunt Grace said. "What she did wasn't easy on her either. It may be hard to believe but she acted out of love too."

"There's no need to defend her. She hasn't changed. She won't stand up to my father any more than she stood up to Pappaw." Jack sighed upon seeing their puzzled looks. He gritted his teeth. "They're taking me off the school. They're taking me away from London."

Izzy raised her voice. "They can't do that. You can stay if you want to stay. You can live your own life."

Jack shook his head. "They're moving back to America this summer."

"Stay here," Izzy pleaded, "you have us." She turned to her mother. "Tell him!"

A look of sorrow filled Aunt Grace's eyes. "They won't support you any longer," she said in a low voice. It was easy to forget how well Grace knew Jack's parents.

"That's right. They won't." Jack saw the look of disgust on Izzy's face. "They feel I've betrayed them in changing to the Acting department. They feel like I betrayed the memory of my grandfather by quitting the piano. And they are right. I did betray them. But they betrayed me too." He looked towards Izzy. Her expression mirrored the anger and frustration he felt inside. "Betrayed *us*."

"There has got to be something we can do," Izzy exclaimed. "You can work here in the bar, can't he Mum?" It was the first time Jack heard Izzy call Grace 'mum' again. They'd be alright those two. With time.

Grace looked startled. "Of course he can. I was going to look for someone to help out in the weekends. But…"

"No matter how many extra hours I work, I won't be able to afford it, Izzy," said Jack.

Izzy crossed her arms but didn't say anything. The seconds

ticked away on the clock above the door. Silence hung in the room until Izzy had an idea. "Why don't you try to talk to Margaret?" she asked her mother. "Would you do that?" Both Jack and Grace tensed up. "It's the only thing we haven't tried yet. She is bound to listen to you, isn't she?"

Grace looked from Izzy to Jack. "I don't know. I haven't talked to her in so many years. I doubt she'll even want to hear me out. And I'm not sure—"

"Could you?" Jack chimed in. "I realise it's a lot to ask, but they won't listen to me. Could you help to make her see reason?"

Grace sipped her tea. "I don't condone you keeping secrets from your parents all year, Jack."

"Can't you see why I did it? They had my whole life planned out for me from before I could even walk or talk. But I want out. That's not the life I want for myself and they refuse to acknowledge that. They refuse to acknowledge anything that doesn't fit in the box they built around themselves and around me. I want our relationship to improve. But I have to get them to listen first. I won't move back to America, I won't."

"Jack, calm down," his aunt told him. "I'll give it a try. But I wouldn't expect any miracles."

Jack got to his knees. "Thank you, Aunt Grace." He scrambled to his feet and pulled his phone out of his pocket. He scrolled through his contacts. "I'll send you her phone number." The sound of an incoming text came from Grace's pocket. "Better to call her during the day, when my dad is at work. I'm not sure he'll like you calling. He might hang up." He shot his aunt an apologetic look.

Grace heaved a sigh and got up to her feet. "Why don't I order us some Chinese food? Any takers?" Izzy and Jack readily accepted the offer. Jack's stomach growled at the thought of food. He had barely eaten anything all day. Seated around the little table portion after portion disappeared on his plate. He and Izzy were seated on the carpet while Grace sat in her armchair. The fairy lights surrounding the café gave of a warm orange glow as the other lights were dimmed in strength. For the first time in a while Jack's chest felt lifted of the burdens that had kept him down. Both Aunt Grace and Izzy had managed to turn his day around. A day that Jack felt was hopeless and wasted at the start now ended with a feeling of hope. Aunt Grace would talk to his mother. She might be able to convince her to stay in England. She might be able to convince her to keep supporting Jack financially. All was not lost. And for today, that was enough.

RAINDROPS TRAVELLED DOWN THE WINDOWS. Soft music played through the stereo. Only a single lamp in the common room was turned on. Christina's head rested on Omar's shoulder. She held his hand between hers, carefully placed in her lap. She whispered words Jack couldn't understand from the doorway. If he was subtle, he could still turn around and leave unnoticed. As soon as the idea popped up in his head, Christina raised her eyes. She let go of Omar's hand.

Omar got up and stretched his back. A dull stare filled his eyes. He put a hand on Jack's shoulder upon passing him and left the room without another word.

Jack looked at Christina questionably. "What did I walk in on?"

She patted next to her on the sofa "Idris isn't doing well. He can't go home as planned. He has to stay in the hospital."

Jack was sorry to hear it. "If only we could do something for him."

"I know, right? I hate to see him like that." She didn't expand any further and changed the subject. "I've been looking for you all day." Concern was evident in her voice. She held up her hand when Jack wanted to speak. She looked him in the eyes and what he saw surprised him. She seemed close to tears. "I'm sorry I haven't been myself this past week. I've been stressed out about

246

school. I should have been there for you this weekend and instead I've treated you horribly."

Jack scooted over and hugged her. "You're my best friend, Christina. Do you know that?"

She nodded against his shoulder. "And you're mine."

Jack leaned back and propped up his legs on the sofa. "It's been a while since you and I talked about things, hasn't it?"

Christina nodded. "I guess so."

"My parents know I quit playing the piano."

Christina heaved a sigh. "I already thought so. Was it as bad as you expected?"

Jack had to think about that one. "Yes and no," he said, coming to a conclusion. "It was more of a relief in a way. I'd been holding on for that secret for too long. It wasn't healthy anymore. In that sense I'm happy it's out in the open."

"I get that," Christina said. "It must be quite a weight lifted of your shoulders."

Jack agreed. "On the other hand I was right for keeping it a secret. They're taking me off the school. They're moving back to Boston and I'm afraid I'll have to join them."

Christina's expression remained unchanged. "You can't be serious. That's absolutely horrid."

"That's not the end of it. We found out that Izzy is my sister. And Alexander kissed me again. Well, we kissed many times... But then I completely messed up any chance I had with him."

For a few seconds it was silent. "Izzy is your sister? How?"

The door to the common room opened. Alexander walked inside, his gaze falling on Jack and Christina. Jack's heart skipped a beat. How much of the conversation had he heard?

"Hey Alexander," Christina greeted him. "How are you? Will you join us for a bit?"

Jack eyed her suspiciously. She ignored him completely.

Alexander didn't seem to trust her either. "I'm fine," he said slowly. "I was actually..." He pointed towards the door. Christina, however, could be very convincing. "Alright, just for a minute."

All eye contact with Jack was avoided when Alexander took a seat opposite from Jack and Christina. Jack on the other hand couldn't keep his eyes of him. Alexander had told Jack he liked him, and Jack had pushed him away. That had really happened. The reality of that conversation hit Jack as he stared at Alexander's beautiful face.

I'm a complete mess, Jack had said.

But that's OK, Alexander had responded.

Jack's attention got pulled back to the room when Alexander started talking. He had zoned out completely. "Me?" Alexander asked Christina. "I'm still working on some details for our play." It was the first time he acknowledged Jack's presence.

"Interesting," Christina responded. "Do you guys still need to rehearse a lot?"

Jack could see what she was doing. Alexander seemed startled and didn't reply. "I made a timetable," Jack said, towards Alexander.

Alexander nodded but didn't look at Jack. "Send it to me by mail."

Jack felt awkward with Christina there, yet at the same time he was grateful for her presence. She urged him to go on with her eyes. "We still have to film the tree to project on the screens for the decor," he continued.

"I know, I'm going to film it tomorrow morning."

That stung, seeing as they had originally planned to do it together. "I can join you. It's a team effort. Where were you planning on going?"

Alexander finally turned to look at Jack, a glare on his face. "I was thinking Regent's park. There should be a spot that's quiet enough."

"Don't you think something like Hampstead Heath would be a better fit?" Jack had got to know London pretty well since moving there. Alexander looked even more annoyed than before, making Jack regret speaking up in the first place. "Regent's park will be lovely."

"No, you're right. Hampstead Heath it is." Alexander shifted in his seat.

"I'll join you." Jack eyed him hopefully.

Alexander got up abruptly. "Don't bother. Goodnight, Christina."

CHAPTER TWENTY-FIVE

THE DAYS WERE LONGER and warmer, yet early in the morning Jack shivered from the cold. It was one of these days where it was cold in the morning and warm during the day. Jack got dressed in short blue dungarees with a white t-shirt underneath. He had awoken early, at sunrise. No movement was to be detected in the residence hall. No sound was to be heard but the coffee machine brewing at six in the morning. Jack poured the coffee into a thermos, which he packed in his backpack with some fruit and a few croissants. Then he waited.

"Seriously?" was the exact way Jack had expected to be greeted by Alexander.

Jack offered Alexander a smile. He had waited in the kitchen for a little under an hour, cramming lines in his head for his Scene Studies examination until he heard movement in the hallway. He grabbed his bundle of papers and hurried to the lift where he encountered Alexander on his way out.

The sun stood high in the sky when Jack and Alexander got off the bus at Hampstead Heath. Birds sang and flew from tree to tree. Colourful flowers were plentiful. They walked around in search of a tree well suited for their purpose. Jack tried to keep up with Alexander as he scoured the park from one place to the other. They had barely spoken ten words to each other since leaving the residence hall.

The brisk walk up the hill made their chests rise and fall. Jack held his hands in his sides as he breathed deeply, taking a moment to admire the mesmerising views over the city and the park. He allowed the peace of his surroundings to clear his head.

Alexander started walking again, this time at a slower pace. They walked in silence until an enormous oak tree caught their eye. The setting was exactly what they needed. A quiet backdrop of forestland with no signs of the city behind it.

Alexander dropped his backpack with camera equipment in the grass. He handed Jack the tripod and rummaged in the bag. Jack pulled the tripod out of its bag and set it up as efficiently as possible. Alexander secured the camera on it and selected the required settings. He looked at the screen, making slight adjustments to the frame. "This shot will do," he murmured. Alexander fixated his gaze on the camera screen as the seconds ticked by.

Jack on the other hand had had enough of the silence. "I figured, since we need half an hour of recording, it would be more fun if you had some company."

Alexander ignored him but did raise his eyebrows when Jack grabbed a chequered picnic blanket out of his backpack. Jack placed it on the grass close to the camera set-up and made himself comfortable. Alexander only sat down after another minute of stubbornly ignoring Jack. He left as much space as possible between them.

Jack stared at Alexander's back, a look of sorrow in his eyes. "I owe you a huge apology, don't I?" Nothing "Here it comes. I'm sorry for the way I acted this weekend. I never wanted to push you away, Alex. I really didn't."

"You can stop that," Alexander said in a low voice.

Jack shook his head even if Alexander couldn't see it. He still hadn't turned around to face Jack. "You need to hear this. The other day, when you came into my room after my parents had just left, was the worst possible timing ever..."

Alexander tried to get up to his feet, but Jack shifted closer to him and held him back by his arm. "No, listen to me, please. What happened that day was one big misunderstanding. Everything you said, I had wanted to hear that for such a long time." Jack took a deep breath to calm down and released Alexander's arm.

"Don't bother, Jack. Just leave it be. After the performance we can go our own way. Two more weeks. We'll be fine."

"You're in luck if that's what you want," Jack said, a bitter edge to his voice. "My parents are moving back to Boston and I'll have to join them. Unless I find a way that will allow me to stay in London without my parents' support, I'll have no choice but to go."

At last Alexander turned around. "You're not going." It wasn't clear if it was a question or a statement. "You'll find a way."

Jack stared into Alexander's eyes. "Perhaps." The longing inside of him grew by the minute. No matter if he would have to leave or if he could stay, he wanted to spend all his time with Alexander. "I like you too. You do know that, right? Some people tell me being subtle is not my strong suit." Jack chuckled and even Alexander's expression brightened for a split second. Jack tried his best to keep the desperation out of his voice. "I have enjoyed spending time with you and I don't wish for that to end. I want to be with you. Experience more things with you. Go to the theatre more often, talk until dawn, share our work, laugh, touch, kiss... This wasn't nearly enough time with you."

Alexander looked down. "I need to be with someone who can let me be myself. And let that be enough. I don't want to feel anxious to be better all the time."

Jack placed his hand on top of Alexander's. "You don't have to be better. You're fine as you are. More than fine."

"I have to stop punishing myself for being happy," Alexander admitted. His eyes squinted against the light of the sun.

"You deserve to be happy," Jack whispered. He edged closer to Alexander, their sides now touching. "You. Deserve. Happiness."

They stared at the green field in front of them. "That's why I didn't want to get close to you, in the beginning. I can't stand the thought of people leaving anymore. I can't trust anyone to stay. I needed some certainty."

"You and me, Alex. One hundred per cent."

Alexander's lips curled upwards. "One hundred per cent," he repeated with a nod of the head.

They sat there for a few moments, each caught up in their own thoughts, until Jack reached out for his backpack. "Do you want some coffee?" He took out the thermos of coffee he had prepared along with the fruit and croissants.

Alexander accepted the reusable cup Jack offered him. "You sure did come prepared." He sipped his coffee and looked at Jack who took an enormous bite from a croissant. "Are you going to share those?"

Jack grabbed the food and placed it between them. He chewed away his croissant and took an apple. "I can't believe assessments and exams start next week already. How the time has flown by this year. It's a good thing we don't have any classes this week. We can use all our time to study."

"You call this studying what we are doing now?" Alexander joked. "In that case I like studying a lot more than I thought I did."

Jack laughed. He pointed towards the camera that was still recording in the grass beside them. "We're working on a school project, so it counts. It's called multitasking."

A comfortable silence fell between them. When half an hour had passed, Alexander stopped the recording. He held the camera between them and replayed the footage. "What do you think? It could work, right?" All seriousness had returned to his voice.

Jack nodded. "The tree is centred and there is a nice sense of depth in the shot. It'll work just fine." The answer seemed to satisfy Alexander as he put his camera away.

Neither Jack nor Alexander made any attempt to get up despite being finished. They had made a lot of progress in the last weeks on their play. Bit by bit Jack started to feel ready for the performance. With the decor almost finished there wasn't much left to do anymore except the final rehearsals. "Our whole play, the script you wrote, it's in honour of your brother, isn't it?" Jack asked. "Your other plays as well. The ones you let me read earlier. Almost all have death or loss as a prominent theme in some way or other."

Alexander's smile disappeared and made place for a troubled expression. "Writing has been an excellent escape for me to let go of things. Everything I don't want to say out loud, everything I feel, I can write it all down."

"Art, in its many forms, is a beautiful way to process emotions without directly saying them out loud. And you do it so well. You write beautifully. I'm sure Viktor would be proud of you, if he knew what you had accomplished." Anything Jack said right now could shut Alexander down, he knew that much. They had gone down that road so many times. Yet this time it was different. Slowly and carefully they were building the trust between them, discovering that they could turn to each other in times of need as well as times of joy.

"I sometimes feel like he's slipping away from me," Alexander admitted. "It all happened a while ago and my mind has been so filled with anger and hurt that it makes the details hard to recollect. I've pushed everything away and I think it worked. I can't hear his voice as clearly anymore. Can't see his face anymore unless I try really hard."

Jack's grandfather popped up in his mind. He tried to picture him and realised that he couldn't. Not fully. As always he saw his grandfather behind the piano, playing the piece he had composed for Jack. Only his back was visible. *Turn around.* But he never did. "You won't forget him," Jack said for both of them. "We carry our lost loved ones close, always."

Alexander turned his head and looked Jack in the eye. "I believe you."

"You better."

Jack grinned like an idiot on the walk back down the hill. He tried to refrain himself from skipping and gave in a couple of times. Alexander could roll his eyes at him all he wanted, he was clearly amused.

The front row seats on the upper level of the double decker bus were still empty when Jack and Alexander got on. Jack always aimed for that spot and pulled Alexander behind him to get there before anyone else. They observed the passing streets, both with a grin on their face. Jack's heart skipped a beat when he felt Alexander's hand on his knee. He kept on staring outside, as did Alexander. He leaned into Alexander, so their sides were touching. The whole thing felt foreign to Jack in the nicest way.

Startled by how quickly they had reached their stop, Jack and Alexander got up and grabbed their backpacks from the floor. They hurried outside right on time before the doors closed behind them. They strolled to the residence hall, both enjoying to just walk next to each other, doing anything in their power to prolong the moment for as long as they could.

AFTER A LESSON-FREE WEEK, the time for assessments and juries had arrived. Jack felt ready to show his teachers what he was made of. The common room had never before been quieter while jam-packed with students twenty-four seven. Jack and Ava spent most of their time together as they had the same assessments. Their time was either spent writing papers, rehearsing for their juries, or rehearsing their play for the recital with Alexander. The week flew by and what seemed like a lot of time at first, felt a little tight at the end. Before they could apprehend it, their first jury was right around the corner.

Jack awoke early and for once had no trouble getting out of

bed. With a grumble or two he turned off his alarm and sat up straight. He threw his legs over the side, counted to three, and got up. A hot shower woke him up and got him ready for the day. Walking back to his room he saw Christina pounding his door.

"Oh good, you're awake." With her handbag on her shoulder and her sheet music in hand, she looked ready to leave.

"You do know the exams don't start for two more hours, right?" Jack asked her. No matter how he prepared himself for something, Christina somehow always beat him to it.

Christina rolled her eyes and turned around to leave again. "I wanted to check in on you to see if you were up."

"Break a leg," he shouted after her.

Jack took a seat behind his desk and stared at the script for his Voice exam. He knew the lines by heart but wanted to go through them one final time. He'd have to deliver a speech, written by himself, in two different accents. He didn't know which accents he'd have to bring. Those would be selected at the moment of the exam. He opened his repertoire for the day but had trouble reading through it. He saw the words, but they didn't stick with him. A knock on the door made Jack jump up. "Yes," he shouted.

"I wanted to check in on you," Alexander said. He closed the door behind him "How are you holding up?"

"Terribly," Jack exclaimed. "I'm forgetting everything I'm supposed to know. How is it even possible that I'm confusing Cockney with Northern Irish in the same sentence?"

Alexander closed the open folder on Jack's desk. "Don't go over it again now. You're too nervous."

"I thought I was ready, but I'm not. I'm forgetting the lines as I read them."

"That's because you're panicking. Don't try to rush it. You said your lines aloud to me last night. I know you're ready."

Jack gave in. He took his notes from Alexander's hand and stuffed them in his backpack. "What about you? Are you ready?"

"Of course," said Alexander, who looked as calm and collected as ever. He took a seat on Jack's bed with his back against the wall.

Jack zipped up his backpack and put it by the door, so he'd resist the urge to go over his lines again. He took a seat next to Alexander and rested his head on his shoulder. "I'm happy you're here," Jack murmured. They sat like that for a while, their faces close together, feeling each other's warmth.

Another knock on the door brought them back to reality. Alexander nudged Jack in the side. Jack's heavy eyelids fluttered open. He had almost fallen asleep again. Stifling a yawn, he stretched his body and got up.

Ava stepped inside without waiting for a reply. Despite their upcoming exam she seemed to be in a cheerful mood. A little too cheerful. "Oh good, I thought you were still sleeping. Hi Alexander."

"Why does everybody think that?" Jack grunted. He grabbed his backpack and ushered the others out. "Let's get going."

The three of them walked to school together. "I implemented every advice Mrs Hendrix has given me. They'll see how much I have improved." Ava held her head up high and walked with confident strides.

"Good for you," Jack encouraged her. If only he could feel the same level of confidence.

The hallway was lined with chairs for those waiting their turn. They had all been given a different timing to arrive, but as Lewis came right after Gallagher in their list of classmates, Jack had accompanied Ava to keep her nerves under control. She didn't seem to be needing his help, however.

Soon enough Ava got called inside. Jack closed his eyes and focused on his breathing exercises. It helped until Ava came back out again, a smile gleaming on her face.

"Jack Lewis!" Mrs Hendrix called out.

As soon as Jack walked through the door into the familiar studio where he had spent so many hours of his time over the last year, his nerves disappeared. He became excited to show the judges what he had prepared. He had such joy in what he did and loved sharing that with others. Preparing for these exams, preparing for the creative recital, it was such hard work but so worth it once everything came together. While Jack had no idea what the future would bring, what even the next months would bring, he was there in that exact moment.

JACK LAUGHED HEARTILY, clutching his stomach.

Alexander merely grinned. "I told you it was ridiculous." He shook his head and composed himself until a frown appeared on his face. "Jack, turn around. Is that Izzy?"

"What?" Jack turned around and saw Izzy standing in the cafeteria of the Institute. She scanned the room and when she spotted Jack she walked over in a hurry. Despite her smile, Jack got the horrible feeling that something wasn't right. No text, no call, showing up without warning.

"Have you decided to become an actress?" Alexander asked, when Izzy had taken a seat next to Jack.

Jack was too concerned to joke. "Aren't you supposed to be in Brighton? What's wrong?"

Izzy shrugged. "I study a lot better in the flat here. Helps me focus. I know too many people in Brighton. It would tempt me too much to go out all the time."

Jack nodded. That didn't answer his question at all. He didn't say anything else. He stared at Izzy in anticipation, waiting for an explanation.

Izzy looked towards Alexander before returning her attention to Jack.

Alexander got the hint. "Can I get you anything to drink, Izzy?"

"No," Jack said, before Izzy could even respond. He held out his arm to Alexander and motioned him to remain seated. He

258

didn't break eye contact with Izzy. "Anything you have to say you can say in front of Alexander."

"Alright," she said hesitantly. "Mum called Margaret last night, as she said she would."

"Oh," was all Jack managed to say. His stomach dropped and his whole body tensed up. This could only mean one thing.

Izzy's smile had disappeared. Tears glistened in her eyes. "I'm so sorry, Jack. She tried to convince your parents, I know she did. They wouldn't budge. They're moving and not giving in. They'll only support you if you join them."

"That's blackmail," Alexander said through gritted teeth.

Izzy shot him a concerned look. She turned to Jack again. "We can check if there are scholarships you can apply to. Or financial aid support. Or—"

"I don't need financial aid, I need my parents." Jack hated how pathetic he sounded. He wanted to plead his case to Izzy, but that wouldn't help one bit. She couldn't do anything about it. The desperation inside of him had nowhere to escape to.

"If we don't find a solution, the worst-case scenario... If you move to America at the end of the summer, you'll have to research drama schools. Apply for auditions."

Jack shook his head and opened his mouth to speak, but he didn't get the chance to say anything. Alexander shoved his chair back and got up. He grabbed his backpack and walked away.

"Alexander, wait," Jack called out. He watched Alexander's back as he left the room. "I can't breathe. Why do things have to be this way?"

Izzy had no satisfying answer. "I'll wait here if you want to go after him."

Jack didn't need to hear that twice. He left his stuff behind and caught up with Alexander, who was walking right outside of the Institute. He ran down the stairs and zigzagged through some tourists. "Alexander," he shouted, breathing heavily. The anger in his voice surprised him. He grabbed Alexander by the arm. "Don't leave me like that!"

"You're the one who's leaving," Alexander spat out. Jack was surprised by the anger in Alexander's voice as well.

"I'm sorry. I don't know what to do anymore. We'll figure something out." Neither of them believed that for a second. Alexander looked away from Jack, but Jack wouldn't have it. He flung his arms around Alexander's neck and hugged him closely. It was the only thing he could think off to do. Alexander softened up and eventually threw his arms around Jack's waist. He buried his head in the nape of Jack's neck.

Finding a solution didn't seem realistic but Jack would try nevertheless. Apart from the life he had built up in London there was no way he could leave Alexander behind. Jack could lean on Alexander, with his down-to-earth personality. The thought of not seeing him anymore was too much too handle. Jack pulled back and stared at Alexander's face, trying to etch every last detail of it in his memory. "I love you, Alexander," he said. His heart was beating fast and his face flushed red, but he had to say it before it would be too late.

Alexander put his hands on either side of Jack's face and kissed him tenderly. "I love you too," he whispered against Jack's lips. "Very much."

CHAPTER TWENTY-SIX

THE DAY that Jack had worked towards for such a long time had finally arrived. It took a while for that to sink in. He couldn't grasp the reality that it was happening today. He met up with Alexander and Ava in the theatre. Each of the performances had been given a time slot during the day to test their set-up on stage. Alexander instructed Ava and Jack on what to do, his eyes glistening with life and excitement. They worked quick and precise and were happy to find everything in working order. They laid all the props in the centre of the stage, tested the projection of the tree on the screens, and marked their places on stage as it was bigger than the studio they had rehearsed in.

"Make sure to use the space you're given. Act big. Everyone needs to see you, even the grandmas in the back," Alexander said for the third time. He stopped talking when Rachel and Christian appeared backstage, each carrying a box filled with props. They didn't even try to keep it down as they marched on stage, talking in loud voices. Alexander whistled as loud as he could, gaining their attention. "Do you mind? We have five more minutes."

Christian raised his eyebrows. "Don't overreact, Henderson. The stage is big enough for all of us to prepare at the same time."

Alexander crossed his arms and scrunched up his face in

disgust upon hearing Christian use his last name. "Wait your turn in the hallway or we'll go over time." He stepped back to Jack and Ava with a glare on his face.

"Remind me never to get on your bad side," Ava joked.

Alexander didn't laugh. "Start positions," he barked.

The nerves came out of nowhere. They were well prepared, ready to perform, and still had most of the day to get ready. But no matter how prepared he was, nerves overthrew Jack as he thought of the approaching performance.

Out at lunch, Jack's mind drifted everywhere but at the present. The hours ticked by mercilessly, no matter how Jack begged time to stop going on. He didn't want to leave London, which he had grown to love in all its imperfections. He didn't want to leave his friends, who had been by his side through it all. He didn't want to leave the school, which had become a second home. He didn't want to leave Alexander, who he had fallen completely and utterly in love with.

Alexander followed Jack back to his room after lunch. They had a few hours to kill before they had to get ready to leave for the theatre again. Jack leaned against his desk while Alexander kicked off his trainers and got comfortable on Jack's bed.

"I told Omar about us," Alexander said out of nowhere. "I was surprised you didn't already tell him. I actually thought he knew."

Jack stood up a little straighter, trying to hide the grin at Alexander's mention of *us*. "How did he react?"

"You'd like to know that, wouldn't you?" Alexander held a playful grin around his lips. Something Jack was only now getting used to. "Let's just say he was surprised. There was a bit of shouting involved."

Jack grinned. "I thought he must have noticed somehow."

"So did I," Alexander agreed.

"You do realise this might be one of our last days together, do you?" Jack asked him in all seriousness. They stopped laughing.

All week they had been tiptoeing around the inevitable fact Jack would soon be moving across the world.

"We still have all summer before you have to leave, right?" Alexander said, less cheerful than before. "You can come over to Enfield and I'll come over to Alston."

"What? And meet your parents?" Jack asked in a high voice. "You can come to Alston but I'm not sure my parents would be happy to see you. No offence."

Alexander shrugged. "Tell them I'm your friend. As for my parents, I'm sure they'd like to meet you." He got up from the bed and stepped up to Jack until their bodies almost touched.

"They'll see it in the way I look at you," Jack said in a low voice.

The room grew silent, the only sound came from the street noises below. Jack got lost in Alexander's big amber eyes with a sense of desire that came from deep within. He rested his forehead against his, enjoying the warmth of having Alexander close to him. It was Alexander who closed the space between them with a soft kiss that sent sparks racing through Jack's body. Hungry for more, Jack kissed Alexander back with more force, his hands tangled in Alexander's hair. Out of breath, he drew back.

Alexander didn't leave any time for Jack to catch his breath. He closed the space between them again and pushed Jack against the wall. He took Jack's hands and held them above his head with one hand, while crashing his lips to his with a passion that made Jack's legs tremble. Still holding Jack's arms above his head, Alexander used his other hand to explore the exposed skin underneath Jack's shirt.

Heart beating fast, Jack wriggled out of Alexander's grasp and dragged him towards his bed. Driven by an uncontrollable urge of longing, Jack pushed Alexander on his back and crawled on top of him, leaving a trail of sloppy kisses down Alexander's neck.

"Lock the door," Alexander whispered in Jack's ear.

With everyone out preparing for the show, Jack and Alexander were able to enjoy one afternoon together knowing no one would interrupt them. They had gotten so caught up with each other they ended up late to leave for the theatre. Flustered, Jack put together an outfit which he would wear to the reception and held it over his arm in a garment bag. Noise filled the hallways of the residence hall as students ran around getting ready. Jack on the other hand couldn't get that stupid grin off his face.

They ran into Ava on their way out. "Has anyone seen Christina this afternoon?" she shouted.

Jack and Alexander both shook their heads. "Haven't seen her all day," Jack said.

"Seriously? What have you been doing all day?" Ava ran back into the hallway, followed closely by Jack and Alexander.

"Nothing!" Jack was quick to defend himself while Alexander just grinned. For such an important day, he was surprisingly relaxed.

Ava knocked on Christina's door. "Are you ready?" she shouted. No response came. "What should we do?" Ava asked Jack. "Do you think she would have left already?"

Jack moved to the front. "Christina, you better be dressed, because I'm coming in." He waited for a few more seconds before turning the doorknob. The door gave in.

Christina stood in the middle of her room, pale as a ghost. "I thought I was sure, but now I can't decide." She pointed to the dress on her bed.

Jack took a moment to look at her. She wore a tightly fitted black dress with a low cut back. The dress on her bed was black as well. "You look lovely, as you always do." Jack tried to sound reassuring and offered her a smile. He grabbed her long grey coat from her coat rack and handed it to her. "Let's go."

A TINY GAP between the heavy red curtain and the backstage area offered Jack and Ava a peek at the audience that poured in. The growing noise of chatter filled the theatre as people looked for their assigned seats. Technically, Jack and Ava weren't allowed to be there, but Jack wanted to see if his parents had stuck to their word and would show up. There were so many people which made it hard for Jack to recognise them.

"Mrs Hendrix is going to be looking for us," Ava whispered, looking around.

"Yes, she is," Mrs Hendrix said out of nowhere.

Jack's heart pounded upon hearing his teacher's voice. He spotted his parents entering the theatre, tickets in hand. He sighed in relief yet swallowed in horror at the same time. If he could only still convince them to let him follow his dreams. They had promised to give him a chance. He knew it wouldn't sway their decision on moving back to Boston. Jack's father's business was growing, and they had to do what was best for Lewis & Burton's Instruments. There was, however, still a glimmer of hope nestled deep inside of Jack. A hope that they'd see with their own eyes how much Jack loved to act. He hoped they could find it in them to forgive him for lying and get on board with his plans. No matter how their relationship had crumbled under the weight of each other's deception, Jack loved his parents and wished to restore the bond between them.

"You're not supposed to be here," Mrs Hendrix said in a strict voice. "Go get ready backstage."

Ava and Jack apologised and followed her into the dressing room where the rest of their classmates were scattered around in little groups.

They hurried over to Alexander, who sat on a chair in the corner, glaring at them. "How nice of you two to show up. I swear you're trying to kill me."

"Relax," Jack said with a grin on his face. "We're right on time." He took the seat next to Alexander and rested his knee against his.

Mrs Hendrix clasped her hands together. Wearing a black off-shoulder dress with a slit in the side that came up to her knee she looked a world apart from her usual self. "Showtime, people!

Only a few more minutes until the dancers open the show. You know what that means, time to get in your costumes and get your make-up done for those who haven't done so already. And remember, no eating or drinking once in your costumes except for water. Make sure not to sit anywhere dirty and don't get any wrinkles in the costumes because the audience will notice. Keep it down in the hallways and when you step backstage you don't say a word to bring anyone out of their focus, is that understood?" She looked around the room as her students nodded. She smiled even brighter. "That only leaves one other thing for me to say. The most important one. Have fun."

Excited whispers filled the room as Mrs Hendrix closed the door behind her. Christian took it upon himself to install the television which was set up for them to follow the performances. Most of them gathered around the television to have a good view and applauded when the curtains opened. It had been a nice surprise to find out the show was being filmed.

People entered and left the room. Some were still going over their lines. Others were warming up. It was a hectic affair. Amidst the chaos, Jack found he did the opposite. He calmed down and didn't want anyone to talk to him. He watched the dancers perform from the corner of the room. He could just make out the television screen amidst all his classmates' heads. Watching the others numbed his nerves. Though when it was their turn to go backstage, the nerves rushed back at once.

The audience had a twenty-minute break between watching the dancing performances and the acting ones. Jack and Alexander found a quiet spot in the hallway away from their fellow students.

Five minutes remaining. Please return to your seats, it sounded through the intercom.

Jack's heart skipped a beat upon hearing the announcement. They were the ones to start after the break. "Alex," he whispered, frozen where he stood. "What if this is the last time I get to act on stage?"

"Look at me!" Alexander snapped. "Don't let it consume you, remember? You've got this. Enjoy this moment. Get out there and show everyone, including your family, how brilliant you are." Ava and Christina appeared in the hallway, looking for them. "Time to go. Don't ruin my script, OK?"

Jack, Ava, Christina, and Alexander walked down the hallway in complete silence. At the door leading backstage one of the stage assistants held up her hand, listening to her earpiece. They waited until she nodded and opened the door for them. Jack and Alexander went to the right wings while Christina and Ava walked left.

The silence before the show. The coldness of being backstage. The familiar sensations rushed back to Jack. No matter how prepared he was, nothing could prepare him for the overwhelming thrill of performing on stage.

Through the intercom, the audience got instructed to get back to their seats. *Not long now.*

Alexander stood behind Jack and whispered in his ear, "Empty your mind. Focus."

Jack took a calming breath. He turned around to look in Alexander's eyes. Alexander, who put his hands on Jack's waist and leaned in to kiss him. Jack drew back and placed his hands on Alexander's chest to keep the distance between them. Confusion was written all over his face. They weren't the only ones backstage. There were stage workers and other students around. Even Mrs Hendrix walked around here somewhere. He turned to look at a bemused Alexander who took a step closer to Jack, closing the distance between them again.

"Who cares?" Alexander leaned in and this time Jack let him. He let him kiss his worries away. "Good luck," Alexander whispered in his ear before giving him a little push in the direction of the stage.

Jack shook it off, he needed to focus. Performing felt a lot like a drug. Once you had had it, you wanted more. Jack vividly remembered his first time on stage in January. Performing made him feel alive. Made his heart beat ten times faster. Made him feel part of something more. It was the biggest satisfaction he had felt in his life. With that feeling in mind he could do it. Alexander had reminded him of that with a single kiss.

The stage assistant placed their picnic blanket and basket on the before agreed spot. At the same time the screens for the projection came down from above, attached to invisible threads the audience would never see. The piano was rolled out. Everything happened at once in a choreographed routine. A minute later, everything was set for their play.

Jack bounced from one foot to the other in order to get warm. He stretched his neck, then his arms. One vital difference made this performance more special than any other time Jack had performed. The audience no longer consisted of fellow students and teachers. This wasn't an exercise anymore. This was the real thing. They were all briefed on the scouts present in the audience. Their families were there along with friends and people who had bought tickets just for the fun of it.

Jack felt the familiar peace rush to his head. Everything around him went quiet. Goosebumps formed all over his arms. His breath got steady. In that moment, he smiled. He was ready. Jack walked out on the pitch-black stage and took his place behind the picnic blanket. His arms rested by his side. His head hung low. This was it, all he had worked for. The curtain opened. The audience applauded.

Jack played the part like never before. He didn't simply act the role, he became it. He found the right timings for his dialogue and Ava played the counterpart perfectly. Christina's music fitted the piece like a glove. All their hard work, long hours, and preparation came together in one cohesive play.

Jack and Ava took their bows and were met by a deafening applause. Part of the audience stood up, clapping and shouting. Adrenaline rushed through Jack like a high fever. This feeling could never get old. He stretched out his hand to Christina, seated behind the piano, who got up and joined him and Ava for a bow.

Secondly, he stretched out his hand to the right wings, where Alexander had been watching. The audience kept on clapping as Alexander stepped on stage. Jack flung his arm around his shoulder and kissed him on the cheek before taking their third and final bow. The curtain closed, but Jack's heartbeat didn't return to normal.

Jack couldn't hold himself back any longer and crashed his lips on Alexander's ecstatically. Alexander responded by throwing his arms around Jack, pulling him as close as possible. They were ushered off stage as the next props were set up. They left the stage hand in hand. Ava stared at Jack with her mouth wide open in shock, absolutely flabbergasted. Christina merely grinned.

Walking back to their dressing room, Jack didn't let go of Alexander's hand, no matter who saw. This felt right, how it was supposed to be.

They dressed up for the night. Jack in tailored trousers with a white shirt and his grandfather's suspenders. It had been a while since he had worn them but tonight he wore them with pride. Alexander changed into a dark suit with black trainers underneath. Ava wore a long flowy dress and heels, which enabled her to look straight into Jack's eyes for once.

The three of them watched the rest of the performances in front of the television in a relaxed manner. The musicians still had to perform. More than that, Christina had received the great honour of closing the entire show with her piece. They rooted for Omar, as he performed in his chamber music group. The entire Drama department had finished by then and huddled around the television in their fancy clothes, a lot chattier than before. They had started the celebration early.

Everyone went quiet for Christina's piece. How this had all become reality Jack had no idea. His eyes beamed with pride as Christina took her place behind the grand piano. She invited the audience into the story she had created, moved them with the melody of her song in her own enchanting way. Tears glistened in

Jack's eyes when she let the last note linger. She stood up, and received her well-deserved applause

Mr Norbury entered the stage for a final word to the audience. As soon as the last words of his speech had left his lips, cheers erupted from everyone watching backstage. The biggest burden dropped of Jack's shoulders and he felt nothing more than utter happiness for himself, for Alexander, and for his friends.

The inevitable time to get back to reality hit Jack like a thunderstorm. He followed his classmates to the foyer of the theatre where the reception was being held. The audience was already there, sipping champagne or orange juice. The room broke out in applause when the students entered through the double doors that connected the foyer with the backstage areas. The excitement Jack had felt evaporated when he scanned the room for his parents. Ava rushed by him as she had spotted her family who were waiting for her. They engulfed her in hugs and presents.

Jack walked on, Alexander by his side, until he spotted Izzy and his aunt drinking champagne at a high table. He took Alexander's hand and dragged him along. "I had no idea you were coming after all," he told his aunt, beaming. "Did you watch the show? How did you like it?"

Aunt Grace put her hands on Jack's shoulders. "I'm proud of you! That was a great performance. And how smart you look." She looked over Jack's shoulder. "You must be Alexander."

Alexander stepped forward and shook Grace's hand. "It's a pleasure to meet you," he said politely.

Jack grinned at him. He hadn't seen Alexander like this before, all courteous and polite. Jack saw his parents approaching. They stopped at a table a little further away. Jack's mother stared straight at Izzy. With a jolt Jack realised this must be the first time she had seen Izzy since she was a baby. Jack turned to Izzy with wide eyes. She was looking in the opposite direction, her mouth set in a thin line.

"Mum, can we go somewhere else?" she asked Grace through gritted teeth.

Jack nodded. "You go, I'll find you later."

It was just him and Alexander. "Why don't you go talk to your parents?" Alexander suggested. He walked away before Jack could say anything in return.

With his head held high, Jack walked over to his parents. He had no idea what to expect. The last time they had been in the same room hadn't ended very well. Nevertheless, he approached his parents with a sense of hope. They must have seen how much he loved acting.

"You look lovely, darling," Jack's mother greeted him. The smile on her face didn't fool Jack. Tears glistened in her eyes at the sight of her son. Jack hugged his mother and felt nostalgic for a time not so long ago where they all got along.

"We're not staying much longer," Mr Lewis told his wife. "Jack, I don't know what to say to you. What a horrible situation. Your grandfather would turn in his grave if he saw you like that."

Jack's eyes narrowed. He took a step back and let go of his mother. "Why is it a horrible situation? I'm doing what I love, and the performance went well."

"You were excellent, Jack," his mother said quietly. "We just don't recognise you anymore."

Jack's father nodded and spoke up. "Why would you go out there in front of all these people and make a fool of yourself? Did you see the musicians perform? Did you hear Christina's piece at the end? That should have been you for Christ's sake. Do you want to be made a laughing stock? Be the centre of ridicule and mockery? Because that's the direction you're taking right now."

Mr Lewis stopped his rant as one of Jack's classmates, Rachel, approached them. "Well done, Jack, amazing work." She patted him on the back and cheerfully moved on to the next group of people.

Jack's smile had long disappeared. Despite his anger, he tried to keep his voice down. "If you don't recognise me, that's because you've always pushed me in whatever direction was most suitable for you. Like it or not, this is who I am. I respect you, but I will stay true to myself. You can either accept that or not."

Mr Lewis ignored the distressed look on his wife's face. He narrowed his eyes and glared at Jack. "If you want to continue living under our roof and spending our money, you'll do as you're told. You're going home with us this Friday and everything will go back to normal."

The way he said the word normal made Jack cringe. "Mom. Dad. Listen to me, please. Why are you doing this? This doesn't have to be so hard."

Jack's mother avoided any eye contact with her son. "It's all for the best, darling." She put a hand on Jack's shoulder, but he shrugged it off. "We are upset with the way things turned out. Your grandfather's legacy—"

"Lives on with his music," Jack interrupted her. "Grandpa's legacy is his music that is still enjoyed worldwide. Let that be enough." He took his mother's hands in his and looked right into her eyes. "I've struggled with who I am all year long, wondering which was the right path to take. I'll admit I've been afraid I would have lost Grandpa's respect, but I don't believe that anymore. I'm happy with who I am now. And I'm pretty sure Grandpa would have told me to follow my dreams. Isn't that what he did?" Both Mr and Mrs Lewis had nothing to say to that. It encouraged Jack to go on. "You know I'm right, don't you? He would have been OK with this. He would have wanted me to be happy. To make my own mistakes. To find my own dream. Well, I have found it, and I am pursuing it. Don't you want me to be happy?"

Mrs Lewis threw her arms around her son. "Of course! That's the most important thing of all." She held him to her side as she watched her husband in distress.

Jack's parents' defence crumbled. They were thinking hard, letting it all in. They had tried, and failed, to persuade him. He was standing his ground. Even for his father that must have counted for something. Jack's father nodded, then shook his head, then nodded again. "It'll be good to spend some time together as a family again," was all he had to say. The anger had disappeared from his voice and had replaced itself with something else... something Jack had never heard before... defeat. His father looked suddenly very tired and much older than Jack always pictured him in his head.

Aunt Grace approached the three of them with confident strides. She made eye contact with Jack and smiled at him. Jack held his breath. What was she thinking?

"Margaret," Grace said stiffly, "Jim, good to meet you."

Mr Lewis shook Grace's hand and grunted something in return. Mrs Lewis had tensed up. All the oxygen must have left the room for Jack couldn't take a proper breath. While they were all one family, seeing his parents and his aunt next to each other didn't make sense in his head. They were two separate worlds. Mrs Lewis and Grace had recently spoken over the phone for the first time in many years. Now they were standing face to face. How would they feel? Seeing each other again after more than twenty years apart?

Even if she hid it well, Jack knew Grace was nervous by the way she composed herself. "Did you enjoy the show?" she asked Mr and Mrs Lewis. Twenty-three years of unspoken words on her lips and this was the only thing she came up with.

"We did," said Mrs Lewis. "There's a lot of talent in this school."

"You must be proud of Jack, after all the hard work he put in all year." Grace winked at Jack, which made him relax ever so slightly. It couldn't have been easy on her to come over, but Jack was grateful that she had done so.

Mr Lewis jumped to the defence again. "You don't need to come over here to gloat or try to convince us. We can handle our family business on our own."

Grace remained calm. "I'm sure you can. I only came to

introduce myself and say hello." She turned to her sister. "It's been a while."

"I don't want you to use your bad influence on my son," Mr Lewis spat.

Not many people dared to stand up to Mr Lewis, but Grace was past caring for that sort of thing. "Jack is very capable of making his own decisions," she said. "And what bad influence would that be if I may ask? I have my own business and raised my beautiful daughter all on my own. I think I'm doing pretty well for myself." She went on, in a much softer voice, when no one replied. "How long are you in town for?"

"Until Friday," Mrs Lewis answered in a small voice. She still hadn't looked away from her sister. "We take Jack home then."

Grace nodded. "Why don't you come over to my café tomorrow? It's closed on Thursdays, so it'll be quiet for us to talk. If the three of you are moving back to America, we should at least catch up once."

Mrs Lewis looked at her husband with an almost pleading expression on her face. He offered her a barely noticeable nod. "We'll be there. We're long overdue to catch up." Mrs Lewis almost smiled at Grace.

Grace smiled back. "Great. Jack knows where it is."

Jack eyed her. "I'm supposed to come as well?"

Grace nodded. "We'll all be there."

JACK WALKED THROUGH THE CROWD, deep in thought. The bond with his parents was broken by mutual reasons to distrust one another. It wasn't broken beyond repair, however. Jack refused to believe that. In time they'd learn to trust each other again. He had seen both his mother and father's defence crumble down. They'd be alright with him acting, he knew that deep down.

Alexander stood next to Izzy, in serious conversation. Izzy was clearly distressed, tapping her foot to the ground repeatedly. They both looked up when he approached them.

Izzy avoided looking into Jack's eyes. Her gaze lingered on the table across the room where their parents were talking.

"Izzy," Jack pleaded. "Talk to me."

Izzy finally directed her attention to Jack. "Oh, a picture," she exclaimed. "Of you two together. Here, let me take one." Izzy grabbed Jack's phone from the table. "Close together now."

Jack was about to protest when Alexander grabbed him by the waist. Surprised by Alexander's willingness to getting their picture taken, Jack looked at him with a grateful smile.

"That's perfect," Izzy said.

"Wait, we weren't ready," objected Alexander.

"Izzy, do you want to go?" Aunt Grace had sneaked up on them. "Jack, we'll see tomorrow?"

"Absolutely," Jack said. He didn't have the time to say much more as Izzy hurried away.

"I better go after her," Aunt Grace said. "See you tomorrow. Goodbye, Alexander."

Jack watched them leave with a knot in his stomach. From afar he saw his parents leave as well. He waved over to his mother before they were out of sight.

"They're not budging on moving to America," Jack said with a straight voice. "They might come around about the acting, but we're moving anyway."

Alexander's expression hardened.

Jack took two more glasses of champagne and handed one to Alexander. "To *Faceless Midnight*," he said as he held out his glass.

"To us," Alexander added. They clinked glasses.

Omar's loud voice caught their attention as he thanked his family members who were all gathered around them. He bid his family goodbye and walked over to them. Omar's mother, a tiny older lady dressed in a colourful hijab, waved towards Alexander. "What a night, what a night," Omar greeted his friends. "And you," he poked Jack in the chest, "you sneaky bastard. Getting it on with one of my best friends without telling me anything."

Jack shrugged but couldn't keep the grin of his face. He glanced at Alexander who looked amused. "*One* of your best friends?" Alexander asked in a fake offended manner.

Omar ignored him. "Seriously though, Jack. Good catch. He's a bit rough around the edges but he has a good heart."

Alexander rolled his eyes. "Stop talking about me like I'm not here."

Christina and Ava joined them around their little table. Christina held more than one bouquet of flowers in her hands. She sighed. "Smiling all night is exhausting."

Jack laughed aloud. "Here we all are." He glanced around his group of friends. "We did well, didn't we?"

CHAPTER TWENTY-SEVEN

AN ELATED YET frightful atmosphere filled the hallways that were lined with chairs. Jack waited in front of Mrs Hendrix's office, flanked by Ava and Rachel. One by one they were called inside to receive the news that would decide their fate. Mrs Hendrix had both the pleasure of informing the students they could go through to the second year and the displeasure of telling others they didn't cut it.

With a smirk plastered on his face, Christian walked out of Mrs Hendrix's office. He held the door open for Ava, whose turn it was next. She straightened her back and shoulders before walking in.

"How did you do?" Jack asked, his eyes never leaving the white envelope Christian clutched in his hands. "Can we see?"

Christian took the vacant chair in the hallway and pulled the papers out of the envelope, his smirk never leaving his face. "There are marks and comments per subject. You can fail a few papers and still make it through but nothing much more than that," he explained, while his scores were passed through from Jack to Rachel.

"Did you fail anything?" Rachel asked.

Christian snatched the papers from her hand. "Only our paper on musical theatre history, which was purely a case of not having enough time."

"Still, great marks, Christian." Jack said. He glanced towards the closed door. "It takes so long in there; I wonder what they're discussing."

"All kind of things," Christian said with a shrug. "Mrs Hendrix takes her time to explain what needs improving and what they thought of your evolution throughout the year."

Jack nodded, nerves fluttering through his stomach. He looked up when Alexander approached them. "Any news?"

Jack shook his head. "Not yet. You? How did it go?"

He smiled. "Made it through everything. They'd be happy to have me again next year." Alexander glanced towards Christian, sitting next to Jack, and gave him a curt nod.

Smiling widely, Jack jumped up and engulfed Alexander in a tight hug. "I knew it!"

"Jack, you can come in now." Mrs Hendrix stood in the hallway. Ava came out after her.

"I'll wait for you," Alexander said. "Good luck."

Ava passed Jack, bumping into his shoulder as he made his way to Mrs Hendrix's office. He wanted to shout out after her, but she already stormed off. Jack closed the door of the office behind him, shutting out the hallway chatter. Since the performance last night, he thought he didn't care about his marks anymore. No matter what they would be, it wouldn't change the fact that he wouldn't return next year. Now that he sat here however, right in front of Mrs Hendrix, getting good marks was the most important thing he could think of. Mrs Hendrix had done so much for him throughout the year. All his teachers had. Jack wanted to make them proud. Show them they were right in selecting him to join the program. Never before had he worked so hard for something, had he loved something that much. The marks were important.

"You can turn that frown upside down, Jack. I won't keep you waiting any longer. You got through with high marks." She held the smile of a proud mother. She took the envelope on top of the stack and pulled out the papers. She turned them towards Jack. "Here you'll see how you did on each of the subjects. As you can see you passed all the exams, juries, and academic work. You have delivered outstanding work."

Jack went over the subjects, seeing marks higher than he would have dared hope for.

"The performance of last night only confirmed what's reflected here," Mrs Hendrix continued. "You played with such integrity. We are all very proud of you and would love to see you back in class next year."

The words sank in. Jack didn't feel fully present in the room. "Thank you." Now he had to decide what would have been worse. Failing his classes so it wouldn't sting so much to leave or pass and be forced to leave anyway.

"I thought you'd be more pleased."

"I am! This is much better than what I had imagined. It feels so good, seeing that I can do it. That my gut feeling was right, but…"

Mrs Hendrix frowned. "But what?"

"I have some problems at home. My parents are moving back to Boston and I'm supposed to join them. I'm sure Boston has good acting schools as well, but it's not the same."

Mrs Hendrix was taken by surprise. "I hope you'll stay with us anyway. I would love to continue teaching you. Two more years of education here will prepare you for life on stage. I can look into scholarships with you if you'd like. See if you'd be eligible to apply."

Jack had to try his best not to burst out either shouting or crying. "That would be great," he managed to say.

The atmosphere in the room had changed noticeably. Mrs Hendrix handed him the envelope with his marks. "There you go. You can send in Rachel now."

In the hallway Jack was met by a curious Alexander and his curious classmates. He plastered a smile on his face. "I made it through."

"Let's get out of here." Alexander grabbed Jack's hand and

tugged him along around the corner. Alexander nodded towards a closed classroom. "You should go in there. I'll see you back in the residence hall." He kissed Jack on the cheek and walked away.

Jack didn't ask any questions but knocked on the door Alexander had pointed out. No reply. He knocked again and turned the doorknob, pushing the door ajar. His heart broke as he peeked inside. Ava stood in the middle of the room, sobbing uncontrollably. She had wrapped her arms around herself, her shoulders shaking up and down with every shallow breath she took. Jack stepped inside, tears forming in his eyes, and closed the door behind him as gently as he could.

"Oh, Ava. I'm so sorry for you," Jack whispered as he put his arms around her. Ava rested her head against Jack's chest, unable to say anything. He held her close and caressed her hair. "Ssh, it's going to be OK. You tried your best."

Trembling all over, Ava opened her mouth to speak. "I've lost everything now. My dignity, my pride, my hard work. Everything is gone and I'm so tired."

THE BELL RANG as Jack led the way into The Imagination Factory. Grace welcomed him with a reassuring hug. He didn't want to think about the fact this might be one of the last times he'd see his aunt. Jack had moved across the world almost nine years ago and he could do it again. He'd adapt if he had too. The big difference was that Jack had been a child then. Now he had his own life and that made it a lot more difficult to leave everything behind. As a child he had been home-schooled in America. He had never had many friends his age. His parents and grandfather were the only people that mattered to him at that point and they had been right there with him when they moved. More was at stake now. There were others he didn't want to leave behind. Alexander popped up in his mind. Alexander, who had been so careful in choosing who to open up to, had made the wrong decision. *You and me, one hundred per cent.* It hurt, knowing Jack wouldn't be able to live up to his own words.

Meanwhile, Jack had taken a seat at the table in the middle of the room next to his aunt. His parents were seated across from them.

"Isn't Isabel joining us today?" Mrs Lewis asked her sister carefully.

Grace forced a smile on her face. "Izzy is upstairs." It was the first time she had said Izzy instead of Isabel. "She knows you're here. She'll come down if she wants to."

Grace stood up and prepared them some drinks. The only sound in the room came from the coffee machine and the clock that ticked on. When she returned with the drinks, she held something else as well. A small square box with a string wrapped around it. She placed the coffees and teas on the table and played with the little box in her hands. Everyone's eyes followed as she slid it over to Jack. "It's your choice, Jack."

Jack twisted the little box around in his hand. "A gift? For me?" He pulled the string, his curiosity spiked. He opened the box, looked inside, and saw... His eyes shot to Aunt Grace, eyebrows raised. "This can't be—? Is this—?" He took a breath and tried to control his racing heart. "What is it exactly?"

"What do you have there?" His mother chimed in. She tried to peek inside the box but couldn't quite see its content.

Jack took out a set of keys and held them up around his finger. "It's my choice," he murmured.

"I've been thinking of a way to set this whole situation straight between us." Aunt Grace turned to Jack's parents. "Trust has been broken between us all. What kind of a family are we?" Nobody answered. Grace turned back to Jack. "We can turn the attic into a studio. I've started construction works last year with the idea to sublet it to a tenant but never finished it."

"No," Jack's mother cried out. "You're not keeping my son here."

Jack's father put a supporting hand on his wife's shoulder and turned to Grace. "Go on."

"He can work here in the weekends as a way to pay rent. Then all that's left is school. Perhaps he'd be able to get a scholarship to help him out." She turned to Jack and addressed him directly. "It's an option. You don't have to do it. But at least the choice will be yours."

Jack was left speechless. His mother was close to tears. "I won't have it," she said with a trembling voice. She clung to her husband. "Can't we stay here, Jim? Do we have to move?"

Mr Lewis tried to calm his wife down. "We do, Margaret, you know we do. Everything has been signed for. Besides, your sister is right. This has gone on for long enough. Let's try a different approach. One that works for everyone in this family." He took a deep breath and settled back in his chair, staring Jack straight in the eye. "It's time for Jack to be his own man."

Jack's eyes lit up in surprise as the words sank in. He could hardly believe his own ears. "Thank you," he breathed. He got up at the same time as his father. The two men walked over to each other and hugged each other for the first time in a long time. Jack held his father in a strong embrace as a huge burden lifted of his shoulders.

"No," Jack's mother cried out again, "I won't go without you, Jack."

The defeated look in his mother's eyes made Jack hurry over to her. He kneeled beside her and took her hand in his. "It's OK, Mom. We still have all summer to spend together. You guys will visit, and I will come over during holidays as well. We'll make it work."

Jack's mother nodded and tried her best to compose herself. "Thank you for keeping an eye on him," she told Grace. "And thank you for… everything else. I have never properly gotten the chance to thank you." All the unspoken words hung between them in the air. Neither Jack nor his father broke the silence between them.

"Jack, why don't you go upstairs and check out the attic? Izzy will show you where it is." Aunt Grace made it sound like a suggestion, but Jack took the hint.

He walked through the curtain behind the bar into a dark hallway. His eyes needed some time to adjust to the light. He walked a few steps up the staircase. "Izzy?" He ascended the stairs until he was on a landing. The sound of a television caught his attention. "Izzy?" he asked again as he followed the sound to what must have been his aunt's living room.

A talk show played in the background, but nobody watched it. Izzy sat on the windowsill and stared outside. Jack took a seat opposite from her, trying to catch her eyes. Eventually Izzy's eyes met Jack's. "My mum told you? Good." She lifted her head, which leaned against the window. "Will you accept the offer?"

"I'm supposed to think about it, but I already have my answer. My parents are turning around as well. My father more than my mother, surprisingly."

"That's amazing news," Izzy said in a low voice. Jack had rarely seen her this quiet. "Are they leaving?" She returned her gaze outside. "I thought if I sat up here I could get a glimpse of her when she left."

Jack shook his head and lowered his voice. "No, they're talking downstairs. They wanted to get rid of me." A mischievous smile appeared on his face. "We can sneak down and listen in on them?" If Jack thought it would cheer Izzy up he was wrong as she only shook her head. "I'm grateful you showed up after all yesterday. I didn't expect you would anymore."

"Neither did I. Only when my mum was getting ready yesterday did I decide to come. Luckily they still had a few tickets left by the door." She averted her gaze from the window and hugged her knees. "I wanted to see you act. It wouldn't have been fair that I had to miss it because of her. On the other side, if I'm being honest, I was curious to know what she'd look like."

"We can go down if you'd like to meet—"

"No," Izzy interrupted him. She got up and walked towards the door. "Are you coming? I'll show you the attic."

Jack hurried after her as they climbed another flight of stairs. Izzy opened the attic door with the key Jack had been given. Once inside she turned on a single lightbulb that hung from the ceiling. It was a bit dark and construction was still undergoing, but Jack grinned as he took in the room. The floor was made of dark wooden boards, identical to the ones in Aunt Grace's flat. Some walls were already painted white, a paint roller still chucked in one of the corners. Jack had expected a cramped little attic space, but it was much bigger than that. The main room was about the size of the common room they had in the residence hall. Then there was a separate bathroom which didn't have plumbing yet. With a bit of work they'd be able to turn this into a cosy place Jack could call home.

Jack hugged Izzy goodbye and re-joined his parents. They were ready to leave and were talking with Grace by the door. The atmosphere was still uncomfortable although lighter than it had been when Jack had left to go upstairs. Aunt Grace gave Jack a big hug. "I'll miss you while you're in Alston. We have gotten quite used to your company. Why don't you come over soon so you can help me finish the attic before the start of the school year? If you don't change your mind about moving to America of course."

"I won't," Jack said. "I'm coming to London for a few days in two weeks. I'll see you then."

Aunt Grace smiled. "For visiting friends?"

Jack nodded but didn't expand any further.

"Did you have the pleasure of meeting Alexander yesterday?" Grace asked Jack's parents.

Jack's heart dropped in horror. "Let's not push it, Aunt Grace. Today has been a good day." He let out a nervous chuckle.

Mrs Lewis looked at Jack as she threw her arm around his shoulder. "Is Alexander one of your friends?" she asked. "He wrote the play you performed, didn't he?"

Jack ignored the stern look on his father's face and opened his mouth to reply until footsteps made him look up. It couldn't be. But as he looked towards the curtain in the back, Izzy stepped through it. Her poker face expression didn't give her thoughts away, but Jack knew how uncertain she must have felt.

With her head held high she halted next to Grace and broke the painful silence. "I thought I'd meet Jack's parents before they left," she explained, mostly to Grace. She crossed her arms and for the first time ever she looked Mrs Lewis in the eye. The woman who had given birth to her was a total stranger. "It'll be the only chance before they move to America."

Mr Lewis stepped forward and held out his hand. "It's nice to meet you, Isabel."

He turned to his wife who had turned pale. She nodded. "Yes, very nice," she whispered. She couldn't keep her eyes of Izzy. "You're all grown up."

"That's what happens when you don't contact your family for over twenty years," Izzy said.

Aunt Grace nudged her in the side.

Mrs Lewis opened her handbag and rummaged through it, taking out a photo with slight creases in it. She handed it to Izzy with a trembling hand. "This is from the last time we saw each other, in Dallas, where you were born."

Izzy looked at the photo with a frown. Her eyes met Jack's for a brief second. He didn't need to guess what she was thinking. The missing photo from the album in Brighton. On it was a much younger version of Mrs Lewis. The fact she was younger there than Jack was now hit him hard. She had been only a teenager. In her arms she held a little baby. There was no denying that the look in her eyes was one of pure love.

JACK SCRAMBLED to his feet and rubbed his hands together to shake of the dirt. He kneeled and moved the skylight back into place. He squinted his eyes against the brightness of the sunlight.

Omar, Christina, and Alexander were already seated on the roof, laughing and talking in loud voices. Jack could hardly contain his excitement as he joined his friends. Alexander spotted him first and eyed him questionably.

"Why the long faces?" Jack couldn't hide the grin on his face. He would be a terrible poker player. "Haven't you heard? I'm not going anywhere. You'll have to put up with me for a few more years at least."

Christina and Omar gasped. It was Alexander's reaction Jack was most interested in. The smile on his face had disappeared. "Are you serious? Don't say that if you're uncertain."

Jack nodded. "Very serious."

Alexander broke out in laughter and engulfed Jack in a hug. Jack nearly fell backwards and had to keep his balance not to fall to the ground. "Can't breathe," Jack gasped.

"Too bad," Alexander muttered in his ear.

"Who would have thought it would end like this?" Christina asked, completely relaxed and carefree. Her legs rested on top of Omar's lap. She wore a yellow sundress which popped against her dark skin.

Jack looked towards Alexander and grinned. "I certainly didn't." Alexander didn't pay much attention as he was too busy admiring the view from the roof. It was all new and uncertain, and Jack and Alexander were different on many levels, but at least they had a fair chance to find out what they could mean to one another.

Four sets of eyes turned to the skylight. Ava climbed out with some difficulty and walked over to the group. She was dressed more casually than usual and didn't wear any make-up. Her tears had all dried up and were replaced by a smile. Nobody dared to say anything. They all looked at her as the realisation hit that they wouldn't see her again in the near future as she was leaving for Ireland in the morning.

"I'm so proud of you all," Ava said. As soon as she had spoken up, tears filled her eyes once again. "I'm sorry. I'm happy for you, truly." No matter what she was going through, she was genuine in her well wishes to the others and that was one of the many reasons why she was a wonderful person.

"What are you planning to do? Any ideas?" Jack asked her softly. "You're the reason I got into acting in the first place, I'll never forget that. I'll be eternally grateful for all the help you have given me." It didn't seem fair.

Ava spoke up before Jack could go on. Her voice had gained in strength. "Don't feel guilty, Jack. This is how it works, we all know that. I pulled the short end of the straw. This wasn't meant for me. I'd love to find out what it is I'm meant to do with my life and I'm sure I will."

"Are you going to be alright though?" Christina, who at first couldn't stand the sight of Ava, had grown to care for her. These last few months the girls had grown towards each other without anyone noticing.

Ava shrugged. "I might not feel alright at the moment, but I know I will eventually. I'll find my place. I'm ending the year on a happy note. This is our last night all together. Let's enjoy it."

It hit Jack that she was actually leaving.

As the night progressed, Jack thought of how lucky he was. Lucky in every possible way. Looking back at his life exactly one year ago he could find but few similarities. Initially he had never had the intention of turning his whole life around like that. If he would have known what rollercoaster he was about to embark on, he would have been terrified. All the changes, all the misfortune, and all the happy coincidences had helped shape him into the person he was today. It had taken him a while, but he had finally found what he was passionate about. He now knew who he was and what he wanted to do in life and that was something to treasure. Finally, he was free. Free to make his own choices. Free to think for himself.

As he looked to his side, at the mesmerising view over London, he was once again reminded of the endless possibilities that laid before him. He rejoiced in the fact that this time around, it would be his own choices he would make. By this time next year new experiences would have changed him once again. The more he experienced the more he learned. Both the good and the bad. That was the art of becoming. Jack felt in his whole body that all roads were open to be explored, and he was truly free.

THE END

ACKNOWLEDGMENTS

Taking the approach, *write something you would like to read yourself,* I embarked on an amazing journey. Four and a half years later, *The Art of Becoming* sees the light of day. A dream come true. Would it not have been for the wonderful support I was lucky to receive these past years, this book wouldn't exist today.

From the early stages of writing until the finish of the book, my parents, partner, family, and friends have generously bestowed their excitement upon me. Their enthusiasm kept me going in times I thought I'd never be able to complete the book. Specifically my mother, Kathleen Buytaert, who listened, advised, and was there for me every step of the way. Thank you for your patience and wise words.

The NaNoWriMo organisation helped me start this project all those years ago. The amazing community of people I have met there helped me finish it. A specific thank you goes out to the wonderful NanoVlaanderen group, who made writing a social event and who were always there with motivational cheers.

Thank you Kathleen Buytaert, Louise Vincqueer, Elizabeth Kluskens, and Sander Fierens for beta reading this novel when it was still in its early stages. Both your kindness and remarks have helped further develop this story. My editor Tiffany Shand helped bring the story to the next level and provided feedback in a time where I was too close to the project to make sense of it.

Thank you Fredericke Decoster, for transforming my ideas into a beautiful cover. You helped bring my vision to life.

Last of all, I want to thank every one of you who are reading this book and keeping my dream alive. Always remember that with hard work, determination, and some support, dreams really can come true if you put your heart into it.